The Giant Singer

The Sibylline Saga: Book Two

Anna Cackler

Book Cover and Illustrations by Anna Cackler

Author photo by Carla Evans

For Isaac and Bear

Contents

Author's Note

This book includes scenes that may be distressing to some readers. Please refer to the appendix at the back of this book for a complete list of these sensitive topics.

Take care of yourselves, loves.

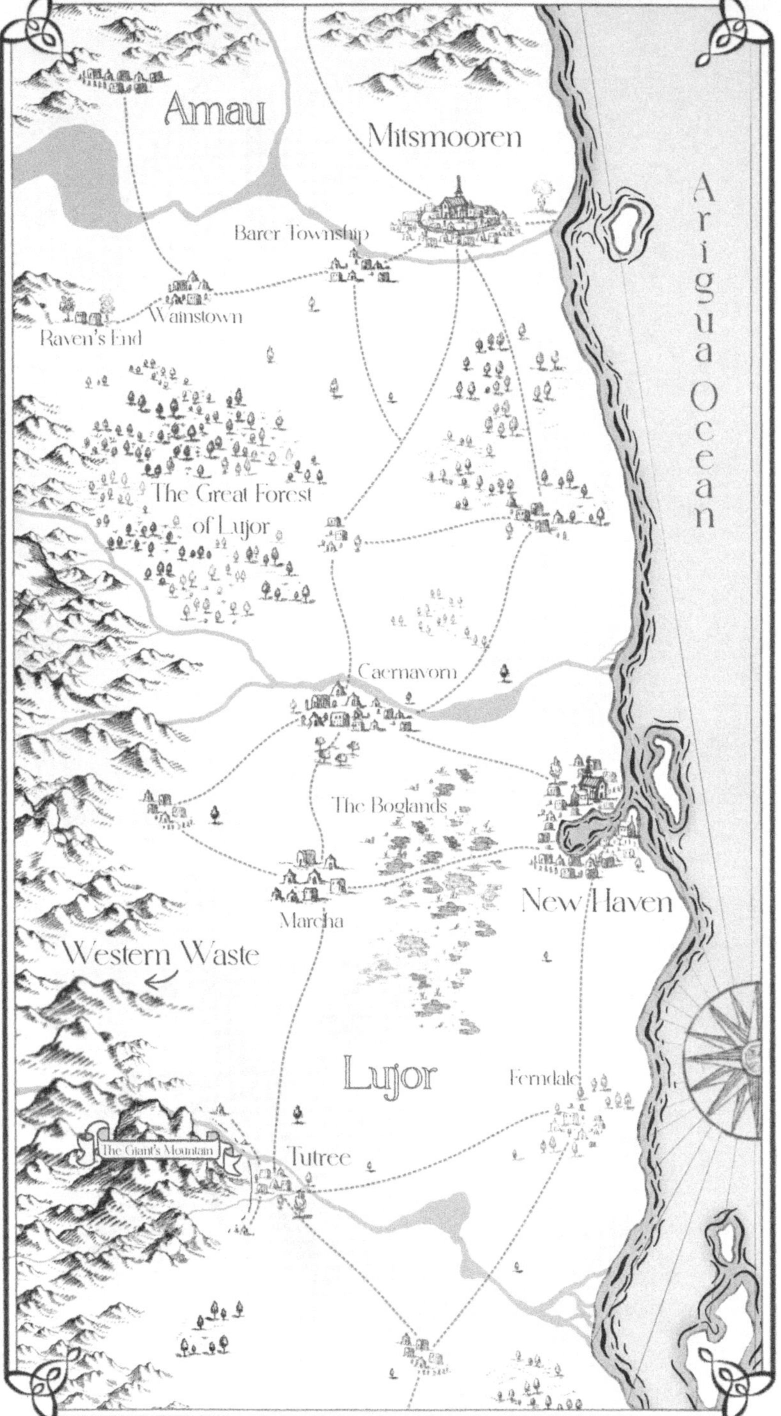
Amau
Mitsmooren
Ariguа Ocean
Barer Township
Wainstown
Raven's End
The Great Forest
of Lujor
Caernavorn
The Boglands
New Haven
Marcha
Western Waste
Lujor
Ferndale
The Giant's Mountain
Tutree

Prologue

On the western edge of town, two women sat on a stone overlooking a meadow.

One woman was thin and strong, with long dark curls tumbling down her back and a few braids to keep the worst of it out of her eyes when the wind blew. Her two young daughters were playing in the meadow below, with hair just like their mother's. This woman's name was Zoya.

The other woman was shorter, rounder, and sharp-eyed, with ash blonde hair in a no-nonsense pile on her head: Nikita.

Nikita had no children of her own and never would. The nature of her job wasn't conducive to raising children. And though that wasn't one of the reasons she'd gone into the field of cartography, it certainly didn't hurt.

The two women sat close together, leaning against each other like the old friends they were. They didn't say much, just watched the children down below as they played. The women were far enough to give the girls a sense of being grown up and alone but close enough to make sure they didn't get into any real danger or, the Old Kind forbid, cross the low stone wall on the western edge of the meadow.

The girls chased each other, squealing with delight. They passed in and out of view as they ran through the trees, little blurs of activity and giggles. Both of their fathers were long gone—one lost to the grave and the other to restlessness—but Zoya had worked hard on her own to make sure her daughters grew up happy.

"Are you sure you want to take both of them on?" Zoya asked her friend.

Nikita nodded, her eyebrows raised in a pensive expression. "Yes, definitely both of them. Casting a wide net. In case one of them doesn't take to mapmaking, I'll still have a spare."

"How optimistic of you."

"Realistic," Nikita corrected.

"Well, there's no harm in having two apprentices, I suppose." Zoya sighed. "And they're such good girls. Edith especially. She's very attentive."

"Hm." Nikita's eyes followed the younger sister, the faster of the two: Nora.

"And we live so close. It really is an excellent arrangement. They can come home for lunch every day. They were forever running up the hill last fall to pick the peaches, and your house is closer than that by half."

"Hm." Still, Nikita watched the faster of the two girls.

Nora was slightly shorter, darker skinned, and more reckless. She tackled her sister, and both girls went rolling. It was a good-natured tussle over Nora's favorite stuffed rabbit.

Zoya let out a little gasp and a laugh. "Oh, I don't even want to *think* about the grass stains they're getting on their knees."

"If a girl doesn't have dirty clothes after a good play, then she's doing something wrong," Nikita said.

"Says you, who doesn't have to wash the clothes."

The meadow where Edith and Nora played was bordered on the western side by the Wall, though that was a generous title. It was only a few feet high, made of stone, with a poured flat top where the girls retreated to sit and chat. Nora had rescued her stuffed rabbit and was making it walk along the Wall while Edith wove a tiny flower crown for it.

And beyond the Wall was nothing remarkable—just more land, with a few trees here and there. No monsters. No dangerous ground or roaring rivers. Just a gentle rise going about a mile until the ground sloped sharply upwards into the foothills of the Giant's Mountain.

It was beautiful, really. The mountain created a dramatic backdrop in vivid greens, blues, and stone whites for the town of Tutree. It sprawled upward to a gentle peak often shrouded in a mist of low clouds. The mountain was likely a paradise for wildlife, but no one could really know for sure. And that was because no one ever set foot on the Giant's Mountain.

Not ever.

Even now, while the two girls sat talking on the Wall, they kept their attention on their game, and their gazes never wandered to the west. The stuffed rabbit had a second flower crown draped over its ears, and Edith was busy weaving a third. Nora's focus was entirely on getting the rabbit to balance just right against her leg so it appeared to sit upright on its own.

Neither of the girls noticed a handful of other children approaching from the direction of town. And the two women on the rise, they had no reason to think anything bad might happen in the meadow below.

They watched the new children approach Nora and Edith. But what looked at first to be a friendly conversation between friends quickly turned nasty. One of the new boys laughed loudly, and Nora shouted something her mother couldn't quite hear.

Zoya stood up, but Nikita put a hand on her arm. "Let's see how she handles it. Lord knows that Xander boy could stand to be put in his place."

"I never liked him," Zoya said. "He's turning out to be just like his father. Pushes buttons just to get a reaction out of people."

The children below were shouting properly at each other now, and Zoya anxiously shifted her weight from one foot to the other. She wanted to protect her daughters, wanted to hide them away from the ugliness of other people.

Nikita was right, though. They were growing up, little by little, and they were brave, smart girls.

But the boy, Xander, snatched Nora's stuffed rabbit away, holding it just out of reach. Its flower crowns fell apart and scattered on the ground.

"Give it back!" Nora screamed loudly enough for Zoya to hear her clearly, even from a distance. Nora stood on the Wall, her little fists clenched at her side. She was ready for a fight, and she launched herself at the boy.

Xander tossed the rabbit to a friend at the last minute. The friend hauled his arm back and threw the toy as far as he could.

Which, as it turned out, was pretty damned far.

The stuffed rabbit arced through the air, sailed over the Wall, and landed with a plop in the tall grass beyond.

Edith screamed and ran to the Wall. She stopped with her hands on top of it, staring at the spot where the precious rabbit had disappeared into the grass, but she didn't dare go any further.

Nora, on the other hand...

"Nora! No!" Zoya took off at a sprint down the hill when her daughter vaulted the low Wall and stalked toward her toy. Zoya blanched in a panic as she ran, fast as her short legs could carry her, toward the fighting children. She leaped over the wall without hesitation and snatched her daughter up by the waist.

Nora kicked and screamed, but her mother carried her back across the Wall, her rabbit left behind.

"Mother, no! Bunny!" Nora roared in anger. "Go back! We can't leave her!"

"No, Nora! Bunny's gone. You just have to let her go."

Zoya set her daughter down in the grass but had to immediately catch her again when Nora tried to beeline toward the Wall for a second time. Edith stood off to one side, crying great sobbing tears of confusion and anger.

Nikita arrived on the scene just in time to grab Xander by the arm before he could escape like the rest of the children, who had scattered the moment the two women came into view.

"I think we need to go have a talk with your father, young man," she said to him. "And Bill's mother too. He can run as much as he likes, but I know where you both live. Let's go."

And off Nikita went with a protesting Xander—"Get off me! Let go!"—back toward town, leaving Zoya to deal with her children on her own.

"Bunny! Bunny!" Nora cried, with the great angry tears of a child deeply wronged.

Zoya picked up Nora and began the long walk home. Edith followed dutifully behind.

"I know, my darling. I know. Those boys treated you abominably."

"I hate them! I hate them!" Nora wailed. "Why did he do that? My Bunny!"

"Shh," Zoya said. "I know, my darling."

They continued like that the entire walk home. Nora refused to be consoled. But Zoya put both girls to work peeling potatoes for an early dinner, and they spent the next hour happily planning all the ways they would get their revenge.

"I'll accidentally drop ink all over Xander's favorite shirt!" Nora announced.

"We can throw eggs at his window!" Edith suggested.

"No, no, even better! We can hide eggs in his mattress, and they'll rot and stink, and he'll never know why!"

That set both girls to giggling. But Zoya just rolled her eyes. Nothing would come of these threats. At worst, the boys would get a few dirty looks and some childish insults when they bumped into each other at the market. But for now, the girls were satisfied they had regained control, and that was what mattered.

Except, that night, Nora had to go to bed without her bunny, and Zoya had to watch helplessly from the doorway while her daughter silently cried herself to sleep.

Maybe it was the silence of the tears that did it. Zoya wasn't sure. To be honest, she didn't think very hard on the *why* of it all. All she knew was that an injustice had been done and the Wall wasn't there to punish or contain. It was there as a reminder of what lay beyond in the Western Waste, up the Giant's Mountain, and beyond. A sacred place. A place of hope.

And a small justice like this, that was in the spirit of the Wall, wasn't it? A little hope?

So Zoya crept out of the house well after the moon had set, when the night was at its darkest. She walked back to the little meadow by the Wall, where her daughter's heart had been broken, and she crossed it. Zoya walked with her head held high to the spot where the stuffed rabbit had landed. She had to search for several minutes in the dark, but eventually she found the rumpled toy. Zoya swiped off some stray dirt and grass, but Bunny was just fine otherwise.

Back home, she crept into her daughter's room and knelt by the bed.

"Nora, love," she whispered, shaking the little girl's shoulder.

"Wha?" Nora asked, her voice sleep-heavy and thick with crying.

In answer, Zoya tucked Bunny under her daughter's arm, then pulled the blanket tight around them both.

"Bunny?" Nora breathed a sigh of disbelief.

"Shh," Zoya said. Her eyes held a warning.

Nora understood immediately. Bunny was back, but she must remain a secret. No one outside of their family could ever know that someone had crossed the Wall to fetch her.

But Nora didn't care about that. She hugged Bunny close and buried her little face in its fur. "Thank you, Mother."

"You're welcome. Go back to sleep."

Zoya patted Nora's arm once more, then got up and closed the bedroom door behind her. She checked on Edith next, who had been much easier to console than Nora had been.

Edith woke up when the door squeaked. Her bright eyes shone in the dark.

"Did you find her?" Edith asked softly.

Zoya smirked. She should have known. Edith always knew more than she let on.

"Yes, I found her."

Edith rolled over with a sleepy sigh. "Good."

Zoya closed the door with a small smile. That night, she settled into her own bed and slept the sound, contented sleep of a woman who knew deep in her bones that she had done exactly the right thing.

A Promise

Deep within the Western Waste
    and far from prying eye,
    rooted firm in myth and mist,
    that's where the Giants lie.

Waiting, sleeping, dreaming all,
    the Giants bide their time.
    Expectant for the one who calls,
    the one who makes the climb.

Have faith, my dear, and listen well.
    The Giants will ne'er succumb.
    When they hear the Clarion call,
    the Giants, they will come.

In your hour of greatest need,
    look deep into the West.
    Rooted firm in myth and mist,
    that's where the Giants rest.

Part One
The Map Maker

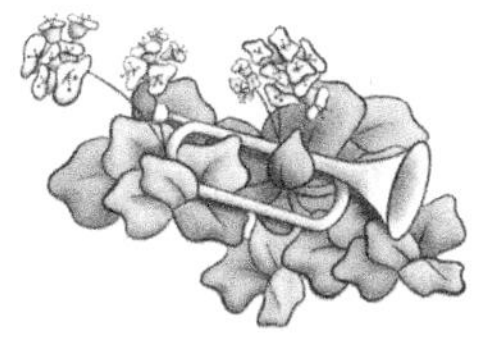

One

Nora

Sometimes, I get lost in the paper.

I get so caught up in the process, in the repetitive nature of each step of making paper, that I lose hours at a time. There was a music to it too. It was in the gentle *thump, thump, thump* of the great hammers as they pulped up the fabric scraps in time with the water wheel outside. It was in the rushing of the water itself, which turned the creaking, squeaking wheel. It was a comforting song to me after all these years.

That morning, alone in the paper mill before the workers arrived, I dipped my mould and deckle over and over into the soupy pulp. I had to shake it just right to get the fibers to lay evenly. It took a steady, even hand. Too much effort could ruin it, make me have to start all over with a fresh dip.

But I didn't have to start over, not anymore. My arms knew this dance, and my paper was perfect every time, thank you very much. The music of the mill rattled out a gentle beat while I dipped the mould over and over again, straining out sheets of fine, creamy paper pulp. The water dripped back down to the vat, adding a bright staccato to the song of the mill.

After every dip, I removed the deckle and flipped the mould onto the growing stack to my left. The paper fell away from the screen in an even wave. Perfect. I laid a sheet of woolen felt over it and then started again.

Dip, shake, deckle, flip, felt. Over and over.

And the stack of paper grew—a precious pile of cream-colored potential.

Tutree wasn't a big town, not by any means. But we had the rivers, and that meant we had water mills. Most of the mills were for grain, but we also had one weaving house and one paper mill, and that was worth being damn proud of. This far west, so close to the mountains, we had to make everything ourselves. Trade didn't come this way often.

There wasn't much to our mill. It didn't even have walls, just a long roof supported by sturdy columns over the workstations. There was a proper stone structure for the great water wheel, but that was all. The pulp vats stood sentinel to the right of the creaking wheel, overlooking the river and the road beyond that. My favorite place to be.

Our paper mill was small, but we made the most of it. At least, I certainly did. I'd been going there every morning before lessons since I was ten, just to learn how paper was made. Though I wasn't allowed a second apprenticeship and wouldn't have given up cartography for anything—what other profession would pay me to draw?—no one could stop me from peering under the paper millers' elbows while they dipped their moulds into the pulp.

And no one seemed to mind me too much. The millers just laughed and answered my questions. They even let me dip a few times with the smaller moulds. It wasn't long before I began working alongside them during any stolen hour I could find. And soon, my paper was as fine as any produced by the true millers: smooth and crisp.

Nikita never understood. Though she didn't stop me from

going to the paper mill, she certainly gave me enough grief for it. "If you have so much energy in the mornings, Nora, you can come to lessons early instead," "I can think of a million better things for you to do with your time, child," "You always come in here stinking of the mill, Nora," or "Why do you care so much about paper, anyway?"

That last one was the single question I could never answer. Because if Nikita—a fellow mapmaker and artist—didn't already know, then how could I possibly explain my fascination with paper? With the way it smelled and felt and how it could become *anything*? How a story could be written on it or a portrait painted? How something imagined could be made real and shared?

I smiled at the memory of Nikita's consternation as I stood in that same mill ten years later. The sun began to rise over the Greater Apgatt River and shone on Nora the Mapmaker, wrist-deep in pulp, with water running down her elbows. Lost in the paper.

I laid down yet another sheet of the delicate paper onto the pile and scratch-rubbed my sweaty forehead with one wrist and a sigh. The pale flakes of wet paper stood out in high contrast against the dark skin of my forearms.

The stack was taller than was wise. The press would take longer to dry it out, but it would be fine in the end. The mill workers would be arriving soon, so I needed to get out of their way.

I wheeled the cart of stacked felt and paper over to the press and loaded the sturdy board on top with a grunt. Next came the weights, arranged as evenly as possible. Water began to drip away from the stack of paper when the weight of the stones bore down on it. I would come back later tonight to hang up the sturdy sheets to dry completely in the airing shed.

"Nora?"

I startled and whirled around.

My mother, Zoya, was coming up the hill, looking incredibly annoyed. Her dark, curly hair, the twin of my own, aside from the streaks of well-earned silver, hung in a heavy braid over her shoulder. Wisps of it fluttered in the gentle breeze.

Alarm zapped through my chest like lightning. Mother never came up to the mill. She had too much to do on her own without following me all over town at the crack of dawn.

"Mother? What's wrong?"

Mother shook her head and waved one hand as if to say, *Nothing!* But then a grunting noise came from down the hill, just out of sight, and Mother turned her eyes to the sky.

"The Old Kind only know," she muttered to herself.

And behind her came the one person even less likely to visit the mill than Mother herself.

"Nikita? What are you doing all the way up here? What is going on?"

My cartography mistress groaned and leaned heavily on the wooden railing alongside the steep pathway. "I'll never understand why you come up here, girl," Nikita said.

I glanced back at the tall stack of wet paper I had just loaded into the press. "For the view mostly. But why are *you* here?"

"She came by the house, looking for you," Mother answered for her. "Refused to wait or leave a message. I tried to tell her—"

"I'm right here!" Nikita butted in, indignant.

Mother turned her attention to her old friend. "I tried to tell *you* that you shouldn't be climbing this hill, the way your hip has been acting up! And now look at you!"

"Pfft. I'm fine," Nikita said, but she failed to hide a grimace of pain.

I knew better than to push the issue, but her last wince was really quite alarming. "Can I get you a stool, Nikita?"

"I don't need a damned stool!" she spat, but she leaned against the sturdy railing to take the weight off her right leg. "I'm not staying up here in this awful wind anyway. I just have to tell you one thing, and then I'm off back home."

"All right, then. Out with it," I said.

Nikita turned and looked pointedly at Mother, who stood off to one side with her hands on her hips.

Mother's eyebrows shot up in amusement. "You are absolutely insane if you think I'm leaving."

"Have it your own way, then," Nikita said. "Nora, you are wanted on a job. Head down to the Council Room to meet with the mayor and two others. They will have all the details. I would take you there myself, but you made me climb this damn hill, and now I can barely walk." She nodded once, pleased with a job well done, and turned as if to head back down the hill.

"That's it?" Mother shouted, incredulous.

"Whoa, whoa, whoa," I said, arms out in a placating gesture. "Stop right there. What job?"

"I could have passed that message along!" Mother said.

"You don't send me on jobs! Four years, I've been qualified, and you won't let me go anywhere!"

"I can't believe you came all the way up here for *that!*"

"You said our only job was translations and copying! You said we don't *go* on jobs! Not while the war's on!"

"You're not going to be able to get out of bed for a *week* after a climb like this, and I won't be stuck taking care of you, mark my words!"

Nikita rounded on us both. "First of all, of course you'll take care of me. Don't be ridiculous. I won't be able to keep you off if I beat you with a stick every time you come within six feet of me with a compress or a bowl of soup. And second of all"—she glared at me—"we don't take jobs, not here in Tutree. But we take *this* job. Or at least, you do. Because I won't make it on this damned hip. I can't believe you made me climb up this damned hill just to find you! You and your paper!"

"No one made you climb this hill, Nikita," Mother said, the color high in her cheeks.

I ignored Nikita's jab about the paper mill. "What in the hell are you talking about, Nikita? What job?"

"The job we train for. Why do you think I made you learn Old Ambic? Cartographers don't need to know Old Ambic, you idiot! Why do you think I make you do all those translations and transcriptions? To keep your skills sharp. Because one day, I knew this call would come."

"Nikita, I swear, you are not making any sense. What is the job? Where am I going? Why? Small words, please."

Nikita clenched her fist around the railing, which was the only thing holding her up at this point. "Go to the Council Room, Nora. Now. They're waiting for you. Said I'd fetch you right away. And"—she sliced one hand decisively through the air—"I cannot stress this enough. This must be an absolute secret. Come up with some excuse for going to the Great Hall. Say you're picking up some documents for me. Or something better than that. I don't know. You're the liar in the family."

"Hey!" Mother spat.

"What is this about, Nikita?" I asked.

"Now. Go. I was going to take you myself, but it doesn't matter really. This job is for you, not for me. If the call had come twenty years ago, then maybe. But it's a fool that tries to make sense of time."

"Is this about the war?"

And for the first time in her life, Nikita had no response for me. Instead, she turned toward mother. "Let's go, Zoya. My hip hurts."

Mother cast a wary glance in my direction, hesitation and fear plain in her expression. But when Nikita stumbled and grasped tightly on the railing, Mother darted after her friend. "Wait, Nikita, stop!"

The two women started back down the path, bickering like old hens, and left me to stare after them in complete confusion.

What in the ever-loving hell had just happened? Mother and Nikita had come barreling up on my pleasant morning and shouted a hole right through it. And now suddenly the air was too dry and the light too sharp. I still had paper pulp drying on my forearms in white flakes, like old skin burned by the summer sun.

Five minutes ago, I had been lost in the paper. Now I was apparently going to war.

Two

The very first map I ever drew was of Lujor, my own country. I was ten years old, and I drew it with chalk on my slate. I wasn't to be trusted with real paper yet.

Edith, my older sister, sat next to me. We had started out apprenticing together. Later on, Edith would switch to fiber and fabric, but on that day, she was with me. We sat comfortably at Nikita's kitchen table, copying maps of Lujor onto our slates, our little tongues stuck out and extremely focused on this monumental task before us.

"Very good, girls," Nikita said from behind our chairs. She was much thinner back then but still quite plump and rosy. "Very good. Do you know what lies past the northern border?"

"Amau," Edith said, her nose close to the slate.

"Excellent." Nikita shuffled through a stack of papers on the table and drew out a second map. "Erase your slates and draw it again, but this time, include Amau to the north."

I stared at the new map she had set on the easel for us to study. The four letters making up the other country's name burned in my eyeballs. Amau. A-M-A-U. The enemy. Not just an enemy, but an evil presence, the villain in every game of soldiers we played with the other kids in town.

But Amau was real, wasn't it? That was the moment I realized it for the first time. Amau was a real place, not just a villain in a game for children. Not just a shadow the grownups talked about in hushed tones after dinner.

There it was, right there on the paper. A country very similar to our own. Amau and Lujor. One stacked on top of the other, taking up space on the same page.

Tutree lay in the southwest corner of Lujor, crammed right up against the base of the Giant's Mountain, where no one was allowed to go. Past that was the Western Waste, mountain after mountain after mountain as far as the eye could see, and none of it suitable for farming.

We were as far away from Amau as it was possible to get, and we were such a small place. A few people would venture out to seek their fortunes, to join the war effort, but we heard little about it otherwise. We sent our tithes, and we accepted refugees. But there was very little else we could do.

And then there was me, a ten-year-old girl tasked with drawing borders. They were just lines of chalk, and yet somehow, they were so much more than that.

"What's it like in Amau?" I asked, finally wiping my slate clean to start the new map.

Nikita let out a heavy sigh. "I went there when I was much younger, helped redraw some maps after the Battle of Chelton. Didn't feel any different than here, if I'm honest. Had a lot more pine trees, more rocks. But otherwise?" She shrugged. "Sometimes, the only difference between two countries is the line we draw between them."

"Did you see the Dragon?" Edith asked.

"Of course not," Nikita said with a sniff. "He's just a man and a general. He was long gone with his army before us surveyors arrived. I'll tell you one thing for sure and certain, girls. Don't put stock into frightening titles and made-up names. The Dragon of Amau is just a man, no different from your own fathers."

I frowned at the map on the easel and stared at the border between Lujor and Amau. "Why did they start the war?"

"You'll have to ask someone smarter than me, love," Nikita said. "Our job is to draw, so draw. Pay attention to your distances and angles. Like this. Look at the way this river curves around Mitsmooren, see?" She pointed at the map, and our lesson continued as normal.

Of course, all that had been before the fires started. Before Amau got frustrated and the Dragon started carting out loads of pitch across the border. The war had turned into something distinctly uglier while Edith and I grew up. Towns were burning, now. Entire cities. We heard of a new disaster every week, it seemed like.

Amau didn't care what was left of Lujor when they won the war. They just wanted to win.

And until that day, when Mother and Nikita came striding up the hill to find me at the paper mill, I had thought the war would never find our little town in the shadow of the Giant's Mountain. We didn't have anything they could possibly want, and we were so far out of their way. Amau desired the capital and the bay. They didn't want us.

But that morning as I made my way into town, I started to doubt. And my comfort in our obscurity began to fade.

The Council Room of Tutree wasn't anything grand. Nothing in Tutree was grand.

The Council Room, where meetings, hearings, and councils were held, occupied one half of a large edifice simply called Main

Hall. It was big enough to hold every adult in town, if we crowded in tight enough.

Main Hall itself stood on the west side of the town square, with the Giant's Mountain looming over it in a grand backdrop. The rest of the building served as clerk offices, mail, storage, and a small library. One of the offices was for document archiving, which was why Nikita's suggested lie about retrieving documents for her was so innocuous.

The market was already crowded with people setting up their stalls for the day, and a handful even called out, "Good morning, Nora!" to me when I passed. But no one questioned me, and the lie was not necessary.

I passed into the cool shade of Main Hall, my heart in my throat. My job day-to-day was spent at Nikita's house, copying maps and translating historical documents. It was one of the least glamorous jobs a person could have. And if you added in the fact that we lived in the ass end of nowhere, it became even less interesting.

Sometimes, I supplemented my time by drawing portraits for people. Those sold well enough, and I enjoyed doing them.

So why, then, was I slipping into the empty Council Room at the crack of dawn? On a secret errand I could only assume was in effort of the war?

It didn't feel real.

I didn't like the empty Council Room. Usually, it was bustling, busy, and full of people shouting either in joy or in anger. Edith and I liked to sit on the ledge along the side and watch the proceedings, taking bets on who would win disputes. My sister usually won. She was always so good at reading people. Usually me.

But this morning, with all the windows shut tight and the lamps cold, it was dark, silent, and a little bit dusty. The only light came in at the cracks around the shutters, striping the rough-hewn benches with bright sunlight.

I only had to wait a few minutes, but it was long enough for my heart to slow back to a steady pace. So, when footsteps finally came down the hall outside, I was steady enough to at least appear calm.

The side door to the Council Room opened, spilling more light into the space.

In walked the familiar figure of Jan, the mayor of Tutree, followed by two people I didn't recognize. I said nothing, staying hidden in the shadows along the wall, waiting to see what they would say and do.

Jan went straight to the dais, where a large table stood sentinel, and she scooted the large oil lamp closer to herself. A match struck loud in the empty air, and she held the flame to the wick. Dim flickering light filled the area, and I got my first good look at the two strangers.

One man was tall and slim, with long salt-and-pepper hair and a tidy beard. He wore simple, old-fashioned clothes with a wide cowl neck, and his hair was pulled half-up into a knot to keep it out of his way. A heavy bag was slung across his body, which he took off to lay on the table next to Jan's lamp.

The other man was harder to make out. He stayed closer to the wall, away from the small light, so only rough shapes were discernable. He was tall as well, but broad. *So* broad. He could have probably lifted me over his head if he wanted to, and the idea had me crushing myself deeper into the shadows.

The second man also had long hair, but it was messy and hastily tied back. Stray pieces had broken away and stuck out, cutting odd shapes in the dim light. His figure was distorted by tools, knives, and supplies packed neatly and hanging from his thick belt, along with a large travel pack riding high and tight on his shoulders.

He was huge.

"We don't have much time," the first man said—the tidy one. He chose a seat and pulled it up to the table to sit down.

He rested his forearms on the tabletop, his long fingers interlocked.

"I know," Jan replied. "Nikita will be back any moment."

"With the younger one? What was her name? Nora?"

Jan nodded. "Yes. Nora. Our master cartographer is an old woman now. It will have to be her apprentice. Though, I assure you, Nora is fully certified."

"And you're sure she can be trusted?"

I narrowed my eyes. Trusted with what?

"I don't see how we have much option either way," was Jan's reply.

I snorted—a little offended, if I was being honest—then winced at my own error.

All three of them swiveled their heads in my direction.

"Who's there?" Jan asked. "Nikita?"

I hopped down from the ledge and wove my way through the benches toward the dais. "What's that supposed to mean? Not much option?"

Jan drew out a chair for me as I approached. She raised one eyebrow. "Where's Nikita?"

I stared around at the others and did not sit down. The broad man remained with his back against the wall, his expression hidden by shadows.

"She said her hip hurt and she wasn't needed anyway. She sent me for some job, apparently. What did you mean there wasn't much option?"

Jan leveled me with a serious expression. "It means that with Nikita unable to travel, you are the only qualified cartographer in town."

"I'm not the only one in Lujor, though. Why didn't you bring one with you? Why me? I'm Nora, by the way."

I held my hand out to the thinner of the two strangers, simply because he was within reach and the other wasn't. He shook it amicably.

The man pressed his lips together, then turned his attention to Jan. "Thank you, Jan. I think we can take it from here."

Jan cast me a wary glance and silently left the room. Of course, that meant I was alone with two strange men, both of them much taller than me, and no one in town knew where I was.

Well, Mother knew. That was something. Mother would tear the whole town apart to help me, if I needed her to.

"My name is Lachlan," the older man said. A small smile played at the corner of his mouth at my brusque attitude. "And this is Eoghan. He's a ranger."

Eoghan nodded politely at me, his face still in shadow, but said nothing.

"Good to meet you, Lachlan. And now may I ask what in the name of all that is holy you two are playing at? What is going on here?"

Lachlan's smile broadened, and the crow's feet around his eyes deepened. He gave Eoghan an appreciative nod. "Oh, yes. I like her. She'll do just fine."

Lachlan stood and drew his bag closer. He rummaged around inside for a moment before pulling out a much smaller leather case secured with a thong wound tightly around decorative iron pegs.

"But it's not 'we two,' I'm afraid. It's just me. Eoghan met me here, same as you did. I have a job for the two of you. A vital mission to end this war once and for all."

I stared at him, one eyebrow raised, my mouth slightly ajar. "Okay?"

Lachlan's smile was serene. "I am the High Reliquary, Nora. I assume you know what that means?"

I snorted again. "No, you're not."

The man called Eoghan shifted his weight from one leg to the other.

Lachlan narrowed his eyebrows in confusion. The leather case paused halfway out of the bag. "How do you mean?"

"What would the High Reliquary be doing in a tiny little town like this, asking to meet with a random mapmaker and a ranger? Alone, with no security or attendants? Who's running the Reliquary if you're here?"

Lachlan settled back on his heels and regarded me closely. "There are many ministers and docents at the Reliquary. I am not needed there every hour of the day. Or even every week of the year. And right now, my duties have called me here, to a tiny little town, to meet with a random mapmaker and a ranger. Alone."

I narrowed my eyes at him.

"Aren't you the least bit curious why?" he asked.

I flicked my eyes to Eoghan, who still leaned against the wall. I wanted to yank him forward into the light so I could get a good look at him. Not that I'd be able to yank him anywhere. By the Old Kind, he was huge. And not huge like everyone was huge. I was a small woman, so everyone was tall to me. But this Eoghan? This ranger? He was a wall of muscle.

I set my jaw and jerked my chin in the direction of the leather case Lachlan had pulled from his bag. "So, what's that, then? One of your relics?"

"Yes," he said simply. "Before we go any further, I need to impress upon you both how vital secrecy is in this matter. The future of our country is at stake. What I am asking you to do is a last resort, and I am not asking it lightly. I would not be here if it weren't absolutely necessary. I need your word."

"Sure," I replied in a small voice. Shitting hell, what was I getting myself into?

"Eoghan?" Lachlan asked.

The other man nodded once in affirmation.

Lachlan took one more breath, then laid the leather case down and slid it across the table toward me.

I hesitated for another second, glancing at both men in turn. Was this some kind of trick? Surely, this Lachlan man wasn't actually the High Reliquary. The Reliquary was the branch of government that curated and protected the cultural and magical history for the entirety of Lujor. The queen herself might as well have waltzed into this dusty town hall at the ass end of nowhere. Alone.

Well, no sense standing around staring at each other.

I pulled the leather case closer and ran my fingers over the decorative iron pegs. They were simple leaves. Pretty, but not ornate. I unwound the thong keeping it closed and lifted the flap.

Inside were four heavy folders, each containing several sheets of antique parchment. I pulled them out with another wary glance at Lachlan and placed the folders side by side on the table.

"Not relics, then," I said.

"Archives," Lachlan said. "Until this moment, I was the only person who knew they even existed."

There was a movement on my right side, and I nearly jumped out of my skin.

Eoghan had finally left his post by the wall to stand next to me, and all I could think was *arms, arms, arms.* His shirt had no sleeves at all, which put his dizzying set of muscles on full display. Dirt and grime had settled into the dips and valleys of his skin, accentuating them. If I poked his bicep, I'd probably break a finger.

I supposed that depended on how hard I poked, though.

And of course, now I could finally see his face properly in the light of the single lamp. He stood peering over my shoulder at the blank folders lying out on the table, but I stared up at him. His short beard wasn't particularly tidy, but it wasn't messy either. He had a heavy brow and a crooked nose, all of it framed by high cheekbones.

But what caught my attention was his eyes. Larger than I expected, bright, keen. Brown as good soil and sharp. They were eyes that saw everything. Not just surface things, but deep-down things.

And when those eyes darted to my face, I blushed. What would a man like that see when he looked at me?

I turned away, annoyed—mostly with myself, but partly with him. Because hell, who gave him the right to look at me like that?

Instead, I focused on the four folders laid out on the table. One by one, I pulled their contents free and spread them out likewise.

Each folder contained sheaves of antique parchment covered right over with handwritten text. The first was in Ambic. This was by far the least aged document, judging by both the language and the lesser browning of the parchment itself. The other three were written in Old Ambic, a dead language. These were much older, with faded ink and parchment so brown on the last one that I had to strain to read it.

I scanned over a few of the pages, my eyebrows drawn together. "They're accounts of some kind of journey. Here"—I pointed to a specific passage on one of the Old Ambic parchments—"the writer talks about the distance to a specific landmark. A stone outcropping that resembles a horse. They sketched it here on the next page." I flipped it up to show Eoghan, who leaned in with some interest.

Did the man even know how to speak at all? What was wrong with him?

"Yes," Lachlan confirmed. "Four accounts of the same journey taken by four different travelers at four different times. A journey that I am asking the pair of you to take again now. The purpose of these archives is to guide you."

The hell was going on here? I lifted page after page, scanning the text. But when one specific word caught my eye, I dropped the pages as if they'd burned me and backed away from the table in alarm.

I jostled Eoghan's arm as I went, registering somewhere in the back of my mind that his arms weren't made of rock at all. Just arms. Couldn't break my fingers on him if I tried.

But I couldn't think about anything at all except that one word I had seen on the parchment. It flashed across my mind's eye over and over again.

Clarion.

"What the hell?" I said breathlessly.

Clarion.

"You see now why this must remain a secret." Lachlan seemed entirely unfazed.

Clarion.

"What is it?" Yes, of course, *now* was when Eoghan decided he had a tongue after all. His voice was deep and smooth, and it dislodged whatever stutter my brain had gotten stuck in.

"He wants us to climb the Giant's Mountain," I said.

I had lived in Tutree all my life. And aside from a couple of trips to the capital with Edith to visit her father's family, I had never left. And there was one thing every person in Tutree knew in their bones: No one set foot on the Giant's Mountain. Not if they wanted to use their feet ever again.

It was just a mountain, really. It loomed over us—a comforting constant in our lives. If I stepped outside Main Hall right now, there it would be, creating the dramatic backdrop of our western horizon. Right there, yet just out of reach.

But it was more than a mountain. It was the final resting place of the Giants. It was a sacred place, untouched by mankind for over a thousand years.

Except...there were accounts of four people who had dared to cross the border.

My fingers traced over the parchments once more, almost afraid to handle them too roughly. "What happened to these people?" I asked.

"Executed." Lachlan's tone was unreadable. "Three of them were before my time. This last one, I was a docent back then. It was done in secret. I didn't learn about it until much later, but I was there in the Reliquary when it happened."

"And now you want us to go? Will we be executed as well? Are you damning us just by showing these to us?"

"Of course not."

I threw out both hands to encompass the dark, empty room, the secret documents, the clandestine nature of the entire meeting.

"What do you mean by *of course?* Because nothing about this makes any sense. And it certainly isn't making me feel particularly safe."

And then, as if he knew exactly how and when to speak to have the most impact on me, Eoghan opened his mouth for the second time. "He wants us to wake them up."

I crossed my arms tightly over my chest and clammed the hell up. I couldn't process this.

Lachlan leaned forward and rested his forearms on the table. "You and Eoghan will set out as soon as possible. As soon as you have prepared yourselves. You will tell no one where you are going. You will take these archives, Nora. You will read them, interpret them, and get yourselves to the Archways. Eoghan is an experienced Ranger. He will keep you safe, keep you alive in the wilderness.

"Once you find the Archways, you will locate the Clarion. None of the four travelers even attempted to find it, out of respect, but you must do so. You will find the Clarion, then take it to the peak of the mountain, where you will sound it in the Cavern of the Giants. And Old Kind willing, the Giants will hear your call and rise up."

I clenched my fists, tucked them deep into the folds of my arms, and willed them to stop shaking. But it wasn't just my fists. It was my entire body. Even my breath shook in my lungs, which could only manage short, gasping pants. Tears welled up in my eyes, but none spilled over. I blinked hard.

This couldn't be happening. I was dreaming. Yes, that was it.

Or maybe I had passed out while dipping paper and had drowned in the pulp vat. That made the most sense. I died making paper that morning, and whatever this was...it was just a drawn-out hallucination in the last seconds before my brain shut down forever.

"What if we refuse?" I asked in a tiny voice. And I absolutely did not dwell on the fact that I'd used the word "we" instead of "I."

Lachlan's expression sagged the tiniest bit. "Every day, new fires are set. Every day, more people die. We are losing this war. Amau will overtake us, and the Dragon will invade New Haven. It is only a matter of time. You don't see it much this far south and west, but it is happening."

He chewed on his lip for a moment, looking unsure for the first time since he'd entered the Council Room.

"The legends say the Giants will rise up when we need them most. They left behind the Clarion for the express purpose of waking them up when we needed them. Now is the time, Nora."

"Why me? Why us? We're nobody."

Why was I still lumping Eoghan in with myself? I didn't know him *at all.* He had said exactly two sentences in my hearing, and that was it.

"It's precisely because you are nobodies," Lachlan said. "You'd be surprised how much gets done by nobodies in this country. No one will ever look twice at the pair of you."

The pair of us. That was it. Settled. Eoghan and I were a set. Neatly done. Just the fact that we were the only two people who knew about these archives, who knew the High Reliquary wanted this done, it separated us from the rest of the country. From the rest of the world.

I glared up at Eoghan, at this stranger I had somehow attached myself to without noticing. My next words came out with a bit of a bite, but they always did when I was upset.

"Say something." The last syllable was laced with a wobble. A plea. *Please.*

He regarded me with those wide eyes. For a moment, I thought there might be a bit of a connection. His right eyebrow twitched, and his lower eyelids rose for half a second. I could practically see the thoughts running through his mind. And if I could just get a little closer, maybe climb right into his skin, I might even be able to hear what those thoughts were.

But instead of saying something profound, comforting, or encouraging, his actual words landed in my gut like a lead weight.

"I'll be ready to leave at dawn."

I didn't know this man, and the little I did know wasn't particularly endearing. But for some reason, I felt betrayed by this cold statement. We were supposed to be a team, but it looked like we would be climbing this mountain alone, together.

Three

I floated through the rest of the meeting like a dream. Eoghan made me write out a list of supplies I would need to gather and pack. Lachlan gave us a few more instructions and impressed on us again and again the need for secrecy. Because if Amau found out where we were going, what we were trying to do, there was no telling what they would do. Kill us before we could succeed? Try and take the Clarion and, therefore, the Giants' loyalty for themselves?

Lachlan packed up the archives and stowed them carefully away, first into their individual folders and then into the leather case. It had been a shock when I realized Lachlan meant for me to keep it, but he insisted. "We won't be seeing each other again. I'm leaving for New Haven immediately. They belong to you now."

Lachlan disappeared through an inner door into Main Hall, and Eoghan followed me outside. I found myself in the busy sunshine of the market square, dazed, with the case clutched to my chest.

The market was in full swing by then. The people went about their business, buying, selling, trading, meeting, and parting. They had no idea the entire world had just turned upside down. I supposed it hadn't for them. Just for us.

"Where are you staying tonight?" I asked. "At the inn, I suppose?"

"Just outside of town," Eoghan said from my left side and *up.* Damn, he was tall. "There's a quiet place on the west bank of the Lesser Apgatt. I've camped there before. Years ago."

It was the most words he'd spoken at once since I'd met him, and they were ridiculous.

"That's ridiculous," I said, because clearly every word that popped into my brain still came shooting straight out of my mouth. "You'll come home with me. Eat a real meal."

"That's not necessary."

The hell was wrong with him? It was enough to drag my attention away from the monumental task we'd been given. I finally looked up at him.

No, not looked. Glared. Because for hell's sake, he was being stupid.

"You're being stupid," I said.

This earned me an honest scowl back from him. "Excuse me?"

Oh, good. He *did* have some emotion in there after all.

"You'll come home with me and eat a real damned meal. And you'll meet my mother. Because she deserves to know who I'll be traveling with. And then you'll help me pack." I waved his list in his face for emphasis. "Were you seriously going to leave me *on my own* to deal with all this, *alone*?"

I clutched the archives closer to my aching chest and stalked off across the noisy square. I didn't need to glance back to know Eoghan followed close behind. His seething was almost audible.

Tutree was a small town. It didn't take long for us to leave the bustling market square behind. The narrow streets and densely packed buildings at the center of town muffled the noise quickly. I had the urge to veer off to the right on Apple Avenue, which led a winding path down to Nikita's house, and wave the archives in her face, ask her if she knew what in the hell I'd been asked to do. She had known I'd need Old Ambic. Had she known why?

But Eoghan was a steady shadow on my left, and I didn't want to drag him into that conversation. I didn't want him to witness me interrogating my mistress about this, like a loon. So my feet cut a straight path through town, no hesitation.

Mother, Edith, and I lived near the edge of town, where the houses had a little space about them. We weren't career farmers, but we were plenty comfortable. We had our own garden, three dairy goats, and a healthy smattering of chickens and rabbits. There was a reason we had been able to afford apprenticeships for two daughters when we were young, and it wasn't my charming personality.

I shooed the goats away from the front gate and held it wide for Eoghan to pass through. The sweet ram butted his head against my hip, begging for attention.

Anyone else might have commented on the cozy little house, with its fresh thatching and bright blue shutters, or the riot of greens in the front garden. They might have petted the goats and asked their names. Our house was a beacon of Mother's love and devotion. Edith and I helped, of course, but this property and these animals were her passion.

Eoghan, however, said nothing at all. He followed me silently to the front porch and made no comment when I shoved the ram with a hip so I could climb the steps and open the door.

In fact, the first indication he was a real human being—and not just a big, silent shadow—came when I went inside and held the door open for him to follow. He hesitated on the porch, brows gathered slightly in the middle, eyes on my knees.

"Come inside, Eoghan."

Mother appeared behind me and looked up at him over my shoulder. "Nora? Who's this?"

"Come inside, Eoghan," I said again. I stepped back further and opened the door a little wider.

And then he did just that. Without any change to his expression or bearing, he simply walked inside, like there had been no hesitation at all. Just like at the Council Room, he planted himself against the wall near the door.

Fine. That was just fine. At least he'd come into the damn house.

"Eoghan, this is my mother, Zoya. And that is Edith, my sister." I gestured at Edith, who stood at the washbasin, with water dripping down her elbows.

I probably didn't need to specify our relationship, because she and I were obviously sisters. We had the same small stature, the same dark curls tumbling down our backs. She did have wider-set eyes and fairer skin than me, though, and she stood a couple of inches taller—a hint of her father showing through. My own father had been nearly as short as the rest of us, according to Mother.

Edith wiped her wet hands on her apron and stood next to Mother, eyes narrowed.

"Edith, Mother. This is Eoghan. He and I have been asked to go on a surveying job."

Eoghan nodded to my family and even managed a, "Pleasure to meet you," which was impressive for him, I thought.

"A surveying job?" Mother asked. She had been there when Nikita first spoke to me that morning, and she knew it was something about the war. Something secret.

"A surveying job," I said with a confident nod, and left it at that.

"When do you leave?" Mother's voice was soft and resigned.

Eoghan and I exchanged a brief glance, but of course, I was the one to answer. "First thing in the morning."

"Well, this is very odd," Edith said with half a laugh. She moved back toward the washbasin and reapplied her rag to the mixing bowl she had been scrubbing before we entered. "Why the urgency? Is that where you were all morning? Mother has been so cagey about it."

"Yes." I pulled out a chair at the dining table and eyed Eoghan meaningfully. *Sit down. Be polite.*

He took a deep breath, but he began to dutifully unbuckle the massive pack, which rode high on his shoulders. Eoghan laid it down carefully. Pots, utensils, and tools hanging off the back clanged when they hit the floor.

I patted the chair meant for him, satisfied he would sit, and fetched down a tin of pound cake from the shelf.

Mother eyed him warily. She had resumed wringing her apron between her hands. I wished there was some way for me to reassure her, but there wasn't. I couldn't lie to her, couldn't tell her the truth. I figured introducing her to Eoghan before we left was the absolute best I could do.

I served out two portions of the pound cake and set one down in front of Eoghan with a muffled clink of ceramic on wood. He stared at the cake like it was something foreign and possibly dangerous.

"It's pound cake," I said in a softer voice, handing him a fork. "Here. Eat. It's good. Made it myself last night."

"Excuse me?" Edith said, eyebrow raised.

"Edith helped," I added, which was patently untrue. I couldn't bake to save my life, and I had spent the entire evening sneaking fingerfuls of raw batter out of the bowl while Edith measured and mixed.

Edith rolled her eyes. "Pfft." She set the now-clean mixing bowl on the rack to dry, then stole my plate of cake. She slid it away right as I was going to slice off a bite, so my fork hit the table instead.

"Hey!"

Somewhere in the midst of our back-and-forth, Eoghan relaxed a miniscule amount. He lifted his own fork and finally began to eat.

Mother sat down opposite him and watched his steady progress through the cake. He didn't look up once.

"So, Eoghan," Mother finally said. "Where's home?"

Eoghan paused for half a second as he took in the question. "Grew up with my Nan near The Great Forest. Haven't been there in nearly fifteen years, though. Home is where I set up camp at night."

"And where's that?"

"Near the Lesser Apgatt, right?" I asked.

He glanced at me before forking the last bite of his cake. "I'll camp in the woods back of your house. It's closer."

"We have a spare cot we can lay out on the floor here," Mother offered, her voice solemn. What must have been going through her mind? This stranger in her house, about to take her daughter out into the wild world, only the fates knew where.

"I'll camp in the woods," Eoghan said with finality. He laid his fork on his empty plate and stood up with a scrape of his chair on the wooden floor. "Thank you for the cake. It was delicious."

"You're leaving?" I asked, unimpressed.

"You said you wanted help packing."

"Yes, and I also said something about a real meal. Don't think I've forgotten."

He let out a barely there sigh. "I didn't expect you had."

Edith laughed. "He's got your number, Nora."

"Yes, thank you, Edith." I gestured for Eoghan to follow me to the back of the house, to my bedroom.

We spent the next two hours carefully sorting through my possessions and packing them into a set of sturdy traveling bags from the storage shed. Eoghan seemed to find himself in his element, because he finally opened up a bit as he directed me about the room.

"Wool, not linen. It'll be much colder at the higher elevations. Linen won't keep you warm if it gets wet...I have a cooking pot. You don't need more...At least two more pairs of socks. You'll change them twice a day. Don't you have any thicker ones?...Do you seriously need all these tools?"

This one earned my first pushback.

"Yes, I need these tools." I snatched my caliper back from him. "How do you expect me to do my job without my cartography tools?"

"You're not going to be mapping anything. You've got all the maps you need."

"Like hell, I won't be mapping." I stowed the caliper carefully into its slot next to my pen knives and rolled up the toolkit into a tight bundle. Admittedly, there really wasn't room for it in my overfull pack. But I needed these. And for hell's sake, now that Eoghan had said they weren't necessary, I would sew an entirely new travel pack if it meant I could get my cartography tools to fit.

"What—" Eoghan bit off whatever charged comment threatened to burst out of his mouth. He took a deep breath in, then let it out. "Fine. But you're carrying it, not me. Every ounce of weight matters."

"I understand," I said, with only a little bit of petulance in my tone. Honestly, it could have been much worse. "I'll carry it."

He eyed my skinny arms and narrow frame almost like he didn't think I could carry the pack empty, much less full. But he kept his mouth shut, and I kept mine shut likewise. There were no more arguments.

Eoghan spent the rest of the afternoon on our front porch, with the cheerful ram dozing on his thigh. Mother and I stared out at him from the window. He didn't seem to be doing anything at all. From this vantage point, his face wasn't visible. But from his posture and the way he leaned his head back against the railing, he might have been just as deeply asleep as the goat on his lap.

"Are you sure about this?" Mother asked in a low voice.

I thought long and hard before answering her. "I don't have a choice."

"There's always a choice, Nora."

I chewed my lip. Outside, Eoghan shifted his weight and laid a gentle hand on the ram.

Mother was right. I had a choice. I didn't *have* to go anywhere in the morning. I could return to the paper mill and hang up my paper to dry in the airy shed. I could spend the afternoon at Nikita's house, translating and copying and drawing. I could spend my days helping Mother with the animals. Or I could join the war effort. They always needed cartographers, despite Nikita's insistence that I stay in Tutree.

"You're needed here," she had always said when the subject got brought up.

Until now, of course. She had practically shoved me out of town herself.

And I was leaving. I didn't have to, but the more I thought about it, the more I knew I *wanted* to. A chance to see the Giant's Mountain with my own eyes? And maybe look upon the Giants themselves?

It had been nearly a thousand years since the Giants last walked the earth. All we had were faded, deteriorated accounts written in dead languages and half-destroyed drawings. And there was no way to tell what was a literal description and what was metaphoric or poetic.

But the Giants were real. They had promised they would rise up in the time of Lujor's greatest need. I wouldn't just be learning history; I would be making it.

I'd get to examine secret archives from the High Reliquary himself and do something that mattered. And in my heart of hearts, I was desperately glad this mission would be sending me in the opposite direction of the front lines.

"I'm sure, Mother," I said. "I'm terrified, to be honest. But it's the opportunity of a lifetime, where we're going. I want to go."

Mother's eyes slid back toward Eoghan dozing on the porch. "And you trust him?"

"I'll learn to trust him."

"Is it safe where you're going?"

I let out a heavy sigh. "Is anywhere safe anymore?"

"Home is safe," Mother said.

I slipped my hand into her crooked elbow and hugged her arm tightly. "Our home is safe, but not everyone is as lucky as us. I can help them. I can stop this war."

Mother pressed her lips into a thin line and drew her eyebrows together. "You're going up the mountain, aren't you?"

I said nothing, just hugged her arm closer.

Four

That evening, after an awkward supper where Eoghan said a grand total of six words—"Please pass the beans," and "Thank you."—I walked him out to the back porch to say goodnight.

"We'll leave at dawn. Be ready to go," he said, shrugging on his pack once more.

"Why dawn?" I asked. "Seems like every journey starts at dawn. I always thought it was just something they said in stories to make it sound more dramatic."

Eoghan's eyes had fallen to stare at my knees—his favorite thing to look at, I supposed. "Can't hike at night."

"But you *can* hike at noon," I countered, with a hint of petulance. "Shoot, we could leave now and get a few hours in before nightfall."

With an eyebrow raised and the corner of his mouth quirked up, he *almost* seemed amused. It was weirdly delightful. An insane ambition to make him actually laugh implanted itself in my chest.

"You want to leave now?" he asked. And for the first time, there was a hint of irony in his tone.

"No." I said it a little too fast, just in case he was being serious.

Someday, I'd make this man laugh. Not today, maybe. But soon. We had plenty of time.

"Dawn it is, then," he said.

Eoghan disappeared around the back of the house and into the woods shading our yard. I watched him go, my eyebrows furrowed, until he disappeared between the trees.

The door opened and closed behind me, and Edith appeared at my side. She mirrored my posture: arms crossed, back ramrod straight, staring deep into the woods where Eoghan had gone. We even had the same curly hair pulled back into hasty braids.

"I like him," she announced. "Bit of a wallflower, but he seems like a good sort of person."

"Hm."

Edith put an arm around my shoulders and turned me toward the door. "Come inside, love. Mother's put on some tea. If we only have one more night with you, then let's make the most of it."

The three of us spent a quiet evening at home. Mother decided all the chores could wait until the next day, so as soon as the bare minimum was done to keep the animals safe overnight, she pulled out a dusty bottle of whiskey to spike our tea with. We sat in our usual chairs near the fire, setting the world to rights, and got more and more giggly as the sun got lower.

I had a bit of scrap paper and my little tin of charcoal in my lap. As we talked, a simple portrait of my mother and sister blossomed into being. It was happy, with hints of smiles and squinty eyes. I exaggerated the light from the fire, the lamps, and the twilight outside, trying to make it even cheerier than it really was.

Because under all the ease and companionship, there was the constant threat of melancholy. This was our last night. Tomorrow, I'd be gone, and only the Old Kind knew when I'd see them again.

Mother must have been thinking the same. Occasionally, she would look at me, and the light in her eyes would dim. But then she'd straighten her spine, affix that smile to her face, and say something rude about Mistress Malacky down the road. And of course, that set us all to giggling again.

We stayed up late, but Mother had a farm to run, and that meant she'd be up with the sun as well. So, we had to go to bed eventually. She hugged me tightly outside my door but refused to cry.

"Don't leave without saying goodbye," she said sternly into my hair.

"I won't, Mother. I promise."

She squeezed my hand one last time, took a deep breath, and turned toward her own bedroom.

But even with the late hour, I couldn't sleep. Finally alone, I pulled Lachlan's archives from the travel pack and spread them out on my desk in my bedroom. I placed my lamp carefully and sat down to read through the pages.

There were four accounts. The oldest was by a man named Lewys, written in Old Ambic. Lewys was very fond of grandiose descriptions of literally everything he saw, but then again, Old Ambic always felt a bit pompous anyway.

The second was a woman called Elaine, who traveled up the mountain with her teenage son. Her account of the journey was very practical. The third was another woman, Tanisha. She was from Amau and was a bit of a stickler for detail. Tanisha had included rudimentary maps and several sketches of landmarks and had even counted her steps in some cases. Tedious, but useful.

The last one was a young man named Luthor, a true adventurer. He wrote daily entries about the views, his girlfriend back home, and his wolfhound companion named Lobo. I admittedly fell a little bit in love with Luthor as I read his account of finding the fabled Archways, about the cliff where he could see all the way to the ocean, and his nights spent cuddled with his hound for warmth. And when I reached the end of his entries, I remembered what Lachlan had said earlier that day.

"What happened to these people?"

"Executed. Three of them were before my time. This last one, I was a docent back then. It was done in secret. I didn't learn about it until much later, but I was there in the Reliquary when it happened."

He had been talking about Luthor.

There were only a few hours left before I had to get up. Eoghan would be at my door at dawn, pack high and tight, eyes on my knees, probably. So I carefully stowed the four archives in their folders, then into the leather case. And the case itself went into my own travel pack, which stood ready and waiting by my bedroom door.

Tomorrow, the adventure would begin.

~

Bang! Bang! Bang!

I jerked onto my elbows with a gasp, staring blearily around at my still-dark bedroom. The house was quiet, and for a moment, I thought I had dreamed the noise. But then...

Bang! Bang! Bang!

The front door.

"Nora!"

Eoghan? My foggy brain struggled to keep up, then I gasped. "Eoghan."

I scrambled out of the bed and promptly tripped over my sheets, nearly hitting the floor before managing to disentangle myself. The way Eoghan had called my name set my heart racing without me knowing why. I pulled open the door just as he raised his fist to knock again.

"What? What is it?"

Mother's door opened behind me, and she rubbed her eyes. "What's going on?"

"Get dressed." Eoghan pushed past me into the house. He went straight for my bedroom, with me trailing behind. "We have to go. Now. Zoya, Edith, pack what you can and get out. Head south. Go on foot or by horse, if you have one. No time for any kind of cart or carriage."

He picked up my pack and made to hand it to me, then paused.

"Why aren't you dressed?"

"Eoghan, what is going on?" I asked.

"What do you mean, get out?" Mother added.

Edith finally appeared in the main room, still tugging on her clothes, as if she had only just thrown them on to cover herself. "What's all the yelling about?"

Eoghan snatched up the pile of clothes I had left out the night before for easy access and shoved those into my hands instead.

"Amau is coming," he replied.

Mother's breath stopped on a gasp.

"I saw them coming up the valley. They'll be here in minutes. We have to move."

"No," I said breathlessly, still clutching the pile of loose clothing.

Mother was already moving, scrambling to the kitchen to gather supplies.

"Yes," Eoghan said. "I've seen it before. They've got wagons backed high with barrels. It's pitch. They're going to fire Tutree."

Edith let out a whimper and hurried to help Mother gather up yesterday's bread and sacks of beans and salt. Even the tin of pound cake was tossed into the bag.

"They wouldn't." I remained rooted to the spot. "We're too far southwest. They don't want anything from us."

"They would, and they are." Eoghan bent low to get on my eye level and gripped me by my upper arms, but I could barely feel it. "Get dressed. Your family can alert the town, but you and I have to go. Now. Get dressed."

He pushed me deeper into the room and shut the door to give me some privacy.

I stood there for a few seconds, still frozen. But the clatter of a dropped pan in the kitchen shocked me into action. Mother and Edith were packing in a panic to *evacuate* our home. And our family was the only one who even knew evacuation was needed.

I ripped off my sleeping shirt and set about getting dressed with steady hands. And then, instead of picking up my pack and opening my bedroom door, I pushed aside my curtains and climbed out the window.

I didn't even spare a glance back at the house while I jogged down the street. As if I would *ever* leave my town, my family and friends, my neighbors, when they needed me. This was one lesson Eoghan would have to learn about me the hard way.

The town was hushed. The moon was long set, and the stars glowed in a blanket of sparkling diamonds in the sky. Sometimes, when I was very quiet and strained my ears, I liked to think I could hear them. That the stars had a music of their own, like the wind, the trees, the birds, and the crickets.

But now, the only sound was the crunch of the gravel road under my booted feet running toward town. Everyone was inside, tucked safe in their beds. The animals were quiet in their barns, and the world was still. Everything seemed perfectly fine.

I slowed to a halt, breathing hard, and stared around.

Everything was perfectly fine. Nothing out of place. Not a noise that didn't belong. Just the crickets, the stars, the wind, and the darkened homes sleeping around me. Suddenly, I felt foolish for rushing out of the house at the word of a stranger.

And so, I spun on my heel and backtracked, then turned up the cart track leading to the paper mill. When I topped the rise and the mill came into view, everything seemed calm. I cast a mournful glance at the weighted stack of paper I had dipped the morning before. In all the excitement, I had never hung them up to dry.

I approached the stone bracket of the wheel, which had been braked for the night. The river below swirled past the diverter.

Nothing more than the swish of water passing over stones and brushing along the bank disturbed the night.

On the opposite bank, the road into Tutree was empty. There was no one, Amau or otherwise. Everything was exactly as it should have been.

Maybe Eoghan had been mistaken? I didn't know the man *at all*, but he didn't seem like a liar or a schemer. What had he seen that made him think an army was coming? Maybe it had been a nightma—

Something disturbed the darkness down the road, barely visible in the distance.

"Oh fuck," I said breathlessly into the night. Panic swooped through my gut so hard I felt nauseous.

But...no. Wait.

I thought I'd seen something out of the corner of my eye, a darkened shape moving in the night. But I must have imagined it. There was nothing there. I peered closer. Only blackness. Nothing at all was audible over the swirling of the water below.

Or had I imagined it? I was so on edge I couldn't tell anymore. But sometimes, when you looked directly at an object in the dark, it seemed to disappear. So I slid my eyes just to the right of the place where I'd spotted the movement and watched the area in my periphery.

There. Fuck. Fuck, shit, damn. There *was* something there.

Many somethings passing before a white boulder that was only just visible in the starlight. People, dozens of them. Maybe more. I couldn't tell in the dark. But there was no reason for such a crowd to be traveling silently in the middle of the night with no lamps. Especially not here, out in the middle of nowhere.

My feet began moving without conscious thought. I passed my abandoned stack of paper and skipped over the rough cart track, back into the village and the main road. I sprinted through town and didn't even feel the ground under my feet or the breath in my lungs. All I knew was—fuck. I didn't *know* anything in particular. I just had to get to the bell tower in the square.

Tutree wasn't a big place, but we had a bell, just like anywhere else. It wasn't manned or anything, and it only got rung once a year, if that. The last time was because a brush fire had been getting too close for comfort. Two years before that, a dam upriver of the Greater Apgatt had cracked and threatened to break. Both times, no actual harm had come to Tutree. No harm *ever* came to Tutree.

Until now.

I skirted around the low wall bordering the square and slammed open the gate of the bell tower. Then I launched myself at the heavy rope and dragged my weight down.

Nothing.

The rope pulled me up to my tiptoes on the upswing. This time, there was a little tap of the clapper on the great brass bell.

I clung to the rope and sagged back down, heaving with all my weight. The rope went lower this time, and the bell finally rang properly.

CLANG!

The rope yanked me up until my feet left the ground.

CLANG!

I dragged it back so low my ass nearly hit the ground.

CLA-CLANG!

Up and down I went, ringing the bell for as long as I possibly could. The effects of my mad dash through the town were finally catching up to me. I couldn't breathe, couldn't think. My heart was a drum in my chest, beating so hard it hurt.

CLANG! CLANG!

Up, down. Up, down.

CLANG!

"Nora! S'that you? What are you doing? What's going on?"

I whirled around on the rope on an upswing and found a

familiar face. Maison and his husband, Cai, the bakers who lived on the square, peered at me through the dark.

I tugged the rope down one last time and finally peeled my fingers away. My hands burned with the effort of gripping the rough rope for so long, but I ignored the pain and yanked Maison inside instead.

"Keep ringing. Amau is coming. They're going to burn the town. They're on the road just outside. Cai, spread the word!"

Maison stared at me with wide eyes but allowed me to tug him into the narrow tower.

"What? Nora?" he spluttered, even while his hands closed over the rope. "Wait!"

"Just keep ringing as long as you can, then get out!" I shouted after him.

Cai was already running to the nearest shops, banging on doors and yelling for the owners sleeping upstairs.

I ran from house to house, hammering on doors. Most of them were already open, with sleepy and confused townspeople staring at me and asking questions. I told them to get out, to run, to only take what they needed, to pass the word! Soon the streets were full of people bustling, yelling, gathering screaming toddlers, pulling goats and horses behind them, and setting chickens free from their coops to flee on their own.

It was chaos. We were not prepared for this.

I tried to help, to keep things in order. "Just move calmly," "No, no. Only what you can carry," "It's all right, sweetheart. Just let me hold you while Mama grabs your bag."

But none of it worked. The panic only grew as more and more people were alerted. Some shouted that we were being crazy, that there was no danger. Who said Amau was coming anyway?

But then came the screams from down the street and the first tinges of smoke on the wind. That was when the true pandemonium began.

People began to run. They stopped talking and started yelling.

Fights broke out around me, and someone knocked into me so hard I stumbled to the ground. The rough gravel dug into the palm of my hand, but I barely felt the sting.

Screaming, crying, wailing, running...Panic, panic, panic. A faint orange glow appeared in the distance.

Fire.

I had done what I could. The town was awake. Even though it was far too late to stop this, at least my warning bell meant no one would be caught in their beds by the smoke and flames. I scrambled to my feet, just to be knocked down again by someone else. A goat clambered over me with sharp little hooves. I threw my arms over my head when a human shoe connected with my thigh.

I had to get up. No one could see me on the ground in the dark. No one was looking anyway. The crowd surged and roiled as people fled south with their children and as many animals as they could drag along behind them. But every time I tried to rise up, something else struck me, and I went stumbling back down.

I needed to get to Nikita, still. With her bad hip, she would struggle more than most. And I owed her a severe berating for keeping secrets, anyway.

Crawl, Nora. Just get out of the road!

But every inch was hard-earned, and the safety of a less-crowded side street was so far away...I wasn't going to make it. Someone tripped over me, and their partner dragged them back up and kept going. A heavy bag banged into me from behind. A child climbed right over me, struggling to keep up with his mother. A man cursed me when his shoe collided with my arm and knocked me down for the tenth time.

And all around me was the noise, the growing stink of smoke, and the raw, metal tang of panic in the air.

Then a large hand closed around my arm, digging into a fresh bruise, and I thrashed against it on reflex. But the grip was painfully firm, and I was hauled upward by my arm. I found myself face-to-face with...

"Eoghan?"

His expression was dark with anger and frustration. Any second now, he would start reprimanding me for running off, for endangering myself this way. For abandoning the archives in my room without telling anyone at all. And even though he'd be right on all counts, I was ready to bite back. Just you dare try, Eoghan. Just try.

"Which way to the Wall?"

"What?" This was far and away the least likely thing he could have ever chosen to say.

Eoghan dragged me toward the side street, where we could at least stand upright without being knocked down again by the crowd.

"The Wall? Which way?" His expression was still dark, and his voice was hoarse with smoke and yelling. Probably from calling for me all over town.

I looked around in the dark, both horrified and grateful for the growing orange glow illuminating our surroundings.

There were actual flames already. Right down the road, fire flicked its way up a thatched roof, and smoke billowed out of windows. I hadn't spotted a single Amau soldier. They were very good. They had snuck in and out like ghosts, and there would be only ashes and death in their wake.

"Uh..."

"Focus, Nora! Which way?"

"Uh, um. There's the bakery. Oh shit, it's on fire. We have to make sure Elliot got out!"

Eoghan shook me and turned me bodily away from the chaos. "No! We have to go! Which way! I am completely turned around."

But I peered over my shoulder, straining my neck in the process. "We can't leave, Eoghan! They need our help! And Nikita! I have to go get Nikita. She can hardly walk these days!"

"We can't help them, Nora! We can't help anyone. But we *can* end this for good. Make sure this never happens again. Which way to the Wall?"

"The archives?"

He shifted his shoulder, and my bag was thrust unceremoniously into my arms. Packed and ready to go, just like I'd left it.

"I'm pretty sure I told you I wouldn't be carrying that."

"Don't start being all high and mighty now, you asshole. Help me get this on." I heaved the heavy pack around, and Eoghan helped me lift it onto my shoulders. After hitching it a little higher with an awkward half-jump, I buckled it across my chest and started walking.

"Where are you going?"

"To the Wall. To make sure this never happens again, remember?"

Eoghan followed dutifully behind.

It took everything I had to keep heading west. More than once, Eoghan had to grab my arm to keep me from veering off down this side street or that alley to help someone load a cart or pass children out of windows with smoke billowing out around them. I screamed my frustration at him and wrenched my arm out of his grasp, but I kept moving forward.

And I might have been able to hate him for it...until we came across a man desperately trying to hoist his elderly father into a cart directly in our path. Eoghan dashed forward and lifted the father with ease, and we were walking again, with the son gasping his thanks to our backs.

I glanced up at Eoghan while we walked on.

"What?" he asked.

"Nothing. This way."

It was quieter on the west side of town. People were still evacuating, but the fire and the panic hadn't spread this far yet. The townsfolk passed by us like ghosts, talking to each other in hushed tones and moving quickly. More than once, someone paused and watched us going in the wrong direction. There was nothing this way except for the Wall, and they knew we'd find no salvation there.

I led us off the main road and veered toward a small park, where Edith and I had often played as children. The Wall was short here. It bordered the park on the western side and was little more than three feet of stone and cement.

"It's not much of a wall, is it?" Eoghan said.

I rested my hand on the poured cement top, which rose only to my hip. "It's enough."

Eoghan glanced around one last time, making sure no one was following us, and climbed gracefully over the Wall as if it were only stone. He paused about ten feet away when he realized I hadn't followed him.

"Let's go."

"It's not dawn," I said.

Eoghan's face softened in the moonlight. The glow of the fires didn't reach us here, but I could still smell the smoke on the wind. He came back toward me and paused, for once not urging me forward. He just waited.

"This wall is the entire reason Tutree was founded, you know. To keep people away from the Giant's Mountain. It was a fort and a wall, and it became a town. And over time, the fort was converted into warehouses and a market and housing. And the soldiers turned their hands to trade instead of patrolling the border." I drew my fingers along the cement and kept my eyes there, on something safe. Something familiar.

"Nora..."

"It's always been here. The border of my world. I never even thought about the land out that way. It was only the Giant's Mountain and the Western Waste. Nothing more to know."

I shrugged against the weight of my pack. Hell, it was heavy. Maybe he'd had a point about my cartography tools.

Eoghan stood silent, a shape in the darkness. He didn't push, didn't question.

"My mother crossed the Wall once, did you know? When I was little. She...I didn't say goodbye to her. Oh fuck, Eoghan. I told her I'd say goodbye before I left!"

"No, Nora. Don't." Eoghan reached over the wall and grabbed my arm before I could turn around. "Don't ever look back."

"But—"

"Zoya knows. Trust me, a parent knows what's in...what's in your heart. No going back."

His grip on my arm was a comforting warmth against the cool night air. He slid his hand down my arm and grabbed mine firmly, then gave a small tug. *Time to go.*

I couldn't see his eyes in the dark, not properly, but I could feel them on me. *Time to go. Come with me. You're safe. We're safe.*

"Help me up," I said in a small voice.

Eoghan gave a stronger tug and helped me up onto the Wall. I fought the urge to hesitate, to savor the moment when I finally crossed the Wall, when I would leave behind the world I had always known.

But I didn't. I just hopped up, then jumped down again. My feet landed in the unremarkable grass illuminated by the unremarkable moon. Eoghan dropped my hand. My fingers felt cold without him.

"We'll walk until dawn, then rest when we can see well enough to find a good camp. But we have to get away from town while we have the cover of darkness. We don't want to risk someone seeing us or following us."

Don't look back. Don't look back.

"Okay. Let's go."

Eoghan nodded once, and we both turned to the west. Toward the Giant's Mountain. Away from the Wall. Away from home.

Don't look back.

Part Two
Waking Up the Giants

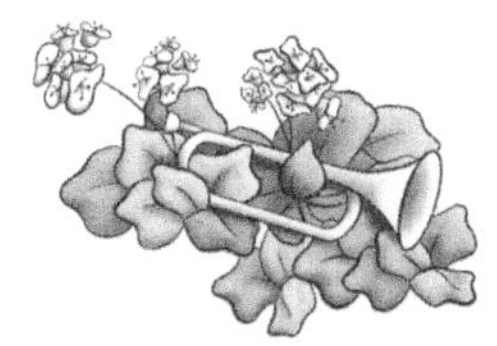

FIVE
EOGHAN

"These can't be natural rock formations." Nora gazed up at the moss-covered arches as she passed under them. "Look at these angles. These are deliberate."

"There are no ruins in these mountains," I answered gruffly. "No man-made anything."

"You can't know that, Eoghan." She slipped her hand into the smaller bag around her waist and predictably pulled out her sketchbook. "The mountain wasn't always forbidden. Maybe people lived up here at some point. You never know."

Her long, dark braid swung when she turned on the spot.

"There are ten of them." Nora stared around in wonder. Her little stick of charcoal flew over the topmost sheet of paper. "All different, but all geometric. Nothing occurs naturally in groups of ten. Especially not rock formations. I mean, look at it! It feels like a room in here!"

Her sketchbook wasn't a book. Books were expensive and meant to last. You didn't bind them until you had words and drawings worth saving. Instead, she carried a leather binder containing a stack of rough paper, which she had pressed herself—a useless skill for anyone but a mapmaker.

Thank the Old Kind she hadn't brought a book. No one would ever see her sketches. Not ever. But I didn't have the heart to tell her so.

In nearly two weeks on the mountain, she had used three sheets: one for notes, one for a rough map, and one for sketching unusual trees or recognizable outcroppings. "So we can find our way home," she explained on the third night, her nose close to the paper so she could see in the firelight.

Home, she said. Nora never talked about the fact that her home was probably gone. Cinder, ash, and bones.

Her drawing of the Archways took up an entire precious page. She indicated folds in the stone with concise, confident strokes, and the hanging moss blossomed in black coal on the paper.

These arches were more than just a landmark. They were the first remarkable thing we had encountered in our ten days of walking. They rose from the weeds and brush in an awkward dome under the high canopy of pines, both alien and natural in this forest shrouded in superstition.

They stood exactly where we expected to find them; Nora's archives had led us here with confidence. If the stories were true, this was the most likely place to find the Clarion.

I eyed the Archways as I stepped past Nora and down under the dome. She was right: it did feel a bit like a room.

The floor dipped downward into a shallow bowl composed of the same limestone, dolomite, and shale as the arches above us. The entire space was empty, save for the tumbled stones and the stubborn weeds growing in the cracks. The morning sun streamed in through the irregular gaps between the arches, striping the uneven floor with light.

"I still don't think it's man-made." I slipped my main pack off my shoulders. The pots clattered against the stony ground when I set it down. "There would be a real floor, not just more ground." I kicked one of the smaller stones with the toe of my heavy, time-worn boot.

"I'm telling you, this doesn't happen in nature," Nora insisted. She slipped her completed drawing to the bottom of the pile and began sketching a second page. "This is limestone, right? The grain is very fine. It's just solid stone." She stood on her tiptoes and laid one dark hand on the nearest arch. It was one of two shorter ones jutting from opposing walls. They each extended about twenty feet across, then ended in a rounded-off edge.

Two short arches right at the back of the room, and eight longer ones stretched across the entire ceiling—for lack of a better word.

"This entire mountain is limestone. And some shale," I reminded her.

"Yes, but neither of those form like this! I keep telling you!"

"But it isn't carved either." I examined the arch nearest to me. "I'm no mason, Nora, but I know one thing for certain. Tools leave either rough-hewn marks, or they leave a deliberate, smooth surface. These have neither. This isn't man-made."

Nora lowered her sketch pad. Her fingers had gone black with the charcoal, as usual. She chewed on her lip, thinking hard. "Maybe it's just weathered?"

"Nora..." I said again, my tone just barely containing my lost patience.

"Eoghan," she responded with scorn, then waved me away. "It doesn't make any difference. We're clearly in the right place. Finally."

I threw out my arms and swung in a circle to encompass the cavernous room. "Are we, though? There's nothing here!"

She lurched half a step back at my outburst, and a startled bevy of pigeons took flight between the arches to the safety of the pines outside.

I was a big man, especially compared to her small, athletic frame. Tall, broad, and sun-darkened, with dirt-colored hair tied into a hasty knot at the back of my head, I was as foreboding as any ranger you might expect to see tramping in from the wild, bristling with hunting knives and furs for trade.

In the ten days Nora had known me, I'd been careful to be as unobtrusive as possible. This was probably my last friend in the world. I didn't want her to be afraid.

Her surprise was short-lived. Nora closed her leather binder, scowling, and wrapped the cord around it twice with a practiced hand. "The archives led us here. These arches are unnatural. We're right on schedule. The Clarion must be here. It *has* to be."

I dropped my hands to my sides with an exasperated sigh. "Fine."

"Just—" She pointed at one of the larger piles of stones on my left. "Just start shifting rocks. We came all this way. We have to at least look for it."

Nora slipped the packs off her back and moved toward a pile of stones near her feet—one large enough to conceal a medium-sized chest in the rubble. There she began heaving stones end over end to expose what lay underneath.

Unsurprisingly, there was only more stone under there.

I watched her determined progress for a full twenty seconds before following suit.

Nora was right. Every day, new smoke rose up in the valley below from another village burning. There was no time for hesitation, and giving up was not an option.

We started in the center, on the assumption it was the most logical place to find the fabled Clarion. When that failed, we continued with the largest piles.

The bright stripes of light crept along the floor as the sun moved across the sky. The only sounds were Nora's grunts of effort and the scrape and thud of stones being overturned.

Whenever I lifted a rock, I half expected to find an ancient chest or a glint of brass. But each time, I was disappointed.

And every time I thought a specific rock wasn't big enough to hide anything important, I always went back and checked under it anyway. Just in case.

After about two hours, Nora stood up and stretched her lower spine with a grimace. "Let's stop for lunch."

I turned over another stone, then another. "Let's finish this section first." A rock tumbled over as I reached for a particularly large one.

"I'm starving, Eoghan. Let's just take a break."

"Have your break," I said with a grunt, hauling on the large stone. "I'll stop in a minute."

"You're going to hurt yourself," she said, one eyebrow raised.

I smirked and opened my mouth to answer, but the stone shifted under my hands. I lost my balance and toppled backward onto my ass. Nora leaped away to avoid being crushed under me, and pain seared through my tailbone when I hit the uneven ground.

"Holy shit, Eoghan! I said you'd hurt yourself! Are you okay?"

She pulled on my arm to help me up, but she didn't have the strength for it. I lumbered to my feet, ignoring the pain, and appraised the stone I had dislodged.

It had only partially come away from its spot, wedged between two other stones in the pile, but a dark gap had opened behind it.

"Holy..." Nora said breathlessly. She darted forward and plunged her hands into the crevice. "You found it, Eoghan. It's here."

She wiped black earth away from a square corner inside the gap, revealing the dull shine of brass fittings.

The air left my lungs in a whoosh. "Holy shit." I stared in shock at the narrow slice of the chest visible behind the stone.

It was real.

There it was, just like they had said it would be. Just like in the stories. A small portion of the chest was visible in the crevice, but judging by the pile of stones I had dislodged, it would be about the size of one of my boots.

Nora laughed out loud as I heaved on the stone with renewed energy. "I knew it! I told you! I told you it would be here!"

"We don't know what's in it," I said. Then, with a roar of effort from me, the stone finally gave way.

"It's the Clarion!" Nora insisted. "What else is it going to be?"

She helped me rock the small chest out of its tight quarters. I set it on the ground and stepped away. We stared down at it, both stunned into silence.

The little box was unremarkable. Made of ancient, scarred wood and held together with hammered brass, it looked a bit like something you'd find in the back of an average closet. A box for knickknacks or old letters.

"It's made of wood," Nora said, wary. "Why hasn't it rotted in all this time?"

The exact same thought had occurred to me too.

"Well..." She slapped my arm with the back of her filthy hand. "Open it. Go on."

I raised my eyes to the unnatural arches above us, exasperated, but then knelt obediently.

There was no lock, only a simple latch. The hinge was so encrusted with filth I had to pry it up with the edge of my knife. I gripped the lid gently—surely, the wood was less solid than it appeared. If the legends were true, this box had been buried under this rubble for a thousand years. Hidden away on the lonely Giant's Mountain, far away from the machinations of mankind.

But the rough-hewn, gray wood was solid as the day it was made. The hinges ground open under my hand.

Dirty black velvet lined the inside, as untouched by time as the box itself. And nestled in the softness lay a small brass trumpet. Nothing special. Just a wide mouthpiece and a single, elongated loop of tubing, which flared into a delicate bell at the other end.

Simple, unadorned, and unremarkable.

Nora crouched next to me and lifted it out. She held it up between her coal-covered hands so we could both see.

Triumph and dread twisted my chest into knots. "Well, there it is," I said, more businesslike than I felt.

"There it is," she replied in a whisper.

"Okay. Let's get going." I gave a decisive nod, rose to my feet, and retrieved my pack without a backward glance.

Nora stared after me, her mouth hanging open. "That's it?"

"What?"

"We're just gonna go? Just like that?"

"As opposed to what?"

She looked down at the Clarion in her hands. Nora held it out in front of her body, as if she were afraid to get too close to it. "We came all this way. Ten days in the wilderness of the mountain, on faith alone. And here it is. This is history, Eoghan. This is why the old pilgrimages were forbidden! To protect this!"

She raised the horn and brandished it at me. It was so small I could have bent it in half with my bare hands.

This little thing? This was where we hung all our hopes?

"This is..." she said, half to herself. "There are no words for what this is."

"What use are words?" I shrugged my pack onto my shoulders. "We came to find the Clarion. That's done. Now we take it and move on."

"But—"

"The sooner we make the peak, the better. Every day, the Amau army draws closer to the capital, Nora. Soon, we won't have a history anymore. It'll go up in flames, just like everything else. Now, let's go. On your feet, mapmaker."

Six

I left Nora to come to her senses and stepped back out into the open air under the pines. This high up, the wind was chilly and fresh. It cooled the sweat on my brow and ruffled through my greasy hair.

The fires still burned in the valley below, but the smoke didn't reach us up here. The wind carried the scents of flowers, grass, soil, and rain. I closed my eyes and breathed in deep.

This.

This was why I had become a ranger. To be in the wilderness, to be free, was my only peace. And thank the Old Kind that I could spend my last days here in this unspoiled place, where no man had set foot in a hundred years or more.

"Help me tie this up."

I turned at Nora's determined tone. She had emerged from the darkness under the arches with the Clarion in one hand and a length of rope in the other.

"You want to tie it to your pack?" I asked.

"It won't fit inside."

"It will be damaged if you fall."

"I won't fall." She held the rope out to me, but I didn't take it.

"Nora..."

"You won't let me fall," she said sternly. She shook the rope in my direction once, insistent that I take it without argument. "You're better at knots than me."

Fine. That was just fine.

She turned around to give me access to her pack, but I put one hand on her arm to stop her. "It will be safer on your front. You'll be able to protect it with your arms."

Nora nodded once, then stood straight and silent while I worked. The straps of her pack crossed her body at a diagonal between her breasts. That was the best place to attach the Clarion. I secured it onto the strap, my fingers quick and practical.

"It shouldn't restrict your movement too much here," I explained.

Her eyes bored into me. She said nothing.

"Is there something on my face?" I pulled the rope under the strap of her pack again.

"You didn't think it was real, did you?" she asked.

Considering where my hands were at that moment, that was not what I expected to hear from her.

"What, the Clarion? Or the Giants?"

"Both. Either. Take your pick." Her eyebrows lowered and she lifted her chin, defiant.

I pulled the final knot tight and stepped back. The Clarion lay secure across her chest. If she was careful when taking her pack on and off, we wouldn't have to untie it until we reached the peak. Not until our last day.

"What difference does it make?" I didn't wait for her answer, but turned toward the west and resumed climbing. There wasn't time to stand around squabbling.

Nora's feet scraped through the scree as she scrambled after me. "Why in the fuck would you come on this mission if you didn't think it would work?"

"Would you rather I didn't come?" I asked, nettled.

"That's not what I said!" She caught up to me, not even out of breath. Nora had grown stronger since our first day out, when she had been green and eager—a fully certified mapmaker excited for her first adventure after being grounded her entire career. These ten days had turned her hard and determined, but her faith was untarnished.

"You'd be dead at the bottom of that ravine if it weren't for me!" I reminded her. It had been a near miss on our fourth day. I'd almost lost her.

"Stop changing the subject!" she snapped. "Why did you agree to climb the mountain? To find the Clarion and wake the Giants? If this is a fool's errand, then that makes you a fool. But you're no fool, Eoghan." She laughed sarcastically and wagged a finger at me. "You're no fool. You came on this mission for a reason, and it wasn't to wake the Giants and end this war with Amau."

I clamped my mouth shut and kept climbing.

Her short legs ate up the ground next to me, going nearly twice as fast as mine to equal my stride. Nora used her hands as much as her feet to scramble up the steeper inclines, the Clarion nestled against her chest.

"So, what? You think we'll reach the peak, sound the Clarion, and then what? Nothing?"

"Maybe," I said, despite my determination to not talk about this.

"Maybe?" she shrilled. "*Maybe*?"

I thought back to the shape of the ten stone arches that had cradled the Clarion, of Nora's expression as she recorded them in her sketchbook.

Maybe? No.

Hopefully, nothing would happen.

"Eoghan!"

"What do you want from me?" I rounded on her, causing her to skid to an unexpected stop. "I'm here, aren't I? We found the Clarion. We're taking it to the peak. We'll sound it. I'm doing everything I'm supposed to do. I'm getting you there. That's the job. What the hell else do you want me to say?"

She met my gaze, unflinching.

"Two days to the top, right? That's what your maps say? Your archives?"

Nora nodded, stubbornly mute.

I gripped her arms, my expression tight, but the words didn't come. All the things I wanted to say to her, that I wanted to protect her from but couldn't. The words dammed up in my throat as I held her gaze.

Damn it, this was why I always traveled alone. My job was to keep her safe. Fool's errand, indeed.

"Just keep walking," I said instead. "Two more days."

I released her and resumed climbing.

Just two more days. That was all we had left.

"We never ate lunch!" she spat at my back.

"Bloody hell," I muttered to myself. I had never rolled my eyes so much in my life as I had done in the last ten days. But my feet stopped their relentless marching, and I hauled off my pack.

We ate the last of yesterday's rabbit in dogged silence. We had long finished off the flatbreads we had brought with us, but Nora had rationed out the dried apricots so we could have a little every day.

I sucked on my portion while we walked, savoring the sweetness.

It was the little things.

We hiked in silence for the rest of the afternoon, stopping only when the sun began to get low. Nora set up camp while I slipped into the woods with my knife and my sling. Squirrels were easy prey this late in the autumn, and I returned to camp an hour later with a whole stack of them.

The two of us ate in silence, sitting close by the fire and watching the sun disappear below the horizon. Nora wrapped herself up in every piece of clothing she had brought with her, and even then, she sat right up against me.

"It's getting colder," she said, tucking her hands under her armpits.

"The air is thin up here." I put an arm around her shoulders, pulling her closer under my own cloak. "We'll have to start sharing our bedrolls if we want to sleep well."

"Fine," she replied, her eyes on the fire.

We sat in silence for a few minutes. I assumed—naively, in hindsight—that we did so in peace. The two of us huddled close to ward off the cold. A healthy pile of meat had been wrapped up in oil cloth, ready for tomorrow. That spot over there, just on the other side of the fire – that would be the perfect place for us to bed down in a few minutes.

The day had been a success. The Clarion glinted in the firelight from where it was still tied to the strap on her pack. Things were going well. According to plan, at least.

But of course, Nora's brain didn't dwell on simple matters. She didn't worry about rations, safety, or cold toes.

"Why wasn't the chest rotten?" she said suddenly into the chilly night air.

"What?"

"The chest. The Clarion's chest. It was made of wood. Why wasn't it rotten?"

I scowled into the dark. "I don't know."

"It wasn't protected from the elements." She plowed on in a soft voice that resonated loudly in my ear. "It was basically buried in the earth. It should have rotted away centuries ago."

"I don't know."

Nora paused long enough that my mind began to turn toward bed again.

"What if it's not real?" she asked.

With an irritated grunt, I got up and began unstrapping our

bedrolls from the tops of our packs. The Clarion glinted at me, mocking the firelight.

Nora wrapped her cloak tighter around herself to compensate for my lost body heat. "I'm being serious, Eoghan."

I stood up, her bedroll hanging from one hand at my side. "What? What are you being serious about? Tell me. Because from what I can tell, there are two options. Either the Clarion is magic and protected the box from time, or else the entire thing was planted less than two decades ago. It's just a regular old trumpet, in a regular old box. Put there by regular people for some unknown reason.

"It won't wake up any fabled Giants, which means there is nothing to stop Amau from plowing over this land unchecked, and our entire country will be wiped off the map from the Western Waste to the Arigua Ocean. Is that what you're being serious about?"

She stared up at me, her eyes wide at my uncharacteristic bout of words. "Is that what you think? That this is all for nothing?"

"Is that what *you* think?" I asked. "You're the one who brought this up!"

"What else am I supposed to think?" Nora's voice rose to match mine.

"It doesn't matter!" I hissed and gestured with her bedroll. "It doesn't matter what you think or what I think. This is the mission, Nora. This is what we were charged to do by the Reliquary. Two people—only the two of us could be spared from the war. A cartographer to navigate and a ranger to keep her alive. That's it!"

Nora glared at me, her face smudged with dirt and charcoal from her drawings and notes. Her mutinous silence should have intimidated me. In the past, I would have clammed up, unsure of my words in the face of such determination.

But with Nora...

"This was only ever a last resort," I said. "No one believes this will work. The only reason we're here is because someone down there"—I jabbed my finger toward the general east, where great billows of smoke were illuminated from underneath by the ravaging fires in the valley—"thinks the old stories about the Giants may have some grain of truth. We are a prayer, Nora. We're just a hope and a prayer."

"A hope and a prayer? A last resort?" Nora launched to her feet and darted forward.

For an instant, I thought she might attack me in frustration. Her stormy expression said as much. But she went to her pack instead and began untying the Clarion from its strap with angry jerks at the rope.

"What are you doing?" I asked.

"I'm going to sound it," she said, picking at one of the knots. "Why wait until the peak? People are dying, right? Cities are burning. Why not do it now?"

"The legends say we have to sound it at the peak, in the Cavern of the Giants. We have to take it to the top of the mountain."

She yanked off the last bit of rope and stood up. The Clarion was small, even in her hands.

"You said it yourself. They're just stories. Who's to say we have to get to the top? Why would it work better there than here?"

"Nora, wait!" Dread filled the pit in my stomach.

But before I had a chance to stop her, she raised the little trumpet to her lips. I watched in horror as she took a deep breath and blew.

The night solidified into sound. A clear, high note much too large for such a small, delicate instrument filled the air around us so that nothing else existed. It drowned out the crickets and the cicadas, the owls and the wind. It silenced my heartbeat and the breath in my lungs. It vibrated into the very earth under us and filled my entire being with raw, unadulterated *life*.

"Nora!" I screamed into the sound, but my voice was entirely overwhelmed.

She squeezed her eyes shut against the din, but her determination was as strong as ever. Nora pushed through despite her agonized expression. She clearly intended to hold the note for as long as she had breath.

After a second's hesitation, I knocked the Clarion away from her mouth with a controlled grab at the instrument. The note died away, leaving a ringing silence in its wake.

She stood shaking and empty-handed in the wake of the Clarion's note, as if the little instrument had taken its sound from her very being. Even the forest around us seemed to tremble in the silence.

No, not silence.

The forest didn't *seem* to tremble. It *really* trembled. The trees shook and lurched in the windless sky, and the air filled with a low, gut-deep rumbling.

Shit.

I launched toward Nora, wrapping her up in my arms and hauling us both to the ground when the earth began to shake beneath us. It trembled and heaved, sending agitated clouds of sparks up from the campfire on our right.

"What's happening?" Nora asked. Her voice was barely audible over the roar of the earth.

"An earthquake," I said.

Just an earthquake. It was just an earthquake. Just a coincidence.

Nora's coal-covered fingers gripped my thick jacket at my sides, and she tucked her head into my chest. I gritted my teeth and held on tightly, hoping against hope the trees would hold their ground and there would be no landslide to bury us alive.

We were supposed to have two more days.

All we could do was wait. We clutched each other for what seemed like forever as the very earth betrayed us, until finally it began to lessen.

The quake slowed in waves, easing off, rumbling again with

force before letting up. Until finally, it slowed to the faintest of tremors, then nothing.

Nora lifted her head and looked around in the darkness.

Our fire had scattered and gone out, though the glowing logs still held enough heat to relight it. I set to work on arranging them once more, adding fresh kindling and a new log to get the flames going. It was as much to busy my shaking hands as it was to combat the chill breeze.

Nora sat, dazed and silent, while I worked. Her eyes fell on the Clarion, where I had dropped it on the ground. She picked it up and turned it over in the firelight.

"It doesn't have a scratch," she said in a whisper.

I took it from her hands without grace and held it close to the new firelight. She was right. Not a single scratch or dent marred the brass. I had dropped it from several feet, and it had been tossed around in the gravel by a violent earthquake. It should have shown damage.

Nora stepped away from the circle of firelight and looked out over the valley. Not much was visible from our camp. The latest fires had burned low, leaving only a gentle glow to outline the ground in a few places, and the moon was a sliver in the night sky. All else was blackness.

"Do you think it worked?" she asked.

"No."

"But the earthquake? That couldn't have been a coincidence."

I eyed the back of her head, which was barely visible in the shadows. Whatever the Clarion had taken from her, she seemed to be recovering.

"It was just an earthquake, Nora."

She turned around and met my gaze. If her faith had been wavering before, it was strong now. The Clarion wasn't a fake. There was no denying its note had been more than just sound.

"We have to take it to the peak. That's all." Nora came back toward me. "It'll work at the peak, just like the legends say. It'll wake up the Giants."

I nodded, watching while she unrolled her bedding.

"To the peak," I agreed.

Two more days.

I banked the fire as Nora hauled off her boots and swapped out her thick, wool socks for a fresh pair. She climbed into the bedroll, her eyes hollow.

I unrolled my bedroll as well, but I didn't lay it out on the opposite side of the fire as usual. Instead I draped it on top of Nora's shivering form, slipped off my own boots, tightened up my hood, and climbed right in with her.

It was a tight fit, but that was the point. She didn't complain, only made as much room as she could. I put an arm over her and pulled her close, sighing at the wash of warmth.

After a few minutes of awkward silence, Nora's nimble fingers pulled open my coat. I glanced down at her, confused. Had she gotten the wrong idea? If she made a move on me, would I object? I honestly didn't know. There were certainly worse ways to spend our last nights on earth.

But then she slipped her arm under my coat and around my waist. Nora nuzzled against the soft, warm wool of my shirt.

I smirked to myself and buried my chilled nose in her curly hair. No, of course not. I was the one getting the wrong idea. She was just keeping warm.

"Eoghan?" Nora said into my chest.

"Hm?"

"You never answered before. Why did you come up the mountain with me? You could have done anything. Gone anywhere. You could have joined the army or led the evacuations south. But you didn't."

I frowned against the top of her head. "I'm a ranger. Lachlan offered me a chance to climb the Giant's Mountain, where no one has been for centuries. A new place. And it very well may be overrun with the Amau soon. How could I say no?"

"So, that's it? That's all it was? Just a new place. Adventure?"

The end of her braid brushed against my hand, and I began twirling the dark, silky curls between my fingers. It was such a little thing, a bit of softness in my harsh world of exposure and loneliness.

"I grew up with my Nan," I said. "My mother's mother. She lived right at the edge of the Great Forest, in a little town that never even had a name. So I spent my entire youth in those woods, days at a time, sometimes. Nan taught me to hunt and how to take care of myself. 'People are mostly good,' she'd say. 'But sometimes, there ain't no people around, is there?'"

Nora huffed a laugh, and I smiled into the dark.

"'You gotta take care of yourself, Eoghan boy.' She always called me that. *Eoghan boy*."

"She sounds nice," Nora murmured into my shirt.

I laughed once. "No, Nan wasn't nice. She was tough. And she took no shit. But she loved the Old Way. The stories about the sibyls and the Giants and the Old Kind. So, most nights, she'd tell me stories. And my favorites were always about the Giants. How they'd been the first peoples of Lujor and fought in the old wars alongside mankind's greatest heroes. They fought until there were no more wars to fight, until Lujor no longer needed defending. So they went away into the west until they were needed again. They forged the Clarion and hid it away in the easternmost mountain of the Western Wild. And one day, they'd rise up again." I heaved out a heavy breath. "And the world would go back to making sense."

I paused, and the sounds of the forest invaded my silence. Owls, night birds, crickets, and rushing wind. A twig snapped just inside the tree line, loud enough to make Nora jump.

"It's just a possum," I said, though I continued to stare into the dense darkness of the scrubby trees. If it had been an animal, there would be more sound: snuffling through dry leaves, mating calls, anything.

But nothing. Only the wind and the crickets and the birds. As if whatever had broken the twig was intentionally staying very quiet now.

I was no stranger to sleeping exposed. If someone was watching us, they would wake me before they got within ten steps of our fire.

Not that anyone *was* following us. They couldn't have been. No one knew we were climbing the forbidden Giant's Mountain. And I would have noticed them before now.

Better safe than sorry. I let Nora's braid slip from my fingers and reached for the Clarion. It had been left lying in the grass next to us, where I could keep an eye on it, but now that didn't feel secure enough. I pulled the little trumpet under the blanket and kept a firm grip on it behind Nora's back.

"What's the matter?" Nora asked, looking up at me.

"Nothing. Just listening. It's a possum or a raccoon or something."

Nora lifted her head and shoulders to look toward the darkened trees. She stared for a few seconds, then dismissed her alarm. She settled back against my chest, and I pulled the blanket up to her ears for her.

"So, you've always wondered about the mountain, I suppose? Because of your Nan's stories?"

"They're just stories," I said.

I felt her smirk against my shirt, and she laughed again. "You don't believe that."

I gripped the Clarion tightly behind her back. Before yesterday, I had believed exactly that. Just stories, distorted through the generations. A symbolic mountain shrouded in superstition. Before yesterday, this was just an unexplored area. An adventure. And yes, maybe a little nostalgia for my Nan's fireside tales.

But now? After Nora sounded this stupid little trumpet, after the very earth moved beneath us? I wasn't so sure.

"They're just stories," I said again, burying my face into the warmth of her curls. "Go to sleep, mapmaker."

Seven

The next day, there was no more talk of motivation or faith. I tied the Clarion to Nora's strap once more, and this time, she adjusted it against her chest with reverence.

The mountain grew steeper as we ascended. In the early days of the journey, it had been a gentle slope with tall birches, elms, and oaks. But as the way went higher, the trees grew smaller. The earth pitched steeper, and the streams ran thinner.

"There may not be much water past here," I said around noon.

Nora crouched next to a burbling spring that ran down the mountain in a trickle.

"Drink as much as you can bear now, and we'll save the water."

She nodded and dipped her cup into the little pool a third time.

I walked to the east toward an outcropping of stone. From there, the entire valley opened up below me—a far better view than any we had seen so far. The fires burned lower today than other days, so even the Arigua Ocean was visible just below the horizon.

This was my home. A small country, inconsequential except for a major port on our coastline. That was visible too.

There, right at the edge of the world, where the startling blue of the Arigua met the sprawling, white city of New Haven. The capital city encrusted the shoreline around a massive bay, the only one deep enough to accept bulk carriers and naval ships for hundreds of miles in any direction. A pivotal stop from north to south.

That was all Amau wanted from us. That was it. One little bay, and the foothold they needed to take the entire continent.

But they hadn't been able to take it. New Haven Bay was well defended with cannons and warships of our own. So Amau had decided to come in the back door. They came in from the north with their torches and their pitch, and they decided to burn us out instead.

Nora's footsteps sounded behind me, but I didn't turn. She put a hand on my arm to steady herself near the edge and looked down at the valley below.

"Shit," she whispered.

"What?"

"Look. Right there. You see?" She stretched out one finger and pointed to the southeast, where a smear of black marred the forest below. "That's Tutree. There."

I stepped forward to get a better look. "Are you sure?"

"Yes!" she cried. "Yes! Look, there's the Greater Apgatt River going south, and right there, where it meets the Lesser Apgatt, that's Tutree. That's home." Her voice trailed off into silence, and her expression crumpled into grief.

Sure enough, the shining rivers met right where her finger fell, just at the base of the mountain. That was where I'd first met Nora in the back room of the Tutree Council Hall eleven days before.

The entire area was a wasteland, even from this height. Amau had gotten very good at reducing an entire village to ash.

"It's gone," she whispered.

"I'm sure everyone got out. You warned them all in time. And your family, they had more notice than anyone."

Nora nodded, but she couldn't tear her eyes away from the black scar where her home used to be.

I gripped her by the arms and made her face me. Her dark eyes slammed into mine, and I faltered. What in the hell did I think I was going to say to her? Her entire family might be dead now. Burned alive. Every person she'd ever known. And why? For a fucking port?

"We have to keep moving," I said firmly.

Nora returned my stare, dry-eyed and pale. Her small hands went to the Clarion nestled across her chest. "To the peak."

She moved away without another word, west toward the peak that loomed overhead.

The view above was just as grand as the one below. A rounded peak of stone loomed above us. It looked so close, but if Nora's archives were accurate, it would take another day and a half to climb it.

We stopped several times that afternoon so Nora could make a note or sketch a specific boulder or tree. She labeled each landmark meticulously in her notes and on her ever-growing map, cross-referencing both with the faded parchments the Council had entrusted to her when we left.

Nora pored over them, obsessing about every detail. She often read while walking, which meant, more than once, I had to grab her elbow to steer her around a tree or stop her from walking off the side of the mountain itself.

"Why are you still reading those things?" I asked when she tripped over a tree root. "We don't need them anymore. That's where we're going." I gestured broadly at the peak above us. It was still a long way to go, but at least the way was obvious now.

"It doesn't make any sense," she said, slowing to a stop. "We have four different accounts to reference here, and so far they've mostly agreed with each other. We came to the ravine right when they said, and that pillar was right where it was supposed to be before we found the Archways and the Clarion. It was right there. 'The pillar stands tall in the west. Follow the morning sun for three hours to the Archways.' But this..."

"What?" I asked, peering down at the parchment. It was written in Old Ambic, which I had never learned to read.

"It says there should be a hollow here. It's very specific. We just came over the sloping hill, then it should be flat for several hours, a bit of a sloping downward, then the final climb to the Cavern of the Giants. All four accounts agree." She shuffled through the antique parchments. "But look. It's completely different." Nora gestured around with the paper.

Sure enough, there was no hollow, just a continuous, gentle climb of tumbled stone. On our right, a sharp drop-off fell away, offering another gorgeous view of the valley below.

"Maybe the earthquake caused a landslide," I suggested.

"Maybe." She pressed her nose close to the page and scribbled more notes.

Nora sat down on a large, flat rock near the drop-off and began digging through her pack for her cartography tools. She opened the leather case smartly and pulled out her compass and a protractor.

I leaned back on my heels. "Do we have time for this?" I asked.

She spread out her map on the rock. "You want to be able to find our way back, don't you?"

"I don't need a map to do that. I travel for a living, Nora. I can retrace our steps all the way back."

"The maps aren't making sense anymore, Eoghan!" she said, not looking up as she began sketching. "They made sense before, but now they don't. Something changed. You really want me to ignore that?" Nora stopped sketching and looked up at me, defiant, daring me to argue with her.

"Fine!" I threw out my arms. "I'll just hunt now. How's that? You draw, and I'll hunt. And then we don't have to stop so early tonight."

"Great," she said, her attention already back on her map.

I took off my pack with less care than usual, unstrapped my snares, and disappeared into the dwarfed trees that clung to the rocky mountainside.

I didn't go far. Just far enough that Nora's muttering wouldn't scare off any rabbits. I had seen a dozen since midday, so it wouldn't take long to catch dinner.

I set up the snares quickly, then headed back to where I'd left Nora to wait.

But before I made it a dozen steps, I slowed to a stop. Something wasn't right. Was it a sound? Or a sudden silence? Or a breath? I couldn't put my finger on it, but the hairs stood up on the back of my neck, and my heart rate accelerated.

A raven glided overhead, the only movement in the quiet afternoon. Something was wrong here. Was it an animal stalking me? Maybe a mountain lion?

I heard it a half second too late. Footsteps running over the loose stones littering the hard ground behind me. I half turned, but it was no use. Pain shot through my skull, and my head snapped around on my neck. The next thing I knew, I lay dazed on the ground with blood in my mouth.

Blackness threatened to overtake my vision. *Sleep. Just sleep, Eoghan boy. Just lay your head down for a minute. You can think later. In a minute.*

I rested my head on the gritty earth. But I had to open my eyes. There was something important. Just open your eyes, Eoghan.

I forced away the darkness in time to watch a pair of black-clad legs running full tilt away from me.

See? The threat is gone. Rest. Only for a little while, then you can get up. And for a minute, I allowed myself the relief of unconsciousness.

Until a startled scream pierced through my foggy brain, like a shaft of light through a shadowed room. A terrified scream. My name.

"Eoghan!"

Nora.

She was afraid. Terrified. Absolutely frantic.

"Eoghan! Ahh! No! Stop! Eoghaaaan!"

I wrenched myself to my feet. My vision blurred and swirled. I bounced off a nearby tree but didn't feel it. I couldn't feel anything. All I knew was Nora was screaming.

Her voice pitched up into a squeal of panic, then came to an abrupt stop.

My vision stabilized in a flash of adrenaline, and I picked up speed.

It was a man. There must have been someone watching us the night before after all, and this was him. He had tracked us here, waited for us to separate, and then followed me into the scrubby woods.

Because he'd wanted Nora. He'd knocked me out, then went after her as soon as I was out of the way.

I stumbled back to the cliff's edge where I'd left Nora.

The man was there. He wore all black and had a short beard a bit darker than the burnt orange color of his hair. The man knelt over her prone body with his back to me, tugging at her chest. For half a second, my vision went red at the thought of all the things an asshole might do to an unconscious woman's body. But then a bit of brass flashed in the sunlight, and I understood.

He didn't want Nora. He wanted the Clarion.

I stumbled forward with blood running down my forehead and into my eyes. The man in black heard me coming. The blow to the head had left me dizzy, and my once-nimble limbs had turned to clubs. I stumbled toward him at top speed.

He was smaller, but he was faster. The man whirled around, a knife in his hand, probably for cutting the Clarion off Nora's straps.

It didn't even occur to me to find my own hunting knife, still sheathed onto my pack twenty feet away. I lunged for him with my bare hands, almost surprised that he stood his ground.

I felt the wrongness in my gut when he plunged his knife into my side. It didn't stop me, though, and his eyes grew wide in sudden alarm.

Large eyes, wider than I was used to. Pale irises, freckled skin, and red hair—he was Amau. This fucker was Amau.

I wrapped my hands around his neck, and he gagged. He yanked the knife out of my side and raised it high, angling to jam it into my neck.

I wasn't too far gone to see the danger. On instinct, I blocked his blow with my forearm and knocked the knife out of his hand. It flew about five feet away, the danger neutralized for the moment.

But I'd let go of his neck, and he had gained a different advantage. The man lunged for me and climbed my body like a monkey. He wrapped himself around my neck from behind, bracing his feet on my waist.

"Just fucking die," he hissed into my ear.

I dropped backward to the ground and landed on top of him. He grunted in pain and loosened his grip, but only just long enough for me to suck in one breath. Then he reclaimed his hold on my neck, and the darkness began creeping in again around the edges.

If he finished me off this time, there would be no one to stand between him and Nora. Would he kill her too? Or would he just take the Clarion and leave her?

Had he killed her already?

No. Not possible. She couldn't be dead.

Blackness edged in closer. I pried against the man's arm around my neck, but he was braced too well.

This man was a killer. And once he had the Clarion, he wouldn't risk leaving someone alive who might go after him. If I died, Nora died.

No.

"Stop it!" Nora's voice once again penetrated the fog in my head. She was awake.

Awake and alive. We still had time.

I opened my eyes. She stood over us, her cartographer's protractor brandished in one hand with the sharp points out.

"Let him go!" she said in a wobbly voice.

I tried a new grip, pulled again, but I could not budge the man's arm an inch.

"Or what, you'll kill me?" He said it almost casually. This was easy for him.

"Yes!" Nora said, but her voice was too high. She took half a step closer and raised the protractor, then hesitated.

"I fucking dare you," the Amau man said. "But you better work fast. Your precious Eoghan is turning blue."

Her entire body shook, and her dark eyes were too wide.

"Go ahead! What difference does it make?" the man taunted, a note of hysterics in his voice. "We're all going to die anyway! It doesn't matter if I play that little trumpet or if you do. We're all going to die when this mountain wakes up! So if you're going to do it, woman, just do it!"

"I will!" she screeched.

"You've got me cornered!" the man announced with a laugh. "If I let go of him, he'll kill me. So either he dies, or I do. You decide!"

There was no time for this. Nora would never be able to stab him. She shouldn't have to do this.

But I could.

I stopped pulling on the man's arm, and my strangled breath stopped completely. Pain seared through my abused neck, but I forced myself to ignore the need to fight for air. Instead, I reached toward Nora, my hand open and asking.

She understood and fumbled the protractor into my hand. I flipped it around in my palm and stabbed blindly over my shoulder. The Amau man dodged, loosening his grip. I stabbed again, and he jerked.

Air. I sucked a precious gulp into my ravaged throat.

I stabbed a third time, and this time I hit my target. The protractor glanced awkwardly off something solid, and the man cried out in pain and anger as I dragged it through his skin.

I rolled over, finally free, to grab him. The protractor had gotten him just over his left eye. The sharp point had dug a gruesome gash across his forehead and temple, almost to his ear.

I hauled back my fist and punched him square in the jaw. My aim was good, but the bleeding wound in my side had made me weak and dizzy. He reared back his head and rammed his bleeding forehead into my nose.

"Argh!" I reeled back with a cry of pain, and Nora screamed.

The man took his chance and scrambled away, closer to the cliff's edge.

I could knock him off. It would be easy. It would be over.

If only I could get up.

Blackness creeped in again. My limbs went heavy and sluggish. It was everything I could do to just crawl in his direction.

Just rest, Eoghan boy. Just rest.

Nora's scream of effort jerked my eyes open. She'd had the same idea as me, it seemed. Nora launched her small frame at him, knocking him off balance. And with a cry of shock, he stumbled too close to the edge and slipped over it.

But he had time for one last revenge. He reached out and grabbed ahold of the Clarion still tied to Nora's strap as he went over.

I watched it happen in slow motion. She didn't even cry out.

For an instant, Nora locked eyes with me. Hers were widened in shock, but her expression was relaxed and calm. Her long, dark braid—so soft—hovered in the air as she went weightless.

Then she was gone.

One second she was there. The next she disappeared over the edge.

Eight

"Nora!" I screamed in a broken voice. "Nora! No!" I scrambled to the edge and looked down.

It was impossible to guess how far it was. A hundred feet? More? All I could make out were the tops of pine trees below the ridge. Their canopies entirely obscured the ground.

She would have hit every branch going down.

How far was it? Could she have survived?

"Nora!"

Pain tore through my side, cutting off my words. I rolled onto my back, clapping a hand over the wound, and glanced over at his knife. It was abandoned on the ground a few feet away, bloody. The blade was a couple of inches long. A utility knife.

But it was long enough.

Blood flowed freely from the wound, and my entire side was soaking wet and sticky.

Okay. Breathe. First things first, my wound. I couldn't do anything else until I stopped the bleeding.

Every movement scorched through my whole trunk. I crawled toward my pack, the one I'd carried half my life. Nan herself had embroidered my name on the top in faded, sky blue thread. I unbuckled the side pocket and pulled everything out: spare socks, twine, sewing kit, salt, bandages. And there, right at the very bottom, was what I needed.

A small aluminum tin, about the size of a walnut. I had sealed it with wax years before to keep it shut and preserve the salve. The precious Athorum. A miracle in the palm of my hand. It would heal any wound and bring a person back from the brink of death.

I ran the tip of my knife around the wax seal and pried off the little lid. The typical sweet stink of rotten fruit hit my nose. This little dab had cost me everything to purchase. Just one miracle. A last resort.

It would heal my wound instantly. But there was only enough for one. And if Nora was alive at the bottom of that cliff, she would likely need this miracle a lot more than I did.

But would I survive the climb down to find her? Had that damn Amau hit an organ when he stabbed me?

If my wound was fatal and Nora was already dead...

No.

I closed the little tin and slipped it into my shirt pocket. Then I began unwrapping a thick roll of bandages. I lifted my shirt and wrapped the woolen strips around my abdomen as tight as I could bear. I covered the wound, but I didn't wait to see if the bleeding slowed. There was no time to waste.

The cliff was absolutely vertical where Nora had gone over with the Amau man, but a little ways south, the slope eased enough that I could slide down on my ass. It was slow going, and I had to stop often to breathe and fight to stay conscious. The pain in my gut swelled to an inferno, and blood seeped through the bandaging.

Just use the salve, Eoghan boy.

No.

I lumbered onward, encountering several long drops, which

nearly caused me to black out. One boulder had to be climbed over. I almost didn't make it.

Just keep moving. One more step. Get a little lower. You're getting close.

That was a lie. I wasn't getting close. Judging by a familiar outcropping high above and far away, I'd gone about half the distance I needed to. It was too far. *She* was too far.

I eased lower and sat on the ground with a miserable groan.

"Nora," I tried to call out. I tried. But it came out as breath.

I leaned back against a narrow pine trunk and focused on breathing. I could picture her, like a dream. In my mind, she came striding out of the woods with her pack on and her soft braid flung over one shoulder, rebellious curls coming undone and framing her face. The Clarion was still strapped to her chest, not a scratch or a dent. Her face was dirty and streaked with charcoal from her sketching. She looked just like I remembered, glowering at me from her rock, with her maps spread around her.

This was how I wanted to remember her. Whole and determined and strong. Not broken and bleeding out at the bottom of a cliff.

I'd let her fall. She said this wouldn't happen.

No, it couldn't have happened. Because Dream Nora was right in front of me, not a scratch on her. I could even hear her voice in my mind.

"Eoghan?"

Just like I remembered. Maybe a little less sarcastic than usual.

"Eoghan? Are you okay?"

Dream Nora slapped me in the face sharply. She sounded worried. Why was she worried?

"Shit, you're bleeding," she said. "Lay down! Let me look at this."

I tried to tell her I had brought her the Athorum, that it would help her if she was hurt, but she spoke over me. "Just lay down, Eoghan. Get some blood to your brain."

"So soft," I breathed as my head hit the ground.

~

I woke with a start, then cringed when pain lanced through my head and neck.

"I swear, Eoghan. Just lay the hell down!"

My eyes popped open, and there she was. Not a dream, but her. The real thing.

"Nora?" I asked in a hoarse voice. Fuck, my throat was destroyed.

Her face swam into view. Not a scratch. Dirty, sure. But hale and whole and frustrated with me.

"*Shh*," she said. "Lay down. You lost a lot of blood. Thank the Old Kind you had that Athorum. Where did you get that? No, never mind. Don't try to talk. That asshole did a number on your throat."

I extended a hand but could only reach her upper arm. She leaned in so I could touch her face.

"You fell," I whispered.

She nodded seriously. "Yup. I did. I fell. All the way. And I hit every branch possible on the way down. But I'm okay. Not a scratch, see?" Nora turned up her face, as if to show off her unmarred skin, then flexed her arms to prove no broken bones.

"How?"

A knowing smirk twisted her mouth. "Well, let me put it this way...I think I figured out why that box didn't rot."

I screwed up my eyebrows, confused.

"The box?" she said. "The Clarion's wooden box? It should have rotted away to nothing, but it was fine?" Nora flicked the Clarion, still tied to her pack on the ground. It let out a faint, metallic ping. "I think it protected me. You guessed right the other night. It's just plain magic."

"And the...man?"

Her expression darkened, and she looked away. "He's dead. I left him back there. Couldn't get to him anyway. He was stuck in a tree."

Good.

"How did he find us?" she asked quietly.

"Tutree."

She nodded her understanding. Someone must have followed us from the beginning. Maybe they had known about our mission, and that was what brought them to Tutree in the first place.

I squeezed her arm once, then let my hand fall.

Nora was full of energy. She moved about, setting up camp like usual. I had left my pack at the top of the cliff, so she covered me with her bedroll and scampered up the slope to retrieve it and her abandoned maps. She even went around to my snares and grabbed a couple of rabbits for dinner.

All I could do was sleep. She woke me up to eat and drink, and then I was out again. At some point during the night, she snuggled in next to me under the bedrolls. Nora had brought the Clarion with her to bed, just in case.

The next morning, I felt much better. The Athorum had done its work, so I was able to move around with relative ease. Only my headache and sore throat persisted.

"I know there's not much time, but we should rest another day," Nora suggested. "I don't think you would make it up the peak in this condition."

"I'll be all right," I whispered. Every vocalization sent stabbing pains through my neck, so I accustomed myself to speaking softly.

"We'll stay here," she insisted. "There's a stream nearby. And you're dehydrated from all the blood loss. Just one day, Eoghan."

I could have fought her. People were dying every day in the valley, but the thought of walking, much less climbing, was unbearable.

"One day."

Nora spent the day with her paper. She still had a whole stack of blank pages left, and this near to the end of our journey, she felt she could waste a few. She sketched birds, trees, and squirrels and even made a few drawings of me. Nora showed them to me with a grin. She had drawn me with an exaggerated scowl.

I rolled my eyes at her, and she giggled.

She was good at it. And after nearly two weeks of hard living, she needed a little peace and artistry. Nora chatted off and on while she sketched, speaking of nothing in particular. I watched her do it, and for a moment, I wondered what it would be like to capture her dark eyes on paper. That intense, focused look.

"What did he mean? That man from Amau?" she asked.

"When?"

"He said we were all going to die when the mountain wakes up. What did he mean?"

Shit.

"He meant..." I trailed off, unsure. Then I changed direction. "You remember...my Nan used to tell me stories...about the Giants?"

Nora nodded.

I cleared my throat with a wince. "She used to tell this one..." Damn, my throat. I skipped to the end. "Said they didn't leave."

Nora furrowed her eyebrows. "The Giants didn't leave? But they went into the Western Waste. They left. And the Clarion will call them back."

I shook my head gently. "No. They would never leave Lujor. This is their home. And the Clarion will wake them up. We came to wake up the Giants, remember?"

"But..."

"They didn't go into the Western Waste, Nora. They *are* the Western Waste. They are the mountains."

She stared at me. "What? No."

"I thought...I thought it was just a story until the Clarion. Until the Archways."

"The Archways?" she asked.

It seemed like weeks ago. But it had only been two days since we had discovered the arches and the Clarion.

It hurt to speak, so I showed her. I rested my hands on top of my abdomen, fingers interlocked in a dome.

"They were fingers?" she said breathlessly.

I nodded. "Not man-made."

She stared around at the pines, the stone, and the grass, as if she could suddenly recognize them as great big body parts.

"But...But why would that mean we're going to die? Why would we die?"

"Landslides." Then I gestured from my shoulder to the ground, indicating a very, very long fall.

If this mountain stands up, we won't stand a chance.

Her eyebrows knit together. "And you knew? This whole time, you knew about this?"

I squeezed my eyes shut. "A possibility."

"That Amau seemed to think it was a *real* possibility!"

I winced at her elevated tone, and she clamped her mouth shut. In fact, Nora didn't say another word to me the rest of the day outside of what was absolutely necessary. She stopped drawing and instead resumed obsessing over the archive documents that had gotten us this far. Nora pored over her own drawings of the arches, trying to see the finger shapes within the stone.

That night, she crammed herself into our bedroll, shivering, and buried her face in my shirt as usual.

"Nora?" I whispered into her hair.

"What?"

"I'm sorry."

She sniffed once, then nodded. "Go to sleep."

I smiled into the darkness.

Nine

We set out early the next day. Our last day. We packed up camp in silence, paused in the small stand of pine trees—our last haven—then without a word, began walking back up the slope.

This close to the peak, the trees gave way completely. The ground was solid stone and tumbled boulders, with only the most stubborn bunchgrass thriving in the cracks. The icy wind bit through our clothes. In winter, this whole area would be snowcaps.

Thank the gods it wasn't winter.

We kept moving.

We climbed for hours, stopping often for me to rest. I wanted to keep on, but Nora could see the struggle on my face. "Just rest for a minute," she'd say, then refuse to budge until I did so.

Her archives began making sense again before long. She pointed out landmark after landmark, guided us to the left to avoid a cliff edge and a dead end, and took us out of the way once to find a tiny spring dribbling out of a crevice. We stopped there for an hour. It took forever to fill up our water skins.

"We don't even have to get to the actual peak," Nora said while

I held my water skin under the trickling spring. "The Cavern of the Giants is about a hundred feet lower."

"Good."

She nodded. "We're getting close. No more stops."

"All right."

Nora stood and looked up at me, her eyebrows furrowed. She opened her mouth to say something, but then she closed it and turned away.

Whatever was on her mind, she was running out of chances to say it.

We found it an hour later. The Cavern of the Giants. Right where the archives said it would be. We stood on a slope twenty feet below and stared up at the dark hole in the stone, bemused.

"It's an ear," Nora said, slightly incredulous.

"That's definitely an ear," I agreed.

There was no denying it. The shell of the ear flared to our right. The shape was blunted with grass and weathered stone, but it was an ear. Even if we hadn't known the Giant lay sleeping beneath us, turned to granite for centuries, we would have recognized it.

This must be why the mountain was forbidden. Anyone who saw this would know for sure the Giants were real.

"That Amau man," Nora said. "He wanted the Clarion. He was going to sound it himself."

"So he said."

"Why would he do that? Why would he want to wake the Giants?"

"Maybe he thought if he called them, they would ally with Amau. But that was never how it worked. Lujor is their home."

"They were only ever fairy tales to me," she said. "I never paid any attention."

The hillside rose gently to the cavern, but the lip of the opening stood about six feet high in the solid stone. Nora put her foot in my hands so I could give her a boost, but then I had to climb up behind her with my wits and a few convenient toeholds. I hauled myself up with a grunt of pain and stood next to Nora.

It was just what you'd expect: a dark, dead-end tunnel with a sloping floor. Only just tall enough for me to stand up straight.

Nora moved forward into the shadows. I wasn't sure what I'd expected, but it seemed strange to not find a platform or a symbol on the floor. Someplace obvious to stand and sound the Clarion.

But there was nothing. It didn't matter. We were inside the Giant's ear. That would be enough. If he was going to hear anything, it would be from here.

"Okay," Nora said with a sigh. She brushed her palms on her thighs, nervous. "Okay, I guess this is it, then. Help me get this off."

She stepped forward and gestured to the Clarion on her chest, but I didn't move.

This couldn't be the end. These couldn't be our last moments. In all my life, I had never cared much about when or how I'd die. But now that the time had come, my body rebelled.

"Eoghan," she said softly.

I set my jaw and began untying the Clarion with confident tugs on the rope. Once it was free, she tried to take it from my hands, but I didn't let her.

"Hold onto it," I said, catching her gaze. "Whatever happens, don't let go of it. Maybe it will protect you again. Maybe you'll get out of this alive."

"It doesn't make any difference. Tutree is gone. Everyone I ever knew..."

"Don't talk like that," I said sternly.

We stood in silence, both of us holding onto the little trumpet.

"If by some miracle..." I said a bit softer. "If we manage to survive this, you can come with me. If you want to. This whole world is about to change. There will be a lot of new maps to draw."

Her mouth stretched into a sad smile, and she nodded. "Okay."

Then she let go of the Clarion and wrapped her arms around my neck instead. I held her tightly to my chest and ducked my head into her shoulder. This wasn't something I was ready for. I'd never be ready. It would never be okay.

But the time came anyway. She took the Clarion from me, tears in her eyes. "We'll make it through. You'll see."

No, we wouldn't. "Okay," I said.

"Hold on tight to me. Maybe the Clarion can protect us both."

That was a long shot, but I didn't care. Regardless of any magical trumpet, we both stood a better chance if we could avoid getting separated. So when she turned to face the blackness of the tunnel, I took my place behind her. I braced my feet wide and locked my arms around her midsection.

"Ready?" she asked.

I nodded against her shoulder. "Do it."

Nora took a deep, steadying breath, raised the Clarion to her mouth, and blew.

Just like before, the entire world solidified into sound. Life and connection and *sound*. It was louder there in the partially enclosed tunnel than it had been in the open air two nights before. So loud that where before it had been painful, now it was unbearable.

But I didn't let go of Nora. Not for anything. Not when the Clarion's note bit into my head. Not when the ground began to shake. Not when a different, older, deeper noise began to rumble underneath the clearer tones.

Finally, when Nora had spent all her breath, the Clarion's note died away. And in its wake came the growling, grinding, rumbling. The tunnel didn't just shake. It moved. It lifted and began to rise away from the gentler slope outside.

"Run!" I cried over the din. I grabbed Nora's wrist and sprinted for the bright daylight at the entrance of the tunnel.

The floor dipped away at an alarming angle, sliding us backward across the sloped floor. Nora screamed, and I grasped for any part of her I could hold onto as we slid violently away from the daylight.

We hit the back wall with a shuddering thud.

"Hold on!" I cried out.

"Eoghan!"

The tunnel began to dip the other way, as if to dump us out into the open air. I grasped wildly at the strap across her chest and hauled us together before we fell out of the Giant's ear canal.

Nora screamed in shock as she was flung out first. I scraped with bloody fingers at the floor, desperate for any purchase, and managed to catch a stone lip right at the exit.

Nora grunted when I arrested our fall. She dangled from my death grip on her pack.

"Don't let go!" she screamed, her eyes wide with terror. "Don't let me go! Don't let me fall!"

Beneath her, the earth loomed hundreds of feet below...and moving.

A large portion of the mountain remained behind as the Giant lumbered upward. It was as if, all those centuries ago, this Giant had laid down against an existing mountain, only adding to its bulk while he slept through the generations. If we acted quickly, we might be able to jump off and land on solid ground.

The Giant lurched, rocking us viciously to the side. My arm was on fire with the strain of Nora's dead weight. And every second we waited, our real mountaintop grew further away.

"Just hold onto the Clarion," I yelled.

"Don't let go of me!"

"We have to jump!"

The Giant lurched again, like a child shaking water out of his ear. Nora screamed again.

Her strap had broken.

She scrabbled at it one-handed for half a second, but she didn't have time. Nora tumbled out of her pack and began to free-fall.

"Nora!" I screamed with a ravaged throat.

No time for hesitation. I let go of the Giant's ear and dove after her.

We were too high. Just the fact that I had time to think it before we hit the ground was proof enough. Nora had the Clarion to protect her, but me? The impact would kill me.

The Clarion.

Nora must have had a similar thought at the same time. She extended it toward me as we fell.

The ground rushed upward at us. My instinct was to spread out, to slow my descent. But I squashed that instinct on a gamble. If I could grab the Clarion, I would be safe.

So I made my body straight as an arrow, diving headfirst toward Nora through the empty air.

I wasn't going to make it.

She strained for me, her wordless cry sharp in the wind.

The ground rushed toward us at an alarming speed.

I reached—reached again. The Clarion was inches away. The ground was too close. Then I made a desperate grab and closed my fingers around the delicate brass tubing.

Half a second later, we slammed into the steep slope and began to roll.

It knocked the breath out of my lungs. My body tumbled limb over limb like a rag doll. I had no control, no sense of orientation or anchor. But there was also no pain. I felt the stones and the earth and the tree trunks as I scraped over them, but there was no bruising or breaking bones. Nothing.

All my focus was spent on keeping hold of the Clarion, and I could only hope Nora was doing the same. We skidded for several dizzying seconds until we slammed into the narrow trunk of a pine tree. The abrupt stop finally made me lose my grip on the Clarion, and for the first time, I felt pain. I skidded another ten feet or so down the hill over stones and tree roots and brush, scraping the bare skin of my arms and face.

"Eoghan?" Nora called down. "Are you okay? Are you hurt?"

"I'm okay!" I replied. I didn't bother to get up, only lay on my back, staring up at the harmless blue sky.

I would never look at the sky the same way again. Not ever.

Nora's scrambling footsteps sounded near my head, and she began yanking on my arm. "Get up. You have to see this."

With a groan, I allowed her to haul me to my feet.

We stumbled to a crumbling cliff's edge, where the Giant had broken away from the mountain. From this vantage point, we could see deep into the Western Waste. As far as the eye could reach, mountains crumbled and broke apart. Huge, stone Giants with lumpy, lumbering shapes rose from their hibernations. They shook away massive amounts of earth, stone, and fully grown trees.

The rumbling went on and on. The real mountain below us shook and trembled as the Giants moved.

Dozens and dozens of them, as far west as we could see.

And our Giant seemed the biggest of all, though not as big as I had imagined. He had only been sleeping atop the mountain, but he still stood higher than three hundred feet, maybe more, and was made of solid stone.

The Giant turned with a bone-deep groan to look for us on the mountainside. Then he bent down so his craggy boulder of a nose was level with ours. His eyes were great, black orbs set in rocky skin, smooth and round like marbles. No iris, no whites. Just more stone.

Nora and I waited, both of us clinging to the Clarion, just in case. The Giant stared us down with his strange eyes, saying nothing. Could he even speak? Would we be able to hear such a massive voice?

Nora elbowed me in the side, hitting a fresh bruise. "Say something."

I shoved her gently to get her to stop digging her elbow in. But she was right. The Giant was waiting.

"Great Giants! We need your help!" I yelled as loudly as I could, but my throat spasmed in pain, and my voice cracked.

"Please!" Nora picked up where I left off. "Amau invades from the north! Lujor is dying! The homeland is dying!"

A crevice opened along the bottom of the Giant's face, forming a jagged mouth. "WAR?"

His voice boomed through the air, almost as oppressive as the Clarion's note.

"Yes! War!" Nora cried. "Save us from Amau! Save us from the north! Fight with us!"

The Giant straightened up and turned west toward his companions. He opened his craggy mouth and gave a wordless roar. The host of Giants returned the call, a bellow of purpose and anger. And as one, they all began to move east and north, toward the burning valley and Amau. Their footsteps echoed as they went.

Nora and I stood clutching each other on the mountainside as they moved away. Their bulky bodies were slow, but their great long legs ate up the distance with every stride. They would reach the Amau army in less than an hour.

We turned toward each other, disbelieving. Had we really done it? Had we woken the Giants and lived?

Nora's expression was a mix of joy, terror, and relief. She smiled through tears, then launched herself at me. With a cry of triumph, she threw her arms around my neck and her legs around my waist.

I caught her, but my legs gave out immediately, and we both went down. My knees barked against the hard ground, but it didn't matter. I held onto her for dear life.

"We did it," she whispered. "I told you we'd do it."

My eyes followed another stone Giant, smaller than the one from our mountain but still a terror. He pulled a fully grown birch tree out of the ground by its roots and swung it laboriously through the air like a club. His feet, wide as a house, tore chunks out of the mountainside when he climbed over it.

They would wipe out the Amau army in great swaths, and our Lujorian soldiers would handle the stragglers. This war would be over in under a day.

"What now?" I asked when Nora slipped off me.

"Where's my pack?"

We both turned to stare at the scar the Giant had left on the mountain when he had risen out of the stone.

"I think it's safe to say your pack is gone," I said, grim.

"Well..." Her hands still shook with adrenaline. "Then I guess now we have to find some new cartography tools for cheap. So, New Haven?"

"That's a long way," I said. There were at least two other cities large enough to find such equipment between here and the coast.

"Yes, and the Giants are moving for the first time in centuries. Lujor is half burnt, and nothing will be like it was the last time either of us saw the lowlands. And we're carrying a very rare, magical object that will likely draw a lot of attention." She held up the Clarion and squinted at me against the afternoon sunlight. "Are you up for it?"

"Don't you want to look for your family?" I asked. "Anyone from Tutree?"

Nora turned away from me and watched the Giants clamber away toward the smoke in the valley. "They would have gone to the capital. Edith's father had a house in New Haven. It's been empty since he died. If we were to find her anywhere, it would be there."

I stepped up and took her hand in mine. The noise of the Giants had become a distant rumble. Slowly, the birds began chirping to each other again in the treetops. I hadn't even noticed they'd gone silent until they resumed singing.

"New Haven it is," I said, squeezing her hand once. "Lead the way, mapmaker."

Part Three
City of Lies
Two Months Later

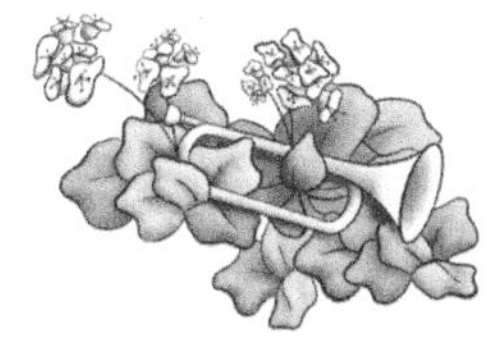

Ten

"I think that man is following us," Nora whispered. "The one with the flat cap."

"I know."

The burly bastard had trailed us all the way from Harp Street. Hounding our steps, moving faster and slower as we did, always just behind, until my heart pounded and my palms began to sweat. Until Nora's breathing picked up and she hurried to keep up with me.

"You know?" she asked, her voice rising. "Eoghan..."

"Just keep walking," I said in an undertone.

"Surely he wouldn't attack a pregnant woman." She gestured to her protruding belly.

In any other situation, I would have said she was right. Anyone looking at her would assume she was at least eight months along. They wouldn't know it was a sham, that her belly was just a bag worn under her shirt. It was the best way we could think of to hide the Clarion and disappear into the crowds.

But tonight? With that look in Burly's eye? I wasn't so sure.

"Just keep walking," I said again.

The town of Marcha was a hub. It had grown around a major

crossroads in central Lujor. The Cathay Main ran north and south, while the Marsh Road went east to west, cutting through the boglands west of New Haven. Both were major roads connecting all corners of Lujor, carrying thousands of travelers daily through the bustling city.

People had flocked there to trade and live a better life even before the war, when the most exciting thing to happen in Lujor was the occasional spring flood in the flatlands bordering the Western Waste.

But after Amau burned half the small towns and cut off supply lines, after the Giants woke up and began roaming the land once more, Marcha became something else altogether. Not just merchants, but refugees. Not just traders, but starving desperation.

That was why we had come to Marcha in the first place. Not only did it lie directly on our path to New Haven, but it was widely known that the refugee camps were overwhelmed and no one asked questions anymore. No one cared who you were or where you came from. No one looked twice at a man and his pregnant wife just passing through, looking for family displaced by the war.

There, we were just two more faces in the crowd.

Except tonight, someone *had* taken notice. Someone had spotted us and decided our heavy packs—or maybe the coin in our pockets—were worth the effort it took to stalk us like this. Had the burly man been following us all the way from the orchards outside of town?

As if she could read my mind, Nora said, "Pass me the coin. I'll hide it with the Clarion."

I glanced down at her determined expression. Her words penetrated the fog of my fear. Coins? That's what she was so concerned about?

She shook her outstretched hand, a second request for the coin in question. "We've been picking those damn apples for a week.

Like hell we're going to lose the funds we need to get to New Haven."

How she could be belligerent instead of terrified was beyond me. A very large man had been following us for many, many blocks. We were about to be mugged. She might be hurt. Or worse, they might realize she wasn't really pregnant at all. All it would take was one person touching her belly, and we'd be screwed.

But I passed over the money bag, and she slipped them inside the false belly she wore under her shirt. In a flash, they disappeared from view, as secure as we could possibly make them.

I didn't care about the coins. Money came and went. Whatever we lost could be earned again. But there were some things that could never be replaced. The Clarion. The pack my Nan had made for me. All the supplies I had carefully collected over the years.

Nora.

I didn't even care that much about the Clarion. I'd give it up in a heartbeat if it meant I could save her. Because so long as I had Nora, we could work it out. No matter what.

Fear could make a man forget his better judgment. I took Nora's hand in mine, pulling her into a darkened alley, but stopped short when two figures loomed out of the dim shadows near the back wall: a bulky man and a slim woman, both leering and ready for us.

It had been a trap. Of course it had been a trap. Why else would that burly bastard have followed us all the way from Harp Street?

"We got a live one, Earl," said the woman in a low, melodious voice.

A bandage wrapped around her head obscured most of her left eye. The skin at the edges of the bandage appeared mottled and scabbed, but it was hard to tell in the poor light what the injury might have been. The woman was skinny and small, with her blonde hair cut short around her ears, and she held herself with a confidence that belied the shitty state of her clothes. She stood like a rich woman, feet apart and shoulders back, but she stank like the gutter.

Earl, on the other hand, kept himself tidy. At least a foot taller than Eyepatch, he stood like a Giant. Lumbering, wide, clumsy. His clothes were hardly better than his friend's, but they were clean and carefully mended. He wore a flat cap on his bald head, angled as though to make him appear jaunty. But he was fooling himself. He just looked mean.

"Eoghan," Nora hissed, slapping my upper arm urgently.

"Back up," I said.

"Eoghan, look..."

I turned in the direction she indicated, angling her toward the sooty wall.

Burly finally made an appearance. The man who had herded us here from Harp Street. He dressed much more respectably than his two accomplices. Where they were dirty and awkward, Burly wore a wool jacket and a carefully pressed shirt. He avoided a puddle of muck leaking out of a compost bin to keep his boots shiny. The man could have been a scholar or a grocer. Maybe even a banker at one of the smaller money houses.

But no. He was a thief. A smart one.

Damn these bulky packs. We could have moved faster without them, but they held everything we owned. Nora and I needed them. From the looks of it, these three muggers thought they did too. Or at least wanted them.

"Don't hurt my wife." I darted my eyes between Burly in the mouth of the alley and the grungy pair lurking deeper in, then gestured to Nora's protruding belly with one hand. "She's pregnant, as you can see. Just take what you want and leave us."

"Like hell!" Nora shouted from behind me.

"Ha! I like her," said Eyepatch. "She's got fire!"

I set my mouth, knowing what was coming. I bent my knees, ready to leap forward the second the opportunity presented itself.

"Fuck you, you little toad," Nora said with disgust.

The smile melted off Eyepatch's ruined face. "What'd you say, bitch?"

Earl threw out a hand and stopped Eyepatch from advancing. "Stick to the job," he said in a deep, rumbling voice.

"I said, fuck you," Nora repeated without missing a beat. "And then I called you a toad. Not just a toad, but a *little* toad. I thought you liked fire, eh? Maybe you only like it when a gal doesn't talk back. Or maybe you just didn't hear me? Your ears as screwed up as your eye?"

Eyepatch bristled, and Earl threw an arm around his friend to keep her back. Burly turned his head just a fraction to yell at his goons.

There it was. The opportunity. Nora was so good at this.

Nora squeezed my hand once and disappeared. She ran full tilt out of the alley, much faster than a hugely pregnant woman should have been able to.

And I launched my shoulder into Eyepatch's gut, taking all three muggers by surprise. It was stupid, reckless. I would almost definitely die, or at best, get out with a severe beating and the loss of everything I owned. But Nora's job was to run, and mine was to make sure no one chased her. No matter the cost.

Because Nora carried the Clarion. And if anyone caught a glimpse of it—or worse, got a hold of it—we were all screwed.

Eyepatch went down with a grunt of lost air, but I didn't have time for anything else. Earl might have looked slow, but he wasn't. Half a second after Eyepatch and I hit the ground, someone grabbed the back of my shirt and hauled me upright. I took the opportunity to kick Eyepatch one more time before a ham-sized fist slammed into my side.

I choked and wheezed, turning in Earl's grip to grapple at his bulging eyes.

"Yaa!" Earl squirmed and tossed me aside with a scream of anger.

I righted myself, squaring off against my opponent while Eyepatch struggled to rise.

What was I doing? I was no fighter. I was a ranger. An explorer. My height and heavy build had always kept trouble away. People assumed the worst of me and gave me a wide berth.

But that part of my life was over. So long as we carried the Clarion, nothing would be normal. Danger would follow us everywhere. Even if no one knew about it, it forced us to keep to the shadows and move in secret. It weighed on us, influenced all our decisions.

Fear of losing the damn thing had sent me down this alley in the first place. Not just fear of losing the Clarion, but fear of what they'd do to Nora if anyone found out what *she* could do because of it.

We had to get the Clarion to New Haven. We had to get rid of it. But first, I had to go through these three.

I reared back my right arm, stepping forward with my opposite foot, fist clenched and muscles tense. But then Burly grabbed my pack and yanked me off my feet. I tried to orient myself, but he jerked me again, pulling the straps halfway down my shoulders.

But it was a huge pack, well-made by my Nan, and she had made it hard to come off on purpose. It belted across my chest to support the weight and protect my back, so it didn't matter how many times Burly tried to pull it off me. It wouldn't go.

"Kick his ass, Earl!" Eyepatch snarled from the ground.

Earl didn't hesitate. He stepped forward and slammed his fist into my stomach. I wretched and gasped at the humid air, scrabbling at Burly's hands on my straps.

"The more you fight, the more he beats you," Burly said calmly. He leaned over me, pulling at the strap across my chest.

This put his nose within range, so I reared back and headbutted him. He staggered away, clutching at his face as blood poured between his fingers.

My victory was short-lived, however, when Earl's fist collided with my jaw. I went down on all fours, and the alley spun.

"You're a tenacious one, that's for sure," Burly said, standing over me. "Just kill him now, and we'll take the pack after. Less hassle—"

His words cut off with a clunking noise, and he hit the ground in front of me. I glanced up and locked eyes with Nora. She stood over Burly with a plank of wood in her hands like a club.

"Your shirt's dirty," she said to the unconscious Burly, sneering.

ELEVEN

I gaped at her. "Nora, what are you doing? Run!"

"He's right," Earl said, stepping toward her. "You should have stayed gone."

Nora heaved back the plank of wood and swung with all her might, but Earl caught it easily and ripped it out of her hands. She staggered backward a step, eyes steady on Earl.

"Run!" I shouted, hauling myself to my feet.

But it was too late. Earl snatched Nora by the arm as easily as Nan used to grab chickens in the yard at dinnertime. He wrenched her around, ignoring her kicks and screeches of fury, and smacked her across the face. She wobbled in his grasp, clutching her cheek in shock.

Red filled my vision. I leaped forward, my own pack halfway off my back, and tackled Earl to the ground. He hit the sticky cobbles with a crash, and I managed to get in one good punch to his cheekbone—right in the exact same place he had struck Nora. I would have beat the ever-living shit out of him, except by this time, Eyepatch had finally gotten to her feet.

I could have handled one of them, but not both. Even with the advantage of a full foot and a hundred pounds over Eyepatch, four hands against two was no contest. They overpowered me quickly, raining fists and boots too fast for me to comprehend. I tried to get up, but they knocked me back down again and again.

"Eoghan!" Nora screamed from the mouth of the alley.

I could only just catch sight of her between breath-stealing blows.

Run, Nora. Just run. And never look back.

But she couldn't hear my silent pleas. And she would probably have ignored them anyway. Burly rose off the mucky ground and went straight for her with a knife to cut her pack off her back. He would no doubt be clumsy with it. She'd be cut to ribbons.

I tried again to get up, only to have Eyepatch's boot connect with my ribs. If she'd been any stronger, bones would have snapped. And then I'd really be useless.

Earl lifted me off the ground by my shirt collar and pinned me against the wall. Blood poured from my nose.

"We just wanted your bags, that's all," he said, shaking his head. "It didn't have to be like this."

"But your bitch wife couldn't keep a respectful tongue in her head!" Eyepatch spat in Nora's direction.

Nora stood quite still while Burly cut her pack from her shoulders, sawing diligently through first one strap before moving to the next. Thanks to the Old Kind, she had the sense to just let him do it without struggling.

But of course, Eyepatch was right. Nora couldn't keep her mouth shut. She never could.

"Respect is earned, you filthy cow," she said. "I doubt you've ever earned a thing in your miserable life."

Eyepatch snarled and stalked toward her.

"Nora, for fuck's sake!" I yelled in a cracking voice. I struggled and kicked against Earl, but my blood-slicked hands couldn't find purchase. My entire body screamed in pain.

Burly's knife popped through the second strap, and he moved to the one that crossed diagonally down her chest. The last one.

But with all their attention diverted, none of them noticed the sixth figure enter the alley. A tall man, with the lamplight from the street flashing across his blond hair, stepped into the shadows. He picked up Nora's abandoned plank of wood and inched silently closer. I scrabbled at Earl's face, desperate to keep him distracted as the newcomer slipped toward Nora's aggressors.

"I think I'll enjoy teaching you a few manners," Eyepatch said, stroking a thin finger down Nora's cheek.

Nora took aim and spit directly in her face, but Eyepatch didn't flinch. She only grinned.

"Yes, I think I'll enjoy it very much, watching you break, little firebrand."

"Don't you touch her!" I ground out, pushing against Earl with no effect.

The blond newcomer took another step closer, but he moved so slowly. He could have swung the hunk of wood four times by now, but he waited. I locked eyes with him, and he set his mouth in determination. *Trust me,* his expression seemed to say.

Like I had any choice. This stranger was our last hope.

Nora clamped her mouth shut, and Burly finished sawing through her final strap. The pack yanked free of her body, and she stood a little straighter. She wrapped her arms around her stomach, angling slightly away from Eyepatch.

Because the second that leech of a woman touched Nora's belly, she'd realize it was fake. And the only reason anyone would fake a pregnancy would be to hide the *real* treasure. And that was one secret we couldn't afford to lose.

Finally, the blond man found his opening. He swung the hunk of wood, which connected violently with Eyepatch's head. The woman hit the ground with a groan of pain.

"No!" Earl roared, finally letting me go. He lumbered toward the unconscious woman on the ground, but I latched onto his back, sending us both down.

Burly took one look at the blond man, hesitated for half a

second of indecision, and ran. He threw Nora's pack over his shoulder and disappeared, abandoning his cronies with the loot.

Earl pushed me off him and landed a sickening wallop to the side of my head. He lunged for Eyepatch again, but the blond man swung his club a second time, and Earl collapsed on top of Eyepatch. Earl groaned, pulling Eyepatch closer through the muck coating the cobbles. He glared up at our rescuer mutinously but did not risk a second blow by getting up.

Nora threw my arm over her shoulders to help me stand.

"Come this way." The blond man ushered us out of the alley and up the street toward civilization. Light filtered down from the busy square a few blocks away, but the blond man led us along a tree-lined avenue and into a decent-looking public house.

My bloodied face attracted several stares from the other drinkers, but nothing more. Clearly, they had seen worse.

"Sit here. I'll fetch some rags." Our rescuer slipped away toward the bar.

While he moved through the room, I observed him properly for the first time. He wore plain but high-quality clothes. Linen and wool with heavy, decorative stitching at the hem of his shirt. He wore thick leather boots and had a finely crafted satchel swung across his body. Respectable, unremarkable, trustworthy. What had he been doing down that deserted, darkened street?

Nora helped me ease into a chair and undid the straps on my pack for me. "Anything broken?" she asked.

I shook my head, my mouth clamped tightly shut.

"I told you this would happen," she said when my pack slid off my back.

"I know," I replied, defensive. I hadn't argued with her when she'd suggested faking a pregnancy to hide the Clarion. It had been a good idea.

But she went on anyway. "I knew this would happen. I knew it. I told you it wasn't safe in a bag." She laid a hand on her false belly.

"You shouldn't have come back for me! What were you thinking? They almost got it! You were supposed to run!"

"I couldn't!" she hissed. "I couldn't leave you there!"

"They would have taken my pack and left me. I wouldn't have been any worse off than I am now."

"Would you have been able to leave me?" Nora asked, her dark eyes intensely focused on mine.

Her left cheek glowed dark where Earl had struck her, and I knew the answer. I would have given up the Clarion a thousand times to save her, but that didn't stop me from being stubborn.

"You shouldn't have come back."

"But I did. It's done." Nora sat down in the chair next to me and accepted the beer the blond man placed in front of her. She took a long, healthy draw and sighed in relief.

"You two were very lucky I happened to be walking by," the blond man said. "Muggings have been common ever since the war ended. People are desperate. You shouldn't be going down empty streets at night."

"Thank you for your help," I said. "I'm Eoghan. This is my wife, Nora."

"Good to know you." He shook both our hands in turn. "I'm Darius. I'm a merchant based in New Haven."

A barmaid arrived with an ewer of steaming water and a stack of clean cloth. "Here you are, love," she said to me.

"Thank you," Darius and I said at once.

Nora immediately set to work cleaning up my face. Her soft fingers on my cheeks sent an ache through my body, relief and comfort so strong it almost felt like longing. As grateful as I was to this Darius character, I wished he wasn't there just then. I wanted to wrap Nora up in my arms, to hold her tight and know she was safe and well. I wanted to make her mine for real, not just go along with this marriage we had invented. We'd done it to go unnoticed in the crowds of refugees who had swarmed Lujor after the war, but every time I called her my wife, it broke my heart a little more.

But I couldn't do any of that. I had to sit in this brightly lit bar and pretend Nora's touch was normal. I had to have a beer with this stranger and maintain a conversation.

"Where are you staying?" Darius asked.

"The refugee camp south of town." Nora wrung out the bloodied cloth. "We're trying to get to New Haven to find my family."

"Maybe I can help you there," Darus said.

"You don't need to do that," I replied. "You've done enough already, and we've made it this far."

Darius waved away the concern with a casual flick of his hand. "It's no trouble. And if I hadn't hesitated so long, that asshole might not have got away with your things."

Nora spared half a glance at him before locking eyes with me. But I couldn't read her expression, and the moment passed.

"I'm a merchant based in New Haven," Darius said. "I'm headed out again tomorrow on the Marsh Road. Ride on one of my wagons. We can travel there together."

"No," I said again. "That's too much."

"Nonsense," he said. "We're so close, and it will cost me nothing. I'm taking two wagons of fleeces. So they'll stink, but they'll be comfortable to sit on, at least. And you'll be there in a day. It's the least I can do. We can't have you walking that far, big as you are, Miss Nora."

"Mistress," Nora corrected, but the fire had gone from her voice.

I recognized the longing on her face. A day. Just one day and we'd be there. After two months of traveling, with weeks to go if we had to prepare and walk with half our supplies gone. It was tempting.

But we'd be putting ourselves in the debt of someone else. We'd be stuck with his caravan for an entire day, and with no supplies, we wouldn't have the option to hop off and start walking if the situation went sideways. There were no resources in the Midland Marsh, just mosquitos.

"Please, let me do this for you," Darius insisted. "I lost family in the war, same as everyone else. I can't imagine what it must be like, not knowing if they're safe."

"It's too much," I said again. "We can't accept."

"Why not?" Darius asked with a shrug.

Nora gritted her teeth and locked eyes with me. Silently, we agreed.

Yes, we'd lost her pack, but we had made it out with the Clarion. And in two days, we could be free of it. We could take it to the Reliquary in New Haven and hand it over to Lachlan, and all this would be over.

All of it. In two days. Done.

"Why don't you sit with us a while?" Nora asked. "Drink your beer and tell us your story. A wealthy trader doesn't just go around giving rides to strangers. Why are you so desperate to help us?"

Darius sat down with a satisfied grin. "How about an even trade? I'll tell you my story if you tell me yours."

Nora locked eyes with him and reeled off our agreed-upon lie. "Our story isn't very interesting. We fled Tutree when Amau burned it a few months ago. We fled into the wilderness. Didn't realize the war ended until a few weeks ago and saw the Giants for ourselves. So now we're headed to New Haven. I have connections there, and it's our best chance to get back to our people. To find out if they survived and where they might have gone."

"You lived off the land all those weeks?"

"I'm a trapper," I said. A small bending of the truth. Trappers were as adept as rangers at living rough, but they wouldn't be sent to climb a forbidden mountain. There was no way to know who might have heard rumors about a ranger and a mapmaker being sent on the mission to wake the Giants. We couldn't risk anyone drawing conclusions.

"A useful trade. Where do you sell your furs?"

"I used to sell them in Tutree, to the merchants who traveled through there. But not anymore."

"Right. Of course."

"Your turn," Nora said.

Darius settled back in his chair, his stein of beer held between both hands in his lap. He studied Nora's expression for a good five seconds, sizing her up. He must have approved of whatever he saw in her face because he lifted his chin and obeyed.

"I had two brothers. Not real brothers, but we grew up together in a workhouse. All of us abandoned, unwanted."

"They still put children in workhouses?" Nora asked, incredulous. "I thought they were all shut down decades ago.

"They're not supposed to. But illegal ones still exist, pretending to be orphanages or foster homes, and that's where my brothers and I grew up. Fletcher was the youngest of us. Brash, confident. And Arlo was the oldest, with me in the middle. Nobody ever gave us anything. We had to take it. And we got good at taking what we needed to survive."

I sat up a little straighter, and Darius noticed the alarm on my face.

"Don't worry, my friend," he said with a placating hand. "I'm not some villain. Though I might have been, once. I did some... very wrong things in my youth. Things I regret very much. It's so easy to keep taking once you get your first taste of plenty."

He shook his head and stared at his hands. The noisy pub seemed to melt away as he spoke, fading into a muted, golden light and a low hum of voices. I watched in fascination when true regret colored his expression.

"I lost sight of what my brothers and I wanted for ourselves."

"And what was that?" Nora asked.

Darius chewed his lip, contemplating the right words. "Peace. Kindness. All the things we lacked when we were children. I was lost for many years, but my brothers brought me back. Gave me a purpose that was more than just take, take, take. So, I went home with them for a time, let my managers run the business for a while. Arlo had done things right, you see. Built his home slowly, found a wife, grew his property by giving and sharing. And Fletch, he only ever wanted adventure. He came home sometimes, full of stories. And I think, those two years at Arlo's house, that's when I really grew up."

"What happened to them?" I asked. "Your brothers."

"Arlo is doing quite well. You'd never know he grew up in a workhouse. He's a proper lord, with power and property and people. He's beloved. But Fletcher..." Darius trailed off. "Fletch died a few months ago, I'm afraid. An accident while traveling."

"I'm sorry," Nora said.

Darius gave a sad smile. "He lived the life he always wanted. None of us can ask for more. Though he would have loved to see the Giants. He passed just before they woke up."

We sat in silence in the wake of his words. The hum of the pub reinserted itself into my consciousness. I wiped at my face with a fresh rag, wincing.

"And so now I'm back at work." Darius sat up a little straighter. "And I try to help people where I can. Live in a way my brothers can be proud of. And letting a budding family hitch a ride on my stinking fleeces is a part of that. And so, Mistress Nora, does my story satisfy you?"

Nora locked eyes with me, relief in the set of her mouth.

We were going to New Haven.

Twelve

The next morning, Nora and I made our way to the warehouses on the east side of town, per Darius's instructions. Merchants, auctioneers, artisans, and breeders for all manner of animals made their livelihoods here, along with everyone they needed to run their miniature empires: errand runners, stablehands, assistants, and clerks.

It seemed like every single one of them had flocked to the warehouse district that morning. Too many people, all together. They milled in and out of the huge, wooden buildings, hauling sacks, pulling mules, and shouting instructions and insults at one another.

And of course, with so many bodies—both human and beast—came smells. Mostly sweat and piss, but plenty of manure as well. It overwhelmed any of the more pleasant aromas wafting out of the sundry houses, things like thyme, onions, and soaps.

No, all we could smell was the piss and the mud.

"Remind me to never get into the merchant trade," Nora said under her breath when we entered the bustling alleys running between the warehouses. She stared around at the general hubbub, eyes wide and wary.

But that meant she wasn't watching her own two feet. I put a hand on her elbow and guided her around a herd of rambunctious goats, all pulling their herder in different directions as he struggled to get them down the street.

"We won't be here long," I said.

"Are we sure we want to do this?" she asked.

"No. But how much longer do you want to wear that false belly?"

She put a protective hand on the bump where the Clarion was hidden under her shirt. "Let's just find Darius and get this over with."

We pressed on to the very edge of town and easily found Darius's crew loading crates into a wagon. The man himself appeared, coming around another wagon loaded down with fleeces.

"Triple check the inventories," Darius said to an assistant while they walked. "The mill says they'll take four hundred raw fleeces, so I plan to deliver exactly four hundred. Ah, Eoghan. Miss Nora." He gave us a welcoming smile when he spotted us and handed a sheaf of papers to his assistant, who disappeared to check another wagon. "You made it."

"Mistress," Nora said.

I elbowed her. She needed to stop drawing attention to herself like that.

But she just elbowed me back, *tisking* like an old angry hen.

"Mistress," Darius amended, a light of amusement in his eye. "You're here just in time. We'll be leaving in a few minutes."

"Can I help you load anything?" I asked.

"Yes, actually. We had to let some of our muscle go this morning, so we're a bit short-handed. Why don't you help Miss Nora up here—you'll be riding on the fleeces. Sorry we don't have better accommodations, but we're traders, not a stagecoach." He cut his eyes at her when he said "miss."

He was a charmer, for sure.

"That's quite all right," Nora said, ignoring his teasing jab. "We're grateful for the ride."

"Not a problem," Darius said with a wave of his hand. "Eoghan, why don't you give your lovely wife a leg up and then come help us load these crates."

"I knew it. He's doing it on purpose," Nora said in an undertone when Darius walked away.

I helped her climb onto the towering stack of fleeces, for appearances sake. A woman this deep into a pregnancy wouldn't have been able to climb anything on her own.

"Doing what?" I asked.

"Calling me 'miss.'"

"Of course he's doing it on purpose." I narrowed my eyes in disdain. "Has no one ever flirted with you before?"

"I'm married. And pregnant. Or at least he thinks so." She settled herself comfortably on the fleeces, thighs level with my face.

I stared up at her, shading my eyes from the sun.

"Men like him take pleasure in charming everyone." I rested a hand on her knee. "It's a game to them. And the more stubborn you are, the more satisfying it is when you fall in love with him. Here, take my pack."

"Don't be gross," she said, accepting my pack when I passed it up to her.

"And you try and keep your mouth shut for more than five goddamn seconds," I said, pointing at her accusingly.

In response, she dropped her jaw and let her mouth hang open, eyeballing me with a *screw you* expression.

I laughed at the disgust in her expression and patted her knee before leaving to help load the last wagon.

I didn't know Darius well, but he was knowledgeable about one thing at least: Raw fleeces stank. Not just animal smell, but manure and grease and just...bad.

Nora got used to it quickly. She lay back, stretched herself out in the dappled sunlight, and went to sleep on the swaying pile of wool. She hadn't had a proper rest since we left the Giant's Mountain.

I sat cross-legged next to her, watching the road disappear behind us. Darius had eight workers, who either drove the wagons or sat precariously on top of loads, just like me and Nora. Darius himself, along with his assistant, rode handsome geldings alongside the wagons. And though the road was loud with the sounds of wooden wheels and rattling horse tack, they all kept up a steady flow of conversation, teasing jabs, and laughter.

If things went according to plan, we would reach New Haven by nightfall. We'd know that very day if Nora's family had survived. And this time tomorrow, we might be rid of the Clarion.

It was too easy. Too good to be true. Something had to go wrong.

And even if it didn't, even if everything went right and we got rid of the Clarion with no incident, what then? Without this blasted trumpet to keep us together, what would happen to us?

"So, how long have you been traveling?" Darius asked.

I whipped my head around, wincing when pain lanced through my battered face. After the beating I'd taken from Burly and Earl the night before, I must have looked like a dead man walking.

Darius had brought his gelding beside the fleece cart. Though his mount was quite large, my pile of wool towered higher. I still had to look down to meet his eye.

"What?" I asked, his words slowly penetrating my distracted mind. "Oh, almost three months. Since Amau burned Tutree."

"That's a long time. Too long for a pregnant woman."

"She's worried about her family." It was the truth, at least. As my Nan used to say, *Always tell the truth, Eoghan boy. That way, when you* do *lie, people will believe you.*

"Understandable," Darius said.

We fell to silence. For me, it was a natural repulsion to talk at all. But for him...what was he thinking? This man we hadn't known before yesterday? This man who was too kind in a world destroyed by war?

"So you say you've seen the Giants up close?" he asked.

"Hasn't everybody?"

"What did you think when you saw your first one?"

I thought back to that moment on the mountain, when Nora and I had first seen an awakened Giant. We had just fallen out of its ear, a hundred feet or more. The Giant stooped down and stared at us with its impenetrable, onyx eyes. Waiting. Questioning. Impossibly huge.

Everything we had hoped for, sacrificed for. Right there in front of us.

"My mind was a complete blank," I said honestly. "I couldn't believe it."

"My first Giant was quite small, actually," Darius said conversationally. "Only about twenty feet high. Scared the absolute pants off me. Of course, we'd all seen them charge the Amau army, but this was my first one up close. Found it poking around the corral where my horses were being boarded in Caernavorn. It seemed curious."

The wagon hit a bump in the road, which sent the fleeces swaying a bit more than was comfortable. I grasped my pack and Nora's thigh to steady her.

"I'm fine," she mumbled, rolling over as the ride smoothed out.

I smirked at her back. Of course she was. She'd say she was fine until she was blue in the face, even if she was on fire.

"What did you do?" I asked Darius. "About the Giant?"

"I nearly shit, of course," he replied with a laugh. "Ran at it, screaming and waving my arms, as if I could stop it from hurting the horses. But it just stared at me like I was an interesting bug, for all the good it did. It wandered off after a while. Some folks found it later. It had gone to sleep in someone's backyard and didn't move again."

"I don't think they want to hurt us."

"No, I agree. I wish they spoke more. Had records or any kind of culture. But they're just...there, aren't they? Like they're just another bit of earth."

"That's exactly what they are," I said. "They're not people. They're walking stone. They're Lujor itself."

Darius smirked up at me. "So the quiet man is a poet, then?" He laughed away my disapproving scowl. "That's not a criticism, my friend. We're all poets at heart. It's just that most of us never learned how to express it."

I looked down at him, at this man who had saved us, who had gone so far out of his way to help us for no reason other than to live up to some ideal from his youth. Being good for the sake of being good.

Nan wouldn't have been so surprised. *Folks is mostly good, Eoghan boy.*

"You're an interesting man, Darius," I said.

He smiled, and a beam of sunlight between the trees lit up his face. Handsome, cheerful, strong. I was suddenly relieved Nora disliked him so much.

"Thank you," he said with a flash of white teeth. "I take that as a high compliment."

I nodded once, perfunctory.

The town of Marcha disappeared quickly behind us, and soon the tottering houses gave way to heavy oak trees and undergrowth. About two hours into the ride, the overwhelming stink of rotting leaf matter and the buzzing of horse flies signaled our entrance to the great marsh. This road had been built to cross the huge bog centuries before and had been the fastest east/west route through Lujor ever since.

Nora slept on and off most of the morning, only rolling over occasionally to make sure I still sat next to her. Eventually, I scooted closer so my thigh butted up against her. That way she wouldn't have to keep checking. She slept better after that.

I couldn't rest, however. Not when Nora couldn't act as my eyes. As sincere as Darius seemed to be, at least one of us needed to be alert. So long as the Clarion was at risk, we couldn't afford to take chances.

So I sat on that stinking pile of raw wool and watched the grass and hardwoods gradually give way to muck and towering cypress.

Giants had become a new normal for the people of Lujor. After they ended the war with Amau, they settled in. Many went back to the Western Waste, but most simply sat down in a convenient place and went to sleep, much like the one Darius had encountered in Caernavorn.

They were more earth than human, though their shape was vaguely like ours. Great, clumsy creatures of living stone with glassy onyx eyes. They ranged in size from ten to three hundred feet. They rarely spoke and seemed to view us as curiosities more than neighbors.

Often, you'd see one lumbering by in the distance, careful not to step on any houses. But mostly, they would be sleeping in a field, with the farmer planting barley around them.

So when someone near the front of the group shouted, "Giant! Up ahead. Look, fellas! It's a biggun!" I thought little of it. But the general shock and awe of the rest of the group that had me turning on the fleeces to look at the road ahead.

My stomach jumped into my throat when I saw it.

Nora popped up next to me, less out of it than I had thought. "Where?" she asked, blinking the sleep away.

There was no need to answer. The damn thing was massive, and it lay directly across the road in front of us. Several other vehicles sat stranded, with our merchant train only the latest in a long line of befuddled travelers.

The Giant was indeed a "biggun." At roughly eighty feet tall, it wasn't the largest Giant we had met in the past couple of months, but it was plenty large enough. Made of dark, jagged stone with thick moss clinging to it, the great thing lay on its back with its head closest to us. A tenacious mesquite tree clung to the Giant's shoulder, its roots buried in the grime-filled cracks between the boulders of its arm.

The only way this beast cleared the road was if he got up and walked away.

"Don't say anything," I said under my breath.

"Oh, for hell's sake," Nora began.

"Nora, please. Not a word. If that thing hears you...Just please. Don't say anything."

She eyed me for several seconds, weighing my fear against her bullheadedness.

Her concern for me must have won, because she faced forward once more with a resigned sigh.

I crawled clumsily to the edge of the fleeces and scrambled down to the road. Nora followed, passing my bag down first before landing on the packed gravel next to me.

Good. I wanted her ready to run if she needed to. If that thing woke up...

No. Focus on the now, not the what-ifs.

Our group wasn't the first one to be stopped, nor the last. Seven vehicles sat stranded on the road aside from ours, unable to go around the great lump of living stone blocking our way.

Several dozen people milled about, all frustrated, tired, and completely at a loss. There was nothing anybody could do. Those who had come by on horseback had dismounted and led their horses carefully around the Giant. They'd found the firmest bit of mud and waded through, hoping the Giant wouldn't decide to get up or roll over.

Two carts and one carriage had tried to do the same and had immediately gotten stuck in the muck. This marsh was impassable, even a foot off the road.

"I could just tell it to move," Nora said under her breath.

"It's not worth the risk," I replied gruffly, my arms crossed over my broad chest. "What if someone saw? What if it took you too literally? Someone might get hurt. *You* might get hurt."

We appraised the Giant from the back of the growing crowd. It had carved an obvious path through the marsh: a wide swath of toppled bald cypress trees and water-filled footprints the size of feeding troughs. The devastation extended to the west and out of sight in the morning mist.

The Giant had clearly stomped through the sucking bog and laid down on the first bit of solid ground it could find: the road.

"There's no telling how long it'll be before he gets up and leaves on his own," Nora whispered, mirroring my posture. She crossed her arms under her breasts, which only served to make her protruding false belly even more pronounced. "We should have gone north and taken the Caernavorn Road. I told you this was a bad idea."

I turned to stare at her, incredulous. "Are you kidding me?"

She waved an irritated hand at me.

"You shouldn't be talking at all," I said. "What if it hears you?"

Nora flapped her hand again, dismissing my scolding. But she lowered her voice even further so I had to watch her mouth when she spoke. "What if we just go around it? You and me? We can continue on foot."

"It's still twenty miles to New Haven."

"We've walked further," Nora said, slightly more audible as her temper rose.

"You weren't pregnant then." I looked meaningfully at her belly and back up to her face.

She narrowed her eyes at me and cocked her head to one side, rearing up to say something cutting, but we were interrupted.

"Eoghan's right," said Darius from behind us. "You can't walk that far, big as you are."

Nora's expression melted from stubborn to ingratiating in a wink as she turned, which brought an appreciative smile to my own face.

"Yes," she replied. "He usually is."

I laughed once under my breath. That must have taken a lot of effort to get out.

Darius returned her friendly smile, then focused on me. "Listen, you're a big man. Maybe you can help us out. We're getting together a few people to try and talk to the Giant. Maybe we can get him to move."

"Yes, we'll come," Nora said.

Darius glanced at her, unsure. He and I were alike: strong, capable, and expendable.

Nora, on the other hand? Even though she was athletic, she was small and hugely pregnant—a fact she had apparently forgotten. Again.

"Giants are dangerous, Miss Nora," Darius said.

"Mistress. And I am perfectly aware that Giants are dangerous."

Darius turned to me, at a loss.

"We'll meet you there in a minute," I said, the subject closed.

Darius frowned, but he didn't argue. "Okay. Be quick, man. We want to get moving." He stepped around us, crunching through the packed gravel past our stranded wagon.

"Nora," I began.

"Don't you dare lecture me, Eoghan."

"When have I ever lectured you? And what happened to not saying a word?"

She gestured vaguely in the direction of the Giant. "Clearly it can't hear me from this distance."

"You don't know that. Maybe you just haven't said the right thing yet. Or the wrong thing, rather."

"I can get that Giant to move."

"Of course you can!" I hissed. "But don't you remember what happened the last time you intervened with a Giant? Back in Ridgewood?"

"Yes, I remember!"

It had been a nightmare. Ridgewood was the first town we had come to after leaving the Giant's Mountain. There had been a Giant there, sitting just outside the city gates, that hadn't moved in two weeks. The people had gotten used to it. There were kids climbing on its outstretched legs and jumping into haybales below.

But when Nora drew close and said, "Aren't you gorgeous?" the damn thing turned and looked at her. That had been startling enough. But then it got up and tried to follow us into the town. One of the kids got tumbled off and scraped up his leg.

People were terrified. The Giant was too big to fit through the city gates, but it tried anyway. The brick wall crumbled under its awkward hand, and Nora screamed, "No! Stop!"

"STOP," the Giant echoed. And it retreated. It pulled away its hand, and more bricks rained down to the street below.

"Stay outside the city, please!" Nora begged while I tried to pull her away. "You'll hurt someone!"

"OUTSIDE," it agreed. The Giant had taken another few steps before settling right down on the road. It managed to crush a small cart before its owner could pull it away, barely saving the mule yoked to it.

Everyone saw. Everyone understood. Everyone was terrified. They tried to grab Nora, tried to pull her out of my arms. But I was too strong for all of them. I managed to push away two people, which made the rest of them falter. I lifted Nora, pack and all, onto my shoulder and fled.

It hadn't been a good situation. We needed supplies, and we weren't able to get them there. No way in hell would we ever set foot in Ridgewood again.

"They nearly got us, Nora!" I said under my breath. "They tried to kidnap you. These people will notice, and they will know what you can do. They will want to use you, don't you understand? They will take you away from me!"

I snapped my mouth shut and stood up a little straighter, unable to look her in the eye. Instead, I focused on the scuffed toes of her leather boots.

The world had changed in the two months since we had climbed the mountain, since that fateful day when Nora had sounded the Clarion and woken up the Giants. Lujor was not the same country it had been when we'd last seen it.

Entire towns and forests had burned in the war. Supply lines had been cut off at the knees. When the armies broke up, bands of opportunistic brigands emerged, scavenging for whatever they could to feed their own families.

The Clarion was a lightning rod. It was only a matter of time before we slipped up and exposed it or until someone who knew about us tracked us down.

We had learned early to hide it—and ourselves—in plain sight. We decided to pose as married refugees displaced by the war with Amau. It guaranteed that we'd be able to keep together without drawing anyone's notice.

It had been Nora's idea to fake a late-stage pregnancy. On our second night back among people, after narrowly escaping a pickpocket, Nora clung to her pack in a panic until we made it back to our shabby room at the public house.

"The Clarion isn't safe enough in a bag," she whispered later that night, fearful of being heard through the thin walls. "What if someone tries to rob us? What if they succeed?"

So we had stayed up late, altering her pack to be worn in the front under her clothes. We stuffed it with our extra shirts, the Clarion nestled inside.

Nora had been my pregnant wife ever since.

And of course, she had been right. Not a month after that day, three assholes had mugged us in an alley.

Nora took my hand firmly and squeezed. "Wherever you go, I go," she said. "That's the deal, remember?"

I nodded, still staring at her boots.

She pushed on my chest with our clasped hands. "Now you say it."

"Where you go, I go."

Nora bobbed her head once and dropped my hand. "There's no telling how long my family will stay in New Haven, if they went there at all. And the sooner we can turn this damn thing over to the Reliquary, the better."

"Okay, but you *have* to follow my lead," I said sternly. My eyes remained on the Giant before us. "The last thing we need is to draw attention to ourselves, and you keep forgetting you're supposed to be pregnant."

She shrugged. "I know."

"We should put some rocks in there or something, give it a little weight. Then maybe you'd walk right."

"Don't even think about it," Nora said, glaring. "I'd like to see you wear this damn thing all day every day." She punched the side of her false belly and adjusted it under her clothes.

"Fucking hell. You are the worst actor I have ever seen." I batted her hands away from herself before someone saw.

Nora grinned at me and slapped my hands away. Then she stalked off down the road toward the sleeping Giant.

Thirteen

Darius had gathered ten other men and women to try and talk with the Giant. Their expressions ranged from overconfidence to curiosity to apprehension as we approached.

We waded through the muddy shoulder and collected near the Giant's boulder of a head, its glassy black eyes hidden in the folds of its stone eye sockets. It did not breathe, so with the lack of sound and movement, it could have simply been an inconvenient pile of rock.

But we knew better. This was a living creature. This was the legacy of Lujor.

"What do we do?" asked someone on my left.

Darius took a deep breath and stepped forward. He got right up next to the Giant's head and opened his mouth to yell. "Great Giant!"

We all stood silently in apprehension. Nora slipped her hand into mine, and I squeezed. When nothing happened, Darius glanced around at us.

"Maybe if we all yell together," I suggested loudly.

Heads swiveled toward me.

"It's worth a shot," a man on my right said.

The group mumbled for a few seconds and came to a collective agreement that we were right. It was certainly worth trying.

So, on the count of three, we all yelled together. A great, bellowing roar of "Giant!"

And this time, to everyone's extreme shock, the Giant moved. A sliver of its glassy eye appeared on its craggy face, and it shifted its limbs slightly.

Everyone took a startled step back. More than once, someone had been injured or killed by standing too near a Giant when it moved. They tried not to hurt us, but they were large and cumbersome. Sometimes it happened anyway.

Nora gasped in excitement, and I pulled her instinctively behind me. The Giant opened its eyes wider and stared at us.

"Great Giant!" Darius tried again. "We beg you to move off the road so that we can pass."

The Giant didn't seem to hear him. It kept its unnatural eye on the center of the crowd, where Nora stood peeking over my shoulder. She gripped the back of my shirt to balance while she rose on her toes behind me.

I squeezed her hand again in warning, a silent plea to do nothing. So far, we had managed to go unnoticed.

The Giant shifted and settled its head against the hard-packed gravel. The sliver of its eye disappeared as it went back to sleep.

The people muttered amongst themselves, encouraged by the small success. Maybe this could be done after all.

"What is he doing?" I said under my breath to Nora, nodding in Darius's direction.

She peered around me. The great blond man stepped forward slowly, hand outstretched toward the Giant's head. His hand trembled, not in fear, but in tightly reined excitement and awe. He glanced around, apparently saw no one watching him, and took another step forward.

"He's going to touch it," Nora said in the tiniest of whispers, slapping my shoulder gently in encouragement. "Let's get closer."

"No. Wait," I hissed.

Darius closed the last of the distance. He reached out one pale hand and, with the greatest of reverence, laid his palm on the cold stone Giant.

Nothing happened. The water birds continued to call, the crickets and the frogs chattered, and the hot and anxious people behind us on the road continued their hum of talk. The Giant remained apparently lifeless.

Darius looked up at the cliff of the Giant's face, his hand steady on the rough stone.

We both stared at him, unsure of what to do. Nora couldn't speak to the Giant in front of everyone. They'd know what she could do in an instant.

So we could only wait. But when they noticed Darius's fearlessness in touching the Giant, a few others dared to step forward as well. At least six men and women moved toward the Giant, arms outstretched.

"Quick," Nora hissed in my ear.

"On the end," I instructed, leading us to the left, myself between Nora and the others. They must not see her talking to it.

We both raised our hands, along with everyone else.

"Ready?" someone asked on my right.

"Be ready to run," another person advised.

I caught Nora's eye. She nodded once, mouth set in determination.

I took a deep breath and angled my body to block her from view. But in that moment, Darius glanced at me over the heads of the others. We locked eyes, and my own widened slightly in alarm.

"Quickly," I hissed under my breath.

But I shouldn't have bothered. Nora wasted no time, as usual. She whispered her instructions to the Giant, and it heard her. Of course it did. The cold, rough stone under my hand trembled, and every person there darted away in alarm.

Everyone but myself, Nora, and Darius.

We stood frozen when the Giant heaved. With the thunderous grinding of stone sliding across stone, it slung one clubbed arm over its body and slammed it into the ground behind me. I ducked and reached for Nora, but she darted away to my right.

"Nora!" I bellowed, but I was forced to stumble even further away when the Giant levered itself upright.

Screams and barked orders rang out from the other side, where the other travelers waited with the carts and carriages. Everyone in our party scrambled for the swampy shoulder and dove down the embankment into the muck below.

I lunged for Nora, who had dodged and scrambled to the Giant's other side as it slammed its limbs down again and again in an innocent attempt to gain balance. It lumbered upright and towered above us, blocking out the afternoon sun.

The impressive sight stopped Darius in his tracks. He stared up at it, the awe written plainly on his face. He took a stumbling step backward, his neck craned painfully back.

I could not get to Nora without going under the Giant's legs. She sprinted away from the towering creature.

"Stop!" she screamed to me, holding out one hand to halt my progress. The Giant steadied himself on his blunt legs. "Just stay back! I'm safe!"

The Giant's massive head swiveled in her direction. A crevice wedged open along the bottom of its face, and its tremendous voice thundered over us. "BACK," it echoed, rattling my ears.

I darted forward in alarm. "Nora! Run!"

"No!" Darius called from behind. He ran toward her as well.

Nora realized the danger an instant later, when the Giant obeyed her words. It took one step backward, but there was nowhere to go. Its stubby leg slipped on the steep slope of the embankment and skidded into the marsh at the bottom. It swung out its arms in an attempt to maintain balance, splintering the cypress trees on that side of the road. Fractured timber slammed into the ground from fifty feet up, splattering mud.

But it was no good. The Giant couldn't save itself. It toppled toward the road, Nora directly in its path.

No. Not again. Too many times, I had nearly lost her, and it just kept happening. I sprinted as fast as I could, arms pumping, legs churning through the packed gravel.

I wasn't going to make it.

What difference would it make? None. Even if I could get to her in time, it wouldn't matter. There was no escaping a falling mountain. Of all the times she had cheated death, this would be the time she would succumb.

The Giant toppled to earth as fast as any stone. Nora sprinted for the embankment, but there was simply no time. She only got in two frantic paces before the Giant slammed into the road. It landed with such shocking violence that my feet skidded across the gravel and I hit the ground as well. Darius rammed into me from behind, both of us completely winded.

Human and equine screams cut through the air as the ground shook. Horses thrashed in their traces, and at least two broke free to gallop away down the road, away from danger. Birds took flight in the trees, and cries of alarm filled the silence left after the echoing noise of the falling Giant.

"Nora!" I screamed in a cracking voice, scrambling back to my feet.

The Giant lifted both arms and pried itself up again.

There would be so much blood. She had been directly under its chest, only feet from the embankment. There would be nothing left.

I ducked under the rising Giant, heedless of the ongoing danger, and scrambled toward Nora's body in a crabwalk. And to my utter shock, she sat up, eyes wide with fear.

No blood. No broken bones. Not even a scratch. She was barely dirty.

I halted in front of her, shaking from head to toe, and followed the line of her arm with my eyes.

Her hand disappeared under the hem of her shirt and into the false belly she wore to hide the Clarion. The little trumpet had saved her life twice already. It had kept her safe when she had fallen off a cliff and again when we had tumbled out of a Giant's ear, landing a thousand feet below. Not a scratch.

She only had to touch it, and the Clarion would protect her from all injury. That Giant was the size of a mountain. It should have squashed her like a bug.

I launched forward and gathered her into my arms. She immediately dissolved into sobs of terror.

"It's okay," I muttered into her hair. "You're okay."

Darius skidded up to us and knelt. "I thought for sure it hit her, but she's okay. Any broken bones?"

Nora clung to me and shook her head. "I'm okay," she croaked.

"I told you the Giants were dangerous!" Darius said angrily. "You should not have been there!"

I glared at Darius, but he wasn't one to be intimidated.

"What if she'd died! What if she'd lost the baby!"

"That's enough!" I snapped, and Darius wrenched his mouth shut, mutinous.

But I didn't care. Darius had nothing to do with any of this. I slipped my arm under Nora's knees and lifted her off the ground. She clung to my neck and scrubbed her face on her sleeve.

"Where did it go?" she asked.

I turned so we could both see the Giant. It stood quite still in the marshland on the north side of the road, its legs sunk several feet into the muck. Almost as tall as the towering cypress trees, it gazed down at us.

"SAFE," it bellowed, inciting several more cries of alarm from the stranded travelers.

"Safe," Nora whispered, and tucked her forehead under my chin.

FOURTEEN

"It's still following us," one of Darius's men mentioned to him an hour later.

Nora's grip on my hand tightened briefly, but she said nothing. The muttered conversation of our fellow travelers continued, barely audible over the rattle of the cart wheels on the gravel road.

She hadn't let go of my arm since the Giant fell. Even now, perched safely on the stinking, swaying fleeces, she drew my arm directly into her lap and clung to it like a lifeline, her fingers digging into my skin.

Her blank expression hollowed me out. I wanted to pick her up and carry her away. Just pick a direction and walk, never looking back, until she remembered how to smile again.

Soon. We would turn the damn Clarion over to Lachlan at the Reliquary soon. And then this would all be over.

The man continued, his voice filled with concern and drama. He was enjoying this. "What if it follows us all the way to New Haven?"

"Maybe it will try to enter the city," someone else added.

"It won't."

"How do you know?"

On and on it went. Nora locked eyes with me, her concern written plainly on her face.

The Giant had taken a liking to her, it seemed. As the caravan of coaches and carts sped down the newly cleared road, we expected the Giant to lie down again. Or maybe it would wander off through the swamp to find somewhere else to settle down.

But when the last vehicle clattered away, it lifted one gangly leg out of the marsh with a tremendous sucking sound and followed us.

Its footsteps thundered a slow, ominous beat as we drove away down the road. And Nora clenched her jaw and stared straight ahead, clinging to my arm and refusing to let go.

The Giant *did* follow us all the way to New Haven, and it drew a larger crowd of lookie-loos as we went. Nora cradled her false belly and leaned her weight into me while we rode along, but no one was looking at us. Not when there was an eighty-foot giant ambling down the road.

We saw the city long before we reached it. It settled over the hills and around the great bay, shining almost white in the evening sun. The Arigua Ocean created a magnificent backdrop for it, sparkling every shade of blue and green, with the sky melting into it at the horizon.

"We're almost there," I said, but Nora was able to see the city as well as I could. I needed to comfort her, and I didn't know how else to do it. "You know the way to Edith's house?"

Nora chewed her lip and then spoke for the first time in hours. "Yes. We stayed there several times when we were younger. I know the way."

According to Nora, Edith had owned the house since she was a child, having inherited it from her father. It had been rented out for two decades, with Edith preferring to live in Tutree with her mother and Nora. But with Tutree gone and since there had been a convenient gap in tenants for several months, Nora figured this would be the best place to find her family.

We might be back with her family within an hour. We were so close.

I glanced behind us at the Giant, which still ambled behind us. Nora followed my movement and gazed at it as well, which the Giant seemed to notice.

"SAFE," it bellowed.

The crowds around us gasped and cried out, startled. Some people even laughed about it, as if it were a thrill. I wished I were in their positions. I'd love to find the Giants fascinating. But for us, they were a reminder of just how easy it was for us to be discovered.

Nora nearly jumped out of her skin when the Giant spoke. She turned back around, burrowing even deeper into my side.

"Why does it keep saying that, do you suppose?" Darius asked from his horse.

"Don't know." I tightened my arm around Nora.

Darius twisted around in his saddle to peer at the Giant making slow but steady progress behind us. "It must have *some* reason."

I clenched my jaw and said nothing.

We arrived at the Western Gate soon after.

"We'll let you off here, if that's convenient for you," Darius said. "We'll go around to the south, to enter nearer the warehouses, and I doubt you will find your family there, Miss Nora."

Nora's eyebrows pinched, but didn't correct him. I clenched my jaw harder.

"This is perfect. Thank you Darius," she said. "We can walk from here."

I climbed down first, accepted my pack when Nora passed it to me, and then lifted her down last. Darius seemed to notice her pinched expression when she found her feet.

"Don't worry, Miss Nora. It was a terrifying ordeal this afternoon, but no harm done."

"I'm fine," she said shortly.

"Well." He leaned back on his heels. "It was a pleasure knowing you both, and I hope to see you again in the future. I'll buy you a round if I'm lucky enough."

"Thank you for giving us a ride," I said. "And thank you for helping us last night. You have done us a great service. We won't forget it."

"Don't mention it." Darius clapped me on the arm. "In times like these, we have to look out for each other, don't we?"

Nora glared at him, her expression heavy. She slipped her hand around my elbow. "Let's go, Eoghan. I want to get home before dark."

And finally, we were off and on our own again. I breathed a deep sigh of relief when we walked away from the stinking fleeces and Darius's warm smile. As helpful as he had been, I wasn't sorry to leave him and his carts behind.

To the west, with the beginnings of a fabulous sunset behind it, the Giant finally came to a halt. It hovered off the side of the road and went perfectly still, its eye still following Nora while we slipped through the crowds.

Nora didn't look back, but I certainly did. I didn't like the way it followed us, the way it zeroed in on her.

The crowds were thick here. Dozens, or even hundreds of people gathered about the Western Gate, anxious to get into the city before dark. Soldiers milled about, checking every cart and bag. It was a slow process. But even though the war was over, cautious habits were hard to break. Security was tight as ever, and no one complained. We knew better.

My pack was given a perfunctory search, and no one looked twice at Nora. She got through with the Clarion unnoticed.

And then, just before we reached the city gates, a hand gripped my forearm, causing me to jerk away. I spun to face the stranger: a well-built man in his early thirties, with warm skin and gently curling hair cut short. He smiled up at me, completely unfazed by my glare.

"You'll see her again, my friend," the man said in an unfamiliar accent.

"Who?" I asked.

But the man patted my arm in a congenial manner and slipped off into the crowd.

My gut pinched, and I whirled toward Nora. But she stood at my side, right where she should be.

"What?" she asked, eyes widening in alarm.

I scanned over the heads of the crowd, but the man had disappeared. "Did you see that man?"

"What man?" Nora asked.

I set my mouth, disconcerted. "No one. He must have mistaken me for someone else."

"What did he say?"

"Nothing. That way." I pointed ahead where the crowd thinned, and we pressed onward.

We joined the flow of people entering the city, but another thundering *Boom! Boom!* echoed through the narrow streets.

"It's going around the side," I said under my breath. The people around us cried out in alarm at the noise. "It's not entering the city."

"It won't," Nora said with a sniff. "There are too many people here. They don't like to step on us."

Even as she spoke, I gripped her arm and halted her dogged progress.

Maybe the larger Giants avoided entering the city, but the smaller ones fit inside much better. One such creature—one of the smallest Giants I had seen yet at roughly fifteen feet tall—sat on the edge of the cobbled street, leaning back against a bakehouse. Someone had perched a wicker basket on its head like a jaunty hat.

It turned its head slowly toward us, watching as we passed. It blinked its onyx eyes once but did not move otherwise.

Nora clamped her mouth shut, watching the small Giant warily. She walked onward, determinedly looking away.

New Haven hadn't changed much since the last time I had been there. I usually tried to avoid it, disliking the crowds, the stink, and the noise, but occasionally, I had no choice.

There were plenty of nice things to see and do in the city. Home to more than half a million people, it sprawled around New Haven Bay, coating the surrounding hills in a crust of cobbles, with houses stacked on houses, stairways crammed into corners, and vendors spilling out into the streets.

The biggest markets crowded near the various marinas, where people sold much more than fish and crab. This was where the merchant traders did their business and where the savviest of shoppers came to get wholesale prices on imported silks, citrus, spices, and wine.

But Nora directed me toward the southern coast of the bay, then back down narrow streets and narrower alleys. We stopped before an unremarkable door set into a dingy stucco wall, with a leggy tomato plant in a pot outside.

Nora pulled her cloak tighter about herself, took one steadying glance up at me, and knocked twice on the door.

We waited in silence. I glanced around at the darkened street, but no one moved except a stray cat down the way.

Nora knocked again, and this time we heard noise from inside.

The latch rattled in its socket. The entire door shifted an inch before getting stuck. With another shove, the door finally came free from the jamb and wrenched open.

A young man, barely more than a teenager, stood in the open doorway. The room behind him was illuminated with a few candles. Simple furnishings, a basic cook stove, a bowl of beans soaking on the board near the washbasin.

The man himself cocked his head to one side, displaying the

sharp angles of his face to the twilight outside. His clothes were much too nice for the state of the house, and yet he didn't feel out of place, either.

"Uh, hello," Nora said, drawing the young man's eye away from my imposing height. "I'm looking for my sister. Edith. She owns this house. Do you know her?"

"Nora?" The man lowered his eyebrows in surprise.

His accent was strange. Not like any I had ever heard before. He stuck his head out of the door and peered down the empty alley.

"We're alone," I informed him, my gut clenching. I pinched Nora's sleeve, but not hard enough to pull her back.

"You are Nora?" the young man asked again.

"Yes, I—"

The man ducked back inside the house, shouting, "Edith!"

He left the door open as if to invite us inside. We stepped over the threshold, my boots thumping heavily on the uneven wood floor. Heat washed over us from the cook stove in the corner. The mismatched furnishings were unremarkable, mostly wood softened with faded cushions. A large, cobbled-together shelf dominated the back wall, filled with everything from cooking supplies to clothing, tools, and junk.

"Who is it?" asked a familiar woman's voice from an interior door. The speaker appeared, wiping her hands on an apron.

I had only met Edith once, and only for a few hours. But I would have known her anywhere, just because she looked a great deal like Nora. Her skin was lighter, and her dark curls were a little less wild than Nora's, but not by much.

"Edith!" Nora exclaimed.

"Nora! We thought you were dead!" Edith stumbled forward, arms out, but Nora faltered at the last minute.

Clearly she had forgotten—again—that she was supposed to be pregnant. She arched her body sharply away, trying to embrace her sister without letting her touch the false belly.

Edith noticed. Everyone in the room noticed.

Edith clasped Nora by the arms. "Nora, what is this?" she asked, looking down. "Are you pregnant?"

"Uh," Nora mumbled, then retreated toward me with her arms protectively over her stomach. "Yes. Of course, yes. Edith, you remember Eoghan. We're having a baby."

Edith's eyes hit mine. An echo of Nora's spitfire shone through her haggard expression. "I remember you." She knitted her brows together, looking me up and down. "You're that ranger who came to Tutree right before the fire." Edith glared at Nora. "Three months ago."

I held her gaze, feeling like a stone Giant myself. Nora wrapped herself around my arm.

"It's Eoghan's baby, Edith," Nora repeated.

Hell, she was the worst liar I had ever known. It took every ounce of will I had to stop my eyes from turning skyward.

"You weren't pregnant three months ago, Nora," Edith said, her tone a mirror of Nora's. Clearly, bullheadedness ran in the family. "But you look like you're nearly nine months along.

"It's Eoghan's baby," Nora said again.

The young man's eyes darted back and forth between the women, his mouth twisted into a frown.

"Nora—" Edith began, but I cut her off.

"It's my baby, Edith." I said, leaning forward on the balls of my feet.

The entire room went silent in the wake of my words. Edith and the stranger both turned their full attention on me and shrank slightly. The man fisted his hands at his sides, but he did not move to challenge me.

It was a stupid lie, and everyone in the room knew it. But it didn't matter. We just needed to get through the next few days without anyone asking any questions. Then we'd be gone. And all this would be over.

Nora anchored me by my arm. I forced my focus onto her

desperate grip, the way she held on for dear life. Both to hold herself up and to hold me back. She needed rest. Nora needed to recover properly after nearly dying that morning.

"Edith," Nora said, her voice steady. "We're looking for Mother and Nikita...and anyone else who might have escaped Tutree." She swallowed hard.

"Where have you been, Nora?" Edith asked.

The young man hovered behind her.

"We had a job, remember? Me and Eoghan. Where's Mother?"

"She went on south to Ferndale, to live with your Aunt Maeve. She was well when she left. I expect to hear from her any time, saying she made it safe."

Nora grinned up at me, tears in her eyes.

"I told you," I said.

"Shut up." She slapped my arm and turned back to her sister. "What about Nikita?"

Edith's expression tightened. "I don't know. We didn't see her again after we ran."

Nora's grip tightened on my arm. "Oh."

Edith's eyes flicked down to Nora's false stomach. Did she realize it wasn't real? Or did she think we were simply lying about the identity of the father? What explanations were rifling through her sharp mind?

"Who is your friend, Edith?" Nora asked.

"This is Garet." Edith placed a hand on the young man's shoulder. "He's been staying with me the last few weeks."

"Good to meet you, Garet," Nora said.

Garet gave her a smile that could have been friendly if his eyebrows hadn't been drawn so tightly together. Nora and I both waited for him to say something, anything. But he stayed stubbornly silent.

"Do you need a place to stay?" Edith asked, her hands clasped in a tight knot in front of her stomach. "We don't have much, but you are welcome. Supper will be ready soon, and you can have the storeroom. There's space to make up a bed in there."

Nora nodded, swiping at her eyes. "Thank you, Edith. Just for a night or two. We won't be staying in New Haven long."

"Will you go to Mother in Ferndale?"

Nora glanced up at me again, hesitation in her eyes.

"Yes," I answered for her.

Where you go, I go.

We ate the watery beans in relative quiet. Where the two sisters might once have chatted and joked, now they sat in dogged silence, making small talk about the weather and reconstruction after the war. Every time Edith brought up the Giants, Nora fell conspicuously quiet, and her face went pale.

Garet spent the entire meal watching us, a thoughtful expression on his face. He rarely spoke, and when he did, it was in broken Ambic: "Give salt, please, Edith," and "You have name, Nora? For baby?"

For that one, we simply answered that we hadn't decided yet.

After a while, conversation petered out altogether. Nora no longer clutched at my arm since we were seated around a table, but she barely lifted her eyes out of her bowl of beans.

My knee bounced under the table. I wanted to drag her to another room or outside or into the wilderness. I wanted to talk to her for real without anyone else listening in. I wanted to give her proper food, with thick slices of meat and seasoned greens and maybe a cake. She deserved pound cake and tarts and...Anything except this weight around her front and the Giants following her around.

Edith watched her too, the worry clear on her beautiful face. But after several repetitions of "I'm fine" from Nora, Edith stopped asking.

After dinner, Edith led us to the storeroom just off the kitchen. She dragged out a narrow straw mattress and old linens, gone soft with age and countless washings, and left us to sort ourselves out on the floor.

And if it was a bit strange that neither sister seemed interested in catching up beyond that, I couldn't bring myself to care. All I wanted was to get Nora alone so I could check in with her properly.

The instant the door clicked shut, Nora stripped off her shirt and turned her back to grant me access to the straps of her false belly. I undid the clasp between her shoulders in silence.

She slipped the bag off, then let it fall unceremoniously to the floor next to the mattress. It hit the wood with the muffled *clank* of brass wrapped in fabric.

"The sooner we get that thing to the Reliquary, the better," I said. "We'll go first thing in the morning."

She nodded without looking at me.

"Are you all right?" I asked.

Nora turned around in nothing but her trousers and her undershirt, slim and lithe once more. She closed the distance between us and buried her face in my chest.

I froze for several seconds. I had seen Nora afraid before, but never like this. Never this broken.

She felt my hesitation and pulled away. "Sorry," she said, wiping under her eyes again.

Her sheepish apology triggered something in my brain. Holy shit. She thought I didn't want her to touch me.

I wrapped my hand around her upper arm and drew her into a tight embrace. She melted into my chest with a muffled whimper, and I held her closer in response.

The feeling of her against me sparked a sharp memory of the first time we had shared a bedroll—two months before, on the Giant's Mountain. She had snaked her arm under my jacket and pressed her nose into my chest, reveling in the precious warmth.

And for a moment, I had thought she'd wanted sex. Because no woman had ever sought comfort from me the way Nora did.

But Nora wasn't like any other woman I had ever met. She didn't balk at my intimidating size or brush me off as just a wall of muscle. Nora saw me for what I was. She saw the softness in me, and it didn't surprise her.

And that morning, I'd almost lost her. I had nearly lost the only person who made me feel at home in my own skin. The only family I'd had since Nan died.

"That was too close today," I said, my mouth pressed into her curly hair.

Nora nodded against my shirt, a short frantic agreement.

"I don't know what I would have done if—" I broke off, unable to finish the sentence.

"Shh!" she said through her tears. She pulled back and took my face in both hands. "I'm too stubborn to die."

A single, humorless laugh broke free of my throat, but my fractured smile wouldn't stick. She shouldn't have been consoling me. It was supposed to be the other way around.

"That wasn't you being stubborn, Nora!" I said. "It was pure luck that Giant didn't—"

"I know!"

"You can't!" I faltered. "Don't...Please don't ever—"

"I won't!"

"Don't go where I can't follow!" I gripped her sides to keep her near. Her skin was warm through her thin undershirt. Warm and alive and real. My chest ached with it.

"Never," she said in a whisper. "Where you go, I go."

I pressed my forehead against hers, and she closed her eyes with a sigh.

"Say it again," I said.

"Where you go, I go."

I kissed her. It wasn't something I could help. I had to kiss her because I didn't know how else to deal with the ache in my chest or the look on her face. Like a drowning man desperate for air, I fell upon her mouth. I wrapped my arms around her, pinning her against me, and her fingers threaded into my hair. She rose on her toes and kissed me back with a hunger equal to my own.

Yes. This.

All fear and uncertainty disappeared. There was only the need and the fulfillment of Nora. She was here, alive and real and on fire in my arms. There was only skin and lips and tongue and breath. I drank her in, melding my body to hers. Needing more. *Always* more.

I had imagined kissing Nora a hundred times since I met her, but I had never thought it could be like this. I'd never felt anything like this before, not with anyone. I hadn't known it was possible.

Nora broke the kiss and stared up at me in wonder, her eyes alight with the first real smile she'd had in a while. It was a small, tentative thing, but it was real.

I should say something, do something. This was definitely not the time to be exploring these feelings and urges. She had nearly died that day. We were clinging to our mission by our fingernails, and we were so tired. But all I wanted was to kiss her again, to feel that smile pressed against every inch of my skin.

Maybe she recognized the look in my eye, because her smile dropped away, only to be replaced with a darker expression. Nora put a foot on a storage box on the floor, stepped up to my level, then launched herself at me. She wrapped her thighs around my waist, and I caught her with a growl of approval.

Fuck the mission. Fuck the Clarion. Fuck the war and the Giants and the Reliquary. Nora was all that mattered. She was all that had ever mattered, from the first moment she had sauntered out of the shadows in the Council Hall in Tutree.

Her sudden weight knocked me off balance, but I had enough sense to make sure we landed on something soft. My knees hit the straw mattress first, and then I dropped the rest of the way, catching us with one arm against the linen sheet.

Nora clung to me as I lowered us gently the rest of the way.

Her soft mouth moved against my neck, sending tremors through my entire body.

"God, Nora," I groaned.

"God*dess*," she corrected with a grin and kissed me deeply, swallowing my laugh.

Having slept next to her for the past three months, often in the same bed, I had thought I knew what to expect. But every touch, every layer of clothing removed, every glide of skin across heated skin, brought delicious new sensations.

And as we made love in that dingy storeroom, on a straw mattress on the floor, I knew for one bright shining moment that everything was right in the world. Just for a while. Right here, right now. We were exactly where we were supposed to be.

Together.

FIFTEEN

"Tell me the truth," Nora whispered later while we lay under the heavy blanket. "How long have you wanted to do that?"

With the lamp blown out, I couldn't see her in the dark, but I could feel her. I ran my hand up the smooth skin of her side and considered her question. "Since the first night we shared a bedroll on the mountain."

She snorted into the darkness, dragging a grin across my face. "That's all it took? What, I snuggle up against you once, and that's it? You're ready to go?"

"No!" I said with half a laugh. I drew her closer, and she nestled into me like a contented cat. "No...Well, partly."

She laughed again, her breath blossoming across my chest in a hot wave.

"That was the first night you sounded the Clarion, remember?"

She nodded. "I remember."

"I don't know what it was about that night, but that's when I stopped fighting you," I said quietly. I found the end of her braid behind her back and began twisting it around my fingers. I sensed her looking up at me, even though she couldn't see me properly. "Maybe it was the earthquake or the stories about Nan. Or maybe it was just that you were so soft and warm. I don't know. But I didn't feel so alone anymore."

She reached up, and her fingertips brushed against my bottom lip. Heat flushed through my face, and I kissed her fingers.

"And then," I said breathlessly, "after the Giants woke up and we survived, that's when I started to think of you...to think of the future. With you."

"Hm."

"And what about you?" I asked. "How long have you wanted me?"

A smile colored her voice. "Since the first moment I saw you in that Council Hall in Tutree."

I laughed, and she giggled in response.

"No, you didn't."

"Yes!" she insisted. "I thought you were so sexy and rough and strong. And these arms, holy hell. But then you were a giant ass for days. Wouldn't say a word to me."

My laughter rumbled in my chest, and she pressed her smile into my skin, directly over my heart.

"But after a few days," she continued, "I realized you were just quiet in general. And then...after that Amau man attacked us on the mountain and you nearly died...I just thought...I didn't know what I'd do without you. I mean, I could finish the climb on my own and get the job done, but it wouldn't be right without you. And then, at the peak, right before I sounded the Clarion, you asked me to come with you afterwards." She looked up at me in the dark. "I knew then I'd follow you anywhere."

I held her closer, as if I could make us one person if I held tightly enough, and thought back to that man, the stranger who had taken my arm right outside the city gates.

You'll see her again, my friend.

His words hit me like a warning bell. I had only ever loved two women in my life: Nora and my grandmother, Nan. There had been no one else in the world I cared to see again, all passing friends and acquaintances.

Nan had died eight years before. Her passing still hurt, but it was an old wound.

That left Nora—the only woman who could possibly be taken away from me.

I knew better than to dismiss the man's words as coincidence. There was no such thing in a world where sibyls and Giants walked the earth. But if I was careful, if I kept her close until we were far away from this city, maybe it would come to nothing.

"We have to get rid of the Clarion," I said.

She nodded against my chest.

"I know it protects you, but it brings danger as well," I continued.

"I know."

"We can't carry it around forever. We have to figure out how to pass it to the Reliquary secretly. Right into Lachlan's hands. No one can know they have it. Could you imagine what Amau would do? They'd burn the whole place down just to get the Clarion from them."

"Sleep, Eoghan."

"I can't sleep. I can't—"

"*Shh,*" she whispered. "We're safe tonight. We did what we came to do. We found my family. Tomorrow, we'll figure out what to do about the Clarion."

"Nora—"

"And then once we get rid of it, we'll go to Ferndale to see my mother."

"Nora, please," I said, my hand tight on her hip.

"And then after...we go anywhere. Someplace new, where I can draw maps and you can hunt and explore. You can take me to your Nan's old house."

I sighed into her hair, and the tightness in my chest dissipated a fraction. "Anywhere? You promise?"

"Anywhere."

~

The next morning, I woke to find Nora on her back, sprawled next to me. I smiled to myself at the sight of her breasts, only just visible in the early dawn light leaking through the dirty window. Memories of the night before set my heart racing. All I could think about was her softness, her warmth, and the way she had molded her body to mine.

But the happy thought popped like a soap bubble when I remembered the Giant waiting for us outside the city. The one that had nearly killed her, then followed us all the way to New Haven.

If we got rid of the Clarion, would the Giants stop listening to Nora? I could only hope so.

I ran my hand across her ribs, shaking gently. She sucked in a sharp breath, then relaxed when she saw me hovering over her.

"Good morning," she said with a smile. Nora levered herself up off the mattress to kiss me heartily.

A little thrill went through me. This was something I could have now.

"Morning," I responded against her mouth.

We kissed once more, then she lay back down and stretched with her arms above her head. My eyes traveled across her naked body while her muscles flexed under supple skin.

"Get a good eyeful?" she asked, sitting up.

"Yes."

"Well, then you'll really enjoy this," she said casually. Nora threw back the blanket and stood up, displaying a gorgeous view of her ass.

I screwed up my mouth in a rueful smile. "You know me so

well," I said while she went about collecting her clothes and the false belly.

When we emerged from the storeroom, Edith greeted us from the back corner of the main room. Her wheel clicked steadily as she spun her flax. Something was loose on it somewhere. I clenched my teeth at the noise, but it was impossible to ignore.

"Good morning." Edith glanced up only once before turning her attention back to her work. *Click, click, click.*

"Morning, Edith," Nora said, hovering near the open front door. "Where's Garet?"

"He had business to attend to in the city today."

Click, click, click, click.

"What business? The market, I suppose?"

"Yes, the market," Edith amended with a reassuring smile. Her dark hair glowed in the light flooding in through the open door, and the flax slid through her fingers with expert grace. She fed two bobbins at once from a single distaff, occasionally dipping her fingers into a pot of water next to her to lay the fibers as they twisted together.

Click, click, click.

I stared at Edith's blank expression. My gut twisted, just like her thread. Something was wrong here. Something had been wrong since we arrived the night before. I pinched Nora's sleeve. "We need to get going."

"Yes," Nora agreed. "Edith, I'm sorry, but we have to get going early today. We have business in town as well, but then we want to move on as soon as possible."

Click, click...click...click. The wheel slowed to a stop when Edith's feet stilled on the treadles. "But you'll be staying here one more night, surely?"

"Maybe," Nora said.

"No," I answered at the same time.

Nora glanced up at me, eyebrows furrowed, but didn't argue. I pulled a little harder on her sleeve, telling her without words, *Let's go!*

"We'll stop by later today to say goodbye before we leave," Nora said smoothly. "I want to follow Mother to Ferndale as soon as we can."

"And have the baby there, with her to help," Edith added.

Nora nodded quickly. "Yes. Exactly."

My eyes darted between the two women. The dread in my gut solidified into something identifiable. The sisters were more alike than I realized. They had the same tells when they lied: fidgeting, avoiding eye contact, agreeing too easily.

"Thank you for letting us sleep here last night." I pulled Nora toward the door.

"Of course," Edith said. "Anything for family."

"We'll see you later," Nora said, and we slipped out into the early morning sunshine.

"She's hiding something," I whispered to Nora, moving away from the dingy doorway.

"What could she possibly be hiding?" Nora asked, her voice equally low.

I glanced backward down the alley and stared at the open window, where Edith had been sitting just inside. We should have been able to hear her wheel clicking, but she hadn't resumed working.

"I don't know, but I don't like it. Let's get this done and get out of here."

SIXTEEN

The Reliquary.

The cultural and historical heart of Lujor.

A major arm of the government.

Its entrance butted directly against the seawall so as to be on display to the heaviest traffic through the Georgian Canal. The Reliquary was responsible for collecting and maintaining—and sometimes containing—the notable artifacts from Lujor's past: important documents, treasure, works of art, pieces of magical significance.

Their Grand Gallery housed these items for public viewing. I had never really thought much about them, aside from a passing appreciation that our government valued culture enough to establish such an agency. And I certainly had never thought the Reliquary would become an important aspect of my personal life, and yet here we were.

These were the people who had charged Nora and me to climb the Giant's Mountain. Lachlan had provided Nora with the secret archives—accounts of previous illegal climbs that had led us to the Clarion and the Cavern of the Giants.

Those accounts had been lost on our trek. I wasn't looking

forward to having that conversation with Lachlan, the High Reliquary himself, but what more did he want? We had woken up the Giants and ended the war. Besides, most of the landmarks on those archives were long gone, so they were worthless anyway, aside from any historical context.

After we left Edith's house, we made our way to the southern side of the Georgian Canal and entered a half-filled restaurant right on the docks. We chose a table overlooking the water, taking advantage of the convenient view of the Reliquary across the canal. Even this early in the day, dozens of people entered the Grand Gallery in a steady stream through the enormous doors that stood sentinel at the top of a wide, sweeping staircase.

The server brought us thick slabs of rye bread slathered with plum jelly, and we stared over the water at the impressive columns and stained glass windows, nursing strong coffee in steaming mugs and discussing possibilities.

"We could throw it in the bay," Nora suggested with a raised eyebrow. She sat with her elbow on the table, her chin in her hand.

"Someone would see."

"So we take a boat way far out," she suggested with a *why-not* shrug.

"The boat captain would see."

"So we just rent the boat, not the captain." She frowned and cocked her head, clearly proud of her reasoning.

"What if Lujor needs it again?"

Nora deflated on her stool. "Well, what do you suggest then, Eoghan? Because I can't stay pregnant forever." She pulled on her false belly to adjust the fit, and I rolled my eyes.

"Will you please stop messing with that?"

She hissed like an angry cat. "I'd like to see *you* wear this stupid thing all day!"

"Stop it." I passed her the last bite of my bread. "Here. Eat this. We'll get that thing off you soon. I promise."

"How?" she asked, taking my offering and jamming it into her mouth.

I shifted my weight in my seat and raised my coffee to my lips. I gestured across the water at the Grand Gallery. "It has to be the Reliquary. We have to give it to Lachlan. There's no alternative."

"There has to be an alternative, Eoghan," she said. "Because the Reliquary is not an option. How would we even get in contact with Lachlan without drawing suspicion from *someone*? Look at it."

I glanced for the millionth time across the calm water as a rowboat went by.

The Reliquary was a massive governmental organization. It employed hundreds of docents, collectors, artists, ministers, and craftsmen. And on top of that, hundreds of people flocked in and out of the Grand Gallery every day to view the relics on display.

"We can't just walk in there and ask for Lachlan. We would have to go through who knows how many people in order to get to him." Nora gestured with one hand at the Grand Gallery entrance. "No way could we keep it a secret from all of them. Someone would find out. Someone would talk. And Amau would burn the whole Reliquary to the ground in order to get it."

I set my mouth in dissatisfaction. Though I already knew all this, hearing her say it out loud really hammered home how impossible it was.

"What we need," she went on, "is to pass it to Lachlan himself. The top brass. Right into his hands without involving anyone else."

I wiped a hand over my eyes, sighing inwardly. "Nora—"

"No, no, hear me out," she said, ramping up. "We just go straight to his house, knock on his door—"

"Nora, come on. Do you really think we could just walk up to the High Reliquary's house? Shall we take a stroll directly into the queen's private office while we're at it?"

"Well, no," she answered in a deadpan. "We have no need to talk to the queen, Eoghan."

"What in the hell are you two talking about?"

Nora and I swiveled around on our stools to find Darius, who had appeared behind us in the restaurant. His steady blue gaze moved leisurely from her to me and back again, an amused smirk on his mouth.

"We're just"—Nora searched for words in the most obvious way possible—"trying to decide...hypothetically, you know...how hard it would be to...talk to the High Reliquary?"

I slid my eyes over to Nora, one eyebrow raised.

But Darius took her atrocious lie in stride. "In that case, Eoghan's right. Going to his house is a nonstarter. What you *should* do is catch him in the street."

Nora glanced at me but said nothing.

"It's too bad we're past the Harvest Parade," Darius continued. "All the ministers join the processional. You could easily run into him that way. But even without the parade, it's not impossible. It would only take a few days' watching to learn his routines and plan an encounter while he's on his way home from the Reliquary."

I looked back to Darius, incredulous. He laid out the ingenious plan like he was getting ready to do the weekly shop.

Darius plowed on without noticing my wary stare. "You could probably head him off at a corner or something. Pretend it was by accident, then pull him into an alley or empty shop. How did this come up anyway? Why would you ever want to talk to the High Reliquary?"

Nora waved away his question. "Just a passing what-if? That's all. Just passing the time. What are you doing here, Darius? Did your trading go well this morning?"

"It's still wrapping up, actually." He crossed his arms over his broad chest. "I rarely bother with the haggling anymore. But the market's up, and my goods were top shelf. I'm confident I'll be going home with a decent profit. I'll be meeting my men at the harbor in just under an hour."

"Then what are you doing here?" I asked.

Darius shook a finger at me. "Now, that's the interesting question, isn't it?"

Something was wrong. He was too casual, too relaxed. What the hell was he doing here? This city was much too big and this particular restaurant much too insignificant. This wasn't a coincidence.

He had come here on purpose. The realization hit me like a ton of bricks, but his easy posture made me hesitate. I fingered the strap of my pack, everything I owned on this earth within reach.

Always be ready, Eoghan boy. You never know when you'll have to make a run for it.

"I had planned to take a few days to finish up here," Darius went on. "Really make sure things went smoothly, ruffle as few feathers as possible, but Edith says you'll be moving on today. That means I'll have to be a bit more blunt."

"Edith?" Nora said breathlessly.

I had never been a talker. No hesitating, no second-guessing. I latched onto my pack with one hand and swept my stool out from under me with the other. In one smooth motion, I lobbed it at Darius with every ounce of strength I had. My bruised muscles screamed with the effort, but it was enough.

Darius dodged the heavy stool flying for his face. I grabbed Nora's arm and ran.

The restaurant erupted around us. Other diners screamed and dove out of our way. A server dropped her tray, spilling oats and shattered crockery over the cobbles under our feet. I half pulled and half dragged Nora behind me.

Darius's voice rose above the general din. "You're clever, Miss Nora!" he shouted with a heavy grin in his tone. "A fake pregnancy! I never would have guessed!"

"Mistress!" Nora screeched back at him.

We rounded a corner, and he disappeared from view. I buckled my pack across my chest while we dodged the pedestrians and market stalls lining the winding avenues.

"Keep moving," I said to Nora, glancing back at her.

Angry tears welled up in her eyes. Her mouth was clamped so tightly her lips had gone completely white.

It didn't take a sibyl to read her thoughts at that moment. Edith had betrayed her. Her own sister had sold her out to this stranger. This con artist and thief.

"Nora," I said, my hand tight on hers. I refused to let her slow down. We had to keep moving.

"I'm fine." She swiped viciously at her eyes.

I nodded once and faced forward once more—only to stop short with a grunt of surprise.

Earl, the mugger from Marcha, stood solid as a brick wall in the narrow street. The entire right side of his head was purple with bruises where Darius had slugged him with that hunk of wood, his eye swollen shut.

Nora slammed into my back, then sucked in her breath when she laid eyes on Earl.

"Shit," she hissed.

Earl nodded in agreement. "Hello, again," he said through a heavy frown. His tone vibrated with anger, with revenge.

We didn't bother to answer. Nora and I turned and sprinted the opposite direction down the road, swerving to the right when Burly stepped out in front of us.

"Shit!" Nora squealed again.

We sidestepped the second mugger. Would Eyepatch turn up next? I whipped my eyes from one shadowed doorway to another, expecting every second to spot her leering face half-concealed with bandaging.

"That way." I guided Nora ahead of me, up a set of narrow stairs running between two buildings.

We emerged onto a raised courtyard crowded with potted

trees: plum, apple, and peach. Their thin branches hung low with nearly ripe fruits of all colors and variety. The houses up here were of a different class than the market down below. From here, the Grand Gallery was plainly visible from the eastern side of the courtyard, which overlooked the water and the docks.

"They're coming," I said, following Burly and Earl with my eyes.

They were pushing through the crowded market below, heading right for our stairwell.

"Here, take it." Nora fumbled with her false belly. "They think I have it. They won't chase you."

I stared while she hauled her shirt up and unbuckled the bag underneath. "But—"

"Just take it, Eoghan."

"But we don't want them chasing you either!"

"They're chasing me anyway!" She ripped the Clarion out of the bag and held it out to me. It reflected the morning sun in a dull, brassy shine. When I hesitated too long, she pushed it at me. "Take it!"

"I'm not leaving you!"

"Fine, but take it!" she said, her voice rising.

I grasped her face between both hands and kissed her full on the mouth. Once, then again. I savored every second of that short embrace, every ounce of heat and passion I could get. Tried to convey to her in the pressure of my mouth that this was not the end. This would not be our last kiss.

I pulled back and looked her in the eye. "Put it in my pack."

She nodded and did as I instructed. I jerked and shifted while she crammed the Clarion in amongst my things, yanking the straps tight as soon as it was in.

Thudding footsteps and heaving breath announced that Burly and Earl had finally reached the top of the stone stairs.

"Go! Go!" I shouted, urging Nora forward.

We ran. Past the pruned fruit trees, past a couple strolling along in the shade, on toward the other side of the courtyard where another staircase continued upward to the next level.

But we only took a handful of steps up before Nora skidded to a halt.

"You really shouldn't bother running," Darius said from the top of the staircase. He descended casually toward us, taking one step at a time. "And there's no need for anyone else to get hurt. Just hand over the Clarion, and you can go on your way."

"No," I said flatly.

I gripped Nora's arm, guiding us backward. Darius continued to advance. I angled us away from Earl and Burly, back toward the view of the Grand Gallery and the bay below. Another alley exited the courtyard on the north corner, barely visible from this angle. If we were careful, we could get close enough to run for it without any of these assholes getting between us and it.

"I'm afraid that's not an option," Darius said. "You seem like lovely people. I've really enjoyed our time together, short as it was. But I'm afraid the time for delaying is over. Hand over the Clarion, and this can all be done with."

"Why do you even want it?" Nora asked, clearly stalling for time as I continued to maneuver our position. "The Giants are awake. The war is over."

"The war isn't over until Amau and Lujor are united once more," Darius said simply. "My brother's vision is not complete."

I momentarily forgot about our escape route. The shock of what Darius had said washed over me. "Your brother?"

"Arlo," he said. "The Dragon of Amau."

Nora's fingers tightened on my hand.

Amau. Fucking Amau. It was always—*always*—down to what Amau would sacrifice in order to get a foothold in this damned war. To get access to the Port of New Haven. To line their pockets. To...

Wait, what had he said? Until Amau and Lujor were united once more?

But Darius hadn't finished. He didn't gloat over the revelation, didn't savor the shock in our expressions. Darius simply continued talking, as if we knew what the hell he was talking about. "And don't worry. I don't blame you for Fletcher's death. We all knew the risks of joining the war effort, Fletch more than anyone."

"Wait," Nora said. "What? Who's death?"

"Fletcher's." A shadow passed across Darius's face. "Our youngest brother. You met him on the mountain two months ago. He failed to get the Clarion from you, so now it's up to me." He spread his hands wide and shrugged, as if to suggest it was simply his brotherly duty.

"The Amau man," Nora breathed. She glanced at the drop-off on our left.

The redheaded Amau man who had attacked us. Of course. He had tried to kill me and take the Clarion from Nora, but she had pushed him off the edge of a cliff.

No. No, Nora. Don't.

The idea hit me at the exact same moment it hit her. But where she saw a plan, I saw her—two months previous—falling over the edge of a cliff, apparently to die at the bottom. She had floated there for half a second, her long, brown braid weightless, before she had disappeared.

She'd had the Clarion then. It had protected her. But she'd just stuffed it into my pack, where it couldn't save anybody.

Did she remember? Did she care?

"I'll find you," Nora said.

"Nora..." I hissed the warning, but she was already running. She sprinted full force toward the drop-off, arms pumping, braid flying out, false belly flopping against her thighs as her legs ate up the distance.

"No! Stop her!" Darius cried out.

Burly and Earl tore after her, but she had a massive head start.

I should be fleeing toward the northern corner of the courtyard while Darius and his men were distracted. I should be thinking of the Clarion, of the possible disaster that might come if Amau got their hands on it.

Nora was sacrificing everything to protect it. To protect me. I should make the most of that sacrifice.

But instead, I followed the others to the edge, surprise distorting my face. All I could see was Nora's braid, her slim hands cutting through the air when she leapt over the edge of the courtyard.

All four of us reached the low wall at the same time, all out of breath in shock, leaning far over to see where Nora had landed.

I must have been holding my breath, because air flooded into my lungs in a wash of relief. Nora landed on the pavement below with a graceless roll. She stood and looked up, hopping a little on one foot.

Nora met my frantic stare for half a second, then ran.

That was when I realized my mistake. I locked eyes with Darius, who leaned over the wall next to me. Red flashed across my vision. My hands itched for his throat. My muscles bunched in preparation to fight, but it was no good. The bruises on my face and body were still too fresh, too deep, and I'd never stand a chance against all three of them at once.

I'll find you! But Nora couldn't find me if I were dead or captured, so my only choice was to run. I turned on my heel and sprinted toward the alley mouth.

"No!" Darius's voice floated behind me. "Not him! Follow the woman! She's got the Clarion!"

A quick glance over my shoulder confirmed that none of the three were showing any interest in following me. They had turned and run for the stone staircase we had originally come up and were heading for the street below, where Nora had gone.

Seventeen

It had been a long while since I had spent time in New Haven, but I'd been here often enough to know my way around. Nora's street followed the seawall for nearly a mile, crowded with market stalls, vendors, restaurants, and pedestrians. Her progress would be slow.

On the upper level stood the middle-class residences. Squat, tidy little houses were crammed in so tightly that one had to turn sideways to get through the alleys between. Skinny shade trees and flower beds brightened the space.

Hardly anyone used this avenue except the people who lived in these specific houses. With almost no one to dodge, I rose up on my toes and sprinted as fast as my aching body would allow. I could cut her off in half a mile when this avenue dipped to meet the main thoroughfare.

I'd beat her there. I'd find a place to hide. I'd grab her, and we would tuck away, out of sight. Darius and his goons would never see us again.

And then we would throw the damned Clarion into the ocean, just like Nora had suggested in the first place.

I ran, leaping over chickens and bushes, ducking under low

branches, tossing aside strangers who didn't get out of my way fast enough. The road sloped downward, right where I had expected. I nearly lost my footing when my speed increased with the steep grade. With a burst of effort, I willed my feet faster, more cunning, and just barely managed not to fall and roll the rest of the way down.

I skidded around the corner, eyes peeled for Nora's curls in the crowd. My chest heaved and I fought for breath, but I'd made it.

She couldn't have gotten this far yet. I still had time.

With one eye on the oblivious crowd, I scanned the edges of the street for a dark doorway, a kiosk, or hanging fabric we could hide behind. There, that weaver at the mouth of the alley. The weaver's bright cloth hung from sturdy racks on the street, placed to draw shoppers toward her stall.

A small Giant sat sprawled near the flapping fabric. It must have been there a long time because several brooms and mops leaned against it. And behind the Giant stood an open door, only blackness beyond.

There. That's where we would hide.

I turned again and scanned the crowd for Nora.

"Eoghan!" Nora called.

The spark of hope in my chest burst into a bright flame. I stood a little straighter, eyes wide, but I couldn't see her.

"Eoghan! This way!"

Nora's voice came from a long way off, it felt like, and not from down the road where I expected her to appear. I turned toward the alley where the weaver had set up her stall.

"Eoghan! Hurry!"

I set off running down the alley, leaving the crowded thoroughfare behind.

She must have taken a turn somewhere along the road, gone down an alley or two. Nora had been to the city before as well. And as a mapmaker, she probably understood it better than I ever could.

The alley curved to the left, and the noise of the bay, the marina, and the busy market road faded into a muffled, distant hum. Chickens and cats went about their business in the corners. A small child ran past me in the opposite direction, her face smudged with dirt.

"Eoghan! This way!"

I turned down another alley on my right, which ended in a flight of stairs going up, and I paused.

Clotheslines criss-crossed overhead, with faded fabric whipping in the strong sea breeze funneling between the stucco walls.

"Up here! Hurry...before they catch us!"

Nora's voice echoed down the stairs, clear as day. But where was she? I should have caught up with her by now.

"Where are you?" I called, fearful of being too loud in case Darius made another surprise appearance.

"Just hurry up!" she said, her voice tinged with impatience. "We don't have much time!"

"Wait for me!"

"Hurry up, Eoghan!" Her voice grew fainter, as if she moved away from me as she spoke.

"Wait, Nora!" I sprinted up the stairs, taking them two at a time. At the top, out of breath and thoroughly confused, I turned to look to the right, then left. More deserted alleys branched away, but still no sign of Nora.

"To the left!" she called.

I followed her voice further away from the docks. I glanced up and saw a man's face looking down out of a window, but he disappeared the second he caught my eye, slamming the shutters closed behind him.

Fear washed down my body in an icy ripple. "Nora!" I shouted.

"I'm here!"

Her voice sounded directly in my ear, and I spun to the right.

Another alley, this one a dead end only a few meters back. And at first, my heart fluttered because there she was! Nora stood at the back of the alley, calm, well, and whole. She had lost Darius and his goons. She'd gotten away clean.

Except...

That wasn't Nora.

A woman stood at the end of the alley. Mostly unremarkable, she wore fine clothes in simple cuts. A loose, white shirt. Long, flowing pants that billowed around her legs in the wind. Her arms were bare, the brown skin glowing with warm undertones in the morning light. She had twisted her dark hair into a single, heavy braid, which hung over her shoulder.

The one thing that stood out was the feathers. She had fastened three feathers into her hair. Long, broad, heavy things. A green magpie feather, a striped owl feather, and an iridescent black sickle feather from a rooster.

They fluttered in the wind, shining like jewels.

Dread filled my body from head to toe. The confusion, the fear, the loss of Nora—the sudden realization that I had been fooled—struck me with the force of a raging bull.

But it didn't matter. None of it mattered. Because whatever had brought me here, it was too late. I was caught.

The only thing that existed in the entire world was one horrible, sickening thought: I couldn't move. My entire body froze on the spot. Every muscle betrayed me, turned to stone. I couldn't take a step, twitch a finger, or shift my weight to alleviate the ache slowly building in my shoulders under my pack.

Dread flooded through me. I couldn't react, couldn't run or fidget or scream. There was only an aching clarity as my body turned to fire.

I could breathe, and I could blink. But that was all.

I had never given much thought before to what fear felt like. Because always, when fear came, I focused on survival, on getting out, on getting away. But now, I had no choice but to wallow in it trickling down my limbs and into each fingertip and toe. My heart pounded against ribs that wouldn't budge. Every inch of my skin crawled.

And every second that I couldn't react to the fear, every second that I couldn't move, the fear grew.

The woman did not move. The sickle feather, being the longest of the three, caught the gentle breeze and fluttered wildly. Her pants billowed, smooth as silk.

I could only stare at her.

Her eyes were dark as coal with flecks of gold. Her brow lowered in a sad frown, and she took a deep breath.

And then my hands turned against me. They lifted toward the buckle across my chest and removed my pack from my shoulders. I twisted around, my movements graceful and sure, and lowered the pack to the ground. With deliberation, I began untying the top flap.

Stop! Eoghan! Stop! I screamed at myself internally, but it was no use.

My hands dipped into my pack and wrenched out the Clarion. My pack slipped sideways and thudded on the ground. A tin of salt fell out and rolled a few feet before clattering to a stop.

I walked toward the woman with the feathers, holding the Clarion before me. As I approached, she held out her hands. She had bitten her nails to the quick.

Focus, Eoghan! Stop! Run!

I stretched out my arms and gently placed the Clarion in her hands. Her fingers closed around the dull brass.

She put one warm hand on my arm and said something in another language with complex vowel combinations and short words. I had never heard anything like it. And though I couldn't have repeated her words for the life of me, I understood them. The meaning pierced into my mind, brushing the unfamiliar words aside.

"You will see her again, my friend."

The dread in my gut fractured into panic.

Nora.

I tried again to fight the hold this feather woman had on me, but I was entirely powerless. Her mental grip held my body perfectly still.

She let go of my arm and wrapped her fingers around the Clarion once more.

I blinked.

I swear, that's *all* I did.

I blinked, and the woman disappeared. Her hold on me ceased so abruptly I fell over. My knees collided with the dusty cobbles, and I coughed and wretched.

You will see her again, my friend.

All thoughts of the Clarion and the feather woman fled my rattled brain, leaving only one focus: Nora.

I scrambled to my feet, ran right past my open pack on the ground, and sprinted out of the alley in the direction I'd come from. Then I raced down the stairs, back along the empty alleys, and out past the weaver and the little Giant, with its mops and brooms on the main sea road.

I turned left and pushed through the crowds, screaming as I went. "Nora! Nora!!"

Nothing. Only strangers surrounded me, startled faces, worried at my frantic cries.

But then...

"Eoghan!"

I whirled around toward the water, and there she was. Nora this time. The *real* Nora.

She stood on the deck of a ship moving steadily toward the mouth of the bay. Darius held one of her arms, a sharp knife only just visible at her side. Earl, Burly, and a bitter Eyepatch flanked him on the deck, all leering at me.

Darius leaned in to say something to Nora that I couldn't hear, and my fists clenched at my sides. I wanted to rip him to pieces, to pull his filthy hands off her. But they were too far away, moving too fast on the swift ship headed toward open waters.

Nora glanced at Darius once, her face limned with disgust. Then she opened her mouth to convey the message. "Don't follow us!" she called, her voice cracking. "Stay here."

Darius flashed the knife at me to be sure I saw it, then tucked it back out of sight at Nora's side.

I stalked along the seawall, following the ship, knocking people roughly out of my way as I went, keeping level with Nora and the bastards who held her. "She doesn't have it!" I called. "She gave it to me! Let her go!"

Darius shrugged. His handsome mouth pulled up on one side. He said something softly to Nora.

"They don't care!" she called sadly. "They don't need it if they have"—she hesitated, and Darius jostled her—"me."

"The Giant Singer herself!" Darius called out joyfully.

Eyepatch crossed her arms behind him.

A stranger knocked into me while I powered down the street. "Hey! Watch it!" he cried in alarm.

In response, I grabbed him by the shoulders and pushed him over the seawall. He hit the water five feet below with a splash and a roar of outrage.

"I will find you!" I bellowed at Darius. "I will never stop!"

Darius frowned, put out. He took my threat as an inconvenience. With a few words I couldn't hear and a gesture at his goons, he set my fate. Eyepatch stepped forward, raising a longbow she couldn't have been strong enough for. But she pulled back the line like it was nothing and took aim at my head.

Other people watching the spectacle screamed and dove for cover, leaving me a clear target. Nora screamed, reaching for me.

"No! Safe! Keep him safe!!"

The impulse to hide or to dive into the water to chase them warred within me, rooting me to the spot. I could only stare down

Eyepatch as the ship slipped past me, daring her to fire. My heart pounded audibly in my chest.

Thump, thump, thump!

Eyepatch's shitty grin widened, and she released the arrow. Time seemed to slow as it arced toward me. She had excellent aim.

Thump, thump. Boom! Boom!

My heartbeat changed from thumps to earth-shattering crashes of stone against stone, and a huge, clumsy hand made of rock appeared in my peripheral vision. The Giant had gotten up and had come after me. It had heard Nora's command to "Keep him safe!" and followed it to the letter. The Giant, only six feet taller than me, wrapped me up in a bear hug and turned with me in its arms. Eyepatch's arrow glanced off its back harmlessly with a tinny *clack!*

"Let me go!" I yelled at the Giant.

It held on tightly while I wriggled and fought. I ripped at its stone arms, tearing the skin off my fingers and bruising my feet with my kicks. I might as well have been fighting a brick wall for all the good it did.

With one final, fruitless heave, I wrenched around in the Giant's grip to watch Darius's ship slip smoothly past the buoys and out to sea, taking Nora someplace only the old gods knew.

"Nora!" I ignored the shocked exclamations from the crowded street around me. "I'll find you! I'm coming for you! Let me go, you stupid, fucking rock! Nora!"

The ship turned to sail around the jetty and out of sight.

The street fell silent. The entire crowd stared at me and the Giant that held me. The only sounds were of the gentle waves slapping the seawall, gulls overhead, and my breath heaving in and out of my lungs in angry gasps.

Finally, the Giant put me down and stood passively beside me. I slouched on the street, staring at the empty space of water where the ship had gone.

"Nora."

Part Four
Of Dragon Bone and Gristle

Two months later

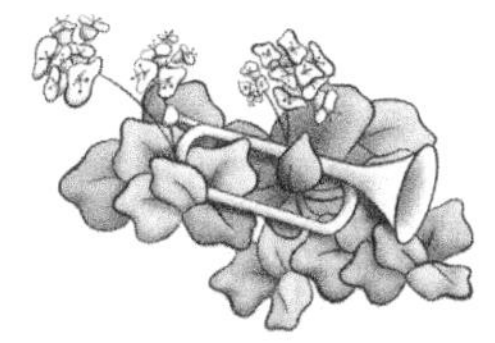

EIGHTEEN
NORA

They hung a portrait of Fletcher in the hall outside my room. I was almost positive the Dragon put it there on purpose to punish me.

It was working.

I stared up at Fletcher, the sunlight slanting across his two-dimensional expression. He was handsome. Clean cut, fine features. Dark red hair and beard. A mischievous twinkle in his green eyes. Wide mouth ready to smile. A raven sat on his shoulder, nearly blending in with the dark background.

The artist had done a magnificent job, not just with his likeness, but with his spirit. A few months ago, I might have thought him handsome, but I couldn't now. Because when I looked up into his eyes, I only saw death. I saw his body broken, twenty feet up in a pine tree, a splintered branch protruding through his gut. Blood bubbled up between his lips and dripped into his beard, his green eyes accusatory.

"They say he died on the Giant's Mountain," came a voice from behind me, and I nearly jumped out of my skin.

I whirled around to glare at Isla, who Eoghan had always called

Eyepatch. In the shock of seeing Fletcher smiling down at me, I had forgotten she was even there.

She had taken off the eyepatch weeks ago, revealing a hideous scar marring her otherwise pretty face. It cut across her eyebrow and down her cheekbone. Her eyelid had healed wrong, stuck half-closed over an eye that no longer worked. It gave her an almost quizzical expression, like she was on the verge of arguing a minute point of syntax over a round of beer.

But Isla was never one to be quizzical about anything. She stared up at Fletcher, just like I had done a few seconds earlier, her mouth twisted into a look I had never seen on her face before. Regret? Nostalgia?

"Did you know him, then?" I asked.

Isla took a deep breath and turned away from Fletcher's portrait. "Of course I knew him. *Everyone* knew him. Keep up."

I rolled my eyes at Isla's back, tired of this game. Isla had lost some of the manic anger she'd had when they had mugged us in Marcha, but that fire was still there. It was an angry simmer under the surface, just waiting for someone to stoke it again.

The Dragon had assigned Isla to me as a punishment as well. Apparently, he was very astute when it came to finding my sore spots.

"So, where are we going?" I asked, trotting to keep up with her. We slipped past closed doors and curtained windows and I took in every detail. I hadn't been allowed to leave my room in the two months I had been a guest at the Dragon's fortress, so this was my first and best opportunity to get an idea of the layout of the place. Maybe it was a sign my strategy had finally begun to pay off.

"There's no need to talk." Isla stalked ahead of me toward a stairwell at the end of the hall.

A massive urn nearly as tall as I was stood sentinel in the hallway outside of my room. I eyed it when we passed, making a mental note.

I tried to spy through the slitted windows cut into the walls of the circular stair, but the light was so bright outside it was hard to make out any detail. Besides, it looked like any other fortress town: smaller buildings crowded around, animals of all shapes and sizes, people milling about, market kiosks, and walls. So many walls. If anything, my glimpses through the narrow windows made my plans seem even more hopeless. The town spread as far as I could see, with nothing but wilderness beyond.

Not that wilderness was a barrier for me. In fact, if I could just get to the safety of those trees, I'd be home free. I had learned enough from Eoghan about living wild. Combined with my training as a mapmaker, I could disappear to the south and never be seen in Amau again.

No, the wilderness wasn't the problem. The problem was the city standing between me and the trees.

So I kept my eyes peeled, grateful that Isla didn't want to look at me any more than I wanted to look at her. I counted steps and doors, moved as slowly past windows as I could without drawing the notice of my guard, and constructed a mental map.

We didn't go very far. Isla led me down two flights of stairs and to a heavy exterior door right on the ground floor landing. The sunlight outside slammed my eyes shut. I grasped at the doorframe to keep my balance and squinted through tearing eyes.

"Don't be so dramatic," Isla said, though she narrowed her eyes just as much as I did, obscuring her ruined eyelid.

"Don't be such a bitch." I blinked hard while my eyes adjusted, forcing them open.

Isla had led me out into a walled garden. One of the useless kinds rich people kept for pleasure. A flagstone path wound between patches of bright flowers, and shrubbery softened the institutional feel of the stone walls. A small fountain burbled in the center, designed to look like a wild, stony spring. Water tumbled over mossy stones into a shallow pool, where bright orange and white fish swam lazily between the water lilies.

No vegetables. No herbs or berries. Just flowers and ivy.

It was quaint, considering the size of the fortress as a whole, but plenty big enough to be useful for someone else. A garden patch this size could have fed an entire family. But no. Someone had planted primroses and marigolds instead.

Isla turned to me, her sneering mouth open to reply to my retort, but a man's voice stopped her.

"Yes, Isla. Do try to be a bit less bitchy."

The man sat casually on a garden bench in the shade of a redbud tree, leaves gone bright yellow with the chill of an early autumn. His arm lay thrown across the back of the bench, and his ankle crossed over the opposite knee.

My voice died in my throat. The man was beautiful. Glossy brown hair pulled into an artfully messy bun. Broad shoulders, big hands, kind eyes. The only marks on his angular face were laugh lines and a thin scar cut through his left eyebrow. He wore rich but simple clothing: a white linen shirt and canvas pants with tall boots. A blue vest hugged his muscled chest. Color and style, but not overdone.

"Yeah, yeah," Isla said with good-natured belligerence. "I'll try."

The handsome man smirked. "Try a bit harder. Nora is our guest."

"But it's so much fun," Isla said, like a younger sister who had her big, scary brother wrapped around her little finger.

I turned to stare at my jailor. Isla's expression had melted into something...likable.

Her eyes flicked to me when I turned, and she flashed an annoyed look.

"You're the worst, Isla." The man's deep voice rumbled with affection. "Give us a minute, would you? Go annoy someone else. Maybe Calumn has something useful for you to do."

"I didn't ask to babysit this pain in the ass." She hooked her thumb in my direction.

"I didn't ask to be here at all," I said, hackles rising. "Seems to me, the only pain in the ass here is your precious Dragon. Kidnapping people and starting wars. Why don't you go tell him how annoyed you are with me, and maybe he'll send me away to make you happy?"

Isla opened her mouth to bite back, but the man on the bench sat forward, elbows on knees. "Okay, that's enough. Go take a break, Isla. I want to talk to Nora for a bit."

Isla snapped her mouth shut, glared at me once, then disappeared back through the door where we had entered the garden.

The only door, I realized, looking around. That door at the base of the narrow stairwell was the only way in or out. There was no gate in the stone walls—at least, not one I could see. This was a private garden, not for just anyone to wander in off the street.

Not like they would want to. What a useless flower patch. The fish in the pond didn't even look very appetizing. Fish weren't supposed to be orange like that.

"Come sit down, won't you?" The man slid over to make as much room as possible on the bench.

I crossed my arms over my chest and looked at him sideways. "I'd rather not."

"Suit yourself," he said, leaning back.

"Who are you?"

The man laughed, and it melted my resolve a little. His laugh was like warm honey on a fresh biscuit. All golden and sweet.

This was the sort of man featured in fairy tales, adventure stories, and romances. He was no Eoghan, but I still wanted him to like me for some reason. Like I could be the damsel in distress, the forlorn princess locked away in the tower, and this could be the handsome prince who rescued me. I could see the sketch forming in my mind of two lovers reaching for each other in this very garden. Though the princess in my mind's eye didn't have my face. She had a prettier, slimmer bone structure, flowing hair, and wistful eyes.

It was a lovely picture, but it wasn't real. And thank all the Old

Kind of the earth and the sky that I realized this small fact before the man answered my question. It saved a little bit of my pride.

"My name is Arlo," he said with a friendly smile.

My heart stopped in my chest, and I froze like a rabbit on alert. "The Dragon?"

"Yes, the Dragon," he said with a rueful expression. "It's a useful name for politicking. Very dramatic. But you can just call me Arlo. Everyone does who knows me."

I turned my head toward the door without taking my eyes off him. This was the bastard who had done it all. He had invaded my country, had burned my hometown, had sent Fletcher to kill us and Darius to kidnap me. This man was directly responsible for tens of thousands of lives lost and for countless villages being burned to the ground.

This was no handsome prince. This was the devil.

"So," I said slowly, gathering myself. This was the opportunity I had been waiting for, though I never could have guessed my patience would be rewarded so richly. I had hoped to find a weakness or a linchpin of some kind. But the man himself? That was a fortuity I wouldn't let pass me by. "Finally, we meet. It's an honor."

"I'm sorry it took so long." Arlo adjusted his weight on the bench. "My wife and I have been away, unfortunately. But I did leave orders that you were to be kept comfortable. How do you find your rooms here in the Keep?"

I narrowed my eyes. "What game is this?"

He scrunched up his perfect mouth and shook his head. "Game? No game."

"You're the Great Dragon of Amau. Someone like you doesn't make small talk with prisoners of war."

"You're not a prisoner, Nora." Concern laced his voice. "You're my guest."

I raised my eyebrows. "Oh, so I can leave, then? Go back home to my family?"

Arlo's eyebrows drew together ever so slightly. "No, I'm afraid I can't allow that."

"Right." I waved one hand in vindication. "It doesn't matter how fancy my prison is, *my lord*. It's still a prison."

"But it is fancy?" he asked, raising his eyebrows like a friend trying to cheer me up. What kind of warlord was this?

I scowled at him. "There's no proper light in my room. They boarded up one of my windows, and the other faces a brick wall. I can't see to draw."

"You also can't see the city to make your maps," he said. "But if it's light you crave, I'll instruct your guards to bring you here to this garden as often as you like. Bring your paper."

"And paints," I cut in. "Charcoal I have. But I need color."

His smile quirked up on one side. "Whatever you like, just ask."

"Because I'm your guest?"

"Yes."

"Why?"

"Why what?"

"Why am I your guest? Why did you give me the fancy prison? Your Keep isn't big enough to house everyone you've captured in the past year alone. You must be putting them somewhere. Why am I here and not with them?"

Arlo cocked his head to one side, scrunching up his eyebrows in teasing amusement. "Because you're the Giant Singer, of course."

"The what?"

"The Giant Singer. You have a touch of the Old Kind in you. Probably because you were the one who blew the Clarion and woke them up. You are family."

That one got a real laugh out of me. "What?" I burst out. "Did you say *family*?"

He nodded, smiling with me. "Yes. You are my wife's sister. That makes you my sister."

"I already have a sister." I only just bit back the word "dumbass" from following up that statement. "And your brother Darius coerced her to betray me in New Haven. What family I *did* have, you took away. So pardon me for asking you to try again. Why am I here? It's been two months. I deserve to know what your plan is for me. What? You think you can convince me to command the Giants for you?"

"No," he said flatly. "I've met enough people like you to know what bullheadedness looks like."

"But you clearly don't want me to help Lujor command the Giants."

"Of course not. If you set the Giants against me again, I'll never make it back to New Haven."

"So, what? You'll just keep me here under lock and key my whole life?"

"Or until the war is over," he said with a shrug. "Whichever comes first."

"I thought the war was already over?" I spat at him, sarcastic. "The Giants decimated your army four months ago. Is that not enough to make you stop?"

"It was a setback, sure. But I am a patient man. Soldiers can be replaced. Weapons can be rebuilt. I have a whole armory full of them, and the next push is already planned. This war isn't over until I get back to New Haven and retrieve what is owed to my family."

"The Queen stole something from you, did she?"

The Dragon smiled at me, amused. "I've said too much."

"I think you said exactly what you meant to say."

His smile grew.

"I've heard at least three different motives for this war since the summer, and none of them make sense. I think you're doing it on purpose. What's your real reason for this?"

"To gain the bay at New Haven," he said calmly. "For trading purposes."

"Right." I stared at the Dragon, my jaw working in determination. "Why did you say that about your wife? That she's my sister?"

He waved the question off with a lazy sweep of his hand. "I don't mean biologically. I mean spiritually. She's like you. In touch with the Old Way. Though you are a fraction of what she is. She is excited to meet you, of course."

"So bring her down. I'm interested to know what sort of woman she is, by your description."

He shook his head with a rueful grin. "Unfortunately Nora, I don't trust you yet. And my wife is very fragile. There's no telling what will come out of your mouth."

"What if I promise to behave myself?"

Arlo barked out a laugh. "Ha! I don't trust you as far as I could throw you."

I shooed away a bee buzzing past my shoulder on its way to an azalea bush. "So, what? You expect me to just sit here, twiddling my thumbs forever? Alone? Is that it? Give me access to a few flowers, and you think that's you being kind?"

"Nora," he said in a long-suffering tone.

That was how Eoghan used to say my name. I hadn't heard Eoghan's voice in two months, and the realization sent a stabbing pain through my heart.

"What?" I snapped. Fuck diplomacy. Fuck escape. I just wanted to scream at this horrible, handsome man. I wanted to tear up his fancy, useless garden and throw the root balls directly in his face. Maybe get a worm or two down his white shirt.

"I know you have family and friends that miss you, but you pose too much of a threat to me and my work. I simply can't let you go back there. There was a man, correct? Eoghan?"

"Don't say his name," I growled.

He raised both hands and bowed his head with respect. "Fine. I understand."

"Understanding is an empty gesture." I crossed my arms over

my stomach to keep myself from rushing at him with nails and teeth. "What good does your understanding do me now? Will it bring me home? Will it keep my family safe? Will it reunite me and Eoghan?"

"No."

"So why do you say it? To tease me? To mock me?"

"No."

"Do you say it because you think it absolves you? You're a heinous, evil man, but at least you understand the pain you've caused?"

He leaned forward, eyebrows furrowed. I had finally gotten to him.

"Would you rather I be completely unaware of the pain I've caused?"

"Would it make any difference?"

"Yes," he said sharply. "I could have done so much worse."

"Ha!" I laughed once without humor. "So just because you could have done worse, that means the villages you've burned, the people you've killed and rendered homeless, that's all okay, then?"

"You're putting words in my mouth. I never said those things are okay. But war means making hard decisions."

"So you had to do it, then? Because of the war?"

"Yes!"

"Bullshit!" I screeched. "You can't say war forced your hand when you started the war in the first place!"

"I didn't—" He broke off, flexing his hands open and closed, open and closed.

Good. The fucker deserved to be upset. It was poor justice, but it was the best I could do at the moment.

"I can see why Darius likes you," he said with a grim expression.

"Darius can go fuck himself."

Arlo rolled his eyes and stood up. "I can see this conversation isn't going anywhere productive."

I threw my hand out as if to say, *Well? What did you expect?*

"My second purpose for bringing you out here was to introduce you to my spiritual advisor. She is another of your sisters in the Old Way and has been anxious to meet you."

"I can meet your advisor but not your wife?"

Arlo's mouth twisted upward, like I had told some kind of joke. "The Owl can handle your bullshit. Stay here and wait for her. She won't be long, I'm sure. It was a pleasure to meet you, Nora."

"I wish I could say the same."

Arlo let out a heavy sigh. He went to the only door, the one leading to the spiral stair, and closed it behind him. The sound of a lock clicking into place reassured me that I had the garden to myself...at least for a little while.

I went straight to the bench where he had been sitting, vaulted onto the wisteria lattice behind it, and climbed as high up the wall as I could. The lattice didn't go high enough for me to get on top, but I was able to stretch just enough to peek through a decorative slit in the wall.

Through the narrow opening, a tower appeared. Brown brick, slender, with a belfry at the top. An iron bell, polished to a dull shine, glinted in the afternoon sun. Judging by how the shadows fell in the garden, that put the bell tower to the northeast of my bedroom and a bit north of this garden. I tucked this information away, adding it to my mental map, along with a few other landmarks I had managed to spy on our way down the stairs.

If only I could see a little more down...

I stood on my toes. The lattice creaked under my weight. I dug my fingers into a crack in the wall, prying myself up just another inch.

Yes! There! A huge warehouse on the south side of the bell tower. Another landmark, another detail.

You're going to hurt yourself, said a woman behind me.

Except she didn't say it, exactly. The words sounded in my

mind, but my ears only heard the birds, the wind, and the muted bustle of a busy town on the other side of the wall.

I slid down the trellis, scratching up my hands when the flimsy wood and wisteria bark dragged over my skin. Teetering on unsteady feet, I spun to face the silent speaker.

A woman with dark hair and tawny skin stood beside the far wall, nowhere near the entrance to the garden. She wore a cozy, cable-knit sweater to ward off the early autumn chill. A city girl at first glance, she was around my age and appeared to be moneyed. No holes in her clothes, and though her boots were scuffed, they were made from fine leather.

But she couldn't have been a city girl. Not with all those feathers in her hair.

Her glossy braid was so covered in feathers it was difficult to tell how long her braid actually was. Magpies, rooster, pheasant, goose, duck, raven, starling, robin, owl—feathers of every color and species. Dozens and dozens of them.

She gazed at me calmly, waiting for me to speak first.

"Are you the spiritual advisor, then?" I asked.

She nodded. *I am the Owl.*

I grimaced, turning away. "A sibyl?"

The woman nodded again.

"Do you have to talk in my head like that?"

I do not know your language. Meaning is easier than words.

"You said you're the Owl? What does that mean?"

It is a title.

I didn't quite manage to hold back my sneer. "Dragons and owls. What's next? Does a dolphin handle the state accounts?"

The woman snorted out a laugh. She said something to herself in another language, like repeating my joke in appreciation.

I stared at her amused expression, and my distrust melted slightly. Something about her felt familiar. Maybe it was the look on her face or the way she held herself with her hands relaxed at her sides. She wasn't too pretty, the way the Dragon was. And her clothes weren't so stylish or expensive.

"You'd expect a spiritual advisor to have a bit more pomp." I gestured to her hand-knit sweater. "You don't even have a fancy hat or a staff or anything. Just some feathers."

"Some feathers" was an understatement. She had too many to count.

I've always collected feathers, ever since I was little.

I sidled away from the wisteria lattice I had been climbing, drawing attention away from the broken limbs and scattered blossoms. "Is Arlo's wife a sibyl too? Because I'm not. And we're supposed to be sisters."

I don't know what Calliope is. She claims to be human, but she isn't. Her mind is entirely empty. With that thought came the mental image of a wide, open space. A sleepy wood with a high canopy. Not empty of thought, but emptiness itself.

"Arlo says she's fragile."

The Owl's mouth curved into a sad smile. *Yes. In some ways, she is.*

I hugged my arms to my chest, unsure of what to do or say. This woman was one of the Dragon's allies. She had helped him wage war on my country. This Owl was no different from my jailers and guards.

I am not your enemy.

I scowled at her. "Stay out of my head."

She held my gaze steady. *I read your expression, not your mind.*

"If you're with *him*, then you are my enemy."

What makes you think I'm with him?

I narrowed my eyes and tapped the fingers of one hand on the opposite elbow. A double agent? A plant? What language did she speak? The one word she had spoken aloud...I couldn't place it. It didn't sound like anything I had ever heard before.

"Where are you from? What language do you speak?"

I come from a country called Derehan on the eastern side of the Agrigua Ocean. You won't have heard of it before.

"You could be making that up."

I could be. But I'm not.

Visions flooded my mind. Memories of places I had never been. A deep, dark forest full of twisting trees and climbing moss. Walled cities with squat stone buildings and steep thatch. Wide fields, dramatic waterfalls. I saw people dressed in strange fashions, a festival around a raging bonfire, and a family dinner. Everyone spoke that unfamiliar language—swooping vowels, smooth consonants. Their language sang out of their throats like music.

One of the faces was strikingly familiar. A young man with a sarcastic smile. "How do you know Garet?" I asked.

Garreth, the Owl corrected. *He is my nephew.*

"He was at my sister's house in New Haven." My fists remained tight at my sides.

He was protecting her from Darius's men. They were harassing her, trying to get to you.

I chewed on my lip. Why would she protect Edith from Darius and not me? "So why are you here, then? "

Because of you.

"What do you mean?"

Another vision came to my mind, but this time, I knew the place. A cold night, most of the way up a savage, lonely mountain. Two people lay cuddled up in a single bedroll near a banked fire, speaking softly to each other in the dark.

A man's voice floated on the gentle breeze. A voice so achingly familiar it broke my heart. "'You gotta take care of yourself, Eoghan boy.' She always called me that. Eoghan boy."

"She sounds nice," my own voice replied.

The man laughed once. "No, Nan wasn't nice. She was tough. And she took no shit. But she loved the Old Way. The stories about the sibyls and the Giants and the old magics..."

"Stop it," I said out loud.

The vision faded away, and I swiped under my eyes with agitation. The Owl swam into view before me.

"You were there that night? It was you Eoghan heard in the darkness?"

She nodded. *I heard the Clarion call in the night. All the way across the ocean.*

"So how did you end up here?"

The Owl turned her head slightly, as if she were listening to a far-off voice. After a moment, she answered. *That is a long story for another time. I came here to warn you.*

Fear clenched my gut. A sibyl's warning was nothing to scoff at.

You are taking too long to escape. The moment the Dragon finds out about your child, your time will be up.

The clench of fear turned to icy horror. The breath stopped in my lungs, choking me. I forced myself not to wrap my arms protectively around my flat stomach. "What?"

He will wait until it is born, then kill you. He will claim you died in childbirth and give the baby to his wife to raise. She has always wanted a child but cannot conceive. She will raise it happily. She will consider herself to be the baby's "only family" and its rightful guardian.

I stumbled backward until my body slammed into the stone wall. The garden spun, and I clutched at the bench to keep my balance. "No," I said breathlessly.

It is the vision I saw.

"No!" I swallowed hard against the nausea.

I had spent months—*months*—pretending to be pregnant with Eoghan's baby. I'd done it to hide the Clarion and to help us disappear into the crowds. Just another refugee family displaced by the war.

But the night before Darius had kidnapped me, our deception had become the truth. And now—

Oh fuck. Oh no. I knew I needed to escape soon, before the

baby grew too large to manage. But I had never considered that the Dragon could be so heartless, so cruel. I never imagined he would try to take my baby—the only piece of Eoghan I still had.

I stared up at the Owl. Her expression mirrored mine: Horror, helplessness, tears.

"Help me. Get me out."

I can't.

"You can!" I said in a harsh whisper. "You're his spiritual advisor. You can do anything."

I must remain his spiritual advisor. I must remain blameless. You have to do this yourself...and soon.

"I can't! I've been trying for two months! They're watching me all the time! I can't get out!"

You can. You will find a way. The future does not always happen the way I see it. You can change this.

I screamed in frustration. The wordless cry echoed off the stone walls in the narrow garden. Silence followed, as if by screaming I had emptied out my entire body.

The lock on the stairwell door clicked open, and we both turned toward the noise. Isla appeared around the heavy door, scowling at me.

"Are you crying?" she asked, disgusted.

I glanced at the place where the Owl had been standing, but found only empty air. I turned on the spot, taking in the small garden in a quick glance. There was nowhere for a person to hide. She had disappeared.

"Come on. Back upstairs." Isla held the door open for me.

I lurched to my feet, sniffing hard and scrubbing my face dry, then walked stony-faced past Isla into the darkened stairwell. Counting steps as I went, I catalogued landmarks flashing by the narrow windows: a market square, a city wall, a bakehouse, a clothesline.

If the Owl said I could change my future, then in the name of the World Mothers and World Fathers, I would change it.

Nineteen

Isla escorted me back to my room in silence. We both went past Fletcher's portrait without a single glance in his direction, but she paused in my doorway, leaning on the handle.

I glared at her. "What?"

"Arlo says you met the Owl."

"So?"

"What did you think of her?"

I thought back to the expression of wretched grief on the woman's face when she refused to help me.

"I think every person in this Keep is an asshole."

"She can hear your thoughts," Isla said with a shudder. "No one can keep her out."

"You have some thoughts you don't want her to hear?" I crossed my arms before quickly uncrossing them when I realized how it pulled my shirt against my flat stomach.

Isla's good eye landed on me, but her voice lacked her usual venom. "Doesn't everyone?"

My hackles rose at her informal tone. Isla should be angry. She should be mean. That way I could be mean back. "We're not friends."

Isla rolled her eyes and disappeared into the darkened hallway, where Fletcher's painting stood sentinel. She locked the door behind her. Or rather, she locked my prison cell.

The Dragon had been right about one thing: My prison was fancy. A comfortable bed, pillows stuffed with real down, a wardrobe full of fine clothes, meat with every meal. I truly felt like a guest, except that my door remained locked at all times with a guard sitting outside. And the fact that my main window had been boarded up so tightly only a thin rim of light leaked around the edges.

So you can't draw your maps.

Ha! If Arlo didn't want me drawing maps, he shouldn't have let me out of my room at all.

Finally alone, I went straight to the desk and pulled out a crisp, fresh piece of hot-pressed paper. I had been given an entire stack of the precious stuff, with real graphite to draw with, though I still preferred the coal out of my stove.

In the bottom left corner of the page, I drew the hall outside my door, including the large urn, the stairwell, and the frivolous garden. I noted each step and marked every window, even the curtained ones in the hall where I couldn't see out.

Then I added the bell tower and the warehouse I had spotted through the slit in the garden wall, approximating angles and distances with a practiced hand.

Holding my work up allowed me to see it more clearly in the ambient light coming in through the window facing the stone wall. It only took up one corner of the page, hallways and streets ending in blank paper. It would have to do until I located more landmarks to connect.

"It's a beginning," I said out loud. "It took two months of patience, but it's a beginning."

I turned to face the portraits on the wall, where familiar faces stared back at me. Edith, Mother, Nikita, the wise old eyes I imagined Eoghan's Nan had.

And of course, Eoghan himself. Bright eyes, square jaw, greasy hair, dirty face, but steady. He stared out at me with a constancy I desperately missed.

My mouth quirked up into a tiny, self-indulgent smile. "I called Isla a bitch today. Right to her face."

I shifted my eyes to another drawing of Eoghan. In this one, his eyebrows pitched up into a long-suffering frown. I could almost hear his rumbling voice. *Hell's sake, Nora. When will you learn to keep your mouth shut?*

My smile widened. "Probably never."

The smile melted off my face and my imagination faltered. The drawings were just paper and charcoal. Eoghan wasn't there. No one was.

I looked around at the quiet, comfortable room, dim in the light of the boarded-up window. My hand fell to my abdomen. Soon, the baby would begin to show.

I was on my own. And I was running out of time.

"But I can't just leave," I said to Eoghan's drawing without looking at it. "I have to do something. I have to hobble the Dragon somehow."

But how? I thought back to our conversation in the garden. Arlo knew Isla well. He cared about her, but that didn't seem like enough.

But his wife, on the other hand...Now, there was a possibility.

My wife is very fragile. There's no telling what might come out of your mouth.

I sat up a little straighter on my chair. His wife. Callie-oopy something. That was the weakness. Assholes always showed their hand when they got overconfident.

He had told me what he didn't want me to do. So that was exactly what I *would* do. I would find his fragile wife and see what came out of my mouth. And I knew just how to begin.

~

On my second night in the Dragon's Keep, I figured out how to get out of my room.

It wasn't that hard. It was a bedroom, not a prison cell. The interior wall was made of oak paneling, and with some careful prying and inspecting, I had found the one that could be lifted away. Behind it lay the back of another wood panel, which, when removed, gave access to an empty guestroom on the other side.

It had taken about a week of hushed, paranoid work to hide my efforts and still make the exit accessible, but then I was set.

The loose wall panels were always a last resort, though. There were too many obstacles between me and the woods outside the city. Just because I had overcome the one hurdle of my bedroom door didn't nullify guards, gates, and walls. And I couldn't afford to have my freedoms restricted even further.

But the Owl's warning had changed everything. I had to get out, no matter what. And in the two months I had been playing the perfect guest, no one had underestimated me yet. I wasn't getting anywhere.

So that afternoon, after Isla had left her post outside my door to be replaced by a guard called Oren for the evening shift, I moved the straight-backed chair hiding the loose oak panel from view.

I brought nothing with me, not even paper or graphite. There were only a few hours before Oren let the maid in with my supper, and I needed to move fast. I pried away the panel with my fingernails and popped out the one on the other side. It clattered into the dark, empty room, and I cringed.

"Don't come in. Don't come in," I said to Oren under my breath, staring at my closed bedroom door.

After a few seconds of silence, when the door didn't open, I allowed myself to breathe again. I crawled through the narrow gap between the wall studs and into the empty room. I picked up my wood panel by the makeshift handles I had attached to its back and settled it back in place.

If anyone came into my room and found me missing, at least they wouldn't be able to tell how I had gotten out.

I replaced the second loose panel and stood to face the room.

The windows were shuttered tight—a fact that had disappointed me greatly when I had first discovered the room. I hadn't risked opening them for fear of being noticed, so I hadn't been able to map the city that way either. And being on the third floor, it was an unlikely escape route anyway.

Through the gloom loomed a large four-poster bed, the twin of my own. Dust cloths had been draped over chairs, tables, and dress forms, muffling their shapes and giving the room a ghostly feel.

I slipped between the spectral shapes to the door but hesitated.

This door would be on the same wall as my own, where Oren sat bored to tears. Probably picking his nails again. If he saw me coming out of this room...

I shook my head, my hand on the knob. "Get it together, Nora," I said. "There's no other way."

Before, I had thought it would be impossible to open this door without being spotted. But thanks to Isla taking me out for a little walk, I now knew there would be a great, glorious urn standing sentinel in the hallway between me and my guard. It wouldn't be a perfect cover, but it was a hell of a lot better than nothing.

I turned the knob slowly, grateful it didn't creak or groan. At least the Dragon had enough pride to keep his house in order. But judging by the way he had spoken to me that morning, a lack of pride had never been his flaw.

I opened the door a millimeter at a time, my temple pressed against the wood.

Slowly. Patiently. A little more. Just a little bit more. There!

The door opened just enough that I could peek out of the crack toward my own room. I smirked with sarcastic surprise. The urn was just there on my left, right where I expected it to be. And around the curve of the urn's neck, I could see Oren in his chair, picking his nails. Of course. He would never get them to grow if he didn't leave them be. And he was always complaining about it.

With a sigh of relief, I eased the door further so I could slip through, then closed it without a sound.

Oren never looked up, though he did curse with a hiss of pain. Probably bit his nail too short again. Idiot.

I hunkered low to the ground and crab-walked away from Oren and the urn, which hid me from view. When I reached a corner in the hallway, I slipped around it.

I stood up straight, dusted off my skirt, and walked down the hall with my head held high.

One thing I had learned from Eoghan was if you wanted people to overlook you, act like you belong. Don't just act like it, *believe it*. I was relying on the fact that most people in the Keep didn't know I was there. Of those who did know about me, only a handful had ever seen me. And being the home and fortress of a warlord, the Keep teemed with people: Servants, workers, guards, guests, advisors.

It wasn't long before I crossed paths with someone. A scullery maid, her arms full of linens, appeared out of an open doorway.

My heart jumped into my throat, but I forced my hands to remain relaxed by my sides.

She drew closer to me, and every step was agony. This was it. I was going to be caught immediately.

Ten steps.

The young woman glanced in my direction.

Seven steps.

"Good evening," she said in an exhausted tone.

"Good evening," I parroted in a voice that did not sound like me. Too low. Too falsely casual. Eoghan would be dying inside if he could hear me now.

Three steps.

Then she passed me, hitching her load a little more securely in her arms.

Air whooshed out of my lungs. Holy shit, it worked. She just assumed I belonged.

A determined smirk pulled up the corner of my mouth. I could do this.

I moved through the Keep deliberately, never stopping in one place. Every time I encountered a corner, I turned without hesitation. If I saw an open door to a common-use room, I went through it. I passed through sitting rooms, kitchens, pantries, and storage. Hall after hall after hall. People milled about in droves, all bustling with their own employments. No one glanced twice at an apparently busy woman wearing comfortable but stylish dress.

And all the while, I cataloged windows, doors, halls, rooms. The map in my mind grew bit by bit. I spotted the bell tower through blissfully open windows and other landmarks besides. I would never remember it all, but I had time to look again.

In all my wildest imaginings, I never could have dreamed it would be so easy. It was like I wasn't even there. People's eyes skated over me like I was just another brick in the wall. Were these people really so secure? So sure in their own worlds that strange faces in the Dragon's Keep were unalarming?

After about an hour, I circled back to my room. I crouched low in the hallway, slinking along the wall so Oren wouldn't spot me around the urn, and crept back through the door into the empty guest room. After popping out the loose oak panels, I crawled into my room, replacing the straight-backed chair in front of my exit hole.

Then I sat down at my desk and filled in some blank spots on my map.

I stared at the drawing, my tongue between my teeth. It wasn't enough. I would need at least a few more trips through the Keep before I had adequate detail to satisfy me.

Focus, Nora. Eoghan's voice rang clear in my head, and I glanced up at his portrait on the wall. *Find the wife and get out.*

"This map could be useful for the war," I said to his charcoal image.

The map won't be useful to anybody if you don't get out.

"I know! I know!" I said, annoyed.

I folded up the map and slipped it into the top drawer, irritated. The satisfaction of my trip through the Keep dissolved into frustration.

You could just walk out the front door.

I looked up at Eoghan's steady eyes. I had drawn them in black charcoal, but I could see their clear brown in my mind's eye. Brown with flecks of green. Dirt in the premature crow's feet at each outer corner.

It wasn't a bad idea. I had walked around the entire Keep that afternoon, so I could have probably gone right down to the main gates and outside. After that, the risk of being recognized or noticed dropped to about nothing.

I could leave right now. My baby and I would be safe. I could find Eoghan.

"No." My voice was barely audible. "My time here won't have been for nothing." I thought again of the Dragon stealing my child just to make his wife happy. The monster didn't deserve me getting away that easy.

Find the wife.

I pulled the map out again with an angry huff and stared at it. In my hour in the main Keep, I hadn't seen any place the lady of the house might spend her time. I hadn't been brave enough to go into any room that might be private or anywhere Arlo himself might have been, so such a failure was to be expected.

If I was going to find her—and if I wanted to complete my map—I would have to be braver.

Twenty

The next day, I asked Isla to take me down to the garden to draw. I had been supplied with paints, as requested, and these I took with me to reinforce my show of being the perfect guest. Isla sat in a cushioned chair near the only entrance and pulled out a sheaf of paper wrapped in handsome leather.

I glanced at her once or twice out of the corner of my eye, curious as to what she was writing down. She was definitely not drawing. Her pen moved in even lines across the page, left to right, left to right.

"Hm," I said aloud to myself. Isla was a mystery, for sure.

"What?" she barked.

"I said, 'Hm!'" I answered loudly without turning around.

Her rolling her eyes at me behind my back was almost audible.

I spent that morning in relative pleasure. I painted the babbling fountain, taking my time over the reflections of the moss in the rippling water. The paints and brushes were of very high quality. Better than anything I had ever had access to in Tutree.

The corner of my mouth perked up as I daubed an especially large blob of white onto the canvas to highlight the sun reflecting off the water. If the Dragon wanted to give me expensive paints, then by all the gods, I would use up every last drop of them.

And then hopefully, by the time I left, he would be so pissed with me he wouldn't be able to stand looking at my paintings and would burn them all. Every last coin spent on these supplies would have been wasted.

Maybe for my next painting I would use a palette knife. Nothing consumed paint like a palette knife.

"You're very skilled," Isla said behind me.

I jumped. "What?"

"I said, you're very skilled," she repeated, a touch of annoyance in her tone.

I glanced around at her, unsure of what to do with this compliment. "Uh, thank you."

"You're welcome."

She set aside her writing and came to stand next to me. I glanced up at her, then away. Then back up again.

"Will you please not hover over me? I feel like you're going to sucker punch me or something."

This time, I got the pleasure of seeing her roll her eyes firsthand. "Have I ever done that?"

"I dunno, Isla." I scooted my chair away. "I seem to remember you ganging up on me and Eoghan in a deserted alley once to rob and beat us."

"Yes, and imagine if you had just given us your packs when we asked for them. Maybe you wouldn't be here right now."

"The Clarion wasn't in my pack, remember?" It had been hidden under my shirt, pretending to be my pregnant belly. "You keep rolling your eyes like that, and you're gonna go blind."

"You're so infuriating."

"Thank you," I said primly, turning back to my painting. "I wouldn't want my kidnapping to be easy for you."

"You're here for a good reason."

"No, I'm not. If I were, you'd tell me what it is. If I were here for a good reason, then I'd stay of my own free will. But you know that I know I'm nothing more than a prisoner with a comfortable cell."

"You should trust Arlo."

"Ha!" I laughed out loud. "Give me one reason why."

"Because he does not lie," she said, matter-of-fact. "There are things happening here that you do not know about, so you're just going to have to trust us when we say we're doing the right thing. Well, at least, the *necessary* thing. If you understood, you wouldn't be so obstinate. At the very least, you are safe here."

"Bullshit, bullshit, bullshit. You sound just like every other over-dramatic, woe-is-me, nobody-understands-me asshole I've ever heard. I have even less sympathy for people who have systematically burned an entire country for no good reason." I waved my paintbrush around to emphasize my point, lobbing globs of the expensive paint on the stones.

"Will you watch what you're doing!" She bent down to wipe up the paint with her bare fingers. "If you're going to be so disrespectful of this garden, then you're not going to be allowed back down here."

"It's just paint." I wiped the brush as dry as I could get it in a towel. Then I dropped a used brush into a jar of linseed oil to soak the rest of the paint off the bristles before selecting a fan brush from the generous collection they had given me.

"I have spent years cultivating this garden. It used to be moldy storage." Isla scrubbed at the quickly drying paint with her sleeve pulled up over the heel of her hand.

Isla had built this garden? And here I thought it had been servants assigned to build a peaceful retreat for the Dragon's wife.

"Here." I dipped a corner of the cloth into the oil. The paint came up with just a couple of swipes.

"Thanks," she said, standing upright again. Isla took my cloth to clean the paint off her hands.

I looked at her properly for the first time. Something seemed off about her face. The scarring around her eye had faded dramatically over the last week or so. Even the bit that had healed wrong, pinching her lid shut in an awkward position–it seemed to have corrected itself quite a bit.

"Your eye is healing remarkably well."

"Yes," Isla said, almost uninterested.

"The scarring was very bad, but it's fading fast."

"I'm tougher than I look."

"But it was scarred all to hell. It was healed wrong. But now it almost looks normal."

"Okay?"

She was being obtuse on purpose. "How?" I barked at her.

"The fuck do you care?" Isla asked.

"Oh, I don't know. There's a war on. Maybe others could benefit from whatever healing methods you have. Athorum couldn't do that. It leaves the scars behind."

Isla ignored me completely.

"So how did it happen, then? Your eye?"

She rubbed the cloth against the heel of her hand, then paused. "A few months ago, I went to a bar looking for a fight. I found one."

"Why were you looking for a fight? Seems like a stupid thing to do."

"Grief makes people stupid." She passed me back my cloth. "I paid for it. What's done is done."

I chewed on the inside of my lip for a few seconds, torn between the urge to piss off Isla and the desire to comfort a person who was obviously hurting. In the end, my optimistic nature won out.

"What happened to make you grieve like that?" I asked in the kindest tone I could possibly muster. I had to be especially polite after all the shit I had put her through. She had deserved it all and more, but maybe not right now.

Isla stared at the upper corner of my painting, her arms crossed over her chest, her eyebrows drawn. She screwed up her mouth, opened it, closed it. Then she just said, "We're not friends."

"I never said we were."

Isla nodded once and went back to her seat by the entrance. I turned to my painting and scooped out a healthy amount of yellow onto my palette, with just a dab of blue and a good amount of brown. After dipping the fan brush into the hasty mix, I added more highlights to the moss.

"Fletcher was my brother," Isla said from behind me.

I froze, my brush hovering over the canvas.

Once again, I saw those green eyes in my mind, accusatory even in death.

"Not like Arlo and Darius. They're not his brothers, even though that's what they call themselves. They met in the workhouse. But Fletcher and me, we're blood."

I lowered my brush to my lap but did not turn around. Something told me that if I looked at her, if she felt seen, she would clam up.

"I got put in the girls' home. Didn't see him for years. I was nearly grown, destined for the streets. No skills, no connections. My options were the whorehouse or a fishing boat or the laundry. No matter what, I'd be ruined forever. Stuck in poverty and pain. But then, he came for me. All three of them came. I knew Fletcher wouldn't forget me. I knew that someday he'd come for me. And he did. After they were able to leave the workhouse, the first thing they did was come get me."

Once again, my mind's eye pictured vivid scenes. Three handsome young men stealing through night-darkened alleys, helping a teenaged Isla climb out through a window. Moonlight bounced off cobblestones and her bright yellow hair. I would use vivid colors, deep blues, purples, blacks, with bright yellows and oranges for the lamps and reflections. Heavy brushstrokes would convey the urgency of the mission.

That was ridiculous, of course. They had probably walked in

and out through the front door with Isla's possessions over their shoulders and a wave goodbye from the matron. A girls' home wasn't a prison. Not like they used to be in past generations.

"Workhouses and orphans' homes," I said softly. "How did you all end up in a grand Keep like this?"

"That was all Arlo and Calliope."

Calliope! That was Arlo's wife's name. I repeated it over and over in my mind so I wouldn't forget.

Isla continued. "They worked hard, helped everyone they came across. They earned the city state from the Amau Union for 'outstanding service to the country.' We've been here ever since. A ragged group of orphans acting like we know what the hell we're doing."

This time, I *did* turn to face her. "What is that supposed to mean? I thought you trusted Arlo."

She fisted her hands in her lap. "Fletcher was my brother."

Ah. Right. Arlo had sent Fletcher to the Giant's Mountain, and he had never come home. Did Isla know I was the one who killed him? It probably wouldn't matter that it had been done in self-defense. She would only see her brother's murderer, living in comfort and painting in a garden while she got to babysit me.

My eyes darted upward of their own accord, and at first I didn't realize why. But then I saw movement in a second-floor window, just visible over the garden wall. A woman's silhouette behind a sheer, white curtain. She was small and graceful, moving past the window. The woman turned to speak to someone, then walked out of sight.

The curtain was flicked aside, and a man moved into view. Even from here, I recognized that perfect figure. Broad shoulders, narrow waist, square jaw. The Dragon himself.

And that meant the woman must have been the wife, Calliope.

Instantly, I started counting windows, judging angles, referencing this turret against that balcony. And the map in my mind grew.

"War is an ugly thing," Isla said, her voice low, her gaze on the cobblestones.

I flicked my eyes back to my painting so as to avoid drawing attention to my discovery.

"If only there was some way to, you know, not start wars," I replied.

Isla only responded with an annoyed sigh and went back to the papers in her lap.

That night, I located the entrance to the hall where I had seen Calliope in the window. It took almost my full hour of allotted time, but I managed it at last. The stairwell led off from the main meeting hall. It spiraled up two floors to a wide gallery with heavy doors on one side and windows of thick glass on the other.

There was no one up here at all. The silence beat at me like muffled breathing. And if this was where the ruling family lived, then that meant anyone who might come in would recognize me. Darius, Arlo, Isla...They would all frequent this place, and there would be no hiding from any of them.

My heart pounded in my chest, but I forced myself to keep moving. Don't stop. Just keep walking. One door. Two, three, four. Clearly visible through the windows was Stellwen Mountain looming over the plains—another landmark to help me orient my map.

After counting the doors and taking an educated guess on window placement in the rooms beyond, I judged the third door to be the probable option.

I hesitated in front of it, my hand hovering over the latch.

If this works, what next? What's your exit strategy? Eoghan's voice of reason sounded in my mind, and I latched onto the idea gratefully.

I snatched my fingers up and nearly sprinted back down the gallery to the spiral stair, forcing my feet to take the steps one at a time. Don't lose control. Don't panic. Just go back to your room and regroup.

Like the day before, no one looked at me. I made it down the stairs without encountering anyone, then adopted a mask of calm while I moved through the usual smattering of people in the common rooms. Back through the empty guest room and through the wall into my own.

There, I flopped onto my desk chair and tried to breathe.

Just breathe, Nora!

In, out. In, out.

I dragged out my map with shaking fingers, flexed my hands once to calm them, and then added a new staircase, a wide gallery with six windows, and four more doors. Judging by the dimensions of the rooms I had already mapped, I estimated the size of the new ones.

What's the plan?

Eoghan's drawing eyed me steadily.

"I've found the wife," I said.

Yes.

"I've drawn the map. At least, enough of the map to be useful."

Yes. Then what?

I frowned down at my map. "Then what" indeed. I wanted to hurt the Dragon, but I also needed to get out alive. This map needed to get to New Haven, to the Cartographers Guild, so it could be used for the war effort.

I needed to find Eoghan. I needed to find a safe place to have this baby. I needed to find my mother in Ferndale.

I could get out right now if I wanted. Walk right out the front door. But I had to hurt the Dragon first. I *had* to.

No bright ideas came to me.

With a huff of irritation, I took a fresh piece of paper off the stack and began sketching to ease my mind. I drew the one face I had seen more than any other in the past two months: Isla. I did it in quick, bold strokes of charcoal, struggling to get her expression just right without overworking it. I drew her the way she must have been before Fletcher died, with two perfect eyes and a little less hate in the turn of her thin mouth. The woman who had turned a moldy storage yard into a garden for no other reason than to find pleasure in it.

But when I finished, it didn't look right. Maybe she used to look like this, but not anymore.

With a few vicious swipes, I lowered her eyebrows and drew them closer together. I darkened the lines around her eyes, hinting at a suspicious narrowing. Her new expression was one of determination, no excuses, no barriers.

What would Isla do?

She'd go looking for a fight. And she would find one.

Twenty-One

I started early the next morning, timing my excursions into the Keep between meals and guard changes. I went to the kitchens mostly, helping myself to a couple of knives and travel rations: hardtack, a sack of beans, some dried peach slices wrapped in parchment, a water skin, a fruitcake, and a tin of salt.

Pack light, Eoghan cautioned in my imagination while I hovered over the rack of pans hanging on the wall.

I glanced at the scullery maids passing by. None of them looked at me. One girl started walking in my direction, then abruptly turned around, paused, and wandered off somewhere else.

Quickly! After snatching the smallest saucepan I could find, I hightailed it out of the kitchen.

I made two more trips into the Keep that morning, looking for items that could be useful on my journey. In the butler's closet, I found a whole box of boots waiting to be repaired. I chose the smallest pair with the fewest burst seams and tucked them under my arm.

In the main hall, I snagged a satchel off the back of a chair. Once I got back to my room, I discovered it only held a few supplies for bookkeeping. I left behind the ledger but kept the six copper coins I found in a side pocket. They wouldn't buy me much, but it was better than nothing.

After lunch, I expected to be undisturbed for at least a few hours. It was time to go. I packed the satchel with my stolen supplies, a spare set of socks and underthings, and my map. My house slippers were traded for the boots, and I tucked my pants down into their tops.

The last thing I did before walking out was take down all my drawings and shove them into my little stove. I dropped a match on them, watching while Eoghan's face curled, went black, and dissolved into ash.

These Amau assholes wouldn't have a single image of my people. They didn't need any encouragement to hunt them down.

Things went smoothly, as usual. Shielded by the huge urn in the hallway, I slipped out of the empty guest room. I moved down the quiet hall and into the main part of the Keep. Oren didn't even look up from his fingernails. The idiot.

I stole through the Keep, and no one saw. My heart no longer beat against my ribs. My breath came easy and confident. I moved through the crowds of people with my travel pack secured across my body and a determined expression.

Not only did they not notice me, but they deliberately turned away from me when I approached at top speed. Person after person stopped mid-stride or veered away until I passed.

There was some devilry going on in this Keep. Could it possibly be the Owl? Just how far did her sibylline abilities reach? I had never heard of a mindwalker controlling people. Maybe it was Calliope herself. What had the Owl called her? Not human, but empty?

Whatever was helping me, I wasn't complaining. I set my mouth and stepped into the stairway leading up to the gallery of private rooms, where the family lived.

The hall was empty and quiet. I swallowed hard and walked right up to the third door, gripped the knob, and turned.

The room beyond was beautiful. A handsomely appointed living room with open doorways leading off on either side. Heavy drapery softened the large windows and rippled gently in the breeze. A series of tapestries brightened the drab wall paneling, depicting unicorns moving about a verdant forest. Comfortable sofas and lounges flanked a handsome mantle, the firewood stacked neatly inside, ready to be lit on a cold night. Simple shelving dominated the left wall, full to bursting with books of all shapes and sizes.

The books caught my attention, making me forget for a moment why I had come in the first place. It was a fortune of information. I took a few steps forward and ran my hand over the spines. Not just memoirs and encyclopedias, but novels, adventures, and romances. Handwritten journals and accounts, printed serials, beautifully illustrated fairy tales and children's stories.

I had one of the books in my hands before I could think, flipping through the pages and admiring the artwork. This little stack of bound pages was worth a fortune on its own. And the damn Dragon had hundreds of them. Thousands.

"Hello, Nora," said a low, melodious voice behind me.

I whirled around, clutching the book to my chest.

And there she was. The Dragon's wife. It had to be her. Average height with a shapely figure. Her hair was the color of flax but with a tinge of green when the light hit it just right. Her eyes were huge for her face and a strange color. Black and iridescent green, like the wings of a beetle.

At first glance, she was just a woman, but the Owl was right. Calliope *couldn't* be human. She just couldn't. It was something about the way she looked at me, like the darkness of a dense forest peeking out between the trees.

"Are...Are you Calliope?" I asked.

She smiled and stretched a graceful hand toward me. "I am. Come and sit with me, Sister."

I took a hesitant step forward, still clutching the book to my breast. What in the hell was I supposed to do? I had found the wife, but now what? Eoghan's voice in my head went conspicuously silent, and I remembered it had never been him at all. It was just me, making half-formed plans and charging ahead without purpose.

Why hadn't I just walked out? What had I been thinking?

"Come," she said again. Everything about her was unhurried. She spoke slowly and articulately, and she crossed to the couch with deliberate, calculated steps.

I perched on the edge of the suede couch, still clutching the book and leaving plenty of room between us.

"I am glad we are finally able to meet," Calliope said with a sincere smile. "Arlo has told me much about you."

"What did he tell you?"

"That you are headstrong and capable. That you draw beautifully. Maybe one day, you can paint my portrait."

"Uh huh," I said, eyes flicking to the door.

"Do you like books?"

I stared at her, completely thrown. "Ye-yes."

She held out her slender hand for the book I held. I jerked, unwilling to let it go. Not because it was valuable, but because it felt like a piece of armor. Like just by holding it, I was safe.

But it was only a book, and it was hers anyway. I passed it to her, and she opened it to the title page.

"Ah, yes. This one is beautiful. Fairy tales about the Old Kind. And such lovely illustrations. Arlo likes to read to me, but this one must be looked at as well." She closed the book and held it back out to me. "You should keep it, Sister. You are an artist. I like it, but you would love it better."

I took the book back. Calliope folded her hands gently in her lap.

"What are you?" I blurted out.

She cocked her head to one side, her flaxen hair falling onto her shoulder. "What do you mean?"

"What are you? Where did you come from?"

Calliope's pert mouth slipped into a confused frown. She leaned away from me, looking around for a polite escape. "What? I don't understand."

But I didn't care that this sweet woman was in distress. I dug in my heels and pushed harder. "Why did Arlo start this war? What does he want?"

"I-I don't—" She cast around and stood up, backing away from me.

Don't fall for it, Nora. She's putting on a show. This is the Dragon's wife. No innocent woman willingly slept next to the devil every night.

"He wants to help people," Calliope said. "Sister, please!"

"Help people?" I asked with a snorted laugh. I gripped her forearm, holding her hand up between us. A sapphire on her ring glimmered in the sunlight. "Where did he get this ring, then? Spoils of war, no doubt!"

"Stop!" Calliope wrenched her arm out of my grasp. Her skin slipped through my fingers too easily, like she was coated in soap or slime.

I glanced down at my hand, then froze. A gray substance coated my palm and oozed between my fingers. I spread them out, and the stuff slumped into the creases of my hand.

Clay. Gray, wet clay.

"What?" I breathed.

Calliope held her arm close to her body. The clay coated her arm right where I had gripped her. But it sank into her skin, absorbing like thin paint wicking up into the bristles of a paint brush. Soon, it was just skin again.

I held my own hand away from me, watching in horror. But the clay didn't sink into my skin the way it had done to

Calliope. It just sat on the surface, already drying a bit around the edges.

The door to the gallery slammed open, and we both jumped in surprise. Arlo strode through the door, fury turning his handsome face into a mask of rage. He came right at me and gripped me by the upper arms, hauling me away from his wife.

"Having fun sneaking around my house?" he snarled at me.

"Arlo, don't!" Calliope said behind him. "She's just scared!"

Arlo ignored her. "Maybe you're right. An actual prison cell would be more appropriate."

"Arlo! She is my sister!"

"She can't be allowed to wander the house, Calliope," Arlo said with grim determination.

I writhed and pulled against his grasp, but he held me too tightly. My arms screamed with the pressure of his fingers. There was no clay between us to help me slip free. Not like with Calliope.

But while I fought him, Arlo noticed my hand covered in the clay. His eyes went wide, and he grabbed my wrist in a vise-like fist.

"You're hurting me!" I shouted, but I froze at the expression on his face.

Then he did something I never would have expected. He threw me aside by the arm, and I stumbled away, tripping over an ottoman. Arlo ran to his wife, fear in his eyes.

"Are you okay? Did she hurt you?"

"I am unhurt, my love." Calliope showed him her arm and the perfect skin there. No hint of clay or damage.

But I didn't wait to see how this little interaction would play out. I scrambled to my feet and sprinted for the door.

"Stop!" Arlo called, as if that would do him any good.

I slammed the door shut behind me and wedged a decorative table under the door lever. It wouldn't hold him for long, but it would give me a few precious seconds.

To do what? Run pell-mell through the Keep? If it had been

Calliope keeping people from noticing me, then it was a safe bet that protection was over. And if it had been the Owl, then I needed to make it as easy as possible. I had to be calm and easy to overlook. Running for my life wasn't smart.

What I needed was to hide somewhere the Dragon would never look for me, and then later walk out as if I belonged. Just like I had been doing the past two days.

So instead of racing down the hall before Arlo could break his way out of his room, I opened the very next door and slipped inside.

This room was very similar to Calliope's: comfortable furnishings, beautiful tapestries and artwork. There were even books, though not nearly as many.

"Oh, for fuck's sake," said a familiar voice from an inner doorway.

"Damn it!" I hissed when Isla came into view. This was her room, of course. And I was sure the next room belonged to Darius. Or maybe it had been Fletcher's once upon a time.

"How in the hell did you get up here?" Isla asked, then jerked her attention to the wall when crashing sounded from next door.

Arlo still hadn't made it out into the hallway.

"Hide me," I said.

Isla barked out a laugh. "Excuse me?"

"Arlo is going to kill me and steal my baby to give to his wife. That's what the Owl told me that day you found me crying. Hide me."

Isla's expression faltered. "He would never do such a thing."

"Do you wanna risk it? Because I sure as hell don't!"

The crashing turned into splintering, and Arlo's cry of effort became much clearer. My time was up.

"Hide me, Isla!" I hissed.

She didn't move. We both just stood there while Arlo's footsteps thundered down the hall, past Isla's room, and faded into nothing.

The world spun before my eyes, and my chest heaved with the effort of breathing. "Holy shit," I hissed. "Thank you. Thank you."

"I know you killed my brother," Isla said, her voice deadly low.

Shit, shit, shit. "Isla, I'm sorry. I had no choice. He was going to kill me."

"He went looking for a fight, and he found one." A tear pooled in Isla's left eye and spilled over. The scarring was almost completely gone. "He should never have gone looking in the first place."

I pinched my lips together, afraid to say anything that might ruin this sliver of hope I had.

"Disappear," she said. "If I ever see you again, I'll kill you myself."

I hovered at the door, terrified to move. For this one moment, I was a little sad to leave Isla behind. What did she have here, other than her little garden? Nothing. Her brother was gone. She didn't believe in this war.

"Come with me," I whispered. "Right now. Let's go."

She stalked toward me, and for an instant, I thought she might make good on her promise to kill me right where I stood. I stumbled backward toward the door, reaching blindly for the knob.

But Isla reached behind me and wrenched the door open.

"We're not friends," she said, though her voice spoke only of exhaustion. She pushed me out into the gallery and closed the door in my face.

Twenty-Two

The Dragon must have alerted the Keep to my presence. The entire place was in an uproar, though none of them seemed to know what was going on. I slipped through the main hall among crowds of agitated people. Some curious, others fearful and clinging to corners. But at least half of them appeared to be military on high alert.

Front doors, Nora!

You're not making this easy on me.

I flicked my eyes to an upper balcony, where the Owl stood in the shadow of a wide support column. Gone was her cozy cable-knit. Today she wore close-fitting canvas with soft, cotton sleeves and a plain dagger sheathed at her side. Her eyes seemed to glow in the sunlight streaming through the high windows.

She was dressed for battle, prepared for the chaos that had erupted inside the Keep.

I scowled at her, thinking as many foul things as I could.

The corner of her mouth quirked up. *Act like you're afraid. Don't stop until you're out.*

Stupid cocky cow. She had probably alerted the Dragon that I was in his room with his wife. That way, she could keep her cover as his ally.

But her idea of blending in with the cowering citizenry had merit. I hunched my shoulders, widened my eyes, and cried out in fear when a soldier ran past me. It wasn't far off from the truth anyway, so even Eoghan would have been impressed with my acting. I huddled in with a crowd of maids scurrying toward the kitchens but broke off from them at the last minute to head to the main exit.

"You! Stop there!" a voice cried out just when I stepped into the afternoon sunlight.

I froze, unsure if my best bet was to run for it or to try to pass for someone who was supposed to be there. This soldier wouldn't recognize me as a prisoner. I had never met him before in my life.

The soldier grabbed me by the arm, right over the bruises Arlo had left there just a few minutes before. "Get inside, miss! If the Giant makes it past the walls, there's no telling what it'll do. Best to take cover until the all-clear."

"A Giant?" I asked, hope welling in my chest.

"Inside, miss! Now!"

He shoved me back inside, and I took two tentative steps as directed. But the soldier didn't wait to make sure I followed orders. He thundered off down the main steps, along with a crowd of other men and women dressed in fighting leathers and carrying weapons.

There was a Giant at the city walls? That must be the real source of alarm in the Keep. Why had it come now? At this exact moment, when I was ready to run?

I hovered at the top of the steps, watching in confusion while all the soldiers ran right past me. A couple of them shouted at me to get inside, just like the first had done. But none of them followed through. I glanced back up at the mezzanine, but the Owl had gone. What had she done now?

You're not making this easy on me, she had said.

Of course. That cow had brought the Giant here, right on time, to cause enough chaos for me to disappear into. There was no other explanation. These things would have been so much simpler if she had just told me her fucking plan in the first place.

Thunderous booms echoed between the streets below—the sound of rock crashing against rock. I strained upward, as if by will alone I could make myself tall enough to see all the way to the city wall.

If there was a Giant, then this was my way out. It couldn't do too much damage to the city with an entire army up against it, but it could protect me long enough for me to flee to the wilderness.

"Nora!"

I flinched and spun around when Arlo's voice cut through the chaos. He didn't run toward me. A man like that never ran. He didn't have to. Arlo strode purposefully through the crowd. Soldiers and civilians scrambled to get out of his way.

"Gah!" I growled in frustration and ran.

"Nora! Stop!"

Like hell.

I set off down the stairs at a run, tucking Calliope's book into a side pocket of the satchel. I ran through the market, dodging merchants frantically closing up their carts and hauling them away, and into a narrow alley.

Arlo's voice faded when I disappeared behind a building.

A quick right turn at the next street had me running parallel to the main road, shadowing the surge of soldiers rushing toward the wall and the Giant.

A grin spread across my face. Today was my liberation day. No matter what happened, I was getting out. Arlo be damned.

I ran as fast as I could, stopping to walk when I absolutely couldn't bear it any longer. But between two months of sitting around in my locked room and the child growing inside me, I didn't have the endurance I used to.

Arlo was young and strong. Before long, his thudding footsteps grew louder behind me.

I glanced over my shoulder and hissed. Maybe fancy men ran after all. His arms pumped furiously, and his powerful legs ate up the cobbles behind me.

I turned and sprinted down the next alley, dodging a henwife herding her chickens into their little hutches. Grabbing the wire frame of one hutch, I hauled it over, sending the chickens flying pell mell into the narrow space. The woman screeched at me in fury as eggs splattered on the stone below.

"Sorry!" I called between labored breaths.

Arlo stumbled over the hutch and dodged the henwife's stick, buying me precious seconds.

I burst out into the main thoroughfare and hesitated in the bright sunlight, heaving breath in and out, in and out. The wall was on my left. The army gathered around the main gate, preparing to fight. I stood up on my toes to see over their heads.

The Giant wasn't visible, but the noise it made thundered down the streets. Great shuddering thuds and scrapings told me it beat and scratched at the wall, tearing away chunks here and there. It must be one of the smaller ones. Less than twenty feet.

The gates were locked tight, blocking off any exit I could have hoped for. And surrounding the gates, at least fifty meters in all directions, were the bulk of the Dragon's soldiers. There was no getting through, even if the gates had been open.

I was fifty meters away from freedom and help, and I couldn't get to it.

"Shit!" I yelled, heedless of who might hear through their windows. I turned on the spot, swiping stray hairs off my sweaty face. "Shit, shit, shit!"

Now what?

"Stop that woman! Stop her!" Arlo careened out of the alley at top speed, the henwife still screeching after him.

"Shit!" I squealed and sped off in the opposite direction, the stolen satchel thumping against my hip.

Away from the wall. Away from help. But with Arlo right behind me, with his long legs and his endless determination, I had no choice. A handful of soldiers heard his order and joined him in the chase.

I ran headlong into crowds, using the chaos to my best advantage. My body was smaller than my pursuers, so I was able to slip between the alarmed city folk. Other soldiers headed toward the gates and the obvious danger: the Giant. They hesitated, unsure, when first I and then Arlo and his soldiers barreled past them.

I was able to keep just out of reach, but I couldn't get out of sight.

What's the exit strategy? Eoghan's voice echoed in my mind again, the voice of reason.

I dashed around a corner and tucked myself behind a banner for a tailor shop, heaving breath into my lungs in desperate gasps.

"Strategy's shot to hell," I said out loud.

I waited, but Eoghan's voice didn't come back to me. And again, I had to remind myself it wasn't him. It was just me talking to myself like an idiot.

Arlo and his soldiers ran past the mouth of the alley. He and one other looked into the alley and directly at my feeble hiding spot.

I held my breath, but just like in the Dragon's Keep, they didn't see me. One soldier slapped the arm of the man next to her, and they all kept moving past the alley and down the street. Somehow, by some piece of perfect luck, Arlo had lost sight of me.

No, not luck. It had to have been the Owl again. Even now, she was protecting me. How far did her abilities reach?

I couldn't stay there. It wouldn't be long before Arlo started backtracking and found my hiding place. If he asked the Owl, would she help him?

Probably. Two-faced cow.

Move, Nora! Right in front of you. Look up.

I snapped my eyes upward, and they landed on a dark archway across the way. A handful of soldiers came pouring out, pulling sword belts on and latching helmets.

Move. Now. Go.

Was it Eoghan's voice or my own imagination? Or was the Owl nudging me along? I didn't care anymore. A dark doorway was a dark doorway, and it was a better hiding place than the one I had now. After a few hesitant seconds, when no one else emerged, I slipped across the alley and into the comforting darkness of the room beyond.

I fumbled around in the shadowy room as my eyes adjusted. I seemed to have found a back hallway. My hands encountered a cold stone wall only a few feet back from the entrance, which veered off to both sides.

With a screech of pain, I barked my shin against something hard. "Damn it!" I hissed, clutching my leg. I felt around to discover several wooden crates stacked against the wall. Storage. It was the back door of some building, and this hallway was so rarely used it had become a place to store boxes.

I blinked hard, gazing around. A staircase loomed out of the darkness. At the top of the stairs, a lit doorway illuminated the landing.

I glanced behind to make sure no one had followed me inside, then scrambled for the stairway and the light. The stairs continued into further darkness, but I stopped on the second-floor landing. I stumbled up to a railing and stared out over a huge warehouse. It had slatted windows high up on the walls, letting in plenty of natural light.

Very few people remained inside, and none of them looked up to find me on the upper-floor balcony. They frantically dug through boxes, handing out supplies and weapons, then raced out again.

I gazed down at the crates below. Some of them were open,

revealing their contents. Swords, shields, halberds, spears. Armor of all kinds: beaten metal, chainmail, leather. Trunks of arrows stood stacked under several racks of longbows, with everything carefully labeled.

Just below me stood neat rows of trebuchets, nearly two dozen of them, ready and waiting to be pulled out and put to good use. This was why the warehouse had such a high ceiling: So the trebuchets could fit inside. They partially hid me from view while a few lingering soldiers armed themselves and passed weapons to latecomers.

The armory. I had found the Dragon's armory.

"Jackpot," I said breathlessly.

The balcony where I stood went across the entire back wall, with shadowy doors leading off to more rooms. Above me was another balcony on the third floor. Probably more storage. I passed the open doors and empty rooms, scanning the warehouse below for a particular kind of container. But I couldn't find what I was looking for.

Next, I went room to room on the balcony but found only boxes of feathers and arrowheads and workbenches with crates of chainmail ready to be linked together.

I retreated to the stairway in the darkened back hall and went up to the third floor. Far below, the last few soldiers grabbed one last dagger from the rack and ran out the main doors.

Still, no one looked up. Why would they?

Again, I went room to room, and this time, I was lucky. I pushed open the third door and let out a triumphant, "Ha!"

The muted sunlight streamed in through the open door, illuminating stacks of barrels. This was the largest of the storage rooms, and it was filled floor-to-ceiling with barrels of pitch.

I looked down at the main floor of the warehouse one last time to ensure it was entirely empty—no one to hurt, and no one to stop me. Then I set to work.

I wasn't strong enough to do much, but I was able to knock a few barrels onto their sides and roll them out the door toward the balcony. Then I maneuvered them one at a time toward a freight lift and heaved them over the edge.

The first one landed squarely on the edge of a crate of swords and broke apart, splattering black pitch all over everything below. With a wide grin of satisfaction, I ran back and did the same with a second. And then a third.

"Nora!"

I froze, a fourth barrel poised to go over the edge of the lift.

"Nora! What are you doing?" The panic in Arlo's voice was unmistakable. He skidded into view, a handful of soldiers trailing him. Arlo stared up at me, his chest heaving. He threw out his arms to block his soldiers from moving further into the room, almost as if he cared about their safety.

"It's called justice, you asshole!" Shaking with rage, I shoved the fourth barrel over the edge. The pitch splattered over the crates below with a sharp crack of splintering wood.

"Nora, stop!" Arlo called up at me. "You don't know what you're doing!"

I laughed once and shrugged. "I don't know, Dragon. It looks like I'm starting a fire! I'm pretty sure that's something you're familiar with! Considering the fact that you burned half of my country!"

I fished my flint out of my satchel and lunged for the oil lamps tucked into alcoves along the balcony.

"Stop her!" Arlo shouted, running for the far wall. "Go, go!"

They all sprinted for the back stairwell where I had entered, effectively cutting off my escape route. But I had come this far. There was no backing out now. While they dodged between crates and war machines, I bent to light two lamps. The flint threw showers of sparks over the wicks, which caught immediately.

Arlo, however, had reached his target: a rack full of longbows. He snatched an arrow out of a small crate as he ran and nocked it.

"Don't make me shoot you, Nora!" He took aim directly at me, and a little thrill of fear made me falter.

The soldiers slammed into the stairwell. Their thudding footsteps up the staircase were muffled but unmistakable.

There was no time to think, no time to alter my course. I held a lit lamp in each of my hands and stared down Arlo's arrow.

"Screw you," I shouted, and threw the lamp over the edge of the lift.

I didn't wait to see where it landed but instantly ran. The furious *wuff* as the flames erupted below nearly drowned out the *thunk* of Arlo's arrow hitting the wall behind me.

The second lamp I tossed into the pitch storage room. The ceramic lamp shattered, coating half the barrels in oil that instantly caught fire.

"Damn you!" Arlo bellowed. "Damn you, Nora! I will find you!"

"I wasted every drop of that paint you gave me!" I screamed down at him before disappearing into the stairwell. Then I squealed when the soldiers thundered up, only a few paces below.

"Shit!" I sprinted upward into the darkness and away from my pursuers.

I should have saved a lamp to throw at them too.

Twenty-Three

I took the stairs two at a time with legs that felt like lead. I couldn't keep this up much longer. But fear was a powerful motivator, and I managed to stay just ahead of the soldiers coming up the stairs.

I burst out onto the roof and slammed the door behind me, but the first soldier threw it open again like it was nothing. I stumbled away with the force of it and faced them.

Four soldiers, three men and a woman, emerged from the dark doorway onto the flat roof of the armory. Thin tendrils of smoke already wafted out from behind them.

I threw furtive glances around, searching for any way out of the mess I had gotten myself into.

"Shit," I hissed.

There was no way out. I stood on the roof of a three-story building on fire, and there was no way down.

Think, Nora! Think!

"Come with us now! There isn't much time!" The foremost soldier held out his hand to me, easing forward. Smoke billowed out of the door in horrific waves. Not much time, indeed.

I darted my eyes this way and that, and they landed on a familiar steep, red roof. The bell tower!

The soldier tried again while his companions cast worried glances at the smoke. "Now, woman! We can't stay here! Take my hand!"

"No, thank you!" I said cheerfully.

"Leave her!" the female soldier called out. "There's no time!"

The lead soldier hesitated for another second and his friends retreated through the smoke.

"Let's go!" he shouted at me.

I hesitated. With nothing but the ground below me and fire behind, my options were limited. The soldier ripped off his helmet, giving me a clear view of his face. Heavy beard, dark hair, worried eyes.

"What's your name?" I asked.

"I'm Rhyden, mistress." He jerked his hand at me again, begging me to take it. "Please. Let's go. I don't know what the Dragon wants with you, and I don't know why you set that fire, but you'll die up here. Fire is a nasty way to go."

"Thank you, Rhyden. But I'd rather burn than go back where I was. And I'm proud to take this armory with me to hell. You should run. Save yourself. As you said, fire's a nasty way to go."

"On your own head be it, then." Rhyden took a deep breath, clamped his mouth shut, and disappeared back into the smoke.

Alone on the roof, I just had my thoughts and the roar of the growing fire to center me. I had no options. If I went down the stairs, I would be caught. The only other option was the bell tower.

I sprinted to the north edge of the armory roof, right where the bell tower loomed overhead. It had been built just a bit taller than the armory, with the upper window level with the roof. It was only about six feet away, but it was a long way down if I missed. I peered over the edge. At least fifty feet down. To fall would be certain death. I had toed that line one too many times in the past year, and I wasn't ready to do it again.

The chaos in the streets had doubled since I'd entered the armory. The people below scattered away from the main gate. None of them gave a second look to the flames licking out of the high windows of the armory. They were too afraid of what was behind them.

I stood up on my toes and squinted down the street, but the afternoon sun blinded me. A grin spread across my face anyway. I could hear what everyone was afraid of. The Giant continued to pound away at the wall. It would make it through to the city soon.

"Nora!"

I jerked toward the bell tower when the familiar voice called out.

The Owl stood in the window. The feathers in her long, dark hair fluttered in the high wind. A man stood next to her. Tall and lean, with broad shoulders. He stood a little back from the window, gripping the Owl's hand for dear life. Like he was terrified she would fall.

I knew that man. His name was John. He had been one of my guards in my first few weeks at the Dragon's Keep, before being replaced by Oren, the nail biter.

John had always been kind to me. To see him clinging to the Owl like that made my trust in her grow a fraction. Maybe she was on my side after all.

Flames began licking out of the windows below me. The heat was hard to ignore, and smoke began curling around my ankles.

"Jump!" the Owl shouted.

"Jump! I'll catch you!" John called out.

I kept my feet planted firmly on the armory roof. "Why are you helping me?" I yelled.

The Owl's gaze darted to my right, and her eyebrows narrowed in concentration. I whirled around, expecting to find another soldier about to grab at me, but there was no one there.

There's no time for this! the Owl sent directly to my mind, a tinge of frustration in her mental voice. Clearly she had exhausted her knowledge of Ambic.

"Then answer quickly!" I shouted back.

John said something to her I couldn't hear over the angry flames, and the Owl's eyes turned skyward. She said something back to him, then they both disappeared.

I blinked. Where had they gone? Had they abandoned me? Damn it, Nora! Why hadn't I just jumped when they told me to?

A hand closed over my arm, and my stomach dropped out from under my ribs.

I whirled around, coughing. Smoke clogged the air around us. They both stood right next to me, and John had a hand on my arm.

"How did you—"

"Listen carefully," the Owl said. Except, she didn't use those words. I couldn't tell what words she had actually spoken, but the meaning shot clear into my mind anyway. "You don't matter. You've done what I needed you to do."

"Gwen..." John cut in.

"What did I—" I tried to interrupt, but the Owl spoke over me.

"I don't want you to die here, but I will let that happen if I have to." The Owl continued in her own language. The confusion of meaning overlapping her strange words beat at my head in a dull ache. "This is bigger than you. Bigger than me. And I will not let you stop what I have set in motion here. So I need you to jump. John will catch you."

"The Giant will be here soon," John said in Ambic.

He didn't even have an accent. Who *were* these people?

John blinked against the smoke. "It will take you to Eoghan. Take your map to New Haven. Go live your life. But you have to jump now."

"Eoghan?" I said breathlessly. "Eoghan's here?"

"He's in the city," the Owl said, and I winced at the foreign language I shouldn't have been able to understand. "But if you stay on this roof much longer, he will have come for nothing. Now, jump!"

Then they were gone again. I spun on the spot, looking for John and the Owl, but I was alone on the roof. Had I imagined them?

John's voice cut through the smoke. "Nora! This way!"

There, back in the bell tower. What was happening? Was this all a vision the Owl was sending me?

No, it couldn't have been a vision. I had felt John's hand on my arm just a moment ago.

"Nora!"

Jump now, or we'll leave you here.

"Okay! Okay!" I shouted back, then bent double to cough. I tried to take a deep breath but choked on it. Sweat poured down my back and soaked my clothes. It was too hot. I couldn't breathe.

"Jump, Nora!"

Jump now!

If I couldn't breathe, then I would have to jump on will alone. No time to think or prepare. I just had to go for it and hope my muscles held out. Just like that day in New Haven, the last time I had seen Eoghan. The last time I had kissed him, then ran away.

I just had to jump.

I sprinted for the edge of the roof, ignoring the sting of the hot air, refusing to breathe.

Just run, Nora. Eoghan's voice had returned. *Come back to me. You're so close.*

I met the edge of the roof and pushed off as hard as I could, but it wasn't quite enough. One foot slammed against the wall of the bell tower, and my chest collided with the windowsill. Stars blotted out my vision and the last of the contaminated air was forced out of my body. Hands gripped my arms and shoulders, hauling me up painfully over the ledge.

John and the Owl spoke over my head as I lay gasping on the floor. Their words passed across me like gibberish. Smooth, flowing vowels, sharp consonants, long words strung together in an impossible music.

We weren't far enough away from the burning armory, and the smoke fouled the air even here. I choked and coughed while John pulled me up by my shoulders.

"Get up, Nora. You have to keep moving."

"Where's Eoghan?" I gasped with raw lungs. "How do I find him?"

"The Giant will take you to him. That's why it's here." John nudged me toward the curved stair that disappeared into the floor. "Keep moving."

They followed me, and John steered me around the bodies of two women on the floor. They lay in an awkward lump next to the bell's pull rope.

"What? Who are they?" I bent to check on the women, but John kept me moving.

"Sleeping," the Owl said in heavily accented Ambic.

"No one can know we helped you," John added.

"You drugged them?" I asked, alarmed. Drugs were a dangerous game to play. Too much and a person might never wake up again.

The Owl only gave me a condescending look, as if I were an idiot.

"Right." I faced forward once more. "Silly me. You made them sleep."

Then the Owl hissed a word that could only have been a curse. We all stopped on the second floor.

"What is it?" I asked.

After a silent pause, John answered. "She says someone's coming."

We cannot be seen helping you.

I grabbed onto John's forearm and gripped tight. "Don't you

dare leave me! Wherever it is you go when you disappear, take me with you!"

You'll die. Only the sibylline can survive such a journey.

The door to the bell tower slammed open below, and heavy footsteps began on the stairs.

John pried at my vise grip on his arm. "You have to let me go. Gwen, get her off me."

The Owl uttered something that sounded like reluctance, but then...

Oh hell, what was happening to me? Something entered my body, like a worm sliding down my arms and filling up my fingers. It pried at my hands from the inside, trying to make my fists open.

I cried out, fighting the sensation. My arms turned to lead. Moving them took every ounce of will I had, so I spent that will on keeping them still.

Don't let go, Nora. Don't let go.

John jerked his arm, trying to wrench himself free, but I fought the coercion taking my hands from me, and I held on.

John and the Owl started yelling, and the Owl pried at my hands with her own. They tried to drag me up the stairs, but I held on like a leech.

"Stop it!" Tears ran down my sooty face.

"Let go!" John shouted. He pried at my closed hands, digging into my flesh.

I would have bruises from it.

Then it stopped. The leaden sensation evaporated, and my hands felt normal again. I let go of John in shock and stared first at my hands, then at the Owl.

"What are you?" I asked in horror.

But they both ignored me and stared over my shoulder.

I turned to look down the stairs to see what they were looking at.

Rhyden, the soldier from the roof of the armory, stood a few steps lower. His worried eyes danced from the Owl to John, back and forth. He gripped a menacing flail in one hand, but he lowered it slightly when he recognized his city's spiritual advisor and a fellow soldier helping a woman he had been trying to arrest.

"My lady Owl?" Rhyden sounded unsure.

Nobody said anything. We all stood in the darkened stairwell. The roar of the burning armory drowned out the chaos in the streets. Had the Giant made it through the gate yet? Was it close?

"Okay, thank you!" I said into the awkward silence. "Thank you all for saving me. I'll be going."

But Rhyden put out his flail to block my path. The spiked head clanged against the stone wall, echoing up the empty tower. The chain wasn't just a chain, but it was lined with razor-sharp spines. Who had invented this evil thing?

"Let her through," John said.

The Owl hissed something at him under her breath.

"It's over, Gwen," he said.

There followed what could only be called the bickering of an old married couple. John and the Owl began an agitated back-and-forth in their own language. An arms-waving, finger-pointing, screaming fight. Even though Rhyden and I couldn't understand a word of it, we both knew better than to interrupt.

But Rhyden also wasn't about to sit around and watch either. He closed a hand around my upper arm and started pulling me downstairs.

"Hey!" I said, jerking at his grip on my arm. I winced when his fingers dug into the bruises there.

Rhyden ignored me and kept moving.

I tugged on him, but he was strong.

"Hey!" I yelled up at John and the Owl, who were still arguing. When they didn't acknowledge me, I shouted again. Much louder this time. "Hey! Assholes!"

They both whipped their heads in my direction just as Rhyden got me to the second-floor landing. Clean air blew in through a large open window, clearing out a bit of the smoke from the armory next door.

"A little help?" I asked.

John came down the stairs at a trot, faster than Rhyden could pull me down. The Owl followed more slowly.

"Let her go, friend," John said.

Rhyden shook his head. "I'm sorry, John. The Dragon wants her. And she fired the armory. I saw it myself. She has to come with me."

Rhyden yanked me down another step, ignoring my complaints and objections.

"Rhyden, stop." John pulled a short sword out of the sheath on his back.

"Johnny," the Owl cautioned from behind. They exchanged a few more words, though the anger had gone from their voices. Now I only heard resignation. Sadness.

John tried again. "Rhyden, let her go. This won't end well for anyone. Just let her go. She doesn't belong here."

Rhyden tightened his grip on my sore arm. "And where does she belong, then?"

"I won't ask again."

"Then don't."

John's mouth tightened into grim determination, and he flexed his sword arm.

I had only half a second to react when John's steel flashed through the air. With a squeal, I dove for the floor as both men lunged for each other. I winced again and again when the sword and flail met and parried, struck stone walls, glanced off armor.

"Shit, shit," I repeated, creeping down the stairs one at a time on legs that would barely support me. This wasn't the kind of life I had been made for. I was a mapmaker. An artist. I was supposed to go exploring, construct maps, sleep under the stars, and draw pretty things!

But here I was, setting buildings on fire and barely dodging the scariest flail I had ever seen in my life.

"Come on," the Owl said.

I jumped at her voice. She had appeared at my side in that strange way of hers. The Owl took my arm and helped me down the last of the stairs and out into the street. The sunlight was wrong somehow. The whole world was wrong.

Go find your Giant. It's at the western gate, waiting for you. Run.

I hesitated. "What about you? John?"

We'll be fine. Just run.

She nudged me toward the west, then turned and disappeared back inside the bell tower.

I glanced around. Nobody seemed to care about me. I was just a woman, and the world had gone to hell.

It was the smoke, of course. It filled up the sky and turned the sun brown. The heat of the blaze beat at me, even this far away. People had finally decided the burning armory was more terrifying than a Giant at the gate. They had formed bucket lines and had brought pumps and hoses to stop the blaze from spreading.

But it was too late for the armory itself. Everything inside it was ruined. The trebuchets, the bows, the shields, and the leather armor. All of it had turned to ash. Even the metal pieces: swords, plate armor, helmets. They would all have been destroyed. Even if the metal could be recovered, it would have to be smelted again from scratch.

With a small grin of satisfaction, I turned my back on the blaze and moved in the direction the Owl had pointed. That way to the Giant and then to Eoghan. That way to freedom.

I hitched my stolen satchel a little higher on my shoulder and started walking on numb legs. And as I went, I only had one regret.

I wished I could see the Dragon's face now.

Part Five

The Giant Singer

One day earlier

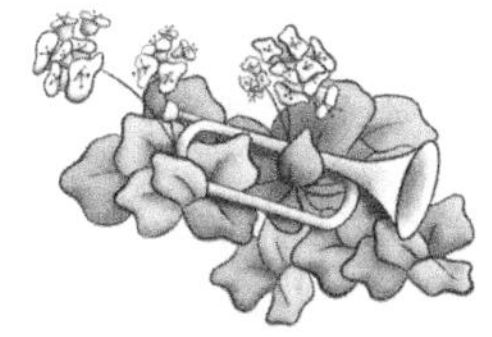

Twenty-Four

Eoghan

In the darkest hours, when my mind couldn't settle or when the burning in my chest could no longer be ignored, that was when I sought out the companionship of the drunkards.

My favorite bar was barely more than a gap in the wall in an alley in Barer Township. It was only a block from the shithole of a room I had rented two weeks earlier, and the unwashed barmaid liked to sneak me free mugs of their piss-poor, warm beer when she could get away with it.

A burly man even taller than me stood by the gaping hole where a door used to be, giving everyone the eyeball as they entered.

"All right, Eoghan?" he asked as I approached.

"Well enough," I grunted back. I strode past him without slowing and entered the dim, candle-lit room crammed so full of tables and bodies there was barely space to move. I welcomed the noise. The raucous laughter and shouting drowned out the voice in my head. The voice that kept me awake at night. The voice that tormented me every hour of the day.

You can't ever escape from the ghost in your own head. But sometimes you could drown it out with beer.

I only made it two steps inside before the doorman's voice called me back. "Ho ho ho! Eoghan! A little help here!"

I paused, my shoulders slumping in irritation.

Fucking hell. Stupid rock tried to follow me inside again.

I turned around and faced the gap in the wall. The craggy face of the stone Giant peered inside. It put one stubby hand on the doorway, and the wall crumbled under its three awkward fingers when it tried to cram inside after me.

Several heads turned to stare in shock and alarm, though the regulars in the bar had long gotten used to my little friend—or so they called the fifteen-foot pile of living stone that followed me around everywhere I went.

I stalked back to the doorway with one hand out. "For hell's sake, you can't come in here."

The Giant teetered backward, straightening up to its full height. Its feet scraped across the ancient cobbles, so loud that more than one head appeared out of the windows above to see what was causing all the ruckus.

"Sit down." I pointed at the wall opposite the bar. "Right there. Sit your ass down."

The Giant peered at me with its curious expression, or so it seemed to me. It was hard to tell if the Giants felt anything at all, much less curiosity. Their rocky faces and onyx eyes gave nothing away. But the way it cocked its head a little to the right, the way it watched me with a steady, unreadable gaze, felt like curiosity.

"Sit," I said again, stabbing my finger at the corner where the wall met the grungy cobbles.

The Giant lumbered to the spot I had indicated, folded itself in half, and scraped down the wall to sit on the road.

I winced when it gouged a deep scar in the stucco of the wall. But really, what had I expected?

Standing a little straighter, I glanced up at the doorman. We exchanged satisfied nods, and I reentered the bar.

The owner, a sturdy woman called Eugenia, passed me a

pewter stein of beer when I sat down at the only empty table. "Listen, love," she said to me, wiping her hands on her apron. "As much as I love to watch you sit here moping in silence for hours on end, your little friend is going to tear this whole building down one day, and I'm afraid that day is going to come sooner rather than later."

"I know, Eugenia."

"We used to have a door, you know. Not that a lack of a door has slowed anyone down, but—"

"So far as I can tell, your business has boomed ever since *my little friend* and I started drinking here," I reminded her with a tilt of my head. The Giants had been awake for nearly four months by then, but they were still a source of novelty for people in the city.

"There won't be any business at all if the roof collapses," she said with the patience of a mother who had heard one too many excuses. "If you can't keep it under control, you can't come in at all anymore. And that's the end of it."

I grimaced. She turned on her heel and stalked away into the crowded, dusky heart of the pub, her skirts bustling side to side in the wake of her purposeful stride.

I leaned heavily back into my chair, clutching the stein between both hands hard enough to bend the handle a little. Damned, stupid Giant. How long would he dog my steps? Cast a shadow over my life?

Keep him safe!

I shuddered as the memory of Nora's voice pierced through my head and brought the beer to my lips.

Not tonight. Not again. I just couldn't anymore.

I downed the beer in one long, breathless go, then slammed it onto the tabletop. I raised one hand to call the barmaid over, then froze in shock. I wasn't alone anymore.

Two figures sat across from me. A man with thick, brown hair curling gently around his ears. A smaller figure in a hooded cloak of fine, gray linen, with a pattern of diamonds about the hem in a lighter gray color. A woman, judging by the way she sat, her legs crossed one over the other. My suspicion was confirmed when I noticed the end of a long, brown braid peeking out from under her hood and two delicate hands folded gently in her lap.

In the time it took to down my stein of beer, two people had dragged over an extra chair and sat down opposite me. Except there had been no noise of chair legs scraping across sticky floors. Their clothes were still, as if they had been sitting comfortably for a while.

Like they had been there for hours.

I hadn't sat down at an occupied table, had I?

"Hello, old friend," the man said. Something about his voice was familiar.

He wore unremarkable clothes: lightweight cotton shirt, a dark leather jerkin, a simple sinew bracelet with a carved bone amulet. But his face was strange, his skin a little darker than I was used to seeing in these parts. His eyes were wide-set, and his nose was a little long over a well-kept beard.

"I know you," I said with narrowed eyes, but I couldn't place him. Where had I seen this man before?

"Yes. My name is John. This is my woman, Gwen." He gestured at the figure seated next to him, though she still didn't reveal her face.

"Where I come from, we don't keep women as slaves," I said with a sour expression.

The woman's shoulders jerked, and she let out a, "Pffi!"

John smiled, disarming. "You misunderstand. She's not my slave. She is what you might call my wife."

"So call her your wife, then." I shifted my weight.

Gwen turned toward John, her face still hidden, and spoke to him in another language. Her words were unfamiliar, full of swooping vowels and sharp consonants. It had a musical quality to it, almost like the cadence of a poem.

That feeling of recognition plucked at me again. I had heard this language before. I had...I knew it. For some reason, the sound of her words brought forth the memory of humid, salty air, sand-colored stucco, square buildings, and fabric fluttering in the breeze over empty stairs.

You will see her again.

The realization hit me like an angry bull crashing through a fence. These two people had been in New Haven the day Nora had been taken. This man had spoken to me in the crowd. And this woman, this Gwen person, she had taken the Clarion from me. She had distracted me and had drawn me away from Nora. This woman had taken over my body and forced me to give up the one thing Nora and I had sacrificed everything to protect.

She was the reason Nora had been taken in the first place.

My lip curled up in a snarl of anger. "You!" I hissed, muscles bunching. I began to rise.

But just like that day in the alley, my body betrayed me. I sat gently back in my chair, my hands in my lap, my face relaxed. The fury flooded through me in hot waves, but I could not act upon it. I could only feel it. The other drunks went about their noisy business, completely unaware that anything unusual was happening.

"Be at peace, my friend," John said. "We are here to help you."

I opened my mouth to speak, then paused for a second, surprised my jaw obeyed me. "Like you helped me two months ago?"

"That was a necessary betrayal," John admitted. "Nora needed to go to Amau as the Dragon's prisoner. But the time is coming now for her to escape. That's why we're here."

"She needed to go?" My rising voice was at odds with my relaxed posture. "According to who?"

Me.

I flinched internally, though only my face showed any hint of the shock. Gwen's voice sounded clear as day in my mind over the racket of shouting men, scraping chairs, and clanging dishes. The woman was sibylline. She must have been, considering the way she used my body like a puppet. But to hear her in my mind was an entirely different sensation.

"You? And just who are you?" I asked.

Gwen lifted one delicate hand to her hood and revealed a sliver of her face. She looked just how I remembered from the day she had taken the Clarion: medium dark skin, wide eyes, smooth brown hair full of feathers.

"She is the Owl," John answered for her.

"Is that supposed to mean something to me?"

"The Owl is the Dragon's spiritual advisor."

My eyes widened in furious shock. If I had been able to move, I would probably have tossed the whole table. "You're the Dragon's people?"

"Peace, my friend."

I turned my angry gaze onto John next. "Stop calling me *friend*!"

In the past two months, no change had come over the Giants. I hadn't heard the Clarion's ethereal call. I had finally dared to hope that the witch who had taken the Clarion, the witch I now knew to be Gwen, hadn't been with the Dragon at all. If she had taken it to him, he would have used it right away. But every day that went by with nothing, my hope crept a little higher.

But now...

"Where is the Clarion? Did you give it to him, then? To the Dragon?"

The Clarion is safe. Gwen's voice was tranquil in my mind. *I have hidden it where no one can ever find it. When I am finished, I will return it to its rightful owners.*

I narrowed my brow. "Finished with what?"

A great evil has been done in Amau. I am working to right it before it spreads to the rest of the world. I needed Nora's help, but her time is almost up.

"And how do you expect her to escape?" I asked. My voice began to shake. "Don't you think I tried? I can't get within a bowshot of that Mitsmooren. I've tried. Many, many times, I have tried! Why do you think I settled here? It's as close as I can get without drawing suspicion."

This much was true. I had tried going to Mitsmooren straight away and had even made it into the outer city, which sprawled away from the wall. But with that damned Giant in tow, I drew every eye. Even if I could convince it to break down the wall, what then? It would be me against an entire army. I couldn't do Nora any good if I were dead.

After a few weeks, I figured out that the Giant listened to me a little. If I said the right thing, really leaned on the idea of "staying safe," I could get it to wait for me. I could get it to sit down outside the bar or wait two streets away while I went and asked about a job in Mitsmooren. Anything that would result in papers and authorization to get through the gate.

It never lasted, though. The longest I could get the Giant to wait was about an hour, and then the *boom, boom, boom* of his footsteps would creep up on me.

So I stayed away. I rented out a shitty room in the nearest farming community, and I bided my time. For what? I had no idea. My little friend was very well known at that point. Everyone knew it was in the community, and everyone knew who it followed around. No one had a job for me. There was no way in.

I blundered on, my caution spent. "Every day, I am looking for another way into Mitsmooren. For some employment within the city. Some errand that will get me through the gate. But I can't get anywhere with my little friend following me around. I have nothing. I have no one. Lujor won't risk any men this far north. I can't—"

My words broke off as the anger, frustration, and bone weariness took their toll.

Fucking hell. Where was the barmaid with more beer?

John raised one hand, placating. "There is no way into the city. The Dragon is very protective of his people, and he knows that, as his military center, Mitsmooren is at greater risk. That is why he took Nora. Because he knows only the Giants can break his walls."

"Yes, and only the Old Kind know where she is, how she's living." I scrubbed my hand over my grubby beard, trying to wipe away the urge to cry like a child. Only afterward did I realize I had control of my body back.

Gwen remained passive, her face only partially visible under her hood. If she had some reaction to my barely controlled rage, she didn't show it in her expression.

"Nora is living in a comfortable room," John said. "She is missing good light to draw by, and she has no company aside from her guards, but she is well. She doesn't want for comfort."

"You think that makes it better?"

"It's better than her shivering in a cellar with nothing but stale bread to fill her belly," he said with a bit of an edge to his voice.

His sharp tone snapped my mouth shut. I wanted to scream, to shake these two, to argue and put them in their place. I wanted to call in my little friend and tell him to swipe his stone arm across them and wipe them both off the face of the earth.

But John wasn't wrong. At least Nora wasn't living in filth.

"Even better if she hadn't been taken at all," I said, stubborn. "And don't think I've forgotten your roles in bringing that about."

I'm not sorry for helping Amau kidnap Nora, Gwen said to me silently. *Her actions in Mitsmooren will result in thousands of lives saved. Tens of thousands. I know she has been unhappy there, angry. But I have made sure she was kept in comfort. And now I am working to get her home to you.*

"What did she do?" I asked.

She has not acted yet, but she will soon. The day she escapes, she will set a fire that will delay the Dragon's battle plans for months. It is time we desperately need.

"We plan to stop this war, but we need time," John said. "With

Nora's help, no more battles will begin before our plans are finished."

"If you're the Dragon's spiritual advisor, then why can't you just tell him not to attack?"

I only have so much influence over his choices.

"You can't just force him to act how you want?"

Gwen's response to this was a steady, unamused gaze. She ground her teeth, barely holding on to some harsh comment that would surely stoke the fire of my anger.

"What?" I barked at her. Please, say something. Anything I can latch onto and turn into a weapon. It didn't matter how petty.

John raised his hands, clearly desperate to rein in both of our tempers. "What's done is done," he said with a note of authority. "We cannot change the past, and our plans can continue, no matter what happens to Nora. So it's up to you, Eoghan. Do you want our help getting her out or not?"

I gripped my empty stein until my knuckles went white. What I really wanted was to toss the table over and storm Mitsmooren myself. To hell with both of these conniving bastards.

But deep down, I knew there was no way. I had tried so many times, and never once had I gotten close to finding out where Nora was being held within Mitsmooren, much less getting her out.

"Seems like I don't have much choice, do I?" I said through gritted teeth.

There is always a choice, Gwen replied in my head.

I jabbed my hand at her. "Don't get semantic with me, witch."

I'm not being semantic, ranger. It is a fundamental truth. There is always a choice. And I hope, when the moment comes, you'll remember it.

Then she said something to John in that musical language and disappeared. One moment, she sat calmly across from me. The next, her chair was as empty as if she had never been in it at all.

John turned to face me, unruffled. "You sure know how to get under her skin."

"How does she do that? Where did she go?"

"Back to Mitsmooren," he said, raising his hand to get the attention of the barmaid. "She can't stay gone for long. If her absence is noted, we'd be risking discovery."

The barmaid brought us two steins of beer and winked at me. "Who's your friend, Eoghan?" she asked, the dimples showing on her ruddy cheeks.

I took the stein from her hand a bit more roughly than I intended. "He's not my friend."

She threw up both hands. "Well! If you say so." She strode off with a huff.

John gestured at the barmaid's retreating back, and his face crinkled into an unmistakable expression of, *Was that really necessary?*

My gut churned with guilt. The girl had always been kind to me, and she didn't deserve my bad mood. But I was so deep into my self-dug hole of fury that I couldn't claw my way out now. "I don't need your judgment," I said into my stein.

John shrugged. He took one sip of his beer, made a face, and put the stein back down. "We'll need to set out right away so that we're ready to enter the city when Gwen gives the word. It's all down to the timing Nora sets. When she's ready to go, we have to be ready as well."

"And just how are we supposed to get into the city? Will your witch woman blink us in and out again?"

John shook his head. "No. It would kill you to try. Only sibyls can survive the journey through the void."

"So how, then?"

"There is a secret tunnel that goes under the wall. You'll be guided to it when the time is right."

"And why can't Nora get out that way?" I asked, my voice rising. "If there's a way, why hasn't she taken it?"

"You misunderstand," John said patiently. "Gwen and I cannot be implicated in Nora's escape. If we want to end this war, we have to remain entirely above suspicion. That's why we need you. Gwen could walk Nora out through the front gates, and no one would be able to stop her. But then our time at Mitsmooren would be over."

"So I'm your scapegoat."

"Yes," John said, leaning back in his chair. "The difficulty is making sure you're seen doing it. We need to make a big commotion. A diversion."

I drained the last of my shitty beer and plunked my stein down onto the table. "Well, as to that. I've got a possible solution in mind."

"What?"

"I think it's time for you to meet my little friend."

Twenty-Five

The journey to Mitsmooren was short—only a two-day walk. We avoided the roads as much as possible to draw less attention from other travelers, but the way was easy enough with the trees set wide apart from each other and the ground firm, stone and hard-packed soil.

"What's to stop the Dragon from killing Nora the minute he knows a Giant is close?" I asked. We had left straight from the pub, stopping briefly at my rented room to collect my supplies and the pack Nan had made.

John walked backward next to me, his attention fully on the Giant. It lumbered behind us, its feet crashing into the stony ground with every step like miniature earthquakes. It was a sound I had long gotten used to, but John was entranced.

"You know, this is only the second time I've been so close to one awake," he said. "It's fascinating to watch how it moves."

I glared over my shoulder at it, annoyed. "Did you hear my question?"

"Gwen isn't worried," he said with a shrug.

I drew my eyebrows together. "And that's supposed to be enough for me? The word of a witch?"

John shifted his pack on his shoulders and resumed walking forward. "When the time comes, the Dragon won't be in a position to hurt Nora. She will be in the wind before he can do anything about it. She's been sneaking around the Keep for days. Popped out a piece of paneling in her room." One side of his mouth curved upward in appreciation. "It only took her two days to get out. Took her longer to figure out how to get around without being seen, but she got there in the end. She's very good."

My teeth ground together. I knew Nora was good. I didn't need him bragging about her, as if he had a right. As if he knew her.

John continued in a more somber voice. "She has at least four drawings of you up on the walls. You and some others. But you're the only one I recognize. She talks to you."

"Stop talking," I said, my fists clenched.

Nora sitting alone in a room, talking to her drawings. Penned in, unable to move. It must be killing her.

"She is strong," John went on, undeterred. "She will make it through this."

"Stop talking!"

This time, he obeyed. He did not cower, but he also seemed to realize that the conversation wasn't helping anything.

I glared ahead, subconsciously timing my steps with the Giant's. One, two, three, four, *boom!* One, two, three, four, *boom!*

Focusing on my steps steadied my heart rate. Get it together, Eoghan. John and the witch were offering to help me, and I needed them. I couldn't afford to chase them off by being disagreeable.

But the image of Nora alone in her dark room intruded on my thoughts once more. *You won't let me fall.*

Breathe in, breathe out. One, two, three, four, *boom!*

What I wouldn't give for a beer.

We stopped well before dusk. John hadn't said anything since I'd asked him to quit talking, so I didn't know what sort of woodsman he was. But any worries I had on that score were quickly put to bed. He walked all day, apparently without tiring, and when we agreed to stop, he set to work putting together an efficient but comfortable camp. John collected wood with a selective eye, avoiding anything too rotten. And once it was lit, he rolled a large stone closer to the fire's glow and sat on it like a cushioned stool.

"Do you travel much?" I asked.

"Is it that obvious?"

My response clogged in my throat. Nora's name had almost come bounding out of my mouth, like everything was okay.

Breathe in. Breathe out.

"When Nora and I first..." I swallowed hard. "When we first met, she'd never been in the wild before. Our first night on the mountain, she went off into the brush to gather wood and came back with all the wrong things. Green wood, rot, and a pile of tinder so large she must have thought to burn only twigs all night long."

John's mouth quirked up appreciatively.

My own face did a strange thing. It pulled in all the wrong directions, an expression I distantly remembered. A smile? "She'd grown up with a stack of seasoned wood in the shed. She'd only ever had to gather tinder for the cook fire."

The ghost of a grin lingered on my tired face. It felt good to remember her. I had tried not to think about her for so long, but maybe that had been a mistake.

John spoke into the growing silence between us. "I was an emissary for many years before Gwen and I married. I stopped traveling to be with her."

"And now you're doing it again?"

John shifted his weight on his rock and dragged his bag toward himself. He dug through it until he produced a small case of sewing supplies. "She and I have traveled many places together in the last few years. But this is the first time I've had to sleep rough in a long time."

"What's the longest you've been apart?"

"Seven months," he said. "But that was before we married. That was the last journey I made alone. I just couldn't do it anymore."

"Until now?"

He shrugged and pulled a shirt out of his bag next. John turned it this way and that until he found a seam that needed repaired. "She'll be here before long," he said casually.

And of course, that reminded me that this woman he loved... she wasn't just *any* woman.

The sound of the crackling fire did very little to comfort me. John sat across the fire, the warm light illuminating the angles of his face. He focused intently on the shirt in his hands, the bone needle glowing in the darkness when it passed in and out of the fabric. John worked meticulously, his forehead smooth and his expression calm, as if repairing that shirt was the only thing in the world to care about.

"Are you like her, then?" I asked, surprising myself more than him.

John didn't look up. "Like who?"

"Your woman, as you called her."

"Gwen? What do you mean?"

"Can you spy on my mind like she does?"

John's mouth pulled into a lopsided grin, but he didn't take his eyes off his work. "No, I can't do that. Not usually, anyway."

"So, what *can* you do, then?"

He looked up at me, eyebrows raised. "There's no need to be nervous of me, Eoghan."

I glowered at him and resisted the urge to pull my rough cloak tighter around my shoulders. Don't give him any sign of discomfort. "I'm asking you to be plain with me."

John sat up a little straighter, finally lowering his mending to his lap. "I can speak mind to mind with other sibyls, like Gwen. I can feel what others feel around me, and occasionally I can hear their thoughts, though it's distant and hard to control. I can survive passing between the worlds, but I cannot do it myself. Gwen must take me through. I have enough awareness of my own mind to shield myself from most sibyls, but not the stronger ones usually."

"So she can get into your head, and you can't stop her?"

"No one can stop her."

He held my gaze steadily, entirely unperturbed by the appalling things he said.

"What?" he asked.

I shook my head, unsure of how to continue without offending him. Half-formed exclamations and shocked denouncements chased each other around my mind, each clamoring to be said first. But my mouth was always the easiest thing for me to control. I clamped it shut in consternation.

"Out with it, man," John said.

"How can you stand it?" I spread my hands wide, my cloak clutched in each fist. The cold night air rushed in behind the movement, but I didn't care. "How can you be so trusting?"

"My trust wasn't easily won, Eoghan." His accent came a little thicker when he finally gave in to the emotion. His vowels elongated in agitation, and the cadence of his voice danced, adding stressed syllables here and there. "What difference does it make if she has the ability to overpower me? Most people have that power. *You* have that power. You could stand up now and kill me, and there would be very little I could do to stop you. I'd fight back, but you're bigger than me."

"I wouldn't—"

"And what about your Nora? She could do the same. Kill you in your sleep, steal everything you own, and abandon you."

"Nora would never do anything like that," I said, my voice far too loud in the night.

"And neither would Gwen," John said, hands raised in a shrug. "You've only just met her. You've only ever known her as she is now. I've known her my whole life. We've been together for years. I have seen what she has sacrificed for other people, her regret when she makes mistakes, and the choices she has made to control herself. When I say I trust her with my life, I mean it."

He held my gaze, daring me to argue with him.

A prideful man might have goaded him to save face, but pride had never been my vice. I shook my head again, lost in thought. "She just doesn't seem real."

"What does that mean?"

"It means she feels like a character out of a fairy story. And not one of the good ones. She..." I pulled my cloak tighter around me and hunched closer to the fire. "I don't know what I was thinking, coming here with you."

"You were thinking about Nora," John said quietly. "You were thinking you'd try anything to get her out of Arlo's grasp."

I rested my chin on my arm and glared at the fire. "Can your witch really get her out?"

"Gwen could walk Nora out in broad daylight, and no one would be able to stop her. We only need you to take the blame so she can keep her cover. That's all. The minute we arrive, that's when Nora walks out."

"It's too easy," I said. "It can't be that easy. Something has to go wrong."

John turned back to his mending with a raised eyebrow. "It usually does."

If John's witch came to him in the night, I didn't hear her. I slept hard, my back to the fire. But then again, I had always slept better out of doors, where I could smell the dirt, the grass, and the dew. Where I could focus on the wind in the trees instead of my own breathing.

We set off early the next morning and made it to the outskirts of Mitsmooren before noon.

"We should stop here," John said at the tree line. The outer city was visible in the distance to the east. "The longer we can go without alerting the Dragon that a Giant is nearby, the better. And here he can hide in the trees."

I glanced up at my little friend. The Giant stood about twenty feet back, apparently stoic. A clump of hanging moss had gotten stuck on its shoulder and dangled like midwinter garland.

"How long do we wait?" I asked.

John shook his head and let out a heavy breath. "I don't know. It won't be long, though. Gwenna will let us know when Nora makes her move. And then we'll need to work quickly to create our diversion."

I crossed my arms over my chest. "I don't like waiting."

A look passed over John's face, there and gone before I could comment on it. But his opinion on how long I was willing to wait was obvious. I had spent two months sitting around, doing nothing. What difference did another few hours make? Or another day?

The honest answer was "none." But that didn't take away the itchiness in my feet or my erratic heartbeat.

So even though I went along with John's decision to wait, even though we set up camp about fifty yards back from the tree line, where my little friend would go unnoticed...I couldn't settle.

"I'm going for a walk," I said.

"What about him?" John gestured at the Giant with a stick he had been whittling into a spit.

"We'll stay out of sight," I said dismissively.

I strode away from the cozy light of the fire, and soon the smooth strokes of John's blade against the stick dissolved into the general noise of the forest: wind, critters scuttling through old leaf litter, the calls of birds.

And of course, the *boom, boom, boom* of the Giant's footsteps behind me. The ground shuddered, and the trees shook around me as we passed. It had become the rhythm of my life. Everywhere I went. *Boom, boom, boom.*

We went a good ways north, as far from camp and John as possible. Then I stopped. The Giant's crashing footsteps fell silent.

"Sit," I said to it. "Right here. Sit down."

The Giant's deep gaze leveled on me. Its eyes were like the blackness between stars on a clear night. Endless.

"Please," I said, a note of pleading in my voice. Please just sit down, you useless lump. "I need you to wait here. If you follow me, I won't be safe."

A jagged crack opened in the lower part of the Giant's head, and he spoke. "SAFE."

I cringed. Birds took off in alarm from the nearest tree, but its voice wasn't as large as some other, bigger Giants.

"Yes, safe," I confirmed. "I need you to wait here so that I will be safe."

The Giant cocked its head to one side in its usual way. As if I were a dog trying to speak.

"*Please.*"

Then, with a great grinding of rock against rock, the Giant sat down where I had indicated. It levered itself down like a boulder bending in half, uprooting a small tree on its way down. It wasn't graceful or quiet. Hopefully John couldn't hear all this racket back at camp.

"Thank you," I said. "Wait here. I will come back safe."

The Giant only stared while I backed away slowly. I took one step, then another. Another.

The Giant didn't get up.

I took two more steps.

The Giant stayed where it was.

Then, fists clenched with anxiety, I turned and sprinted with purpose to the east. If I was fast enough, I could make it all the way into Outer Mitsmooren, do some scouting, and then get back before the Giant decided to follow me and make a fuss.

If I was fast enough, I could do something useful while I waited for the witch and her grand plans.

If I was fast enough, I could outrun that voice in my head. *Her* voice.

Keep him safe!

Twenty-Six

The city of Mitsmooren had spilled outside of its walls a century ago. Such things always happened to walled cities. When too many people flocked to a place that couldn't grow, they simply built their houses and shops in its shadow.

Outer Mitsmooren was at least twice the size of the city proper. Winding, narrow streets like these usually had the best and the worst of everything. Bread, beer, meat, and company ranged from the seediest and most foul to the best you've ever had—if you only knew where to look.

Finding the best the locals had to offer was something I had made a science of in my many years of traveling. So I strode into the streets, my hood up to hide my face, and blended right in.

I found a mediocre public house and settled in at the bar with a lukewarm stein of beer. There, I drank a little, trying not to relish it too much. Around me, the locals conversed loudly about everyday things: the outcome of a boxing match the night before, a recent tax increase, some man's pig that had gotten stuck under a fence.

After about fifteen minutes, I got up and found another

public house. It was more of the same there. Useless day-to-day gossip, laughter, and back slapping. At a third tavern, I overheard a woman telling her neighbor that she was having trouble finding someone to travel to Caernavorn to pick up an order of indigo. I almost turned around to ask about it, purely out of habit. A few months ago, I would have jumped at such a job. It was easy coin for a light load.

But no. I was here for Nora. First, I get her out. Second, we run. Third...

I chugged the last of the beer in my mug and plonked it onto the bar top. I had no idea what step three was. All I knew was my time was running out. The Giant wouldn't wait forever. I had to get back before it decided to follow me and blew what little cover I had.

But then a familiar voice cut through the general buzz of conversation around me. "Excuse me, did I overhear you saying you needed an order from Caernavorn?"

I froze, gripping my empty mug with white knuckles. That voice had haunted my nightmares for two months. The voice of a friend-turned-traitor. A kidnapper. A blackmailer. A lying sack of shit.

I dared to turn a fraction and look at the speaker out of the corner of my eye, confirming my suspicions.

Darius stood there with the woman and her neighbor, looking handsome, approachable, and solid. The Dragon's brother. The man who had stolen Nora and taken her against her will to be a prisoner in this godforsaken city.

"You did, sir," the woman replied with energy. "You're not looking to earn some coin, are you? I can't lie, you'd be doing me a real service."

"I may be able to help you," Darius said in a friendly, businesslike tone. "I'm a merchant, you see. And I travel to Caernavorn with some regularity."

They continued speaking, working out an arrangement

between them, but their conversation dissolved into a loud buzzing in my ears. Fury drowned out everything else. All sense, all purpose. The only thing I could think about was pulling my hunting knife out of my belt and jamming it into his belly.

Yes, a slow death. That was what Darius deserved.

"Care for another?" the barman asked me. His voice cut through the fuzz in my ears and brought me back to the present.

"What? No."

"As you like," the barman replied, but I had already turned away again.

Darius concluded his business with the woman and shook her hand to seal the deal. He waved one final farewell to someone on the far side of the room and made for the door.

I slipped off my stool and followed him. All thoughts of the Giant waiting for me at the tree line had completely fled my mind. Here was the man who had ruined my life and hurt Nora. Fuck the Owl, fuck John, and fuck the plan. New mission: find a way to fuck Darius over in any way possible and use him to rescue Nora. I wasn't sure on the details of that last part, but things would work themselves out.

Darius pulled a blue knitted cap over his blond hair as he stepped into the sun. He followed the alley to Wall Street, which ran the circumference of the wall around Mitsmooren. He strolled along, his hands in his pockets, not a care in the world.

I followed behind at a good distance, allowing plenty of people to fill the space between us. It was a major road, with vendors lining the right side. Occasionally, Darius stopped to peruse a fruit stall or clasp hands with an old friend, but he made steady progress while the sun began its slow descent to the west.

The wall itself was impressive. It rose about twenty feet high, composed of stones two feet across. The mortar was as solid as the day it was packed in. Most of the moss had been scraped away, and no buildings had been built against it. The Dragon kept his fortifications in good order.

It had the traditional four gates, one in each cardinal direction, with regular guard shacks standing sentinel along the top. It was well-manned, but I didn't spend too much time staring up at the guards patrolling the wall. Nothing drew a soldier's attention more than eye contact.

Besides, I only had eyes for the bastard who had brought us here in the first place.

I followed Darius for more than an hour, almost all the way to the northern gate. Surely at some point it would have been faster to cut directly through the main city, rather than skirting around the wall.

What was he playing at?

Just as this thought occurred to me, Darius veered right, away from the wall, and disappeared down a narrow alley between a butcher and a chandlery.

I leaned against the wall of the chandlery, pretending to study a broken fingernail. I glanced down the alley just in time to see a door close at the back of the building. After waiting another two seconds, I walked casually down the alley where Darius had gone before.

The door was plain, set in a simple wood frame at the back of the chandlery. I opened it as if I belonged there, stepped inside, and closed it behind me with a sturdy click of the latch.

The room was dark, but enough light leaked through the smoky windows to illuminate a massive stove along the right-hand wall and racks full of drying candles. Most of the area was taken up with crates of wicks, flour, salt, and lime. A stack of quarter barrels near the back had the letters "LYE" stamped on the sides in bold.

The bustle of customers and busy chandlers in the front room echoed through a partially open door on my left. At one point, a young woman burst through that door. I ducked behind a stack of crates just in time, holding my breath.

The woman had been carrying on a conversation with someone in the store, and she continued shouting her story from afar while perusing a cluttered shelf and selecting a new jar of ink. "I'm telling you, I saw it myself! Harrold caught his foot in the..." Her voice faded to mumbling when she returned to the main store and the door swung shut behind her. A burst of laughter echoed through the wall, and I dared to breathe again.

I stepped up to the door and pressed my eye to the crack. Beyond it was only the backside of a clerk's counter. The woman with the inkpot leaned across it, gossiping with two friends. Aside from them, an older gentleman browsed the shelves of candles, oils, and soaps.

Darius was nowhere to be seen. And if he had wanted to go into the main shop, why would he sneak in through the back door? No, his aim had been here, in this storeroom.

I studied the stacked crates. They were arranged in a curious pattern, sticking out into the room and blocking the path from the main door to the cookstove and drying racks. Why weren't they lined up along the wall?

I stepped around the crates and discovered the answer to that question immediately. Hidden in the shadows behind a shelf of pots and utensils, the wall curved sharply away. Around the curve was a narrow door, like a closet tucked out of sight.

And at first glance, it did appear to be a closet. The little room was simply more shelves, small crates, and pots stacked haphazardly on the floor.

But this had to have been where Darius had gone, right? There was nowhere else to go.

I took another step inside, and the floor creaked under my boot. At first I dismissed it, but the sound had an element of hollowness to it. I bent down and ran my fingers over the floor.

Yes, there. A lip of a door hiding among the wooden planks of the floor. I stuck my pointer finger into a seemingly innocuous knothole and lifted easily. Under the door lay only blackness, with steep, stone stairs leading down into the unknown.

I'd bet my front teeth this had been Darius's path. The chandlery was left behind and I descended into the black.

The stairs went down in a dizzying spiral for a long time. I kept my right hand on the outer wall, letting my fingers slide along the grimy stone, and counted the steps. Forty-four, forty-five, forty-six, forty–

"Shit!" I hissed into the cold, humid darkness. There was no forty-seventh step, only level ground. I stumbled and gripped the wall, trying to orient myself.

My foot scraped along the floor, finding the steps I had come down, and then I faced the opposite way. With both hands out to feel the walls on either side, I moved carefully through the hallway in complete darkness.

I counted my steps again, trying to judge how far I went, but I had lost track of my direction on the spiral stair. There was no telling where this tunnel led.

After sixty-six steps, I jammed my foot into an obstacle. I reached out in alarm but found only emptiness in front of me. Then what had I kicked?

I knelt to find steps leading upward. This was the end already. No twists, no branching. This tunnel was short and direct. It went from the chandlery to...where?

There is a secret tunnel that goes under the wall. You'll be guided to it when the time is right.

I gritted my teeth and started climbing. Fucking sibylline prophetic bullshit. Well, at least it meant I was where I was supposed to be.

At step twenty-four, I realized I could make out the stone walls curving ahead of me. Just barely.

At step thirty, the steps beneath my feet and the grime on my hands were visible.

At step forty, I heard the voices.

"...directly from Leena herself. No one has been allowed inside for months."

I clenched my fists tightly and froze. Darius was ahead. His voice was clear, as if he stood next to me on the stairs.

Up ahead, a rim of light leaked around a narrow door. I crept forward and stood just outside of it, careful not to make a sound.

"Not even the upper docents have been allowed inside?" asked another male voice I didn't recognize.

"No one," Darius replied. "There have been too many cave-ins, apparently. At least, that's the official statement."

"Do we know the real reason?" the other man asked, though his grim tone suggested he already knew.

"No. But there are rumors."

"What rumors?"

A shuffling sound suggested someone shifted their weight from one foot to the other. Darius took a deep breath.

"You remember the reports of the ministers dying of mysterious circumstances?" A pause, then Darius continued. "The rumors are that something in the cavern contaminated them. Caused such intense burns that they fell into comas. It has become erratic, apparently. Unpredictable. They used to be able to get somewhat close, but it lashes out more and more."

"Burns, yes..."

"That's what the rumors are," Darius said. "And it fits with what we know of the Light. Leena says there's something in the caverns besides Athor stone. Something previously unknown. Or at least, previously benign. It *has* to be the Light. Leena was never told about its existence, and you and I both know how dangerous it is."

A long pause followed as the speakers took in this information. What were they talking about? Caverns? Athor stone? Docents dying from some mysterious substance?

Athor stone was the base of Athorum—the most valuable mineral in the world. It could heal anything, bring anyone back from the brink of death. It was produced in Lujor, so it could be hard to come by in Amau. Come to think of it, I wasn't sure *where* it was mined. In some cave, apparently. I had never thought about it much. Perhaps that was part of what motivated the Dragon to invade Lujor?

We had always known he just wanted our port in New Haven Bay. He had made it very clear. It had been in the demands sent to our government right at the beginning. "Surrender New Haven Bay." That was it. Nothing more.

Except Darius had said something that horrible day when he had taken Nora...What had he said? Something about uniting Amau and Lujor?

And here they were, discussing Athor stone. And they had kidnapped Nora, the Giant Singer herself.

"It's grown erratic?" the other voice said with a note of unease.

"Leena only reported the rumors she's hearing on the ground. And the citizens don't know the caverns are even there, much less what's going on inside. But she did make a valuable contact with one of the junior ministers. She said...Just a moment. Let me find it. Yes, here.

"'According to Marcus, the phenomenon has always been there, but it has been miniscule. But over the last few decades, it has grown substantially. He does not know what it is and has never seen it. He is only reporting what he hears through closed doors and gossip among the acolytes. It appears to be little more than urban myth, but I suspect there is some truth in it.'"

"It was small enough when we encountered it. If they're saying it's growing..."

"And with the docents forbidden from entering," the other man said thoughtfully, "it's more vital than ever that we get down into the caverns. And soon. If it's growing and becoming erratic, that means our time is running out. We may need to advance our plans of attack by a few weeks. How soon can we move?"

"Production has been faster than predicted. We have enough

stored in the armory to supply a good-sized army. We could push to the south as early as next month."

"Good," the other man said. "Good. Arrange it."

"Are you sure, brother? Don't you want to ask Callio–"

Darius cut off mid-sentence, and silence filled the room.

I bent my knees, ready to run. Had I made some noise? Had I given myself away somehow? But then Darius spoke again. This time, his voice was oddly calm.

"Nora is in your rooms. She will encounter your wife any moment."

My heart stumbled. Nora? She was where?

"What? How?" the unknown man asked.

"You must hurry, my lord," Darius answered in that strange, tranquil tone.

"Darius, we'll continue this conversation later." The other man sounded agitated.

There was a scraping of a chair against stone and the slamming of some unseen door, and the other man left.

"Ack!" Darius burst out. Then, in an annoyed voice, he said, "I thought I told you not to do that to me."

Silence followed his words.

"I don't care," Darius replied, as if someone were with him in the room. "Find some other way to talk to him. Stay out of my head, witch."

I ground my teeth together. Gwen. John's witch. The Dragon's trusted spiritual advisor who could take control of another person's body. She must have used Darius to pass her message to... whom? Had Darius been reporting to the Dragon himself?

And if Gwen was on Nora's side, if she wanted to help her escape, why had she alerted the Dragon that Nora was roaming around the Keep?

Before I could spiral any further on the machinations of a witch, a rumbling roar echoed through the door. The stone steps vibrated under my feet. It was a bone-deep sound, one I had only ever heard once before, on the Giant's Mountain.

"What was that noise?" Darius asked. "What is happening?"

A pause...

"What do you mean, there's a Giant at the gates? Doing what?" Darius's voice ratcheted down with annoyance.

Fuck, my little friend must have finally decided to follow me to the city. Well, the witch wanted a distraction. Now she had one. But had that great war cry really come from my little friend? He was such a small Giant. I didn't think he was capable of such a roar.

"Nora did this, didn't she?" Darius ranted in the anteroom, agitated. "She called them here, just like you said she would."

Another short pause, then Darius hissed with annoyance.

"Fucking...fine. I'll handle it myself, then. Since no one else can be bothered."

The outer door slammed open and shut a second time, but this time it was followed by the distinctive scrape and click of a latch turning.

I crept up the last few steps to peek through the crack.

The room beyond was empty, lit with several oil lamps set on a desk and in alcoves. I eased the door open, ready to run if anyone appeared, but no one did.

It was a small room, its walls and ceiling made of stones, but clean and comfortable. A large table had been set up as a desk, with cubbies alongside it for storing documents and ledgers. Several cushioned chairs sat around a stove on the far wall, with narrow slits letting in a bit of light.

For all I could tell, it was a private office. A secret office, with two entrances. One through a hidden tunnel in a chandlery in Outer Mitsmooren. But where did the other let out?

I unlocked the outer door and opened it just a crack, pressing one eye to the light. Beyond lay a lush private garden surrounded with high walls. Directly in front of the door stood a large honeysuckle bush, making it hard to see much. This door would be well-hidden, even from those who knew it was there.

With one more glance around the private office, I hesitated at the door. What had Darius and the Dragon been talking about? Athorum? Some report about contamination and caverns?

I turned back to the crack of light spilling around the door, but the documents left behind on the desk called to me.

What if Nora were here? She'd be snatching parchments left and right. *"This is important, Eoghan!"* she would say. *"Why come all this way and leave empty-handed?"*

I chewed on my bottom lip for another second, then set my shoulders. Nora had made it this far. She would last a little longer. I strode to the desk and picked up letters and scrolls at random. There would be time to read and decipher them later. For right now, I simply stuffed what I could into a satchel, which I found on a coatrack by the door.

It didn't take long to gather as many as I could carry. After tossing the satchel over my shoulder, I adjusted it against my main travel pack and eased the garden door open, my heart in my throat. But there was no one around to see me.

The garden was beautiful. Hyacinths, honeysuckle, morning glories, azaleas, and a dozen other blossoms reached for the pale sun in a riot of color and perfume. The space had been designed to make one forget they were in a city at all. Even small trees cast shade over the immaculate cobblestone floor. Orange and red had already started creeping in at the edges of the leaves with the beginning of autumn chill.

At the center stood a lush fountain designed to look like a waterfall in the forest. Water spilled over mossy stones and set a gentle, burbling music over the entire scene.

But I couldn't forget where I was for long.

Above me rose the high stone walls of an impressive fortress. It loomed over me like that first Giant on the mountain. And like that Giant, this fortress seemed to rumble one oppressive thought: "WAR."

I had found my way to the Dragon's Keep. There was no doubt about it. And if the Owl's report could be believed, Nora was in that building right now, making a nuisance of herself, as usual.

A smug smile pulled at the corners of my mouth. I wiped my hand across my beard, smoothing down any stray hairs, and sniffed once. I had finally gotten inside.

There was only one other door in the garden. And behind that door was a single spiral staircase twisting up and away. At the top of the stairs, I burst out into a busy hall. Several people ran by: a maid, two soldiers, and a well-dressed woman. None of them gave me a second look or even a first. They hurried by, calling to each other in alarm.

What had Nora done now?

I followed them to my left, and two boys rushed past me, eager to see the commotion as much as I was. We entered into a main hall, where chaos beat at me from every corner. People crowded about, half of them surging forward to find out what was going on, and the other half fleeing to darkened alcoves. The noise of it bombarded me. Screaming, calling, fear, excitement. Something had stirred up the people of Mitsmooren, and something told me Nora was at the center of it.

"You! Stop there!"

A man's voice cut through the disorder, snapping my attention toward the main double doors dominating the south wall. A soldier had his hand around a woman's arm, but I couldn't see her properly with all the people passing in front of me.

"Get inside, miss!" the soldier told her. "The Giant might be dangerous. Best to take cover until the all-clear."

"A Giant?"

The breath stopped in my chest.

Nora. It was Nora.

Her voice had haunted my dreams for two months, and now here it was, fresh in my ears.

At the same moment, a group of onlookers cleared just long enough for me to catch sight of her brown curls, her dark skin, and the tense set to her shoulders.

My feet moved like clubs, knocking me into people, chairs, and tables. I only had eyes for Nora. All I could make out was the very top of her head and then an elbow in the surging crowd.

I had found her. I had *finally* found her.

"Nora!" I said, but it only came out as a whisper.

"Inside, miss! Now!" The soldier pushed her back toward the interior, two steps closer to me, but there she paused as the soldier ran outside with the rest of his fellows.

A fist closed over my own arm, jerking me back to my own body.

"Hello, old friend," said the familiar, warm voice of Darius.

On instinct, I used my height and weight to twist my arm in his grasp, but Darius was, frustratingly, just as strong as I was. He latched onto my arms and bent them behind my body in an iron grasp.

Nora pivoted as if to face us. Had she heard me? Had she seen me? But her eyes scanned the mezzanine above us with an annoyed expression, and then she turned away again.

"Nor—"

A length of fabric was jammed into my mouth, cutting off my shout. Two others had joined Darius to help restrain me. I fought and kicked, but they had me.

"Nora!" someone else bellowed. Another man, tall but lean, with thick hair and a tidy beard, strode across the chaotic hall toward her, his face a mask of fury.

Nora squeaked and disappeared at a full sprint into the sunlit afternoon.

"Nora! Stop!" the tall man called, breaking into a run after her.

"*Ragh*!" I roared through my gag. But she was gone. I fought and jerked against the ropes being knotted around my wrists. Soldiers engulfed me. There was no getting out of this.

I had been so, so close. She had been *right there*. If I had just come in a few seconds earlier...If I hadn't stopped to gather the papers in the secret office...

There was no use in going over the what-ifs and why-fors. The reality of the situation was that I had been caught. And it was my own damned fault.

Twenty-Seven

Darius and his men took me deep into the fortress, away from the crowds and the chaos, down into the bowels of the Keep. We went down staircase after staircase, and the air grew thick and cool. When the windows disappeared, I could only assume we had gone underground.

The stairwell opened into a wide chamber divided into cells fitted with iron bars. Only two had occupants: thin, filthy men who crept closer to their bars to get a glimpse of the newcomer.

And beyond the prison, through one final door, was our destination. This room was much like the one preceding it, except there were no prison cells here. Instead, there were just a few lanterns hanging from the walls, a rack or two on the left, and a single table near the door. In the center of the room sat a heavy, iron chair. An interrogation chair.

First, they stripped me of everything I owned, leaving me with only my clothes and my boots. That was kind of them, I supposed. They cut the satchel off my body, rifled through every pocket I had, and undid the belt holding my knives.

My captors sat me roughly down and looped rope around my chest. My feet were tied to the legs of the chair, and my hands secured behind my back. I wasn't going anywhere. Someone removed the gag from my mouth, and I swallowed hard.

Darius watched his men tie me down, a curious expression on his face. Like he was trying to solve a children's riddle.

"So, I suppose that's *your* Giant at the gate, then?" he asked.

I ground my teeth together and held his gaze.

Darius nodded to himself, as if I had answered his question. The others stood back, awaiting further orders.

"Yes." Darius scratched his beard. "But the real puzzler is, how did Nora know to act now? When this conveniently timed distraction appeared?"

"What did she do?" I blurted without thinking. "Where is she? What have you done with her?"

Darius ignored me. "But an even more pertinent question is, how did you get inside the Keep?"

"Sir?" said a soldier behind Darius. She held up the papers she had pulled out of the satchel. "These appear to be letters addressed to the Dragon."

Darius snatched the papers away from her. It only took him half a glance to recognize them, and he immediately retrieved every last one from the startled soldier. He jammed them back into the satchel and gripped it tightly in both hands.

"Get out," he barked to his other men. "Now. I want to speak with Eoghan alone."

Darius and I maintained a mutinous silence as the soldiers carried out their orders. They bustled out into the prison we had passed through and shut the door behind them, leaving behind an overwhelming quiet.

Somewhere in a corner, a drop of liquid hit a puddle. Behind me, tiny feet scurried through the dust, then fell silent. The weight of the earth pressed down on me, and my lungs clenched up.

"Well," Darius said with a heavy breath. "I suppose that answers one question, at least. You were in the anteroom. I suppose you followed me through the secret passage. How much did you overhear?"

I grimaced. "Enough."

A corner of his mouth pulled upward. "But how much of it did you understand?"

"Enough," I said again, though my patience was wearing thin. Where was Nora? How far had she run? There had been a man chasing her. Had she been caught too?

I dipped my hand into the waistband of my pants behind my back and pushed until a thin razor blade broke through the fabric. This had been another trick of Nan's. *You never know, Eoghan boy. Maybe you'll never need to have a secret blade. But what if someday you do?*

The razor was tiny, almost too small for my calloused fingers. But if I were careful...If I were slow...

Darius shook his head, amused. "That's a lie. What connections could you possibly make from what we said?"

The razor was pitiful against the thick, rough ropes binding my hands together, but one severed fiber at a time, the cut began to grow. I had to keep him talking.

"I heard that you have a vested interest in Athorum," I said. "And you know something about what's killing the docents in the caverns. And I know the name Leena."

Never mind that I had no idea what caverns they had been talking about, nor how they were connected to the Athorum. But the right people would know. If I told the war guild in New Haven, for instance? That could be tide-turning information.

And of course, Darius understood as much without needing it explained. "Obviously, you're not experienced in spycraft, are you Eoghan? Because you've just given up all the leverage you had."

Another ply of the rope snapped behind my back. I adjusted the little razor in my fingers and began sawing on the next one.

"I'm not like you," I said. "I've never been one to play games."

"Ah. A pragmatist. You do take all the fun out of these kinds of things."

"I'd rather be boring than a masochist," I said with a sneer. "If this is what you call fun, I don't even want to know what you do in private."

Darius raised his eyebrow a fraction.

"Yeah, that's right," I said. "I know some big words too."

He laughed at that, which made me squirm. I wanted him to be angry. I wanted to win this...this...Whatever this was, I wanted to win it. But I was starting to think Darius didn't lose at anything.

Another ply of the rope snapped, and the pressure on my wrists disappeared. I shrugged my shoulders to hide the movement of my hands. "You liked my little joke, did you? See? This can still be fun."

"Oh, Eoghan." Darius relaxed his shoulders with a wide grin. "We could have been such friends, you and I. We are so compatible."

I scrunched my face up in a dubious expression.

"We are, don't you see?" he said. "I need a pragmatist in my life. Someone to pull me down out of the clouds. I can get a little in my own head sometimes. Arlo calls me grandiose—there's another big word for you."

I nodded appreciatively. "Sure." Just keep talking, asshole. Give me an opportunity. Come a little closer where I can reach you.

"But unfortunately, you've made that friendship impossible."

"Oh, *I* did?" I asked. "*I* did that? *My* fault?"

"Hm," he said with a nod. "You informed me yourself that you know dangerous things. So..." Darius shrugged and adjusted his grip on the stolen satchel full of damning letters. "Do you remember when we first met?"

"You mean, when you let your cronies beat me half to death?"

"Yes. I told you a story in the pub after. About where I had come from."

"Some orphanage."

"A workhouse in Northern Amau. Arlo, Fletcher, and I grew up there. It was a hard life."

"Uh huh," I said, unimpressed. What a stupid lie. Workhouses had been outlawed long before I was born. They didn't exist anymore. They had been a cruel and miserable housing solution for displaced children that was barely a step above slavery.

And for Darius to claim to have lived in one nearly a century after the last one had been closed–head in the clouds indeed. It was just proof that he'd say literally anything to get a little more attention. A little more sympathy.

"But it made me strong." Darius shook his head sadly. "I'm not a bad person, Eoghan. I'm not. I just do what has to be done."

"Okay."

"You don't believe me." Darius leaned back against the table. "How would you have done it differently? If you had been in my shoes?"

"I wouldn't have kidnapped anybody," I said with a shrug. I needed him to get closer. I would only have one chance to make a clean attack. My hands were free, but the rest of me was still very much anchored to the damn chair.

Darius shook his head again and ran one hand through his blond hair. "You're not seeing the big picture. You have no idea what kind of pressure I'm under."

"Do you want me to pity you? Is that it?"

Darius glowered, and a little of his handsomeness melted away. "Amau cannot lose this war. The consequences would be disastrous. Not just for us, but for everyone. You and your precious Nora included." His voice shook.

My sarcastic response died in my throat. Was that fear in his tone?

"What do you mean?" I asked.

Darius chewed on the inside of his cheek, considering. "You heard what we said about the docents dying. There is something in those caverns, my friend. Something that cannot be stopped. We have no idea what it even is. Not really."

I leaned forward. "What caverns? Where?"

"The Athorum caverns. Where the Athor stone is mined."

I shook my head. "Where? In the mountains?"

Darius threw out one hand, incredulous. "See? This is what secrets and lies will get you. The most valuable medicine on the planet and no one even knows where it comes from. The people in the mountains call it 'Charinthi,' you know. Claim it's made from the dew of the charinthi flower, which only blooms once a year. Very poetic.

"And in the plains, they call it 'Heart of the Earth' and think the main ingredient is honey. Everyone thinks it's produced by the apothecaries, and there's got to be at least one or two in the next big city who makes it. It's such an integral part of this country that no one ever thinks twice about where the merchants get it from."

"Do you ever get tired of hearing yourself talk?" I hissed. "What caverns?"

"See? This is why I need a pragmatist." Darius tucked the satchel under one arm. "The caverns are in New Haven. Right under the city itself."

I scoffed. "There are no caverns in New Haven. You can't keep a secret like that from everyone."

"It's not a secret. Think real hard, Eoghan. Caverns, docents..."

I narrowed my eyes at him. "I told you, I don't like playing games."

Darius's shoulders dropped. "The Reliquary, you ass. The Reliquary. The caverns where they keep the 'most dangerous relics.'" He crooked his finger in the air to show sarcasm. "That is where Athor stone is mined. And the Reliquary is only there to cover it up. You really are no fun."

I sat back in my chair. "And it's killing docents?"

"The Athor stone isn't."

"The phenomenon, then? And it's spreading? But what is it?"

"Now you are starting to see my difficulty."

"*Your* difficulty?" I spat. "Why is it *your* problem?"

Darius threw his arms wide. "It's everyone's problem, Eoghan. But unfortunately, only a few have the resources to do anything about it. And we have to keep it quiet because there would be panic. And that would make everything harder." He began pacing the narrow, dank room. His boots scraped through the grime on the floor, and the sound echoed around us. "And Lachlan won't let anyone inside. And now we have the damned Giants breaking down our city walls, and people are dying, and you and Miss Nora are running around—"

"Mistress!" I said through clenched teeth.

He stopped short. "Really? Are you seriously sticking to your story on that one? She was never your wife!"

"Like hell she wasn't!" I shouted, clenching my fists behind my back. Come a little closer, you miserable piece of shit. Just a little closer, where I can reach you.

Darius narrowed his eyes at me, looking like he was going to argue further. And then, as if he wanted to be helpful, Darius took two steps forward. He opened his mouth to speak. I tensed my muscles to lunge while he was distracted...

"Sir!" a muffled voice cut through the heavy wooden door behind him. "Sir! Come quick!"

Darius turned when the door burst open and a middle-aged man came frantically inside.

"Fire, sir. We need everyone."

Darius went to high alert. "Fire? Where?"

"The armory. Quickly!"

His message delivered, the man disappeared back the way he had come.

And with that, my chance to get the better of Darius slipped through my fingers. With my feet still tied and with the rope around my chest, I couldn't lunge for him. With him so far away, I lost all advantage.

Darius turned to me, his eyes wide. "You and I will have to continue this conversation later. I think we may be able to call each other friends after all."

I glared at him and clamped my mouth shut.

"But for now," he continued, "wait here. Fire takes precedence."

He turned on his heel, the stolen satchel still tucked under one arm, and exited the room with a purposeful stride. The door slammed behind him.

The candles guttered in the wake of the closing door, and one went out completely.

Twenty-Eight

"R*agh*!" I shouted in frustration to the cold, empty room. Alone, I dropped all pretense and brought my freed hands out from behind my back. I quickly untied myself from the chair and retrieved my things from the table by the door.

The assholes had cut through the straps on my pack, so I had to tie them back together roughly. If Nan could have seen the state of it, she'd go on a terror. I pulled it on, cursing under my breath, and snatched my bandolier on my way out the door.

As expected, a fire in the city had called almost everyone away from their posts. A city full of thatch roofs and wooden buildings could go up in a matter of minutes. This was not something to be taken lightly.

So, when I crossed the dungeon with its two occupants, I only encountered one guard at the entrance.

"Hey! Stop!" he called, but I caught him off guard. I grabbed his wrists to deflect his unbalanced strike and swiped my leg under his. He hit the ground hard, and I was able to drag him into a nearby cell.

The lock slid into place with a satisfying click. I turned my back on the other prisoner's cheering and the guard's swearing and rattling of the bars.

After that, I was free to run as fast and as carelessly as I liked. The Keep had emptied of almost everyone, and the few left behind had no idea I didn't belong. Soon, I made it back out into the sunshine and open air. I paused on the grand steps and breathed deeply.

Except the air was tinged with smoke, and its source was obvious. Only a few blocks away, clouds of black billowed up from an impressive fire visible over the rooftops. The building was too far gone, and the scrambling people would be focused on preventing the fire from spreading.

Screw their town. Screw every last person who lived here. Let it all burn to the ground.

All I cared about was Nora, getting her out, and never coming back to this shithole of a country ever again.

And fortunately, I knew exactly where she was. The Dragon's witch had told me herself: *The day she escapes, she will set a fire that will delay the Dragon's battle plans for months.*

And so I hiked up my damaged pack and set my path toward the billowing, black smoke in the distance. Because that was my wife's handiwork, plain and simple.

I couldn't get within a stone's throw of the fire. The heat was so oppressive it scalded my face and hands. I stood in the mouth of a nearby alleyway and squinted at the blaze, arms up to protect my skin from the heat. The armory? Was that what the messenger had said? Yes, the building was big enough, at least three stories and a full city block, to house enough munitions for an entire army.

No one even tried to save the building in question. Instead, bucket lines and water carts worked tirelessly to wet down the nearby structures, putting out thatch fires from errant sparks before they could spread, and bustling the weak away from the danger in orderly sweeps.

So far, the only buildings lost were the armory itself and some kind of bell tower standing close by. Flames licked from the tower's stone-lined windows, and smoke billowed out around the sharply peaked roof. I jogged a hasty circle around the inferno, my hood up in case Darius made another unexpected appearance. But there was no sign of Nora.

Of course not. Why would she stick around? This fire had been lit some time ago. So where had she gone?

I turned on the spot, dodging a man running from the fire with a goat over his shoulder, and tried to get my bearings. That way stood the Keep, which meant the opposite direction would get me to the western gate, where my little friend was beating down the wall.

The Giant.

My feet began moving without a conscious thought from me. Of course, Nora would head in the direction of the nearest Giant.

The city was in chaos. I jogged along at an easy pace, dodging panicked citizens and soldiers who ran past. Some ran toward the fire. Others outstripped me in sprints toward the Giant at the main gate. Screams, barked orders, and wails of fear competed with the roar of the fire behind and the booming of the Giant ahead.

And everywhere, the smoke persisted. The stink clogged my lungs, and the air turned brown. The smoke blotted out the afternoon sun. Ash floated down like snow, coating everything in gray. The world lost all color around me.

Just keep moving.

Soon the city walls began to appear between the buildings. One last turning in the main thoroughfare brought it into full view. I sidestepped a man pulling two donkeys toward a cart and paused to take in the situation.

A smattering of soldiers tried to keep order over a rowdy mob.

The combination of fear, curiosity, and confusion had created a powder keg. The crowd surged, shouted, pushed. They wanted to see the Giant. They feared the fire. They wanted out of the city.

But with the Giant at the wall, all the city gates would be tightly shut. There would be no evacuations from Mitsmooren today, fire or not.

The Giant had nearly broken through the wall. Great stones the size of ponies lay scattered in the road. The Giant had dislodged them from the wall, and they now littered the street below.

The breach was only just big enough for me to spot a sliver of the Giant beyond. Its glossy black eye peered through the crack and, as if it knew exactly where to look, locked onto me.

"SAFE."

Panicked screams filled the air in response to the Giant's declaration. The people cowered but did not run. With the risk of fire behind them, there was nowhere else to go. Shouts of "Open the gate!" and "Let us through!" rang out through the chaos. But the soldiers held them back.

"SAFE." The Giant's thundering voice rumbled through the city and briefly overpowered the roar of the flames in the distance.

The scattering of soldiers who remained barked orders to each other, though there was nothing anyone could do. They scurried across the wall like ants on a disturbed anthill. The crowd crammed in closer.

I set my jaw in determination when the Giant resumed beating on the wall. Another great boulder tumbled away and crashed to the street below.

Stupid thing. What did it think it was going to accomplish if it got through? How was this keeping me safe? And where was Nora? She had to be here somewhere. One of the many heads bobbing around.

I jogged the last block, eyes peeled. The crowd grew even more panicked.

Just ahead, two soldiers guarding the stairs were overwhelmed by a mob of men. People surged up the wall in a steady stream. A few encountered more soldiers and were met with violence, but there were too many civilians and too few soldiers.

"Nora!" I shouted, coughing. I joined the crowd and scanned over the heads of the people around me. If I could get higher, then maybe I could spot her. Or maybe she was already outside with the Giant? "Nora!"

Someone knocked into me and nearly fell. A woman carrying a baby. I steadied her, and she immediately moved on.

"Nora!"

It was no use. The noise was too much. My voice wouldn't carry more than a few feet in all the chaos. I would never find her in that mess.

A man shoved me, then passed by. I was buffeted this way and that, and more than once, I had to push sweating bodies away with force. But I eventually made it to the stairs and began to climb.

From the top of the wall, I could see the Giant in all its glory. It stood about twenty yards down the wall, right at the main gate. I leaned over the edge and met its eye. Once again, it seemed to know exactly where to look. It peered at me for a full three seconds, then resumed its hammering of the wall.

It had been beating at the barricade for nearly an hour by now. How had it not broken through yet? What was its goal here?

The crowd gathered on top of the wall around me, and other people peered down at the Giant. On my left, two men took a flying leap and landed with a nimble roll on the cobbles below. They shouted encouragement up at the people left behind.

"Jump! It's not so far!"

Soon, more people followed. Children were lowered down and caught by waiting hands below.

Someone else bumped into me and leaned over the edge. It was another woman, shorter than the first one. She strained to see the Giant down the way. With dark curls pulled back in a windswept braid, she reeked of smoke. A black streak of soot marked her cheek, where she had swiped at her face with dirty hands.

Her fingers were black with charcoal.

I stared down at the woman for several seconds, my brain refusing to believe what I was seeing.

"Shit," she muttered under her breath. The woman glared at the Giant on our right. She glanced at the ground, gritted her teeth at the distance, and repeated a little louder, "Shit!"

She didn't look up at me. I was just another body in the crowd. She pushed away from the wall and pressed through the people, trying to get closer to the Giant.

I turned on numb legs to follow the woman's path.

Dirty hands. Soft, dark hair. Pissed as hell.

"Nora?" I said, but the sound barely made it out of my mouth.

She continued down the wall, and the crowd consumed her.

"Nor—?" My voice faltered. She had been real, right? I wasn't imagining her? She had been right there. Right up against me. A little more ashen than the last time I had seen her. A few more lines around her mouth, like she'd been frowning too much. But it was her. It had to have been her.

I pushed people aside and followed. My heart resumed its beating, faster and louder than usual to make up for the way it had stopped a moment before. I couldn't get enough air. I couldn't think.

Nora's dark hair flashed between the milling bodies. She moved with purpose against the flow of the crowd along the top of the wall. If I lost sight of her now, would I ever find her again?

No. I couldn't lose her. Not again.

"Nora!" Yes. Finally. My voice came strong and determined.

Nora's progress faltered. She half turned, hesitated, then pivoted fully. She scanned the crowd, eyebrows furrowed. And then, like the sun parting a storm cloud, her eyes landed on mine.

Her mouth opened in a startled *oh*, and one dirty hand went to her chest in surprise. For what seemed like an eternity, we stared at each other, both of us in shock. But it must have only been a second or two.

Nora let out a single, strangled sob, and her satchel slid carelessly off her shoulder. It hit the ground like dead weight, and she started toward me. My feet began moving. We must have found our way to each other because suddenly, she was in my arms.

The crowd disappeared. The smoke cleared. The Giant stopped its pounding. There was only me and Nora. I held her tight against my body, right where she should have been all this time. I buried my face into the curve of her shoulder, and her arms went around my neck and head. She anchored me to her, and I dug my fingers into her shoulder blades, holding her closer. Her breath came in heavy, irregular sobs against my collarbone. My eyes stung with unshed tears, so I pressed them even harder against her hot skin.

We stood like that for a long time, oblivious to the chaos around us. All I knew was, if I let go of her, if I moved even a fraction of an inch, I would break. I would shatter into thousands of pieces. So I just held her tighter and listened to her ragged breathing in my ear.

But then she shifted, and her cheek grazed across mine. The pressure moved from my heart to my mouth. I needed to kiss her, to taste her. To show her how much I loved her. Right now.

She met my kiss with a different kind of sob: one of relief. It was too rough, all teeth and tongue, but I needed this. I needed her. I put everything into that kiss. Two months of grief, of loneliness and loss. My fear for her, the uncertainty. My knowledge that we would never go through anything like that again. Not ever. I wouldn't allow it.

And with her fingers tight in my hair, her gasps and eagerness, the way she pressed herself into me, I knew I wasn't alone in that resolution.

I pressed my forehead to hers, our breaths coming in heady puffs. Slowly, the chaos around us became real again. The terrified people bumping into us on top of the wall, the crashing of the Giant against the gate, the choking, brown air full of ash. But I still couldn't pull away.

"What took you so long?" she asked in a hoarse voice.

"You attached that Giant to me, you ass."

She laughed out loud, and a grin pulled at my mouth.

"That's the same Giant? From New Haven?" she asked.

"Yes!" I said with a bark of hysterical laughter. "Yes! I can't get it to leave me alone!"

She framed my face with her hands. Her smile pulled down at the corners while she drank in my expression. By the Old Kind, those eyes. There had been times in recent weeks when I thought I would never see those eyes again.

"We have to get out of here," I said. "We should jump. The Giant can distract the guards, and we can disappear through the outer city."

Nora began shaking her head before I finished speaking. "No."

"Yes," I insisted, pulling her toward the edge of the wall. "It's not that far. I can lower you down most of the way."

"No, Eoghan," she said again. "I can't."

"It's the fastest way."

"It's too far. What if I'm hurt?"

What was this fear in her expression? "I'll be right there with you. Just step up here. I'll lower you down."

"I'm pregnant."

I froze, scanning her face. The words didn't have any real meaning. Not quite. *I'm pregnant.* They were just words.

"It's too far down," Nora continued. "I can't risk jumping. I can't. I already did it once today, and I almost didn't make it."

I'm pregnant.

I glanced down at her belly and was almost shocked to see it still unremarkable and flat.

"Eoghan?"

"I—" My voice didn't want to work right, so I just gripped her hand tighter.

A baby. Nora, pregnant. Not one person to protect, but two. Two people, and both of them so much more fragile. More precious.

I'm pregnant.

She searched my face, her eyebrows drawn. "Eoghan, say something."

Just then, a cry rang out from below. We both turned to watch the commotion. A young man must have landed wrong after jumping from the wall. He writhed in pain, clutching his leg as others gathered around to help him.

"Call the Giant," I said. "It can lift us down."

"Those soldiers will see me and attack. They'll know I set the fire by now. I did that, by the way." She said the last part with a bit of pride in her voice.

"I know. I've heard all about it."

"From who?"

"Everyone, seems like." I chewed on my lip, thinking hard. "We can't go to any of the other gates either. They'll be looking for you there as well. And with this attack, those gates will be shut, same as this one."

"I know."

"What was your plan before I found you? Where were you going?"

"To the Giant," she said with a shrug. "The Owl said it would take me to you, and it did. In a sense. I didn't think any further past that."

"The Owl? You mean, the witch? Gwenna?"

"Oh, so she *does* have a name?" Nora asked with bitterness in her voice.

"She brought me here to get you out. That must mean it's possible. We just have to find her."

Nora shook her head. "No. I just left her at the fire. She sent me here to find you."

Two women herding a pack of children bumped into us, and I drew Nora closer. One of the women had a baby strapped to her front with a length of patterned fabric. I stared at its bald head as they passed.

I'm pregnant.

"Eoghan, say something."

But I couldn't process it yet. It wasn't real.

All around us, people clamored for the edge of the wall. Someone had found a ladder and had set it up on the street on top of a cart, but it still wasn't quite tall enough. A mob formed around it, and people began shoving, screaming.

"This is horrible," Nora said in an undertone. "They just want to evacuate."

Two soldiers pushed their way past us toward the growing mob. They were instantly met with violence and were swallowed up by the crowd. Someone screamed, but we couldn't make out what had happened in the scrum.

Nora gripped my coat. "Was I wrong to set the fire?" she asked in a low voice.

"No," I said definitively. "The witch told me you were supposed to fire the armory. She wanted the Dragon's war plans set back. That's why you're here."

Nora's eyes snapped up to mine. "What do you mean?"

"I mean, the witch could have walked you out any time. She told me as much herself. But she waited until now because she wanted you to set that fire."

Nora's mouth curled into an annoyed frown. "I knew she was a cow."

I pulled her a little further away from the ledge when two men nearby started shoving each other. "She has been pulling strings all this time. I don't trust her."

"Me neither."

"I have another idea." I hunched down so she could hear me. "I didn't get into the city through a gate. There is a secret passage that goes under the wall."

Nora threw out her hand in delight. "Yes! That's perfect. Where?"

"It's back at the Keep. In a walled garden. I'm not sure I can find it again, but that's our way out."

"A garden? Was there a fountain? A bunch of flowers, nothing good? And a bench?"

"Yes."

She set her jaw and grabbed my hand to pull me away from the wall. Nora snatched up the satchel she had dropped earlier on our way by. "I know the way. Come on."

It took some effort to push against the flow of the crowd and descend the wall back into the city. But once we made the street, the way was much easier.

Soon, the booms of the Giant's arms on the gate and the screams of the terrified people faded to nothing.

Not everyone had gathered at the gate or had run to douse the fire, but most of the city had. The few who had stayed behind hovered in the doorway to their homes and shops, looking about and shouting news and assumptions to their neighbors.

Eyes followed us everywhere. We were the only ones moving down the street without fear. No one challenged us. Every soldier was either at the gates or trying to keep the burning armory from taking the rest of the city down with it. No one stood at the main steps to the Keep. No one looked twice when we strode inside.

Nora's breath was labored as we entered the cool shade of the Keep's main gallery, but she didn't slow. I followed her confident stride through the gallery, down a hall, up some stairs, down another hall. A few people ran by us, headed to either help with the fire or find loved ones. None of them even glanced our way.

"I've been roaming this Keep for days," she said. "I think the

Owl was keeping people from seeing me. She can do things, Eoghan. She can make people do what she wants."

"I know. She's done it to me a few times. It's..." I trailed off, unable to put the horrible experience into words.

"I've never heard of any sybil with an ability like that. Have you?"

I shook my head. Another man ran past us down the hall. He hugged the wall and kept his eyes forward.

"She might even be doing it now," she said, watching the man as he passed.

"Good. I hope she is. I don't want anything else holding us up."

Nora led us to the top of a spiral staircase, and I recognized where we were. At the bottom of these stairs was the door to the garden. Beyond that, the anteroom and the tunnel under the wall. We were so close.

"Wait." I put a hand on her elbow to stop her. "If the witch is keeping people away, maybe you should take a minute to rest before we make the next run. Catch your breath."

Confusion crossed Nora's face. "What? Why?"

I couldn't get the explanation out. It dammed up in my mouth. So I just gestured at her stomach instead.

Her brow cleared when she realized what I had meant, and then a relieved smile brought her whole face to life. She rose on her toes and pulled me down for a kiss, then another. "Thank you, but I'm okay. The baby's okay. Keep moving."

Her reaction to my concern was too real. I shouldn't have waited so long to say something. Stupid. She had probably been worrying about my silence ever since she told me about the baby.

"Are you sure?" I asked.

"Yes!" she called up at me, huffing and puffing. "I could do this for days!"

I set my jaw and followed after her. "Slow down, Nora!"

She powered down the stairs at top speed and burst into the

sunlight at the bottom. I exited right behind her, but she hadn't cleared the doorway. I knocked into her at full speed and fought to keep us both upright.

"What—"

But then I saw what had stopped Nora in her tracks.

We weren't alone in the garden.

Twenty-Nine

Standing near the burbling fountain of moss-covered stones was a small woman. Her long, blond hair cascaded over her shoulder. She wore a fine green dress, and her hands were delicate and clean. A high lady of the house.

"Hello, Sister," the woman said in a resonant, slow voice.

"I keep telling you I'm not your sister." Nora seized my hand behind her back. Her grip communicated a clear message: *Stay close.*

The woman bowed her head sadly.

"Who is this?" I asked in a lowered voice.

"It's Arlo's wife, Calliope," Nora said.

"Calliope, is it?" I asked the woman. "I'm Eoghan."

"It is very good to finally meet you, Eoghan," Calliope said. Why did she talk like that? So slowly, so carefully. Like she had to think about every sound and every movement one at a time.

"Likewise. Listen, we mean you no harm. We just want to leave." I edged us toward the door hidden behind a honeysuckle bush.

Calliope pursed her lips with worry, her delicate brow drawn. "Arlo wouldn't like that."

"Well, Arlo isn't here, is he?" Nora asked.

"Arlo is always with me."

"Run," Nora said to me under her breath.

"This way," I replied, pulling her toward the honeysuckle.

But we only made it a few steps before another voice sounded behind us. A voice I would happily go the rest of my life never hearing again.

"You are quite predictable, you know, Eoghan." Darius emerged from behind the honeysuckle, shaking his head. He was filthy, covered in soot and dried sweat. "But Nora! Ah!" He clapped his hands appreciatively. "I did not expect arson! Although, I suppose I should have seen it coming. You were always the fiery one. No pun intended."

Instant fury washed over me at the familiarity in his tone. "Do you ever get tired of hearing yourself talk?"

"You know, I could respond to that with sarcasm, but I think it's funnier to just be straight with you. No. I don't ever get tired of it. But I'll tell you what I *am* tired of: the two of you constantly fucking things up."

Nora gripped my hand even tighter, and I could guess what she was thinking. Darius stood between us and our exit. Could we take him? Was it worth the risk to try? If one of us were injured, would we make it the rest of the way to the wilderness? Probably not.

We needed a clean escape.

"Listen," Darius continued. "It has been a hell of a day. Is there any chance at all that you'll come quietly? We can't have you two running off back to Lujor. You both know too much, and with the Giant Singer here..."

"Fuck you," Nora said, annoyed.

Darius's expression dropped to one of determination. "If you like, Miss Nora."

He advanced on us, and Calliope shrank back to the wall, clutching her hands to her stomach. I pushed Nora to the side and met Darius with every ounce of strength I had left.

I don't know how I managed to fight him off. Every muscle in my body shrieked with the effort of punching, dodging, grappling, and roaring in rage. Nora screamed my name when Darius pulled out a knife, and I blocked it just in time.

We tumbled over a bench and rolled through a flower bed. The sweet perfume of tulips and irises tinged the smoky air, and dirt and greenery flew around us.

I managed to straddle Darius, and I shoved his face down into the loamy dirt. He coughed and struggled, but I finally had the upper hand. I unstrapped my hunting knife from my bandolier. It was time to end this. Finally. It all would be over, and we could get away from these hateful people.

But Darius had a final trick up his sleeve. He threw one arm back and twisted at the same time, knocking me off balance long enough to roll over. Faster than I could comprehend, he bent my wrist and snatched the knife out of my hand, reversing our positions. He held the knife to my throat and paused.

"Miss Nora?" Darius called, breathless. "Eoghan doesn't have to die. I still think we can come to an agreement and work together to end this war."

"You mean, work together to win the war for Amau?" Nora asked. "I don't think so. Drop the knife and let him up."

Darius and I both turned at the threat in her tone. During our scuffle, Nora had snatched Calliope by her arm and held a paring knife to the other woman's throat. Gray, wet clay leaked out from between Nora's fingers where she gripped Calliope's arm, but Nora didn't let go.

Darius didn't move. Calliope wasn't his wife, after all. Would the threat to her life be enough?

"Nora," I said. "Just take her and get out. Go."

Nora ignored me. "Let him go, Darius!"

Calliope stood stoic in Nora's grip, her chin up and no fear in her eyes. Nora readjusted her hold on Calliope's arm, and more slimy wet clay squished out around her hand. Was the clay coming from Calliope? And if Nora *did* use her paring knife, would there be blood or just more clay?

I stared at the woman, momentarily distracted. "What is she?" I asked, alarmed.

"She's my wife!" shouted a vaguely familiar voice. "And she is innocent! Let her go. Now, Nora."

Two more people had arrived in the garden: the handsome man who had chased Nora out of the Keep earlier and the woman I knew as Eyepatch. She no longer wore the bandaging around her face, but she had retained the ugly expression of someone hungry for vengeance.

And since the man had called Calliope his wife, that must have made him the famous Dragon of Amau. Arlo himself.

"Screw you, Arlo," Nora said, confirming my assumptions.

"Nora, you don't know what is at stake here—" Darius began, but Arlo cut him off.

"Let him go, Darius!" Arlo said.

Eyepatch hovered at his side, her eyes on Nora with a glare of pure hatred.

"Arlo!" Darius said in an argumentative tone.

"Let him up, Darius. Now. Do as I say."

Darius let out a grunt of frustration, but he stood up and backed away from me.

I rose to my feet slowly, cautiously, and never took my eyes off Darius, who still held my hunting knife in one fist. Taking advantage of the moment, I unstrapped my hatchet next. This one I could throw with confidence if anyone decided to follow us.

"Now let Calliope go," Arlo commanded of Nora. "Eoghan's free. You got what you wanted."

Nora didn't release her hostage. She pulled Calliope backward toward me, her knife pressed against the delicate white flesh of Calliope's neck. Clay dripped down around Nora's fist where she held Calliope's upper arm in a death grip.

"Move away," Nora said to Darius. She gestured with her chin for him to stand near the stairwell entrance with Arlo and Eyepatch.

Darius obeyed, a look of pure annoyance on his face.

"Don't hurt her!" Arlo hissed.

"I'm not even sure I *can* hurt her!" Nora said, incredulous.

As if to test her theory, she nicked Calliope's neck with the barest scrape of her knife. No blood. Only cool, gray clay welled out of the cut, which immediately sealed itself shut.

"See? Did that hurt?"

Calliope held her chin a little higher. She hadn't even flinched when Nora's knife pricked her skin.

Nora shrugged at Arlo, like she had proven some point I couldn't even begin to understand.

Arlo's face twisted in pure hatred. "Just let her go."

Nora edged closer to me so we stood side by side. "Where's the door?" she asked me in an undertone. Because of course, she still had no idea that a hidden door stood behind the honeysuckle.

I brushed some dirt off my arm and gestured behind us. My hatchet glinted in the sunlight, which was tinged brown with smoke.

"Nora!" Arlo shouted.

Darius bent his knees, ready to spring into action.

Boom, boom, boom!

We all twisted in shock when the unmistakable sound of Giant feet on a cobbled road thundered through the air.

"Shit!" Nora and I said together.

Boom, boom, boom!

The crashing footsteps grew louder every second, closer. Faster. The Giant was running.

"SAFE!"

Nora threw Calliope away from us at the same instant I snagged Nora's arm and pulled her back. We dove for the door behind us, and the garden wall on our left exploded. Stone and chunks of mortar rained down in a deadly shower. My little friend had burst through the wall.

"KEEP SAFE!"

Nora and I didn't wait to see what it planned to do next. We disappeared through the doorway into the anteroom. Sitting on top of the cluttered desk was the satchel I had stolen a few hours before—the one Darius had been so keen to recover.

"Wait, wait!" I hissed, doubling back to grab it.

"Hurry!" Nora ushered me through the only other door: the exit into the tunnel.

We groped our way along the tunnel as fast as we dared. Behind us, deafening booms and rumbles told us the Giant was doing its best to destroy everything it could reach. Dust showered down on us in complete blackness, and occasionally even pebbles pecked off my head and clattered to the floor.

"Go, go, go!" I said when we stumbled upon the opposite stair leading up to the chandlery.

We scrambled through the trapdoor, startled two workers in the storage room beyond, and burst out into the smokey air of Outer Mitsmooren.

"Keep moving," I said, directing Nora toward an alley headed south.

Her breath came in heavy gasps, but we couldn't slow down. Not for a single minute. Because there was no way in hell that Arlo and Darius would just let us leave.

So we ran. And when Nora began to slow, I grabbed her hand and pulled her onward.

They came sooner than I had hoped. The sound started low—so low I wasn't sure when it really began. It was a rumbling barely audible over the racket of our own gasps for breath. At first, I couldn't place the sound, but when it grew gradually louder, there was no mistaking it.

Horses. Many, many horses with steel shoes clattered along the cobblestone streets. We couldn't see them yet, but their noise echoed between the buildings.

"We should hide!" Nora gasped.

"No! Keep running."

"I can't! Eoghan, stop! I can't!"

She tugged on my arm until I was forced to pause. Nora doubled over, sucking air in huge gulps. Her legs gave out from under her, and she fell to her knees, retching.

There was no time for this. Now that we were still, the roaring of our mounted pursuers grew even louder. Down that street, I could just make out the first signs of movement. Riders in the distance, barely visible over the heads of other pedestrians and market stalls.

Without thinking, I wrenched my pack off. I threw down the stolen satchel full of Darius's letters. My hatchet clattered to the cobbles. I yanked Nora's pack off her shoulder.

"Get on," I barked.

"What?"

"My back. Get on!" I pulled her up and practically threw her onto my back, where she scrabbled for any handhold she could find. Her shaking legs went around my waist.

"Hold on!"

And I took off running as fast as I could.

Nora wasn't so big. Barely heavier than the pack I had carried my whole life. She wrapped herself around me while we raced toward freedom.

But the riders were faster. When we passed through the outskirts of Outer Mitsmooren, I could hear them shouting to each other.

"To the right!"

"Flank them there!"

"Keep going!"

We passed the last buildings and into the open field outside the city. About half a mile away, the tree line loomed. Dark, dense forest. I didn't know why I had thought it would protect us from the mounted riders. All I knew was that was our goal. Get to the forest. Just keep going.

My legs screamed in agony as they pumped. Nora's grip on my shoulder was sharply painful with every jolting step. My lungs burned. Sweat dripped into my eyes.

And always, the riders drew closer.

We weren't going to make it.

Just keep running, Eoghan boy.

Gods, Nan. I had left behind the pack she had made me. It was gone. Even if we made it to the trees, we would have nothing to survive on.

Just keep running, Eoghan boy. Just keep running.

And so, I did. Left, right. Left, right. I ignored the growing thunder of the hoofbeats catching up. I ignored the pain in my body. Left, right. Left, right. Another step. Another.

The fastest riders caught up to us. A man reached for Nora, but she slashed at him with her paring knife. I almost stumbled when her weight shifted unexpectedly, but it had been worth it. The man cursed and fell back.

Another step. Another. Just keep running.

"Look!"

Nora's voice was too loud in my ear. I couldn't look.

Left, right. Breath in. Breath out. One, two, three, four. In, out. Another step.

Any second, the next rider would snatch Nora by the collar of her shirt. They would pull her off me, and I would go down. We'd both be dead.

One, two, three, four. In, out. Breathe!

"Eoghan! Look!" Nora's voice wasn't fearful or urgent. This wasn't the voice of someone about to be snatched by the enemy closing in. She was hopeful. Excited.

I peered forward at the tree line, still so far away. Too far. I blinked away the sweat in my eyes, and what I saw made me stumble to a stop.

There, in the darkness among the trees, black eyes peered out at us. Black eyes set in stone faces. Some were taller than the trees. Most were a bit shorter. A few were small, like my little friend who had helped us escape the garden.

But there were dozens of them. Giants of lumbering stone emerged from the trees, more than I had seen since that first day, when we had woken them up. They had followed us all the way to Amau, and my little friend had called them to war. The thunder of their advance drowned out the sound of the mounted riders who had been chasing us.

Except our pursuers had disappeared. They had seen the Giants too and had turned tail to flee back to the city.

The first few Giants passed us by and Nora slid off my back. Her shouts of victory were consumed by the earth-shaking booms of their feet digging into the earth. She jumped like a child, punching her fists into the air and shouting encouragement to the Giants reaching Outer Mitsmooren.

I fell to my knees, sucking air into my lungs in huge gasps. Then I collapsed, shaking, onto my back to watch Giant after Giant pass over us on their way to war.

Nora's face appeared over me, grinning ear to ear. "We did it! We're out, Eoghan!"

She fell upon me, pressing kisses to my face, my mouth, smothering me. I couldn't breathe. So with one swipe of my leaden arm, I pulled her down to my chest in a tight embrace.

Nora immediately accepted this and wrapped her arms around my middle. "We did it!" she said into my shirt.

"Yeah," I replied breathlessly. "We made it."

I pushed my fingers into her hair and closed my eyes, listening to the rumble of the Giants.

We had done it.

Together.

THIRTY

We couldn't stay within sight of Mitsmooren, but there was no way either of us could travel in our condition. My legs shook with every attempt to stand, and Nora had gone pale green with nausea and fatigue.

So when the last of the Giants passed us by, Nora called one of them to help us. The Giant was average height and made of dark gray stone, with moss and grass clinging to its crevices. It lifted us both obligingly and carried us away from the battle raging in the city.

At first, the sensation of being carried was terrifying. I clung to the Giant's rocky arm, gritting my teeth in concentration.

"How are you so relaxed?" I asked Nora.

She sat cheerfully on the Giant's left shoulder. The wind blew through her sooty hair, which had mostly come loose from its braid and had become a snarled cloud of warm brown tumbling over her shoulders. "He won't drop us," she said with a shrug.

That was all well and good, but Giants weren't the nimblest creatures. I climbed a little higher and found a better ledge to sit on. There I didn't feel in danger of getting tumbled every time the Giant took a step.

The Giant carried us steadily southward until the sun began to dip close to the horizon. The smoke from Mitsmooren became a vague smudge in the distance. No one could find us here. The Giant hadn't even left any footprints in the deep leaf litter carpeting the forest floor.

It set us down gently, like a human might lower a pet cat to the ground.

"Thank you," Nora said to it with a grave nod.

"THANK," the Giant rumbled.

We had nothing. No supplies, no tools. Nora had only her paring knife, and that was it. The best we could do for the night was to try and sleep, then hopefully find accommodations and supplies in the morning.

Nora deftly twisted her thick curls back into submission, and set to work gathering wood for a fire. I went scouting for anything I could find to eat. This late in the season, there were only dandelions and some wild onions. Nora nibbled at them, then claimed she wasn't hungry.

The Giant lay down and went so still it could have simply been a boulder jutting out of the forest floor. Nora and I huddled close to the fire, both for warmth and to remind ourselves we were finally together.

Neither of us could sleep, so instead we filled each other in on the things we had missed in the last two months. I told Nora all about my attempts to get to Mitsmooren and the visit paid by John and Gwen the day before.

Had it been just one day?

Nora talked about her journeys through the Dragon's Keep and the maps she had drawn. She told me about her tenuous truce with Isla and about the prophecy Gwen had given her.

"That was just two days ago." Nora sat with her head against my shoulder. She spoke in a low, comfortable voice. "That would have been only the day before she visited you."

"Did I tell you she took the Clarion?"

Nora jerked upright. "No. When?"

"The day you were taken. She helped them take you. Or at least, she distracted me long enough so Darius could make his move."

"What did she do with it?"

"She said it was in a safe place. I have no idea where."

It is safe.

Nora and I both jumped when Gwen's voice rang loud and clear in our heads.

And sure enough, Gwen and John stood across from our fire, as calmly as if they had been there all along. Heavy-looking bags weighed them both down and gave them an awkward, lumpy shape.

"By the Old Kind, must you sneak up on a person like that?" I growled.

John's mouth twisted into a grin. "Our apologies."

But Nora had no use for small talk. "What does that mean, *it is safe*? Where is it?"

Gwen pressed her lips together. *It is in my childhood home. Deep in the Sacred Wood, surrounded by runestones that prevent anyone from stumbling across it.*

I stared at her, unsure what to make of this declaration.

"What, were you raised by wood nymphs and mushroom spirits?" Nora's tone dripped with sarcasm.

John laughed out loud. "Don't give her ideas. She'll add it to her narrative."

Gwen glanced up at John and shoved him good-naturedly with one elbow.

"We brought you your things."

John held up what I now realized were our packs: Nan's pack, Nora's bag, and the satchel full of stolen letters. Gwen even lifted my hatchet so the firelight glinted off the blade.

I shot upward, reached for my pack, and ran my fingers over

my name, which Nan had embroidered in faded blue thread two decades before.

I couldn't get your hunting knife from Darius without arousing suspicion, Gwen said when she handed me the hatchet.

"Thank you." I should have said more, should have told her how much this meant to me, to have this last piece of Nan left.

But I didn't need to tell her. She gave me a kind, understanding smile, and I knew the message had gotten through.

"What happened to your arm?" Nora gestured to Gwen's left sleeve. Dark, dried blood stained the fabric of her shirt.

It is an old wound. Don't trouble yourself.

"It wasn't there this afternoon," Nora said.

This afternoon was a very, very long time ago.

"Do you always talk in riddles?"

Gwen smiled and said nothing at all.

"How can we get in touch with you?" I asked.

"You don't," John said. "You have done your part. This war is effectively over. So long as Gwen and I can finish what we started in Amau, it won't start back up again."

"And what is it you're doing in Amau?" I lifted the satchel of letters. "Is it to do with the Athorum caves? Because that seems to be what Arlo is most focused on."

"Go home, my friend," John said. "You have a family now. Take care of them. Go have the life you all deserve."

Thank you for all you've done, Gwen added.

"But—"

Nora's fingers on my arm stopped my protest in my throat.

"What did you do to Edith?" she asked.

Gwen and John both fell silent for a long moment.

Edith is safe.

"That's not what I asked." Nora's tone had taken that hard, determined quality, which was honestly scarier than anything Gwen could do. "Edith betrayed me to Darius. My own sister. She would not have done that unless you did something to her. Forced her hand."

"Edith was being pressured by Darius and his men," John said. "What happened in New Haven was messy, but we did the best we could without giving ourselves away."

"Bullshit," Nora said.

It's not bullshit, Gwen replied.

"Edith helped us because it was the right thing to do," John said. "Go home. Go to Edith and talk to her yourself. What she did was very difficult. But because of her and because you were here in Mitsmooren, thousands of lives will be saved."

The entire world will be saved, Gwen added.

I shivered and drew Nora a little closer. "And just what the fuck does that mean?"

"It means go home," John said. "Your part in this story is over."

He held out his hand for a farewell shake, but neither of us took it.

Nora glanced down at his extended hand, then back up again. "I won't thank you for your part in kidnapping me, but I'm grateful that you helped get me out. And with all due respect, I hope we never see either of you ever again."

John grinned. "Understood. Eoghan, Nora, it was a pleasure to know you."

Gwen hovered in his shadow and said nothing at all. And then, with no fanfare, they were gone.

"Do you really think we'll never see them again?" I asked, dubious.

Nora glared at the empty air where Gwen had stood. "There is something bigger happening here. Something huge. Tell me again about the Athorum Caves. What exactly did Darius say?"

"No."

Her eyebrows shot up. "No?"

"No. Not tonight. Tonight, we rest. Here. There's some hardtack in here and some dried meat. And there's still some water in the skin. Eat something because we both know that 'I'm not hungry' bit was a lie."

"Dandelions are disgusting," she said, taking the hardtack.

"I know."

"Fine." Nora snapped off a mouthful. "But then tomorrow, we're going to New Haven. I want to know what's under the Reliquary."

We ate in companionable silence for a few moments until I remembered one important detail.

"Are you really pregnant?" I asked.

Nora snorted and swallowed hard. "Yes."

"To think, you spent all that time wearing a false belly."

"Oh, I caught the irony," she said.

"I never..." The words got stuck in my mouth. "I never thought..." I cleared my throat. "That this would ever happen for me."

"Did you want children?" she asked.

"I never thought about it much. Not in any real way."

Nora scooted a little closer and threaded her fingers through mine. I studied our intertwined hands, marveling at how right it felt. How well we fit together.

"Well, it's happening now," she said in a practical tone. "And I don't know about you, but I'd say there's a good chance of it happening again in the future."

A laugh welled out of me from some deep place I thought had long dried up. I kissed her fingers, and she took another determined bite of the hardtack.

"As you say, mapmaker. As you say."

Epilogue

Calliope

I loved the light. Hot little candles, elegant lamps, sunshine. Fires roaring in fireplaces, torches, and glowing embers. I loved it, I did.

But sometimes, I missed the dark so much I couldn't breathe anymore. And if I stopped breathing, what would happen to me then?

I sat in bed, clutching the blanket to my chest, and soaked in the quiet shadows. Arlo's soft breaths played a soothing rhythm next to me. In. Out. In. Out. I could just make out the line of his naked back in the moonlight. So beautiful. So incredibly alive.

My fingers stroked through the fall of my blonde hair, and I gazed down at my husband. I had given up everything for Arlo, and he had given me everything in return. The best choice I had ever made.

But tonight, I needed darkness. No candles. No moonlight or stars. Nothing made by man or design. I needed something real.

So I slipped out of the bed, careful not to wake Arlo, and pulled a black, hooded cloak over my shoulders.

No one stopped me. Why would they? The invaders had been

gone for more than a week, and all had been quiet ever since. Life was returning to normal in Mitsmooren.

Two guards at the door tipped their heads at me as I passed. "Lady Calliope," one said in greeting. They knew better than to question the lady of the house if she wanted to feel the night air.

The streets were quiet that night. I took my time, pacing slowly and breathing deep. The smoke had finally cleared, and the air was crisp and clean. Mice scurried in the corners, and wind whistled through the alleys and over the thatch, accompanying the songs of birds roosting in the eves.

"Hello, pretty lady," said a slurring voice on my right.

I paused and gazed around the edge of my hood. A thin, filthy man sat sprawled on a nearby stoop, a brown bottle held loosely in one hand.

The man hiccupped. "What brings you out so late tonight?" he asked with a leer and stood.

"Be at peace, my friend." I pulled back my hood just enough that he could see my eyes in the moonlight.

The man straightened in shock and backed up a step. His expression pinched with wonder and hope. "My lady," he said, giving a real effort to suppress the slurring in his words. "Blessings, my lady. An honor, my lady."

A smile pulled at my lips. I reached out and squeezed his forearm gently. "The honor is mine."

The man's eyes filled with tears of gratitude. He covered the place where I had touched him with one hand, as if to hold onto the feeling for as long as possible.

I pulled my hood back into place and moved on.

The eastern gate was the only one still standing, and therefore it was my only way out. The guards there opened the way for me, following me with their eyes. I passed through Outer Mitsmooren without meeting anyone at all, though late-night revelers talked and laughed down alleyways and inside alcoves.

Outside the city, the road stretched out in pale ribbon through the black fields. The half-moon cast a glow over everything, pressing down on me.

But beyond that lay the trees. And between the trees: true darkness.

I tugged the cloak a little tighter around myself and set off down the deserted road. My feet crunched through the hard-packed gravel. *Crunch. Crunch. Crunch.* Where had the humans quarried this stone? Where had it belonged before it was taken, sorted, and packed down into a road? Was there a scar in the earth somewhere, where these stones had once been?

Before long, I came to the first trees and stepped off into the leaf-littered grass.

Yes. This was what I needed. Beneath the protective canopy of the elms, oaks, and pines, the blackness became complete. The bright shine of my pale hair wasn't even visible anymore. I closed my eyes, no longer needing them, and stood listening to the night birds and the wind. Time slowed, and the urge to hold myself together by sheer will faded.

Out here, in the dark and away from other people, I was free. I was me.

Well, the me I used to be.

Somewhere in the darkness, a grinding, crashing noise broke the silence. I opened my eyes but could see nothing at all.

Another thundering crash filled the night air, followed by the snapping of tree branches. Whatever it was, it was huge. The width of a house and as tall as the trees.

If I couldn't use my eyes, then I would have to use another sense. An older, more mysterious way of perceiving the world around me. I reached out with my mind, something I hadn't done in years, and discovered a Giant sitting among the trees.

He must have stayed behind after Nora left. To what purpose?

It peered at me through the dark, but its stone eyes didn't need light like humans' did. It could sense me just as easily as I could sense him.

Even sitting, he towered over me, half as high as the fully grown trees around him. He studied me, curious. So I stepped forward and reached out a hand to him.

With a great grinding of stone against stone, he shifted his arm to press against my outstretched palm. Life pulsed within him. Older and richer than any other life that existed in humankind. It was something I hadn't felt for a very, very long time.

The Giant cracked open its mouth to speak in his great voice. "WELCOME MOTHER."

I pressed my lips into a small, loving smile. "Thank you."

The Giant lowered its head a little closer. "MOTHER. COME HOME."

My smile faded, and I withdrew my hand. "I *am* home, my son. This is my home now."

The Giant straightened up, regarding me sadly. It stared at me for such a long time, but there was nothing more I could say. I had chosen to live with Arlo. Maybe it was time to stop visiting the darkness. I was human now. Humans feared the dark, and so should I.

So, I turned and walked back toward the moonlight outside the trees. I regained the pale ribbon of road and headed toward the city. My feet crunched through the gravel. I left behind the Giant, the darkness, and my past.

Arlo was my home now. And I would do anything to stay with him.

Anything.

The Story Continues

with Book Three: The World Mother

If you enjoyed this book, please consider leaving a rating or review. With your support, I can keep daydreaming for a living.

You can find convenient links to all the popular review sites on my website: annacackler.com/links

Also by Anna Cackler

The Sibylline Saga

The Forest Witch

The Giant Singer

The World Mother

The Old Kind

The World Mother

The Sibylline Saga: Book 3

With her family by her side, Gwen sets out into a world beset by great stone Giants, guided by ancient prophecy, and nearly torn apart by the delusions of a World Mother.

In this breathtaking conclusion of The Sibylline Saga, Gwen must confront the truth of who and what she is–or risk losing everything.

The Old Kind

A Stand-Alone Anthology in the Sibylline Saga

A grieving flax spinner descending into madness. A fiery rebel stuck between land and sea. Two sisters, divided by faith and determination. An immortal man, and the ravens that watch him from the trees. The Old Kind lurk at the edges of these stories. Almost gone, but never forgotten.

These four stand-alone tales–THE GLASS WHEEL, BLUEWATER, STARSONG, and RAVEN'S END–explore the overlooked corners of the Sibylline Saga universe. These are stories of hope and healing, where the bond between sisters, the bravery to truly feel, and steadfast love can conquer all.

Content Advisory

This book contains scenes that may be distressing to some readers. Below is a list of these topics, drawn up to the best of my knowledge at the time of publication. A regularly updated list can also be found on my website: annacackler.com/books

If, while reading this book, you come across any sensitive topics that need to be added to this list, please reach out to me at anna@annacackler.com and put CONTENT ADVISORY in the subject line.

Mild gore and violence, arson and fire, control of another person's body via coercion (supernatural mental ability), pregnancy (no common pregnancy tropes are included, the pregnancy is not a plot line), kidnapping, isolation. There is a love scene on the page, but it is not explicit.

Acknowledgments

I am so grateful to everyone who has helped me make The Sibylline Saga a reality. I could not have done this without the network of support from both family and from new friends I've made along the way.

Many thanks to those of you who helped me name the Athorum: Gerry Robinson, Jim Meeks, Ashlyn Van Benschoten, Sallie Montuori, and Bear C. It was so fun to brainstorm with you all the ways this mythical cure-all came to be.

I'd also like to thank my many early readers, who helped me polish the series: Zhade, Elizabeth Plass, Brittney Willbanks, Enos Evans, Pam Cemen, and Carla Evans. I couldn't have done it without your feedback and encouragement.

And thank you so much to Lyndsey Smith at the Editing Forge for her tireless work in giving this series its final polish.

There are three other people who have supported me through the ups and downs of being an author. It began with my mother, who told me stories every night and shared her love of books with me. Thanks, Mom, both for the excellent start and your ongoing support and encouragement.

Thank you Chelsea for listening to me ramble and vent with infinite patience. You say you envy my confidence, but that's all fake. You kept me sane when I was barely keeping it together.

And thank you to Kevin, my very best friend and the best husband anyone could ask for. I can't express how much your support and your faith in me has meant.

This series has been an absolute labor of love that began when

I was just a teenager. I am so incredibly proud of it and of myself for getting this far. And I'm can't wait to see what comes next, because this is only the beginning.

From the Author

This story started on a hairpin curve in Puerto Rico.

Neither thing is terribly remarkable. Puerto Rico is entirely made up of hairpin curves and I lived there at the time. I was on my way home from the grocery store, going around a very specific curve on Carretera 108, and a song came on my car radio: Waking Up the Giants by Grizfolk.

It was like I'd been struck by lightening. The idea of seeking an object that was just behind the storm, and a warning to be careful waking up a bigger man, a better man. I'd heard the song a hundred times before, but something about that specific hearing... I had to write this story.

I went home, left the groceries in the car, went straight up to my room, and wrote a three paragraph summary of two wanderers on an epic quest to find a mysterious Clarion and wake up the legendary Giants.

Within a month, those three paragraphs had become a short story: Waking Up the Giants.

At the time, I had already finished writing book one of this series, and I had just sent it off to its first round of beta readers. I had a vague idea of turning it into a series, but honestly I had no idea of where to take the story next.

Waking Up the Giants was just supposed to be a reader magnet. A story in the same subgenre that I could give away to newsletter subscribers.

I didn't know at the time that this short story would change EVERYTHING. Absolutely everything.

It happened when Eoghan was standing on a cliff, looking

down over Lujor and thinking about the cause of the war. It was basically just some background info and setting description. I needed a small detail—the name of the ocean he could see on the horizon.

Usually I'd just mash my hand against the keyboard, then add vowels and remove consonants as needed to make the resulting world pronounceable.

But there was already a word in my head. A place name that I'd used once before to name another ocean: Arigua. I was kind of sad that I'd used such a great name already in The Forest Witch as a throwaway detail. It got mentioned maybe twice in the whole book and the reader never saw it in person.

And then I thought...what if this is that same ocean? What if Eoghan and Nora are on the other side of the world from Gwen, living their lives, playing out their own epic adventures, and knowing nothing at all about the most powerful sybil that ever lived?

So I put some Athorum in Eoghan's pocket and set my two adventurers loose in a world that suddenly got much, much bigger.

That's how I create worlds: one piece at a time. I feel my way through it. Every time I meet a new character, I follow them a little deeper into the story. Every fork in the path gets taken. Every loose thread gets pulled.

Fletcher was just an obstacle on their way to the mountain's peak. He didn't even have a name.

Isla was just a mugger.

Darius was a ride to New Haven.

It wasn't until after I wrote their introductory chapters that they became important. And it wasn't until part four that I became obsessed with Isla—but that's a discussion for after book three...

Made in the USA
Coppell, TX
12 January 2026